"Get up, Julia," Derek Ordered Softly, and the Whole Room Tilted and Became Smaller.

Julia rose to her feet, vowing that he would never know how he made her feel.

At first, his kiss was hard and insulting, as if he was trying to conquer her. Then he began to kiss her gently, persuasively, and she felt an overpowering urge to respond as she never had before. But she could imagine the sense of triumph he would feel if she did, and she forced herself to stay calm and unmoved.

"Is this the way you always are with men, Julia? An ice maiden?"

Never, she thought, had she seen such anger in a man's eyes before. . . .

BROOKE HASTINGS
is an avid reader who loves to travel. She draws her material from many sources: the newspaper, politics, the places she visits and the people she meets. Her unique plots, full of real people who meet love in many guises, make her one of the best new writers in this field.

Dear Reader:

Silhouette Romances is an exciting new publishing venture. We will be presenting the very finest writers of contemporary romantic fiction as well as outstanding new talent in this field. It is our hope that our stories, our heroes and our heroines will give you, the reader, all you want from romantic fiction.

Also, *you* play an important part in our future plans for Silhouette Romances. We welcome any suggestions or comments on our books and I invite you to write to us at the address below.

So, enjoy this book and all the wonderful romances from Silhouette. They're for *you!*

Karen Solem
Editor-in-Chief
Silhouette Books
P. O. Box 769
New York, N.Y. 10019

BROOKE HASTINGS
Innocent
Fire

Silhouette Romance

Published by Silhouette Books New York

For my parents,
Robert and Lillian Hannes.

SILHOUETTE BOOKS, a Simon & Schuster Division of
GULF & WESTERN CORPORATION
1230 Avenue of the Americas, New York, N.Y. 10020

Copyright © 1980 by Brooke Hastings

Distributed by Pocket Books

ISBN: 0-671-57026-9

First Silhouette printing August, 1980

10 9 8 7 6 5 4 3 2 1

Printed in the U.S.A.

Innocent Fire

Chapter One

"Daddy!" Julia Harcourt burst into her father's study, swept across the oriental carpet, and excitedly waved that morning's edition of the *New York Times* in the air. She threw herself into the brown leather armchair next to Richard Harcourt's antique desk, her blue eyes shining with anticipation.

"Guess who's going to be teaching at Middlesex next year?" she challenged. "Listen!

"Weston, Mass. August 18 (NY Times). Middlesex University President Hiram Felker today announced that internationally known artist Derek Veblen will be joining the Middlesex faculty for the coming academic year. This marks the end of a long period of near-retreat on the part of Mr. Veblen, whose only public appearances in recent years have been at retrospectives of his work in

New York and London, and before the United States Congress, in order to testify on behalf of more public funding for the arts.

"Mr. Veblen first gained recognition as a portrait painter in the late 1960s. His subjects have included world-famous political figures, society women and royalty. During the last several years, however, he has devoted himself almost exclusively to painting condemnations of war, terrorism, poverty and racism. In spite of his youth, the thirty-three-year-old artist is considered one of the most important painters of the twentieth century, and his recent reclusiveness has only added to the cult which has grown up around his work.

"According to President Felker, Mr. Veblen will teach several tutorials, both at the graduate and the undergraduate levels. Mr. Veblen was, as usual, unavailable for comment, but the *Times* was able to discover from sources close to the artist that he desires to repay Middlesex University for accepting him on full scholarship when he was a poor student from Boston's North End. In addition, Mr. Veblen has told those close to him that he feels teaching will provide fresh stimulation. His intention to emerge from three years of a very private existence has become the talk of the art world."

"It's quite an important opportunity," Julia said languidly, and then suddenly seemed unable to maintain her sophisticated veneer. She enthused, "Just imagine being able to study with Derek Veblen! I can't believe it!"

Richard Harcourt reached for his pipe. He carefully lit it, puffed several times, and soberly regarded his twenty-two-year-old daughter. Derek Veblen was no doubt a brilliant artist; however, his current choice of subject matter, in the opinion of the urbanely conservative Mr. Harcourt, left much to be desired. He had no wish to have his daughter contaminated by such a man.

"I don't want to put out the fire which that article seems to have ignited in you, Julia," he said smoothly. "But there are hundreds of art majors at your school. I doubt whether more than a few dozen of them will be accepted into Veblen's courses. You may not be one of the lucky ones."

This possibility seemed never to have entered Julia Harcourt's beautiful head. Why should it have done so? She had always had everything she wanted in life—except once. She told her father confidently, "Of course I will. I'm as talented as anyone else at Middlesex. Besides," a slow, knowing smile replaced her previous bland assurance, "not everyone has a father who's been so generous to the school."

"You'll either make it on the strength of your portfolio, young lady," said Richard Harcourt in what he hoped was a stern voice, "or not at all. Is that clear?"

His daughter regarded him innocently. "Yes, Mr. Harcourt." Her eyes gleamed. "I've got a tennis date in half an hour. See you later."

Jill Harcourt had died when her daughter Julia was only fourteen. Julia's older brothers—Thomas, Edward and Douglas—had all been grown up at the time, ranging in age from twenty-four to thirty-two, and it had been natural for her whole family to spoil Julia.

Jill's death after a short, tragic illness had magnified Richard's tendency to pamper his only daughter. It had been natural to assuage his grief, and hers, by showering her with clothes, horses, fancy trips and jewelry. But something was missing. Julia had many friends, but she seemed to trust no one—not even her own family. Her father found her disturbingly self-assured, and disturbingly independent. The winsome, happy child had become a stunning young woman, but she lived her life encased in a shell which nothing—and no one— could penetrate.

Julia walked down the elegant curved staircase, her hand lightly resting on the gleaming mahogany banister. She passed by the full-length mirror in the entryway without so much as a glance at her slender frame. The days when she had been a gawky, uneasy teen-ager seemed very far behind her now.

For the past three years, Julia had been acclaimed as an international beauty. Her shoulder-length red-gold hair, now lightened by the sun, would have made an Irish setter envious; her eyes were no watered-down shade of blue, but deep and bright. They were framed by long lashes, and a small straight nose, perfect teeth, and sensual mouth to make a picture so perfect that more than one cosmetics company had approached her for endorsements of their products.

Today, in a navy and white designer tennis outfit, expensive tennis shoes, and with her hair managing to look glamorous even in a mundane pony-tail, she looked beautiful, glowingly healthy, and she knew it. The fact that her partner would be a Middle Eastern prince did not impress her.

Julia walked slowly over the manicured grounds of her family's twenty-one-acre estate to the tennis court, absently noting the cloudless sky and gentle breeze. Her thoughts were centered on Derek Veblen. Julia knew the reason for her father's lack of enthusiasm; he did not care for Mr. Veblen's politics. The international situation was not Julia's prime concern, but she knew that Richard Harcourt would happily sell his insurance wherever it would profit the firm. If a country's prisons and mental institutions engaged in the torture of dissidents, it was none of his concern.

Nonetheless, Julia was sure that her father would help her—if indeed she needed help. He had always compensated for the small amount of time he spent with her by showering her with every material object she wanted. And Julia admitted that she took full advantage of it.

She looked forward to putting her portfolio in order. Her portrait of her mother, executed last year from memory and photographs—but no. It was too personal, too revealing. She would leave that out. Her latest seascape was coming along well. If she could get up to Maine for a week, she would be able to finish it in time to include it. And the chateau she had painted the last time she was in France—that was worth showing to the illustrious Mr. Veblen.

A lightly accented voice broke into her musings.

"Julia! You are so preoccupied. Thinking of me, I hope?"

"Andy! How nice to see you again." She smiled charmingly and extended both her hands to him as if she were the princess and he the commoner.

Prince Abrahm kissed her hands, then drew her forward to kiss her mouth. She turned her head so that his lips touched her cheek instead.

"So cool," he laughed. "We shall have to find out if a set of tennis will warm you up, Julia."

She marshaled her concentration and launched herself into the game. A less self-possessed young woman might have found it difficult to keep her mind on tennis with a classically handsome prince on the other side of the net. But not Julia.

She was used to princes, millionaires' sons, up-and-coming politicians, rock stars and actors. She had given her heart once—to Mark Glenndale—only to have it shattered. She had adored her mother, trusted her often-distant father, and to what avail? The miserable, awkward seventeen-year-old girl who had been carted off by her father on a round-the-world tour was buried deep inside her. So what if gossip about her supposed affairs filled the society columns? The newspapers were as untrustworthy as all the rest.

Julia knew that everybody except her family and close friends assumed that she must be as experienced as the newspapers implied. More than one of her dates had been baffled—or annoyed—to find out how far from the truth that impression was.

The match was a hard-fought one, but Prince Abrahm's greater height and strength had given him the edge and the final score was 6–3 in his favor. Prince Abrahm relished the victory.

"You play very well. I did not expect such a difficult match."

Julia, who despite their heated game had kept her distance from the prince, reacted more warmly than she had all morning. "Thanks. I enjoyed it. I hate it when men let me win." She looked at her watch. "It's lunch time. Let's change and eat."

The prince was directed to a guest room, and Julia made her way to her own bedroom to change. The bed was canopied with imported, hand-painted floral fabric which cost $50 per yard; the carpet was from the People's Republic of China. Julia had designed her own chests and headboard, which a local craftsman then built from teak. Completely absent from the magazine-perfect room were any of the knick-knacks—posters, stuffed animals, souvenirs of dances or trips—which one would have expected to find in the sanctum of a college girl.

Julia found Andy on the patio, deep in conversation with her father. She wondered if Richard Harcourt were in the middle of selling some insurance to the wealthy prince, then suppressed such an uncharitable thought. After all, the family insurance company had bought her grandfather the magnificent home she now lived in; it paid for her horses and tennis lessons, her designer clothing and exclusive schools. And if her father had begged her to let him take her to Europe for a year to help her "get over" Mark, and then had devoted himself more to his business than to her pleasure—who was she to complain?

Andy rose politely as Julia slid open the glass door between the arboretum and the brick patio. Julia could never pass through that flourishing indoor garden without memories of her mother piercing her heart. The gardens had been Jill Harcourt's domain; both indoors and out, they had been maintained almost exactly as they were eight years ago, when Jill had died. They were a living memorial to the woman who had planned them.

The prince helped Julia into one of the comfortably cushioned seats and then stretched out in his own chair while Richard Harcourt looked on approvingly. Julia knew that Andy was a young man whom Richard Harcourt would consider suitable husband material—wealthy, titled, influential. And if she would find life as an Eastern princess sheltered and boring, she felt it mattered little to her father.

Julia's back became a little straighter, her chin lifted a few degrees higher, and when she spoke, she was regally composed. "Are you looking forward to school this year, Andy?" she asked politely.

"Yes. But I think *you* are the one who read exciting news in the paper this morning, hmm?"

The prince continued suavely, "Of course we are all familiar with Mr. Veblen's famous painting depicting the torture of political prisoners in Odar. He is a genius in his abilities as an artist; it is a most stomach-turning work. Naturally, it is based on incorrect information. I can assure you that such uncivilized things do not happen in my country. Nonetheless, he is brilliant. You of course hope to study with him, Julia?"

"Yes, very much so, Andy," Julia replied, and added coolly, "But, of course, politics is not my strong suit." Almost against her will, her tone warmed. "I only know that the chance to study with someone that talented—well, it's a little overwhelming!" she finished with uncharacteristic breathlessness.

As lunch was served, Julia realized with a certain sourness that her father had managed to steer the conversation toward travel. This had been accomplished in so subtle a fashion that she wondered if the prince even noticed Richard Harcourt's expert manipulation. No matter; the change of subject suited her well enough. Julia was content to eat the delicious lunch and listen.

As the conversation continued over frozen lime pie and coffee, Richard casually suggested to the prince, "Why don't you stay the rest of the afternoon?"

Julia had no choice but to graciously second the invitation. "Yes, Andy, why don't you?"

The rest of the afternoon passed in a pleasant, companionable fashion. They avoided controversy in favor of swimming, sunning and sipping iced fruit juice.

At four o'clock the prince reluctantly left. Julia did not even bother to watch him drive away.

You're a tough little wretch, she told herself later. Oh, it had been a pleasant enough afternoon. The prince was intelligent, handsome and interesting to talk with. But there was no magic. There was no response from her body. There never was—not since Mark.

As soon as she picked up the telephone in the privacy of her room to call her sister-in-law Allison, all introspective reflections were forgotten. Allison was the wife of her youngest brother Tom; Tom had been twenty-seven and Mark Glenndale the same age on that spring afternoon when the two men had appeared at the house for a game of tennis. Allison had arrived an hour later and the three of them had come in search of Julia to make up a fourth for doubles. Julia preferred not to subject herself to the pain of remembering the details of her subsequent romance with Mark, but there was one thing she would never forget. Only one person in her whole family had been willing to take on Richard Harcourt, and that had been her twenty-two-year-old sister-in-law Allie. She had angrily castigated her father-in-law for the unfeeling manner in which he had handled the situation, and spent hours talking with Julia, helping her to accept what had happened. Since that time, in spite of the five year age difference between them, Julia had felt close to Allison.

Julia could picture the smile on petite, brown-haired, brown-eyed Allie's face as she expressed her delight that Julia wished to spend the next week or so in Maine. Julia arranged to call Allison back once her plans were set.

She would approach her father about the trip to Maine later. Julia knew he had a dinner date with Maggie Rasmussen that evening. Her father and Maggie had been seeing each other for the past year. The glamorous, fifty-one-year-old Mrs. Rasmussen was a wealthy widow and had always moved in the Harcourts' exalted social circle.

Julia's oldest brother Douglas had once cynically remarked that if the two of them ever made it to the altar, it would be a merger, not a marriage. Douglas, now forty, was the Harcourt heir apparent.

Like his father, he ate, slept, and breathed work, and relished the prospect of Maggie Rasmussen as a

stepmother. It would add that much more clout to
Harcourt Insurance. As for Julia's view of the impend-
ing marriage, she knew that if Maggie ever became
mistress of her home, she would find a way to spend
very little time here. True, Maggie had never been
precisely unfriendly to Julia; she preferred to pretend
that Richard's daughter was an unfortunate inconven-
ience which one could usually manage to overlook.

The moment Julia stepped out of her father's Cessna,
to be greeted by her open-armed sister-in-law, she felt a
wonderful sense of release. Allison warmly hugged
Julia, then pecked her father-in-law hello. She proceeded to extend a rather stilted invitation to Richard to
spend the rest of the day with them and sleep over at
their home. Before he could reply, his son Tom, who
had been seeing to the car, strode out to the plane,
yelling hello.

Tom's hug for Julia was as warm as his wife's; his
handshake for his father markedly more formal. When
nineteen-year-old Tom had come home for Christmas
vacation one year and announced his plans to switch his
college major from economics to chemistry, it had
created a bombshell that only Jill Harcourt's tact and
influence over her husband could moderate. Tom had
gone on to earn a doctorate in biochemistry. His
graduate work had been in the area of cancer research,
and when he had landed a position with the prestigious
Jackson Laboratory in Bar Habor, even Richard Harcourt was moderately mollified. But a rift had grown
between father and son that could never be completely
healed.

For Julia, Allison and Tom's comfortable home
provided a retreat. They had lived in Bar Harbor, on
Maine's Mount Desert Island, for three years, and
when the pressure of schoolwork and hectic social life

became too great, she would come to spend a weekend with them. Their house was the one place where Julia could drop the layers of defenses that surrounded her to become a little like that open, carefree girl of five years before.

Richard Harcourt replied politely to his daughter-in-law's invitation. "Thank you, my dear, but I've arranged to stop in Boston and spend the night there. I have some business dealings to see to." He kissed Julia on the cheek. "Enjoy yourself, Julia."

A few minutes later, Tom pulled the station wagon into the driveway of their small house, made private by the surrounding hedges. As he carried his sister's suitcase upstairs to the second bedroom, he remarked, "Jules, you'd better enjoy the privacy while you can. Next time you come, you may be downstairs in the den." He smiled proudly at Allison.

Julia's eyes immediately fixed on Allie. The unspoken question she posed was quickly answered.

"The baby's due in late December," Allison confirmed. "And you're the first one we've told."

The next week was as close to perfection as Julia could have wished. Each day was cloudless and warm, with an unusually balmy breeze off the Atlantic Ocean that kept her from becoming too hot as she painted. An impressionistic, craggy cliff rose up the left side of her painting. The surf breaking over rocks and onto an almost deserted beach covered the rest of the canvas. The beach was in the foreground, and as a contrast to this rugged, wild scene, several children were building a sand castle at the shoreline.

Julia painted until noon each day, then enjoyed a picnic lunch and icy swim. Allison would join her after lunch and they would talk and swim before returning home.

Allie was a potter and the fact that she was a fellow

artist endeared her all the more to Julia. Allie and Tom never pried into Julia's private life, and evening conversation had been about family, work, Derek Veblen and Tom's research. Relaxed and satisfied with the progress she was making on her painting, Julia thought how glad she was that she had come to Maine.

Chapter Two

On Thursday, Tom had had to attend an evening staff meeting at the Laboratory. Julia and Allie decided to go to a restaurant in Bar Harbor for dinner. Both loved lobster, and nothing could compare with a boiled lobster that had just been caught.

It was not until they were shamelessly devouring tall crème de menthe ice cream parfaits that Julia began to talk about herself. After four days with Tom and Allison, she felt like a different person. Aloofness and tenseness were an intrinsic part of her character now. Only in Maine, where these traits melted away, did Julia realize by their absence how coolly defensive she usually was. And to become aware of this was to be bothered by it.

She began obliquely. "Allie, do you know how I spent the Saturday before I came to Maine? With an Arabian prince."

Allison asked nonchalantly, "Do you like him?"

Julia shrugged. "Not particularly. That's just it. Allie, he's smart and handsome, and as smooth and diplomatic as Solomon when he wants to be. *Why* haven't I fallen head over heels in love with him? Or with anyone else?" Her voice became low and halting. "Is there something *wrong* with me?"

"I'm no psychiatrist, Julia, but if you want to talk . . ." Allison said carefully.

"Yes. Let's go home and open a bottle of wine or something. Is that okay?"

Twenty minutes later they were sitting in the living room. Soft classical music played on the stereo, the lights were dim, two glasses of amaretto over ice sat on the cocktail table in front of the soft, cushioned sofa.

Julia sipped the almond-flavored drink and wondered how to begin. At last she blurted out, "I don't seem to *feel* anything. Not ever. When the men I go out with touch me, it's either distasteful or nothing at all."

"Julia," said Allie gently, "tell me about your trip with your father. I know you've never wanted to discuss it, but I think it's time. What was it like?"

Julia curled her legs up under her and pulled the clasp from her hair. "Mostly I was on my own. I—I really didn't mind. I've painted since—since mom got sick, I guess. I spent hours and hours in museums, studying all the masterpieces. It's funny, I didn't go to the museums in New York until I had seen the ones in Europe."

"Did your father take you to parties, receptions, that sort of thing?" Allie asked.

"Lord, yes!" Julia's face wore a twisted smile. "And he bought me clothing until it was coming out of my ears. Even though I knew that he just wanted Richard Harcourt's daughter to look the part, I enjoyed it.

"You didn't know me very well in those days, Allie.

At first I was really self-conscious. And I began to realize that every suitable young man Daddy pushed at me saw only one thing—a big, fat dollar sign. I mean, I still had pimples on my face, and braces on my teeth. And my figure was more flat than curved. For a girl who'd just turned eighteen, I was pretty backward. But they chased me all the same."

Allison nodded. "I still remember when you came home for a month—in the winter, wasn't it?"

"Yes. We'd been gone since July. And there was this incredible transformation. I still don't know how I turned out so well."

"It *was* rather astonishing," Allison agreed. "I remember the look on Tom's face when we all went out to dinner the night before you left to return to London. He told me later that his ugly duckling sister had turned into a swan. But he always said you would—that you'd been a beautiful little girl."

"Yeah," laughed Julia humorlessly. "But I was a stupid, ugly teen-ager. How I was ever dumb enough to think that Mark Glenndale was madly in love with me—"

Julia forced herself to remember those few months of utter bliss. Mark had given her a rush that would have made any girl's head swim. He was a former classmate of Tom's who had been teaching at a local junior college. To seventeen-year-old Julia, he was the epitome of a handsome, mature, brilliant man.

Mark had taken her out three and four nights a week, and Richard Harcourt was so often at evening meetings that he had no idea what was going on. Julia took care to sneak out so quietly that even the housekeeper never noticed her absences. Somehow she knew her father would disapprove if he found out.

Blond, blue-eyed Mark was ten years older than Julia

and came to rank just below Apollo in her eyes. All he had to do was look at her and she melted. It was Julia's first real experience with a man, and he had soon overwhelmed her to the point that she was sure she was madly in love with him.

When Mark proposed during a car ride in the middle of June, Julia quickly accepted. No one was at home, so she invited him into the house. They sat in the living room, where Mark had whispered that there was no longer any reason to wait. Julia, though innocent, knew exactly what he meant. She had willingly gone up to her bedroom with him. After all, they would be married soon enough.

He had kissed her several times, then unbuttoned her shirt and unfastened her bra. His own shirt was soon tossed onto the floor. The two of them were in this half-naked state, the lights out, entwined on the bed, when Richard Harcourt walked into the room.

For a moment, Julia froze. The light from the hall cast enough of a glow for her to see that her father was apoplectic. She nervously tugged on her bra and shirt, and sputtered out, "It's okay, Daddy, Mark's asked me to marry him."

Richard Harcourt replied with a spate of language that burned his naive daughter's ears. He all but pulled Mark Glenndale off the bed to take him downstairs to his study, and then as an afterthought looked back over his shoulder at Julia and ordered, "You come too. You'd better hear this."

Trembling, she obeyed. When the three of them were seated, Richard turned to Mark and said in a controlled voice, "So you want to marry my daughter."

Mark replied suavely, "I love your daughter, Mr. Harcourt. She's almost eighteen, hardly a child. I know I can make her happy. I hope you'll give us your blessing."

Julia's father said coldly, "Of course; but that's about all I'm going to give you—or her. Julia has no money, apart from what *I* choose to give her. Let me hasten to assure you that if she marries you, she will see not one red cent of my money. And neither will you."

Richard Harcourt lit his pipe and allowed himself several dramatic puffs before continuing. "I begin to realize that you must have invested two entire months of your valuable time on my daughter, Glenndale. I feel you should be compensated for that."

Julia watched her father open his checkbook with a sense of dawning horror. Why wasn't Mark telling her father to go to hell, that he loved her and would marry her no matter what Richard Harcourt threatened?

Richard held the check up for her to see. "Ten thousand dollars, Julia. Do you think you're worth it?" He then calmly handed it to Mark Glenndale, who took the check and walked out without so much as a good-bye to Julia. And Julia Elizabeth Harcourt walked tight-lipped out of her father's study to be sick in her bathroom.

The spring term had just ended at M.I.T. where Tom was a graduate student, and Tom and Allison arrived late that night to spend a few weeks vacation in New York. Julia had been sobbing in her room when Allison came in. Her calm, gentle manner encouraged Julia to choke out the whole dreadful story. Allison had hugged Julia, then excused herself for a moment to go downstairs. Tom and his father were screaming at each other about Tom's responsibility for introducing Mark to Julia.

No one had ever dared talk to Richard Harcourt as his youngest daughter-in-law proceeded to do. She told him that he was cruel, sadistic and thoughtless. There were a dozen other ways he might have handled the situation, yet he had chosen the one most sure to humiliate and wound his vulnerable daughter. Richard Harcourt's angry interruption of "Now see here, young lady—" was itself cut off. Allison announced that she and Tom were taking Julia back to Cambridge indefinitely, and Julia was only too glad to escape. During the next week and a half Allison was able to make her see that she was well rid of Mark Glenndale. Intellectually she accepted this; emotionally she missed him so much that she felt as if somebody had taken away a vital part of her.

When her father appeared at her brother's apartment, Julia at first refused to speak to him, but he seemed so genuinely contrite that she finally gave in. Her father begged her to put off college for a year to come to Europe with him. He wanted to make up for his behavior. His only excuse was that he loved Julia and had been so blazingly angry with Glenndale that he had not been able to act rationally.

And so it was that Julia found herself in Paris less than a week later. She had even missed her own high school graduation.

She continued telling her sister-in-law about her experiences during that year. "When I got back to Europe, a month later, we sort of picked up where we had left off. I must have seen every castle and museum in England and Scotland. There *was* one difference," she added cynically. "Now when my father's eligible young men looked at me, I could tell they saw more than a dollar sign. Allie, I would look in a mirror, and wonder how it could be *me* reflected back. At first I was flattered by the romantic advances. But then I realized that all my looks were good for was to sweeten the package."

Allison picked up the liqueur bottle and refilled both glasses. "And you began to get very hard, Julia, didn't you? And the longer I've known you, the more layers have been added to that shell. You run around to these jet-set parties and you never seem to meet anybody—*normal*."

Julia agreed, and the sarcasm in her voice was unattractive. "Yes. And the men I meet read all that garbage about me in the newspapers and all they see is a challenge, somebody new to seduce. The idea of sleeping with a girl who they think has been possessed by so many famous men seems to turn them on. Sometimes I even play them along for a bit just for kicks. I've turned into a class A bitch, Allie."

"No you haven't," Allison responded gently. "When you're with us, you're still the same sweet girl you were at seventeen. You've just been hurt too many times. One of these days someone will come along who you'll be ready to trust, honey. You won't let yourself feel anything because you're afraid to. But your instinct will tell you the right time to let go. You'll meet some decent, sweet man who'll sweep you off your feet." Allison smiled and concluded, "You'll see."

"Marriage isn't the be all and end all of life, Allie," Julia objected.

"Don't knock falling in love just because you did it once and it didn't work out," Allie insisted. "If I were to call it puppy love with Mark—"

"I wouldn't bite your head off. I know that now. I was in love with a man who never even existed, wasn't I?"

Allison nodded. "Little sister, I think you're going to be okay. You know yourself better than you want to admit."

Later, a little pang of jealousy stabbed through Julia as she thought of Allie and Tom's happy marriage. She knew that Tom cherished and cared for Allison in a manner which any woman would adore. But Allison gave a full measure of love in return. Julia's deepest fear was that she would never be able to care enough, to trust enough, to do the same.

Julia finished her painting on Monday, and flew home on Wednesday. She was met in New York by a member of her father's staff, who drove her back home to Scarsdale, north of New York City. Ellie, the housekeeper, greeted her warmly, and handed her an official looking envelope with the return address of Middlesex University printed in the upper left-hand corner.

Julia impatiently slit it open and began to read it.

Dear Art Major:

As you no doubt have read, the University is honored and pleased that Derek Veblen will be joining us during the upcoming academic year as a Visiting Professor of Fine Arts. Several hundred of you are art majors, and unfortunately it is not possible for all of you to have the opportunity of individual study with Mr. Veblen.

We are pleased to announce that Mr. Veblen has agreed to teach a survey course in twentieth century art. All fine arts majors will have first preference in enrollment for this course.

In addition to graduate tutorials, Mr. Veblen will also teach one undergraduate tutorial, open to approximately eight students. It is impossible for him to personally interview all of you. The Fine Arts Committee has thus selected those whom we consider to be the most promising students for the privilege of showing their work to him. All graduating seniors will have this opportunity as well. Please bring no more than five paintings with you.

If you are among those scheduled for an appointment, you will find a yellow card enclosed with the date and time. Mr. Veblen's office is in the Sherman Fine Arts Center, Room 204. All interviews have been scheduled for orientation week.

Good luck to all of you.

Sincerely,
Professor James Heilbrohn
Chairman, Fine Arts Dept.

Julia, who would graduate this year, inspected the yellow card. Wednesday, September 6, at 9:15 A.M. She had not planned to return to school so early; orientation week was primarily for entering freshmen and transfer students. But her apartment, which she had sublet to two summer school students, would be free, and she was just as glad to have an excuse to return to school earlier than she had anticipated.

In fact, Julia was honest enough to admit that if it were possible, she would go up to Weston immediately. But her father held a picnic for his staff and associates every year on Labor Day, so she would have to stay in New York to be the gracious hostess on that occasion.

The picnic, as usual, was a smashing success. Ellie was by now an old hand at organizing these affairs, and she had hired a large temporary staff to help her cope with the hundreds of people who swarmed over the Harcourt estate. Richard was in a jovial mood; he was always more relaxed when the weather was cooperative.

There was only one way in which this Labor Day picnic was different from all the others—Maggie Rasmussen was very much in evidence. When her father pulled Julia aside to tell her that he and Maggie had decided to take advantage of the occasion to announce their engagement, she was really not surprised. Julia kissed her father and wished him happiness, then

sought out Maggie to do the same. She received a cold
little peck on the cheek in return.

Julia left for the Boston area early Tuesday morning.
Three and a half hours later, she walked into her
apartment a few blocks from campus.

She had been apprehensive about how clean she
would find it. But Julia was relieved to see that it had
been left spotless. All she had to do was unpack her
clothing and other belongings, and stock up on food.

She had lived by herself the previous year, her first in
an apartment, but this year would be rooming with a
quiet young woman from North Carolina. They had
met freshman year and became casual friends. Melinda
Ashley, with her slow southern drawl and ready smile,
would be a perfect roommate, Julia felt. Of course,
because Melinda was a pre-med student, she would be
studying a great deal of the time.

Between carrying up her personal possessions and
unloading the food she bought, Julia was exhausted. She
put everything away and was asleep by nine o'clock.

She awoke early, then filled the hours between
breakfast and her appointment by cleaning the already
spotless apartment and watching television.

Julia Elizabeth Harcourt was almost never nervous
about anything. But as she stood outside the door of
Derek Veblen's office, she had a sinking feeling in the
pit of her stomach which she hadn't felt in years.

Now she looked at her watch. 9:08. She had decided
not to knock on the door until exactly 9:15. For the
tenth time, she studied the four pictures she had chosen
to bring with her. There was the Maine seascape, and
the French chateau; a muted water color of one of her
mother's gardens, and a portrait of her thirteen-year-
old niece.

Julia stalked down the drab, brown-tiled hall, then back again. Get hold of yourself! she mentally scolded. He's only human, not some god. For three years every professor here has been praising your talent. So calm down!

And in fact, it was as if some protective shield came to surround Julia. In an expensive denim pantsuit with a tee shirt hand-painted with portions of a Chagall stained glass window, she looked cool and beautiful. When, at 9:13, a young man whom she did not recognize emerged from Derek Veblen's office with a noticeably hangdog expression, Julia was unfazed.

A minute later, Derek Veblen poked his head out the door and barked impatiently, "Well, what the hell are you waiting for?"

Julia picked up her paintings and confidently sauntered into his office. Like most professors' offices at the school, it was quite small. The desk was covered with books and papers; the four-foot-high bookshelf was equally disorganized. A dog-eared box of slides, half of which had fallen out, sat on top of the bookshelf. There was a second chair in addition to the one behind the desk, but it was already occupied by a slide projector.

Julia extended her hand and smiled charmingly. "I'm very honored to meet you, Mr. Veblen."

Derek Veblen stared at her as if she were mentally deranged, then pointedly ignored her hand, as if it were contaminated. "The paintings?" he asked curtly.

My God, the man was unpleasant, Julia thought to herself. Artistic temperament she supposed, and silently handed over her work. He looked at each painting for perhaps five seconds. It gave Julia twenty seconds to look at him!

No doubt he was gorgeous. He was dressed in tight jeans and a light blue shirt with its sleeves rolled up to the elbows. Julia had of course studied his work in one of the courses she had taken, and because he was a graduate of Middlesex, his life had received special emphasis. She knew his father had been a German Catholic journalist who was an outspoken critic of the Nazi regime. He had had to leave the country by the latter half of the 1930s.

Walter Veblen had come to the United States and married a young Italian girl. Their son took after his mother in looks—dark hair, penetrating, almost black eyes and tanned skin. His firm, rather thin mouth was twisted into a cynical frown at the moment. From his father, he had inherited only his height. Julia judged him to be a bit over six feet. All in all, Derek Veblen looked vaguely satanic. Julia imagined that most women would find him devastating. She felt nothing.

Walter Veblen had been killed while covering the Korean War, leaving his young wife Clementina to raise Derek and his older sister Ramona. Mrs. Veblen had worked as a seamstress and as a maid, earning just enough to support herself and her children. Somewhere along the line, perhaps as a result of heredity, Derek had developed a blazing social conscience, which was now reflected in his painting.

After a cursory inspection of her work, the artist glanced disdainfully at Julia. "That's all, Miss Harcourt. You can go now."

Julia's heart had begun to thump rather erratically, but she quickly controlled it. In a cool voice, she asked, "When will I find out—"

Derek Veblen shook his head. "You're not what I'm looking for." Then he rudely turned his back to her and began to shuffle through some papers.

Julia would not permit herself to feel angry or disappointed. "Mr. Veblen," she persisted calmly, "perhaps if you could tell me what you *are* looking for,

I could show you other paintings which would meet your standards."

He turned around and stared at her, incredulous. Julia stared straight back. She said patiently, "Mr. Veblen, I want very much to be in your course. I'm sure there must be something I could do—"

To Julia's utter amazement, he threw back his head and began to laugh. "Miss Harcourt," Derek Veblen said with undisguised sarcasm, "are you offering me your body in return for entrance into my tutorial?"

For the first time, Julia's composure slipped. She was mentally counting to three before replying when the artist went on in an amused voice, "I might even be able to summon up the interest to take you up on it. Tell me, do you keep score? Would I be rated from one to ten in comparison with all the others?"

Julia drew herself up to her full 5'6". Two could play his game. She forced her tone to be curious, nothing more. "You tell me, Mr. Veblen, how *would* you measure up?"

He glanced at his watch. "There isn't time to give you a demonstration, Miss Harcourt," he drawled. "I wouldn't want to rush and fail to meet your high standards." His manner was dismissive. Clearly the whole conversation had begun to bore him.

Julia silently gathered up her work. For the first time in over three years she had no pointed retort, no witty comeback. Finally she made herself ask indifferently, "Just what is it my paintings lack, Mr. Veblen?"

For a moment Julia thought that he would simply ignore the question. He had walked her to the door, and opened it with mocking courtesy.

But he answered coldly, "You're a rich little girl who's had everything she wants in life. And it shows in your work. Very pretty, good technique, and sterile as a surgeon's blade. Just like the artist, in fact. No passion, no commitment. Beautiful to look at, but underneath, nothing."

Julia felt absolutely stricken, and any inclination she might have felt to dispute his opinion of her work vanished with one glance at his implacable expression. She picked up her pictures and managed a stiffly proud retreat from his office.

Chapter Three

Julia drove the short distance to her apartment and tremblingly let herself in. She tried to put the conversation out of her mind, but it was impossible. Derek Veblen, in less than five minutes, had put his finger on Julia's very worst fear about herself. *On the surface, beautiful, but underneath, nothing.* Was it really a fair description?

Julia abruptly rejected such a judgment. Hadn't Allie told her it wasn't true? The man obviously had a chip on his shoulder, that was all. He resented her father's wealth and influence; he probably thought that all good artists had to suffer, or some such drivel. It wouldn't have mattered what she had shown him; he would have denied her entrance into the course in any event.

Julia arrogantly decided that she was not about to let him get away with it. By that evening she had convinced herself that she had been dealt with in a capricious, unprofessional fashion. She called her father and simply repeated the details of the conversation she had had with Derek Veblen.

Richard Harcourt, as Julia well knew, could not tolerate any insult to his daughter's virtue. On more than one occasion she had seen him livid over newspaper or magazine stories which linked Julia with promiscuous rock stars or married politicians. It usually took all her powers of persuasion to calm him down and convince him that a suit for libel would only lead to more sensational headlines.

Repeating Derek Veblen's sarcastic comments to Richard Harcourt was like waving a red flag in front of a bull, and Julia knew this perfectly well. No one treated his little girl like that and escaped unburned. He told Julia curtly, "I'll take care of the matter."

Julia passed Thursday in a leisurely manner and confidently awaited her father's appearance in Weston. She was not disappointed. He called at seven o'clock Friday morning to say that she should meet him in the office of university president Hiram Felker in four hours.

Julia took special care in dressing. She washed and dried her hair, then brushed it until it gleamed like a red-gold flame. She wore a white and green sundress, which accentuated her perfect tan, with a pair of high-heeled white sandals which made her long legs look coltish and shapely. When she walked from the parking lot toward the administration building, men turned to stare.

Julia entered the large office of President Felker to find her father, Felker and Derek Veblen waiting for her. Hiram Felker had been a professor of history before becoming president of Middlesex University. Julia remembered hearing that Derek Veblen had been one of his students.

She walked over and shook hands with President

Felker. She kissed her father hello, then gracefully sat down next to him on the couch. Derek Veblen, unlike the other two men, had not bothered to get up. Julia favored him with a cool nod, and controlled the impulse to shudder. My God, he looked furious!

Richard Harcourt got right to the point. "Well, Hy, as you know, I'd planned to make a major gift to the school when Julia graduates in a few months. But there doesn't seem to be any reason to wait." He turned to Derek Veblen. "I understand you have great interest in helping—uh—underprivileged young artists receive the type of education you yourself received here at Middlesex. I propose to endow a scholarship fund to make it possible for two young people in each class to attend Middlesex, all expenses paid. Naturally, I would want you or somebody designated by you to choose the students."

"Naturally," agreed Derek Veblen acidly. He looked angrily over at Hiram Felker. "Hiram, do I really have to sit here and listen to this?"

President Felker smiled smoothly. "Now, Derek, we're talking about a great deal of money. Indulge us with a few more minutes of your time, hmm?"

"I can *indulge* you until your secretary has to call in an undertaker, but it won't make any difference. I don't take bribes." Derek glared at Julia and she could feel herself blushing.

"Mr. Veblen, there seems to be some misunderstanding here," Richard Harcourt put in apologetically. Julia knew her father well enough to pick up the glimmer of respect in his eyes. "It would never occur to me to ask you to accept Julia into your course if you didn't feel she were qualified." He got up from the couch and walked toward a door at the rear of the office. Julia wondered what he was up to. It was obvious that he had decided he couldn't *buy* Derek

Veblen. Her humiliation of a few moments ago had passed, and she was once again self-possessed and aloof.

Richard removed a painting from the closet, and carried it over to set it on the couch opposite Derek. He said in a puzzled tone, "For some reason, Julia has seen fit not to show you her best work. Perhaps it would make some difference in your decision?"

Julia felt queasy. That picture of her mother reflected the artist in her most vulnerable and pained state. It was not a side of her which she liked to admit existed. And, especially after the cruel things Derek Veblen had said to her, she didn't want him to know that Julia Harcourt was anything but the hard, passionless creature he had assumed.

She might have anticipated his cynical reaction. "Who painted it?" he asked curtly.

Hiram Felker said softly, "That's Jill Harcourt, Derek. Julia's mother." He looked at Julia sympathetically. "You couldn't have painted that when she was still alive, Julia. You were much too young."

"No," she murmured in a low voice. "I did it last year, from pictures—and memories. Mom used to sit with her flowers that way, as if she were trying to say good-bye to them—please excuse me a moment."

Julia walked quickly out of the office and into the reception area. She couldn't begin to guess what had made her practically break down that way. After a few deep breaths, she felt much better. When she returned to the office, Derek Veblen was standing in front of the portrait, studying it.

Julia was not about to subject herself to his crushing verdict. Her air of calm was only skin-deep; a stinging rejection from the artist would have undone her. She said aloofly, "I apologize for wasting your time, Mr.

Veblen." She crossed in front of him to pick up the painting.

His hand came down on her shoulder and she flinched violently. Julia could not understand herself. Only two days before she had been alone with the man in a tiny office and had felt absolutely no physical response to him. Now his touch made her skin burn and his closeness made her legs feel weak. What on earth was the matter with her?

Derek Veblen stared at Julia coldly. "If you had brought in this portrait two days ago, we could have avoided this whole ridiculous charade. You obviously have the talent to do quality work. The difference is so incredible that it took me a few minutes of study to believe this was really your work. But I can see that it is."

Julia found it impossible to meet his gaze. Instead she looked at the picture of her mother. Jill Harcourt was seated in her arboretum, surrounded by the plants she had so lovingly raised. On her face were written regret and pain for all she would soon leave behind. It was a wrenching portrait. Derek, his hand still resting possessively on Julia's shoulder, said arrogantly, "If you want to study with me, Julia, you can. But I won't let you get away with painting the kind of passionless, pretty garbage you showed me the other day. The choice is up to you."

Julia nodded tightly. "I'm honored!" she replied sourly.

The artist turned her around to face him, and forced her chin up to look into her eyes. She glared up at him, her body stiff with resentment. "One more thing," he informed her softly. "I don't tolerate insolence from my students, Miss Harcourt. Is that clear?"

How dare he treat her this way in front of her father

and Hiram Felker? Julia, angry and humiliated, all but gritted her teeth and spat out, "Perfectly."

It seemed to satisfy Derek Veblen. He released his hold on her, smilingly told Richard Harcourt that he would look forward to seeing the scholarship fund implemented, and casually took his leave. Julia, relieved that he had left the room, looked over at her father.

A small smile was playing over Richard Harcourt's lips. "I underestimated that fellow. I can even begin to like him, Hiram." He turned to his daughter. "Take care with him, Julia. I think you've finally met somebody who can handle you!"

Julia felt like storming out of the office at that unwanted bit of fatherly advice. Instead, with a perfectly controlled smile, she politely said good-bye to Hiram Felker and her father and, picking up her painting, walked gracefully from the room.

Julia's roommate Melinda arrived Sunday afternoon. She had driven all the way from North Carolina by herself and was thoroughly exhausted. Julia helped her unpack, then made dinner for the two of them and they both went to bed early.

Course catalogues were distributed the next morning. Julia's art tutorial was scheduled for Tuesday afternoons from two to four. An asterisk next to the course listing indicated that the signature of the instructor was required on the registration card. Julia felt like forging it. As eager as she was to study with Derek Veblen, she still dreaded seeing him again. Something about him undermined her usually unflappable composure, and she would not soon forget his rough treatment of her.

Julia had decided to remedy her ignorance about politics with a course entitled "International Relations in Today's World." And of course, she would also sign up for Veblen's course on twentieth century art.

That left one spot open. Julia had started out a year older than her classmates, but had managed to make up a semester's work; she would graduate in January. All her general education and major requirements had been fulfilled by the middle of the previous year.

Finally she settled on "The Psychology of Dreams." She had heard it was fun and undemanding. She neatly wrote in her choices, and on Monday afternoon made her way up to Derek Veblen's office to have him sign her card.

Julia knocked firmly on the door, determined not to let him see that she was anything but perfectly self-assured. She heard him call out "Yeah. Come in!" and immediately her heart began a traitorous thudding.

The office was even more disorganized than it had been the week before. Derek caught Julia's grimace of distaste.

"My graduate assistants say I'm hopeless," he joked. "I can't seem to get all this stuff organized." He pointed to the second chair in the office. The slide projector, now covered with dust, still sat on it. "Put it on the floor and have a seat."

Julia, relieved that he seemed to be in a good mood, did so, then handed him her registration card.

He took it, scrawled his signature in the space provided, and handed it back to Julia. But as she thanked him and rose to leave, he ordered, "Not so fast. You stay right where you are. I want to have a few words with you."

Julia, her face neutral, slowly took her seat. She willed herself not to tremble, lifted her chin and cocked an inquiring eyebrow at the artist.

"My God, but you're cool." Derek Veblen stared at her, frowning.

Julia made no reply. She continued to meet his gaze, her expression bland.

Her seeming refusal to become unnerved by his harsh stare apparently annoyed him. He said dangerously, "If you ever—ever—make the kind of scene you subjected me to on Friday, I promise you you are going to regret it. I value my integrity, Miss Harcourt. You would do well to remember that."

Julia felt hot with embarrassment and more than a little sick to her stomach. But no trace of it showed on her face. Something about his highhanded pronouncement made her mutinous, however, and she foolishly allowed herself to taunt coldly, "Yes sir. Will that be all, sir?"

"I haven't been knighted yet, Miss Harcourt," the artist said sarcastically. "Mr. Veblen—or even Derek—will do." He smoothly got up from his chair and walked around the desk to stand next to her. "I told you, I don't tolerate insolence."

He looked down at Julia for several moments and she calmly met his gaze. But when he softly ordered, "Get up, Julia," the room suddenly tilted and became smaller. Julia rose to her feet, clutching her registration card in one hand. She told herself she'd be damned if she would let him know how nervous he made her.

When his right hand firmly grasped her chin, her deep blue eyes met his angry brown ones, and only icy disdain was discernible in them.

At first his kiss was hard and insulting. When he parted her lips with rough insistence, she made no attempt to resist. Let him think he had no effect on her! His subsequent thorough exploration of her mouth was like nothing Julia had ever experienced.

It was as if he were trying to conquer her, to make her his personal property. The seconds dragged on, but he seemed to have no inclination to give up. He kissed her more gently now, persuasively, and firmly pressed her body against the length of his. Julia felt devastated.

She had never felt this overpowering urge to respond before—not even during her ill-fated romance with Mark. Only her pride kept her from wantonly kissing him back, twining her arms around his neck. She could imagine his sense of triumph, and the thought impelled her to force her eyes to stay open—his were closed— and recite childhood nursery rhymes to herself. Anything to keep her mind off what was happening to her! If her body felt feverish and her legs trembled with longing, she was doing her best to ignore it.

Finally, he drew away and studied her as thoroughly as he might a newly discovered Picasso masterpiece. She tolerated this with bland detachment. "You really are an icy bitch, aren't you?" At least Julia had the satisfaction of knowing that her well-acted indifference had affected him!

"Is that how you are with all your lovers?" he asked with sarcastic curiosity. "Like a damned statue?"

Julia saw the chance to hit back at him, and took it. "Ladies don't answer questions like that one, Mr. Veblen. And *gentlemen* don't ask." She continued frostily, "Perhaps there *is* one thing I could tell you. My response is in direct proportion to the attractiveness and expertise of the man who's making love to me." She concluded airily, "Practice a bit on someone else, Derek. You may improve."

Julia had never seen anyone look so angry. But with a mercurial change of mood, he suddenly began to laugh. "Julia," he shook his head ruefully. "You put it on a little too thick." He grinned at her. "I'm too old to get involved with children, honey. Run along. I'll see you next Tuesday." Still laughing, he ushered her out the door.

Julia's emotions were mixed. On the one hand, she

was relieved that the tension had been broken—that they would not have to greet each other on Tuesday as complete enemies. Derek Veblen had a formidable temper and she had no wish to be on the receiving end of his tongue. But on the other hand, she admitted that she had enjoyed the sense of power it had given her to be able to successfully, even if temporarily, get under his skin.

The artist's private life had often been a source of gossip and speculation in the art world. Rumor had it that his first commission was the mother of one of his fellow students and that the older woman had taken Derek as her lover. This outwardly very proper Boston matron had been delighted with the portrait and had recommended the artist to her friends. How many of those women had been a good deal more than friends with Derek Veblen was a matter of conjecture.

Julia had seen a number of these paintings hanging in the homes of her father's society friends. There was no doubt that even at twenty-two, Derek Veblen had been a blazingly talented artist. He flattered his subjects with stunning subtlety—flaws were down-played, attractive features stressed. And it was all done so skillfully that one would swear the portraits were photographically true-to-life.

Julia supposed that this was only politic. The man had to make a living. Yet his speech about integrity had galled her. Now that he was rich and famous he could afford to have integrity. He had not been so passionate on the subject eleven years ago!

Chapter Four

Julia was delighted with the way her schedule had worked out. All her classes were in the morning, except for Derek Veblen's tutorial on Tuesday afternoons.

The psychology course met Monday, Wednesday and Friday at nine; the international relations course those same days at ten. Both looked stimulating. Julia was asked to keep a journal of her dreams, writing them down before she even got out of bed each day. The psychology reading list was fairly light, and there would be a midterm exam and a final paper based on her analysis of the journal she was keeping

. The international relations syllabus was much more demanding. Hundreds of pages of reading were required each week; there would be one paper, a midterm and a final. The professor warned them that some of the reading was unbelievably turgid; certain brilliant analysts of the contemporary scene, it seemed, had difficulty writing a simple English sentence.

Julia fought her way into the school bookstore; it was mobbed with students who, like herself, had neglected to pick up supplies and books until now. She emerged an hour later laden with over a dozen paperbacks and a host of other miscellaneous necessities. She took everything home and, in a burst of beginning-of-the-term enthusiasm, began to read.

After two chapters of a book outlining the origins of the cold war Julia's head had begun to spin. How was she going to remember all this stuff?

She switched to psychology and found it more to her liking. It would be fascinating to record her dreams each morning, and then attempt to analyze their meaning. As a rule, Julia did not remember what she dreamed, but the instructor had assured the students in her class that with practice all of them would have no trouble with this part of their course work. Her only caution was that they must do the assignment honestly if it were to have any value. Even embarrassing dreams must be recorded, but no one would ever see the details except the student who wrote them down. The professor was interested only in the papers they would write.

Nothing could have prepared Julia for the scene that greeted her Tuesday morning as she walked up the hill to the building where Derek Veblen's art course was being taught. Television cameras from three different Boston stations were in evidence; hundreds of students milled around, waiting to go inside. If Julia hadn't known better, she would have thought that this was a student protest. Obviously the Art Department had anticipated a strong demand for the course; it was scheduled to meet in Hayes Theater, the largest hall on campus. The 750-seat auditorium was usually used only for plays or lectures.

The doors to the theater opened a few minutes before 9:00. Students poured into the building. Derek Veblen walked out onto the stage at 9:15, followed by several graduate students who carried audio-visual equipment. From the number of students standing in the aisles and at the back, it was clear that something had to be done.

Someone handed a mike to the artist and he began to speak. "Hello." He favored his audience with a broad smile. The jacket of his tan suit was unbuttoned; his striped tie was a fraction off-center. To Julia, who sat in the tenth row, he radiated a suave brand of animal magnetism.

"I'm afraid not all of you are going to be able to stay." A groan passed through the crowd. "There's really no fair way to do this," Derek apologized. "If I said the course was going to require twenty hours of work a week, would any of you leave?" Naturally everybody shouted back, "No!" The artist raised his hand for quiet and Julia was amazed at how quickly silence filled the large hall. She had been exposed to Derek's physical attractiveness, and God knows she had been exposed to his anger, but this smooth charm was something new, and Julia was a bit bemused by it.

The artist appeared to ponder the options for a few moments, then said briskly, "All right then. Juniors and seniors and all art majors can stay. How many of you does that cover—raise your hands." About two-thirds of those present did so. "Okay. That looks manageable," he announced. "For the rest of you, tell the students who are taking the course to treat me right." He smiled. "I may be persuaded to give it again in two years."

This seemed to mollify the disappointed younger students, who gave a rousing cheer and noisily filed out of the room. One of the graduate students took the microphone and began to explain how the course would be set up. Derek Veblen would lecture each Tuesday morning for two hours and graduate students would teach smaller sections of up to forty students on Thursday and Friday. Lists for these classes were posted near the Art Department office, and all students with the exception of junior and senior art majors were expected to sign up for one of them.

Derek Veblen then began a brief survey of the material to be covered. Although the course was entitled "Twentieth Century Art," it was clear that he meant to concentrate on lesser-known artists, many of them still living. He assumed that giants like Picasso, Klee and Matisse would have been covered elsewhere. He was especially interested in younger artists who were still working, and he told several anecdotes about his trials and tribulations in obtaining slides of their work to show to the class.

After ten minutes of battle between the slide projector and the determined graduate students, the equipment finally declared a truce and began to work properly. Notebooks were noisily opened as someone dimmed the lights.

"Hey! Don't start scribbling notes on all of this," Derek laughed. "It's just an introduction. We'll start the real work next week, so relax and watch."

Slides of paintings were flashed on the screen, interspersed with the instructor's trenchant and often amusing comments. Before Julia knew it, the two hours were over. She found it almost funny to eavesdrop on the conversations among the female half of the audience. Comments ranged from "I'd pose for *him* any time!" to "Do you suppose we could kidnap him for ransom and forget to send a ransom note?" to simple exclamations of "God, what a hunk!"

He probably took such reactions for granted, Julia thought acidly. His ego was no doubt as big as the Pacific Ocean. She'd be darned if she were going to fall at his feet the way every other young woman in the auditorium seemed eager to do. Besides, he'd called her a child. Let him use his admittedly persuasive charm on more susceptible females. *She* was only interested in his abilities as a teacher.

She picked up a syllabus on the way out. There was a short list of required readings, but Julia was familiar with all of them. She grabbed a quick hamburger at the Student Union, then stopped by the library to read for a few hours.

As Julia approached the studio where her tutorial was being held, she had to admit that she felt a little shaky. Nonetheless, she was the picture of complete confidence as she walked casually into the brightly lit room.

Derek Veblen appeared five minutes late. By now those who didn't know each other had introduced themselves. There were four seniors, two juniors and one sophomore. All of them looked distinctly edgy.

The artist tossed his jacket over the back of a chair and leaned against a desk at one end of the studio. He ran his hand through his already tousled hair. "Sorry I'm late. Did all of you witness my baptism of fire this morning?" he asked, tongue firmly in cheek.

Everyone laughed a bit nervously and said that they had. Everyone except Julia, that is. *She* said lazily, "You were brilliant and you know it. You had all of them eating out of your hand!"

Derek Veblen flashed her a grin. "All of *them*, Miss Harcourt? Don't you include yourself among my admirers?"

She replied demurely, "Of course I do, Professor Veblen. Why else would I be here?"

"Oh, I don't know, Miss Harcourt. Perhaps just to test my patience," he retorted wickedly.

The laughter from the others in the room effectively forestalled any reply, and Julia was thankful for it. Something told her that Derek would ultimately triumph in any verbal battle. She contented herself with giving him a level look.

"I want to have some fun with this course," he was explaining. "All of you have reached the point where I can't tell you too much about technique, brushwork, that sort of thing. Of course, I'll be glad to criticize anything you do—help where you need help." He gazed slowly around the room. "And *all* of you do have some weak points."

Julia felt as if he were mentally adding, ". . . especially you, Miss Harcourt." But his eyes had lingered on her no longer than on any of the others.

He continued, "What I really want to do is to open your minds, expand your areas of interest. I'm going to ask you to do a lot of painting for me, but I want you to understand that I'm not looking for masterpieces here. All I want from you is an attempt to do things you haven't done before—to try new approaches."

Derek stretched his arms above his head, then went on thoughtfully. "The fact that the seven of you are sitting in this room doesn't make you the best or even the most promising artists studying in this University. All it means is that *I* saw something in your work that I could relate to. I have a bias—in favor of emotion—of passion. I own and appreciate works of art from the opposite school of thought, of course. But I can't *teach* that."

He paused. "When Hiram Felker approached me

about teaching here, I made several conditions. I would teach what interested *me*. And I would grade the way I wanted to grade. For the survey course, it's no problem. My grad students will be marking the exams. You have a pass/fail option here. Are all of you agreeable to taking this course on a pass/fail basis?"

Everybody nodded. As if any of us would dare to disagree with him, Julia thought wryly.

"Good. Hold it—I'll be right back."

He strode briskly from the room. The other six students immediately began to discuss him in urgent whispers. Hero worship was rampant. Becky Sterne, a senior with whom Julia had previously taken several courses, said in a low voice, "I expected some brooding misanthrope. I never thought I'd even get into the course—he frowned at my work for all of five minutes, then practically threw me out of his office."

A shared laugh of recognition greeted this confession. It seemed that all of them had had a similar experience. "I wonder," put in Ted Cartwright, a junior, "how he dealt with the people whose work he *didn't* like!" Julia could have answered that he gave each painting five seconds instead of five minutes. But she remained silent.

Derek walked back into the classroom carrying a smoked plexiglass bowl filled with fruit. Everyone stared balefully at this rather mundane object; surely he wasn't going to ask them to paint oranges and apples?

"Ah. All of you are horrified!" he said, amused by the general reaction. "Here's what you're going to do for me. Paint the fruit, but make it interesting. You may never have tried anything cubist—like you, Mr. Clay," he suggested, looking at one of the seniors. "Maybe you should try it now. Or you, Miss Ramirez," and now he was directing his attention to a pretty junior. "You do very gripping, realistic paintings of life's losers. So don't paint me a bowl of rotten, decaying fruit!"

Derek briefly studied each one of his students. A few of them still looked mildly puzzled. "Give it a little thought," he advised, "you'll come up with an approach that appeals to you. But please don't discuss the assignment with each other or look at anybody else's work. Any questions?"

Ryan Kennedy, the lone sophomore in the class, spoke up. "Yes. Can we use any medium we want, and when should this be done by?"

"You can use children's colored pens for all I care," the instructor smiled, "and have it finished by next week." A groan erupted from the students.

"Next week," Derek repeated, laughing. "I told you—none of this stuff is going to hang in the Louvre. You can take the rest of the time to begin the assignment, or leave if you'd prefer. Oh, one more thing. Please leave the paintings you showed me in my office. I want you to be familiar with each other's work." He started toward the door. "See you Tuesday."

All of the students followed him out; most of them did not have painting materials on hand, and would have to buy what they'd need or retrieve them from their rooms.

Julia knew what she *shouldn't* paint—a realistic, detailed picture of a bowl of fruit. She imagined the sarcasm which would greet such an effort.

Back at her apartment she decided that perhaps Derek Veblen would like it if she painted the blemishes. It was true that such an approach would be unacceptable from Lucy Ramirez, but Julia was certain it would be okay from her.

She lay on the couch mentally trying to picture her finished painting, and slipped into unintended slumber. Only Melinda's entrance into the apartment an hour later woke her up. The two girls talked about their courses for a while, then went to their rooms to study until dinner.

After the meal they sat in the living room to watch the television news. Julia wanted to see if there would be pictures of that morning's mob scene at Hayes Theater. When no story appeared on the local newscast she felt a stab of unanticipated disappointment.

She had only to wait twenty-five minutes. Toward the end of the national news, as a picture of the auditorium and the crowds flashed on the screen, the anchorman intoned, "These are not pictures of a student riot of the 1960s. Rather, these young people gathered today at the Hayes Theater on the campus of Middlesex University near Boston—in search of knowledge. They came to listen to artist Derek Veblen speak about contemporary art." Some film of Derek's lecture followed. Then the anchorman said drily to his colleague, "Such enthusiasm for learning gives one hope for the future, doesn't it, Lesley?" He smiled into the camera. "Good night for UBC News."

Melinda's eyes were still glued to the television set. She slowly turned to Julia. "Wow! You didn't tell me he was anything like *that!* Not only is he gorgeous, he oozes charm. How can you sit in a room with him and concentrate on *painting?*"

Julia playfully mocked her roommate. "You're an almost-engaged woman. What would Jim say if he could hear you gushing that way?"

"He'd say I have good taste," Mel retorted. "You haven't answered my question."

"I probably shouldn't admit this. But since you ask, the answer is, I can't."

"Julia! Phone call for you," Melinda shouted.

"Who is it?" Julia came into the kitchen and took the phone.

Prince Abrahm's cultured voice was easily recognizable on the other end of the line. "When may I see you?" he asked in a direct manner. "Saturday night?"

Julia hesitated, finally deciding that a movie could do no harm. Andy readily agreed, telling her he would pick her up at seven.

The rest of the week passed in a routine enough fashion. Julia was finding it difficult to plough through the international relations reading, but she was determined not to give up on it. Was she really expected to remember every name, every date, every fact?

Keeping the journal of her dreams proved an easier task. Some of her nocturnal fantasies were easy enough to recall and figure out. Wednesday morning, for example, she had awakened to recollect visions of fruit surrealistically marching around her bedroom. But what of the dream that she was in a long hallway, with doors on either side? She opened each one in sequence, yet nothing was ever behind them.

She spent hours each day staring at Derek Veblen's bowl of fruit. Other members of the class were often in the studio, doing likewise. But all of them respected their professor's injunction and neither discussed nor compared their efforts.

Julia tried to emphasize the imperfections in the fruit, carefully painting in each bruise and blemish. She exaggerated the distortion caused by the bowl. All in all, she was satisfied with her progress.

On Saturday, Julia went to the movies with Andy and then out for coffee. Once again, he seemed inclined to carry their relationship further than Julia wanted to allow, but he accepted her calm turn-down politely.

Later, back in her apartment, Julia decided that he was pleasant enough. But still, she worried, why wasn't she more attracted to him? Maybe Allie was mistaken—maybe there really was something wrong with her.

Julia spent all her free time that weekend painting. She finished the assignment for her tutorial; she wanted to start work on something different from anything she had tried before. She settled on a portrait of a young girl, and as the idea took shape in her mind, it became clear that the girl was Julia at seventeen. Derek Veblen wanted emotion and passion? All right, she'd give it to him. Gangly, plain Julia at seventeen, in a French couturier's "maison," knowing that all of daddy's money couldn't transform her into a movie star or a model. But Julia was not about to do a self-portrait. The young girl in her picture would look like someone *else*.

"I've been dreading this as much as I've been looking forward to it." The speaker was Justine Brandon, a senior art major in Veblen's tutorial, and her confession accurately represented the sentiments of the other six students in the room as they awaited their professor's arrival.

Derek strode in a few minutes late, just as he had been that morning for his lecture course. Of course he had been electrifying, pointing out important facets of the paintings he was showing with such staccato rapidity that finally a few courageous students in the class had implored, "Slow down!"

Derek had seemed genuinely surprised. "Am I going too fast for all of you?" Almost everyone shouted back

"Yes!" Thereafter he proceeded at a much more leisurely pace, stopping every now and then to relate stories about the artists whose work he was covering, and telling his class, "You aren't responsible for any of this, so don't take notes on it. I'm only practicing in case my paintings stop selling, and I have to hit the lecture circuit!"

But now Julia wasn't one anonymous face in a sea of five hundred, able to relax and thoroughly enjoy her professor's insights and sense of humor. Instead she was one of seven, but no one could have guessed that the beautiful, slightly bored looking redhead was as nervous as all the rest.

Derek had picked up a blackened banana from the bowl of fruit and was regarding it with distaste. "Remind me the next time I do this to replace the banana halfway through. Or to spray it with acrylic coating so it won't ripen and stink up the studio."

The small joke broke the tension in the room, as Derek had intended. He looked at each of his students, amusement in his eyes, then asked, "Okay. Who's going to be the first victim? Is there a volunteer?"

Fourteen hands stayed glued to their owners' sides. No one spoke.

"Miss Brandon. You have the misfortune to come first alphabetically. I promise you that next time we'll start from Z and work backward. Let's see if you've managed to turn a bowl of fruit into a feminist polemic."

Almost all of Justine Brandon's work focussed on the oppression of women. She slowly placed her painting on the easel at the front of the room. Her six fellow students and their professor studied it for several moments as Justine returned to her seat.

The picture was a surrealistic nightmare. The fruit was depicted in extreme close-up; on the outside each piece was perfect. But sections had been cut away, to reveal struggling migrant workers, clawing to escape from inside. And Justine Brandon was almost talented enough to have carried off such a melodramatic theme successfully.

Derek Veblen had begun to laugh. "I see you *did* manage it. But you added oppressed *men,* didn't you? Was that supposed to placate *me?*"

"It isn't feminist, Mr. Veblen," Justine protested weakly. "It just reflects a social conscience."

"A woman after my own heart," Derek said, eyes twinkling. He offered a few rather devastating comments on her work, then said, "All right, let's talk about the picture, and about the type of thing you do. Do the rest of you have anything to say?"

At first, Justine Brandon's classmates were hesitant to be too harsh, but they needed only a few minutes to warm up. Although Julia took part in this merciless dissection, she empathized with the victim. After fifteen minutes, Derek glanced at the clock, and cut off the discussion.

"Don't look so glum," he told a stricken Justine. "Now you get your turn at the rest of them." This thought did not seem to provide much solace to Justine; Julia had never seen her look quite so pale.

In a way, Julia was glad to be fourth instead of last. Better to get it over with! Ted Cartwright and Ned Clay had fared no better than Justine. Derek Veblen began with a few pithy observations, and then leaned lazily back against the desk and let his students take over. His initial remarks could not be called sadistic or cruel; nonetheless, they stung.

By the time Julia walked to the front of the room to put her painting on display, she was quaking inside. Outwardly, however, she seemed calm and unconcerned.

Derek Veblen looked at her work, and a slow smile spread over his face. "Miss Harcourt, you are the only person I know who could paint a bowl of fruit so that even the bruises look elegant," he drawled. "Even with your privileged background, you must be aware that imperfections are *not* supposed to be beautiful." His attention was fixed once more on the painting. For a moment he looked puzzled.

"Were you being ironic?" he questioned.

Julia had no idea what he meant. Her level stare as much as admitted this.

"No, I didn't think so," the artist sighed. "A pity." He explained to the class, "The idea of the very perfect Miss Harcourt taking the blemishes and transforming them into something as outwardly perfect as herself has appeal. Rather a self-parody. Is the meaning clear?" He stared at Julia.

"Yes, Mr. Veblen," she replied evenly. She supposed he meant that for all her outward beauty, she was blemished on the inside. She felt herself redden, and it took all her will power to calmly sit down and pretend his remarks didn't bother her.

He laughed. "Let's see if the rest of you will have more success in penetrating Miss Harcourt's very thick skin." He walked over to Julia. "I hope they will," he said softly. "If you want to create the pictures you're capable of creating, you'll have to let yourself feel."

To Julia, what followed was almost vicious in its intensity. But perhaps it was no worse than what had been directed at Justine and Ted or Ned. Her classmates labeled her a cold little rich girl whose work reflected her inability to identify with what she painted. Only the portrait of her mother, which they had all had time to examine, found favor with them.

And worst of all, through the whole, miserable

fifteen minutes, Julia could feel Derek's probing eyes on her, as though he were waiting for her to crack and run from the room in tears. But she would never permit herself such histrionics. She listened attentively to what was being said, pretending that the criticism was being directed at some fictional person. When she finally looked up, Derek intentionally caught her eye. He slowly shook his head, his face alight with mockery. It was some little consolation to Julia that the remaining three students had to endure similar trials.

When the bell rang signaling the end of the class, Derek quietly asked if everyone could stay for a few minutes. None of them had another class, and they wearily settled back to listen to their instructor. Every ego in the room had been thoroughly mangled; their collective mood was dour.

"I know this hasn't been pleasant for any of you," Derek said gently. Julia considered that the remark should have won a prize for understatement.

"I thought it best to let you rip each other to pieces right at the beginning. Now we won't have to do it again. Keep that in mind if you're ever tempted to repeat what's already been said here today." He smiled warmly. "I want all of you to try to be constructive in your comments in the future. You can leave the withering sarcasm to me."

His gaze rested briefly on each one of them before he asked drily, "Are all of you coming back for more?"

Nods and wan laughs were the response. Julia noticed that all of them avoided each other's eyes.

"Good," Derek said with satisfaction. "For next week, repeat the assignment. And try to keep in mind what you learned today."

"As if we could forget!" Lucy muttered as the others laughed ruefully. The seven students began to gather

up their books and papers to leave, but were once again
checked by their professor's soft, "Hold it."

"I have one more thing to say. All of you did very
well with this." Looks of disbelief greeted that statement.

"No, I'm serious. You were being measured against a
standard which I intentionally set very high. Don't go
away with the feeling that your work is hopelessly
stereotyped, that you aren't capable of doing anything
outside of what most appeals to you. It's not true. And
by the way, you might all try to forgive each other, I'd
say you all came out about even!" Derek smiled.
"Look, I'm supposed to be the expert, and you're all
supposed to believe what I tell you. Cheer up! See you
next week."

Seven only slightly less dejected students straggled
out of the room. None, it seemed, was in the mood to
discuss the two grueling hours they had shared.

The stick and the carrot, Julia told herself. First he
rips our confidence to shreds, then he tells us that it's
only because we're so talented that he holds us to such
high standards.

Was it really necessary for her to entirely change the
method she had come to rely on to cope with her life?
Julia had been playing the aloof heiress for so long that
she doubted her ability to be open or emotional. She
wasn't ready to trust people. Worse, she felt no
particular desire to try.

At home, she treated herself to a long, relaxing soak
in the tub. Melinda would not be home until later so
Julia had time to unwind. She realized that the pretense
of detached interest she had adopted during that fifteen minute blitz of herself and her work had taken
its toll.

Prince Abrahm called that evening to invite her to
go with him to New York for the weekend. He com-

plained sadly that he had been browbeaten into per-
forming certain diplomatic duties; Julia's presence
would make them so much more endurable.

Julia politely declined. She had too much work to do
to take the weekend off. And besides, she asked
herself, what would be the point?

Chapter Five

Although as a senior art major Julia was not required to attend any of the discussion sections for Veblen's lecture course, she had heard compliments about the class led by a new graduate student. She spent several hours on Thursday painting, and by two o'clock felt distinctly uninspired. She decided to take a break and stop by the class.

Max Nyquist, a grad student in art history, stood at the blackboard, writing down key phrases, as the students filed into the room. Julia, because she lacked anything better to do, idly studied him. Powerfully built, trim body; medium height; sandy blond hair. Faded jeans; blue shirt. He turned around and looked at the door. Julia decided that the front wasn't half-bad either: dark eyes, good features.

His lecture was well-organized, concise and interesting. Julia noticed that from time to time he glanced at her, as if unable to help himself.

When the bell rang, Julia was going to leave without speaking to him. Then she told herself that it was only polite to tell him that she had enjoyed his lecture. Maybe he wondered what she was doing in the class.

Several students were gathered around him, and Julia waited patiently until they had gone. When they were alone, she gracefully extended her hand and introduced herself: "I'm Julia Harcourt. I'm an art major—a senior. I heard your section was good, so I decided to stop by to listen."

"I'm flattered," Max smiled. "And you don't have to tell me who you are. *Everyone* at Middlesex knows who you are. So what's the verdict? How was I?"

Julia, who had begun to withdraw after that crack about her local fame, relaxed at the eager note in his voice. "Oh, you *were* good," she assured him. "The idea of the sections is to give non-majors background on criticism, history, that sort of thing?"

"Yes," Max nodded, "but none of it was new to *you*, was it?"

"No. But I wish it had been as well presented when I first learned it!"

"You won't come back, though."

"Probably not," Julia agreed.

"In that case," he said a bit nervously, "may I have your phone number?"

Julia ripped out a blank page from one of her notebooks, and wrote her number and address on it. As she handed it to Max, she saw Derek Veblen walk through the door, and changed her mind about leaving.

"Do you like baseball?" she asked Max, well aware that Derek Veblen could overhear the conversation.

"I grew up in Newton. Rooted for the Red Sox all my life." Suddenly Julia's meaning seemed to become clear to him. "Would you like to go to the double-header on Sunday?"

"I'd never know you were from around here!" Julia teased, mimicking his broad Boston accent. "And

I'd love to go to the game." She cocked her head toward Derek. "I think your boss wants a word with you."

Max tore his eyes from Julia and sheepishly looked around. "I'm sorry, Derek, I didn't even hear you come into the room. I'll just be a minute." He turned his full attention back to Julia. "My car is out of commission. Do you mind taking a train?"

"I'll pick you up," Julia offered. The two of them made arrangements for the date as Derek stood and waited.

Julia had not yet acknowledged her awareness of the artist's presence, but as she passed him to leave, she bestowed a curt little nod upon him. Unhappily, it seemed to entertain him.

Julia walked out of the library Sunday morning, thinking to herself that at the advanced age of twenty-two she had turned into a grind. She had always studied just hard enough to earn respectable grades, and put the greater part of her energies into her social life. Papers were invariably written only as the pressure of the deadline made itself felt; it was not an unfamiliar experience for Julia to stay up all night typing a paper that she would have to turn in at nine o'clock the next morning.

But she had spent most of Saturday researching her term paper for the international relations course—the topic she had chosen was the judicial system in China—and the paper wasn't due until the end of the semester! A thick paperback written by a former United States Secretary of State had consumed whatever time remained after her daily painting stint.

At least I don't have to feel guilty about taking today off to go to the game, Julia mused. It was a crisp, sunny New England fall day, perfect for being outside.

Julia made herself a snack, left a note for Melinda, and climbed into her station wagon.

She easily found the suburban home where Max lived with his family. He was out the door before she was halfway up the walk.

Julia walked up to him, handing him her car keys. "You drive. You're probably just as insane as all the rest of the drivers in Boston."

It was a perfect afternoon, even if Julia ate more junk food than her system could comfortably tolerate. The Red Sox won both games; the small size of Fenway Park generated a feeling of intimacy that contributed to the fun of being a spectator. Max paid more attention to the game than Julia did, but she enjoyed the sunshine and the boisterousness of her fellow fans.

As he pulled into his driveway, Max invited Julia in to meet his parents. After a cup of coffee with his family, he walked her back out to the car, and Julia had the feeling that he was relieved that the darkness hid his expression. He seemed very shy—at least with her! It was such a delightful change after all the wolves she had fended off in her life that she impulsively reached up to kiss him good night.

He caught her in a roughly aggressive embrace, which Julia placidly tolerated. It took a minute for her lack of response to register with Max; then he drew away, mumbled an apology, and helped her into the car. Wolf in sheep's clothing, Julia thought ruefully. It would be nice, if once—just once—she could meet a man who would approach her just as a friend.

Derek Veblen strolled into his Tuesday afternoon tutorial late by his accustomed five minutes. He was carrying a cup of coffee, which he sipped as he leaned against the desk. The seven young people in the room, still smarting from their treatment at each other's hands, had avoided conversation until their professor began to chat idly with them. From the desultory small talk he was making, Julia thought acidly, one would think that this was a cocktail party and not a class-room.

"And you, Miss Harcourt?" At the mention of her name, Julia's head jerked up. She had been off in a world of her own, but Derek interrupted her thoughts with, "How's the international relations course com-ing?"

"Fine, Mr. Veblen." Julia's tone was indifferent.

He lifted his eyebrows. "Ah! You're bored. I can see you want to proceed straight to the matter at hand. Good. We'll begin with you today—bring your picture up and let's have a look." Not a trace of a smile could be discerned on his mouth, but the brown eyes were warm with amusement.

Julia's first effort had met with such a lack of appreciation that she had decided to try a completely different approach. She had never in her life painted anything in the abstract mode; the bowl of fruit in her picture, while not totally non-representational, was a bizarre jumble of angular geometric shapes.

Derek glanced at the picture. "Why?" he questioned drily.

His reaction disconcerted Julia. She didn't know quite what she had expected, but certainly not this mocking amusement. Still standing only a few feet from him, she affected a casual shrug. "Why not?" she drawled in an equally dry tone.

"Because, Miss Harcourt, the whole point of the exercise was for you to put some feeling into what you paint," Derek said with what appeared to be resigned patience. "Did you do that," he indicated the painting, "just for the hell of it, because you didn't want to make the effort to take the assignment seriously?"

After all the hours Julia had spent on the painting, his words stung. "Well, I *do* beg your pardon, Mr. Veblen," she snapped back at him, "but a bowl of fruit just doesn't happen to thrill me!" Then she could have killed herself for allowing her temper to show. She stiffened, forcing the barricades into place.

"Does anything," Derek persisted, and then added so softly that only she could hear, "other than watching someone close to you die?"

Julia would have given anything to hit back with a comment that would devastate him as his cruel words had devastated her. But with six fellow students taking in every word of this exchange, she was not about to enter into a verbal battle with him. So she simply stood there, feeling sick and shaken, yet somehow contriving to look as bored as a Broadway critic at a high school play.

Derek sighed. "All right, sit down, Miss Harcourt." He focussed his attention on the rest of the class as Julia tossed her hair and returned to her seat. "Why don't we talk a bit about the type of art Miss Harcourt was—perhaps—attempting to emulate? Mr. Kennedy, you've done some excellent work, heavily influenced by the cubists. Any comments?"

A lively discussion on the subject, which only incidentally touched on Julia's picture, ensued. She took no part in it, but sat and tried to concentrate. She grudgingly gave Derek credit for manipulating the atmosphere in the classroom from one of hostility among his students to the stimulating sense of cooperation which now prevailed. As for herself, she wanted nothing so much as to be out of the room and away from Derek Veblen. She could not help but notice, as the two hours wore on, that he was much more pleased with everyone else's paintings than he had been with hers.

Five minutes to go. Derek must have just realized the time; he had looked up at the clock.

"I'll be in New York next Tuesday afternoon," he was saying, "but I've got something for you to do that'll take more than a week. Miss Harcourt," he frowned at Julia, "are you with us?" She merely stared coldly at him, waiting for him to go on.

He continued, "One of the most important things anyone can learn, in my admittedly anti-Establishment opinion, is irreverence. Of course," his eyes glowed as he glanced at Julia, "there are those of you in this class who are *part* of the Establishment and might not agree."

I can't imagine whom *that's* directed at! Julia thought, irritated.

"Irreverence and the determination not to kowtow to authority and to the pundits' notions of excellence apply in the art world also. You should be forming your own judgments by this point in your lives. I want each of you to choose a famous artist and paint a parody for me. You can satirize either a body or work of a specific picture. But please," Derek smiled, "not the Mona Lisa. Okay, that's all," he said dismissively.

For the first time in two hours, Julia's eyes lit up. She knew immediately what *she* would paint! But she quickly suppressed her sense of triumph, and put her energies into gathering up her things.

As the bell rang, Derek walked over to place a hand on her shoulder. Quelling her instinctive flinch, Julia looked frigidly up at him.

"Come down to my office with me. I want to speak to you," he ordered briskly.

She followed him out, short of breath and feeling as though a lead weight had settled high in her stomach. Why did he have the power to make her feel so nervous? No one else had that effect on her. She couldn't endure the thought of more chastisement from him. She supposed he just wanted to tell her that it would be better if she dropped his course.

His first words were uttered with a charmingly casual smile. "Do you approve?" With a wave of his hand, he indicated his now well-organized office. "Max Nyquist told me that cleaning this place up should have been the thirteenth labor of Hercules."

Julia was in no mood to appreciate his attempts at humor. These abrupt changes of his discomfited her.

"You didn't ask me down here to show off your immaculate office," she retorted. "If you want me to drop your class—"

"Julia, don't be an idiot!" Derek broke in, clearly annoyed. "This has nothing to do with your class-work."

"But you think I'm hopeless, don't you?" Derek was standing less than a foot away from her, and she had to force herself to look at him. She kept her expression icy.

His gaze took in her hair, her eyes, her mouth. "Was I too rough on you?" he asked gently. "If so, I'm sorry. You're so self-possessed that sometimes I forget how young you are."

As he stood there, looking quietly down at her, a wave of longing washed over Julia. She must be an absolute masochist to feel such a strong physical attraction to him. After all, he was cruel and sadistic, wasn't he? Nice to her one moment, only to hack away at her self-confidence even harder the next! She hastily backed away, sat down in the chair, and tried to look dignified.

Derek eased into his own chair, leaning back and putting his booted feet up on the desk. "One of the advantages of having a clean desk," he observed wryly, "is that it gives you a place to rest your feet. Do you miss the slide projector? If it would make you feel more at home, I'll go and get it back."

"Aren't we being accommodating today," Julia jeered. She still felt much too vulnerable to be agreeable.

"Indeed," Derek laughed, "because I want a favor from you."

Julia looked at him, startled. "A favor? From me?" In her bewilderment, her anger and hurt were forgotten. She couldn't imagine what on earth he could want.

"Umm. But you don't seem to be in a very receptive mood. Perhaps," he teased, "I should take you out to dinner before I ask. Or are you still so upset by what I told you in class that I'd be wasting my time?"

"I wasn't upset," Julia lied. "I wasn't *anything*. I took your class to learn something, Mr. Veblen. I *do* try to listen." She was once again composed, aloof.

"Have it your way, *Miss* Harcourt. You weren't annoyed, or hurt, or upset. You *never* are." Derek rubbed the back of his neck, a long-suffering expression on his face. "I didn't ask you down here to go over all that. And I certainly don't intend to argue with you. Julia—I'd like you to pose for me."

She was totally astonished. She blurted out, "But you *never* do portraits anymore!" A thought struck her. "Is this some scheme to show the moral bankruptcy of the ruling classes?" she asked sarcastically.

Derek Veblen burst out laughing. "God, but you're suspicious. You want explanations? Sure, I'll explain." But he paused for so long that Julia thought he had decided not to go on. When he began to speak, it was in a disjointed manner which was quite different from his usual glib style of expression.

"Hiram Felker is a close friend. He's suggested teaching before but I was too wrapped up in the other stuff. The reason I decided to accept this year was because I felt weary, burnt out." His tone became self-deprecating. "One can only play the impassioned social critic for so long before it begins to pall. It's very trite to say that teachers learn from their students but I do think I'm going to feel stimulated—recharged. I'm tired of death and dismemberment, and torture and hatred. I want to paint something *different* from what I've been drowning myself in for the past three years."

His gaze was thoughtful, intent. "I see something in you that I would very much like to capture. Will you let me try to do that?"

This quiet sincerity was even more unsettling to Julia than his previous harshness. She wondered what it was he wanted to "capture," but would never think of giving in to her curiosity and simply asking. She was all too used to men admiring her beauty; Derek might be a famous artist, but he was undeniably a healthy human male as well. True, she couldn't help the pleasure she felt at his interest, even if it were purely artistic; however, she certainly had no intention of letting him see how he affected her.

"I'm very flattered, Mr. Veblen," she told him politely. "Of course I'll pose for you."

His nod indicated satisfaction. "I want to think about the picture for the next week or so. I'll be back from New York Wednesday night. You're free Thursday afternoon, aren't you?"

She was surprised that he knew her schedule. "Yes. Should I meet you in your office or somewhere in the building?"

"In my office. At noon. We can drive home together."

"Home?" Julia repeated rather stupidly.

"Home. I don't paint here. I have a studio in my house. And there's no sense in taking two cars, I have a meeting on campus Thursday at six o'clock anyway."

"Yes, of course. Is there anything special I should wear?" Julia asked coolly.

"No. You don't need to worry about that." Julia thought she saw the suggestion of a smile tugging at the corners of his mouth, but when she rose to leave, his expression was perfectly solemn. She must have imagined it.

Both Andy and Max had asked Julia out for the next weekend. She had studied so much during the week that she accepted both invitations. She told herself that she deserved some diversion.

With Andy, she attended the opening of a very "in" new private club in Boston. Julia had dated some of the young men who were there, and Andy's reaction to their rather familiar hello kisses was to stay close by her side, clearly seeking to stamp her with his personal mark of possession. Julia did not care to be considered any man's property, but she found herself amused by such masculine posturings.

The party broke up rather late, and she fell asleep in the car on the way home. Andy limited himself to several minutes of restrained lovemaking, to which Julia responded with little more than sleepy tolerance.

On Sunday, she and Max attended a concert on campus—a student string quartet was playing Beethoven. The four instrumentalists were graduate students in the Music Department; two of them played professionally with Boston orchestras.

During the intermission Julia noticed Derek with a young, female assistant professor from the Anthropology Department. The two couples were soon talking amiably about the performance. Max's arm had crept up to drape itself casually around Julia's shoulder. Again she felt the unspoken male desire to possess, to mark one's territory. She smiled inwardly at the thought; Derek was the last person in the world who would be interested in her as a woman. He might find her beautiful enough to paint, but fundamentally he considered her a spoiled child. And his opinion of her talents as an artist was not much better. Max had no need to send out signals to *him*.

Later, Max kissed Julia good-bye outside her door with a practiced thoroughness which she found pleasant if not terribly arousing.

For the next few days Julia was so obsessed with the painting she was doing for Derek's class that she was barely able to concentrate on her other studies. She would sit and work for hours, sometimes missing meals, feeling absolutely delighted with the way things were shaping up. She couldn't wait to see Derek's face when she sprang it on him.

Thursday she met Melinda near the library. They ate a picnic lunch together on the lawn. Melinda had suggested the date, jokingly telling Julia that they never had time to talk except when they passed each other to go in and out of the bathroom.

"I have to keep track of your activities by reading the newspapers," Mel had gibed. The local paper had covered the club opening the previous Saturday night and Julia had been photographed with a group of socialites which included Prince Abrahm with his arm around her shoulder. A picture of her being kissed by the son of a Massachusetts senator had also been featured.

Melinda was laughingly telling Julia about the mishaps she had endured with some uncooperative fruit flies in a genetics course several years before when the twelve o'clock bell rudely broke into the conversation.

"Oh my gosh, I'm supposed to be down at Sherman Hall," Julia wailed, dismayed that she hadn't paid attention to the time. She grabbed her books and fled down the paved walk-way, adroitly dodging through the mass of strolling students who were on their way to lunch or a class.

She arrived at Derek's office, breathless and a little nervous, within five minutes. A knock on the door produced no response.

When the artist sauntered up a few minutes later, Julia turned on him with angry disgust. "I ran all the way down here from the library because I didn't want to keep you waiting!" she snapped. "Why can't you get anywhere on time?"

Derek ignored the tantrum. "If I tell you you look even more beautiful when you're angry, will you belt me?" he asked, grinning.

"Skip the male chauvinist comments and answer the question," Julia insisted peevishly. "Why are you always late? It's inconsiderate!"

"*Am* I always late?" he hedged.

"You know perfectly well you are! You might think of other people! Why should I have rushed down here, just to cool my heels—"

"Well, for God's sake, stop yammering at me and let's go then!" Derek interrupted. "How the hell should I know why I'm always late?" In one of his mercurial changes of mood, he suddenly gave her hair a tug. "I'll try to work on it, ma'am. Can't have my star model frowning at me, can I?"

They walked out side by side, Julia fuming because he had treated her like a pouting child. Derek's psychedelically painted Dodge van was parked in front of the building, quite illegally. In the back were paintings and empty canvases.

"I was wondering what you kept in here," Julia said, unable to keep a fractious note out of her voice. "Where I live, the teen-aged kids furnish them with beds."

"Disappointed?" he drawled.

"Oh, shut up," she replied, and stared out the window.

They drove in silence for several minutes, until Derek asked casually, "Enjoy your date Saturday night?"

Julia eyed him suspiciously. "Why?"

He nonchalantly cut off a red sports car and ignored the driver's angry horn. "You really want to know?"

Julia's first impulse was to yell, "What on earth is that supposed to mean!" But she permitted herself no such emotionalism. She shrugged. "Sure."

Derek's attention seemed to be totally on his driving as he asked bluntly, "When that eastern prince of yours takes you to bed, when he puts his hands all over your body, do you ever feel the blood on them? Do you ever think of the brutalized men in his father's prisons?"

The attack was so unexpected that Julia had to fight down a wave of nausea. Derek's grisly painting of Odarian torture hung in a New York museum where she had seen it on at least two occasions. Now it flashed into her mind. She said, "Andy denies it. He says you're wrong—"

"Don't be naive. It's true, I have photos that were smuggled out that prove it," Derek cut in. "You don't really think he'd admit it to his American mistress, do you?"

"I wouldn't know," Julia informed him frostily. "I don't happen to occupy the position you seem to have assigned me. And it doesn't happen to be any of your business in the first place!"

Silence filled the van. Julia was relieved that the conversation was at an end. But as soon as they came to a back road, Derek pulled the car into the dirt.

"I'm sorry," he said simply. "You're right of course. It's none of my business."

Julia, still shaken by the moral issue he'd raised, stared broodingly straight ahead, saying nothing. Derek's hand reached out to turn her chin toward him. For once she was unable to disguise the bewildered, hurt look in her eyes.

"My God," Derek said softly, "don't look at me like that!"

Julia, mortified by this lapse on her part, instantly lifted her chin; her blue eyes became cynical. "Is that better?" she taunted.

Derek suddenly smiled. "Tell me," he said playfully, "about the picture you're doing for next Tuesday. I have the feeling you're going to exact revenge for every criticism I've ever made of you."

Of course Julia knew that the change of subject was intended to break the tension and restore her good humor. It was blatant manipulation, but she had discovered that she hated being on bad terms with Derek, and so it succeeded perfectly. She couldn't help but impishly grin and say, "You'll have to wait 'til Tuesday to find out, won't you?" And before she could change her mind, she added, "And maybe you're right—about the other thing."

He started the engine. "Derek Veblen on the soap box!" he mocked. "Are we friends again?"

Friends? Hardly the term Julia would use. But she murmured, "Yes," and fixed her attention on the scenery.

Derek's home was located about forty minutes from the campus, north of the town of Concord, where the opening shots of the American Revolutionary War had been fired. He lived in a secluded, wooded area at the end of a long, winding drive. Julia remembered reading that he had bought up all the surrounding property; obviously the man had a mania for privacy.

"My God," Julia said when the house had finally

come into view, "who plows all this out in the winter time?"

"I made an arrangement with a guy who lives a few miles away to come whenever it snows this year. Before, it never mattered. I never had to *be* anywhere. Now not only do I have to get over to school, Miss Harcourt, but you insist I have to do so expeditiously." His sigh was exaggerated. "Life grows more complicated!"

But Julia was already out of the van and looking around at the incredibly lovely setting. Evergreens were interspersed with sugar maples, oak and other deciduous trees. Their leaves had just begun to turn to the vivid yellows, reds and oranges of the New England autumn. "It must be absolutely beautiful here after the frost does its work," she breathed enthusiastically. "Oh, Derek, I'm just going to love coming here to watch it all happen." Immediately she realized that she had unthinkingly used his first name. "I'm sorry—I shouldn't call you that," she hastily apologized.

"You shouldn't?" he repeated, amused. "You mind telling me why not? Especially in view of our conversation in the car."

"Because you're still my professor and I'm still your student," Julia cut in firmly. "I believe in observing the proprieties."

"Do you?" Derek took her arm. "Very out of character for a jet-setter, isn't it, Miss Harcourt?"

Obviously he was determined to think of her as the promiscuous creature of newspaper and magazine articles, Julia thought sourly. In spite of her denials, he probably assumed Prince Abrahm was her lover. But what difference did his opinion make?

He led her into his house, and even if she had not read that it was custom-built, she would have been able to guess after her first brief look. The double front doors led directly into a large living room. It was furnished entirely in browns and off-whites; even the area rugs were neutral tones against the polished hardwood floors. Chairs and couches were arranged in groupings; everything was starkly modern. But the art work! Paintings and sculpture were displayed on the walls and tables. Julia's eye took in bright splashes of color; somber, dreary scenes; wood, metal, plaster.

"Can I see the rest of the house?" The question was a formality. Julia had already begun to walk in the direction of the kitchen. It was large, all stainless steel and butcher block counters, with a sizable breakfast area at one end. The large picture window needed no curtains, there was nothing outside to intrude on the privacy of those dining.

"No dining room?"

"It didn't seem necessary at the time." Derek motioned her to follow him back across the living room, past a flight of steps, through a second door. His bedroom.

The large brass bed and massive oak chests were conventional enough. Some of the artist's own paintings hung on the walls, not the shattering collages for which he had been acclaimed, but abstract acrylics which Julia realized were his work only because of the signature in the lower left-hand corner. The idea of waking up to look out into the woods appealed to Julia. In fact, the idea of waking up next to Derek . . . she quashed the traitorous thought.

"Why did you put the fireplace in the bedroom instead of in the living room?" Julia wondered aloud.

"Because this is where I relax, unwind," he explained. "And the house has a special climate control system to protect the artwork. The smoke and heat from a fireplace can throw it off. Come on, let's go upstairs. I want to get to work."

Julia meekly followed him up to his studio. The house was certainly a bachelor retreat. There wasn't even a second bedroom!

The studio comprised the entire second floor. In addition to floor to ceiling windows it had several skylights to let in natural sunshine. Julia also noticed some klieg lights in one corner.

A bed with satin sheets sat in the middle of the room, and some distance away there was a cabinet for painting materials and an easel with a large blank canvas in place on it.

"I have to mix a few paints," Derek said casually. He pointed toward the far end of the room. "The bathroom's through that door. Why don't you undress while I set up?"

Julia stood rooted to the tile floor, and said in what she hoped was an off-hand voice, "What do I change into?"

"You don't change *into* anything, just *out of.*" His tone became businesslike, bored. "There's a robe in there if you want to slip it on while you wait. But I *did* turn the heat up when I came in. You won't be cold."

Julia wanted to make absolutely sure that they weren't talking at cross-purposes. She could feel a flush rising up her body and prayed that it wasn't obvious to Derek Veblen. "Mr. Veblen," she ventured, "are you saying that you want to paint me—without anything on?"

For the first time since the start of the conversation, Derek looked up from the paints he was mixing. Julia had regained the composure which was so important to her, and coolly met his gaze.

"Is there some problem with that, Miss Harcourt?" There was a slight edge to his voice which told Julia that he was impatient with her protests.

Julia didn't care if Derek Veblen were considered

another Picasso; she wasn't about to take her clothes off for *anyone*. She replied levelly, "No. No problem. I just won't do it."

He abandoned his preoccupation with the paints to stride carelessly over to her. "I think you're serious!" he said as he approached her. "Tell me, what makes it okay for you to be naked in front of your lovers, but not in front of me?"

"I told you before, my private life is none of your concern," she began angrily. "And I have no intention of dignifying your insinuations—"

He cut off this haughty pronouncement with a muffled curse, then told her, "Julia, this conversation is ridiculous. You must have spent a whole semester drawing nudes; you know damn well there's nothing romantic about it! You want to tell me you're pure as the driven snow? Fine, I believe you. Now stop hassling me and get the hell into the bathroom and take off your clothes. I haven't got all day."

Julia could not help but feel intimidated by his highhanded orders, but she didn't budge an inch. "Mr. Veblen, please take me home," she said, trying to come back with an order of her own which *he* would have to obey.

Suddenly Derek smiled, and to her chagrin, Julia wanted to melt. "Think of me as a doctor," he coaxed. "You don't argue with your doctor like this, do you?"

Her doctor was almost old enough to be her grandfather, but Julia was not about to let Derek know that what bothered her most about the whole idea of posing undressed was the physical effect he had on her. If he had been sixty-five years old and fat and bald, she might not have objected. She could feel herself relenting. After all, he couldn't help it if he was sexually attractive to her. He *was* a great artist. Certainly he had no interest in her personally.

She was appalled at her train of thought. She wasn't seriously considering doing as he asked?

He was telling her matter-of-factly, "Take the clasp out of your hair and part it—um—down the center." And then she was being propelled toward the bathroom as if she had agreed to the whole thing.

She stopped dead. "No. I just—I don't want to."

"Julia," Derek said in a voice that he might use to lecture a rather slow child, "I'm sure you have a beautiful body. It isn't anything to be ashamed of. I'm not going to make a pass at you; believe me, that isn't where my interests lie. And I'm not going to paint anything degrading or lascivious. But I picture you a certain way and I want very much to put it on canvas. Please. Don't make an issue out of something so minor."

Julia supposed he was right. She was acting like a silly child, making a fuss over nothing. Derek was an artist, not a lecher. Without another word, she walked into the bathroom and shut the door. She brushed out her hair, undressed, and slipped on the bulky terry cloth robe that hung on the back of the door. It was meant for a man and reached almost to her ankles.

Thank God she was too nervous to be at all aroused by the situation! She tried to seem calm as she sat down on the bed and waited for him.

Derek glanced at her, then said quietly, "Relax. I'm used to edgy models, you know. Let me tell you about the first—no—the second woman I ever painted." He launched into a hilarious anecdote, and followed it up with another story from what he sardonically termed his struggling artist days.

Soon Julia was laughing uncontrollably, and Derek calmly walked over and in the midst of the story he was telling began to issue impersonal instructions.

"And she had this notion," he was saying, "that I should paint her—take off the robe, honey—that I should paint her as some kind of modern day 'Liberty Leading the People.' Her ancestors came over on the Mayflower—lie down, put your head on your arm—and she saw herself as a true Boston Daughter of the Revolution. I could picture her charging up Beacon Hill—let me get the sheet out from under you, Julia— charging up Beacon Hill in a toga, all two hundred pounds of her. It was all I could do to convince her to pose in front of her fireplace. And even then—curl up a bit, hon—she insisted on littering the mantelpiece with her collection of patriotic knickknacks. She called it symbolism."

Julia was so absorbed in this nonstop monologue that it took a little while for mortification to set in. At least he was draping her in such a way that not *everything* showed, she thought with relief.

He finished the story, then began to move the sheet, adjust her head on the pillow and play with the way her hair fell. His face registered only impersonal concentration. But now that Julia had surmounted her initial embarrassment, his closeness was playing havoc with her senses. Every place his hand touched burned. She didn't dare look at him, but stared into space, not focussing on any part of his body. The temptation to reach out would have been too great.

At last he was satisfied and made himself comfortable in front of the canvas. "Perfect," he said softly. "Except for your expression." Julia looked at him, watched a smile spread over his face. "Tell me about all your lovers, Julia."

Blue eyes became frosty; unmade-up mouth compressed. She began to get up.

He raised a warning hand. "No, no. Keep still. Just

keep giving me that 'I'm Julia Harcourt and nobody can make me lose my cool' expression. I want to feel the layers of lucite around you," the artist urged.

Then Julia knew what it was about her that interested him. She wasn't vain about her looks, but there was no point in denying that her body and face were exquisite. Too many men had given her that corny old line about her body being made for love. It was the contrast—the warm, sensual body as opposed to the inviolate facial expression—that he was after.

It was hardly difficult to give him what he wanted. Julia could already feel every one of her defenses moving into place. She stared out the window, at a spot next to Derek's ear, and made her mind blank.

Deep inside, she felt a twisting hurt. If Derek had regarded her as an object of beauty, and had wanted to paint her because of it, she would not have minded. But her coldness and lack of emotion were traits he was constantly expressing his contempt for. And Julia couldn't help but translate that into contempt for her as a person.

She lay on the bed, perfectly still, almost hating him. Her expression was coldly regal; suddenly it didn't matter what she was or wasn't wearing. Nothing mattered.

Eventually her body began to ache with the effort of posing for so long. She tried not to fidget, but Derek quickly noticed.

"You're tired. Okay, get your clothes on and I'll take you home," he said brusquely.

On the face of it, Julia supposed it was a bit ridiculous to draw the sheet around her as she reached down for the robe. After all, Derek had been looking at her naked body for the last few hours.

But he had abruptly gotten up and left the studio before Julia even had time to pick up the robe. She scampered off to the bathroom, quickly pulling on her jeans and turtleneck.

Julia found Derek sitting in the living room, a distinctly brooding expression on his face. Julia stood at the foot of the stairs for a moment, then gave a little cough to get his attention.

Obviously *something* had happened to make him feel very out of sorts. Julia, as a fellow artist, could imagine only one cause. "Isn't it going all right, Mr. Veblen?" she asked with concern. She herself had experienced fits of temper over pictures which refused to take shape as she wished.

He looked over at her, and in some unaccountable manner his eyes felt more intimate now than they had upstairs, when she had been undressed. He seemed about to say something, then shook his head. "Forgive me. Artistic temperament. You were a very patient model, Julia. I'd like to work in a second afternoon, if that's possible. Your Mondays are free, right?"

"Yes. After eleven o'clock. I could do it then."

"Good. Meet me at noon again. I promise not to keep you waiting." He tossed her her leather jacket, and the two of them walked outside to the van.

Chapter Six

On Monday it was easier. Julia arrived at Derek's office at exactly noon, half-hoping he would be late so she could tease him about it again. But he was waiting for her, and pointedly looked at his watch as she approached.

They rode out to his house in silence, Julia studying the scenery and trying to unwind. Because her Monday and Thursday afternoons would be taken up in posing for Derek, she had studied all weekend. Her only break had been to attend a campus production of *As You Like It* with Max. She had received an invitation from Prince Abrahm but had declined, pleading too much work. In truth, Derek's comments about the prince had so upset her that she had decided not to see him again.

As soon as they arrived at his house, Derek told Julia to go upstairs and get ready; he would be up in a few minutes. She undressed; it was easier for her to lie down on the bed without him standing over her, watching. To her delight, the strains of *Eine Kleine Nachtmusik* drifted out of several speakers which Julia realized were built into the walls.

"The music will keep you from getting bored," Derek announced from in front of her. Julia started; she hadn't heard him come up the stairs. "Is Mozart okay?"

"Oh! Yes—fine. Thank you." Unlike the previous Thursday when Derek had simply removed his jacket and tie to paint, he had changed into skin-hugging jeans and a golf shirt; to Julia he looked disturbingly masculine. Why did he have to stand there, studying her as if she were one of his student's canvases?

"Hmm. More like this, I think—" And he began to adjust her body, the sheet, her head. It was a slow form of torture. His impersonal fingers set her body on fire, and she had to struggle to respond coolly to his directions. He was so detached about it, he might have been posing a seventy-five-year-old matriarch.

Julia found her customary focal point by his ear, put a mask of indifference on her face, and listened to the music. Several minutes passed.

"Tell me, Julia. Is the amount of time you spend here interfering with your social life?" Julia, annoyed by the question, looked into Derek's eyes. She had expected to read mockery in them, not this gentle amusement.

"Max Nyquist—how does he rate on your scale of 1 to 10? Is my graduate assistant a good lover?" he asked outrageously.

Julia was about to launch into an icy counterattack when she realized what he was doing. "You're trying to get my goat," she accused. "How come?"

He laughed. "You're too involved in the music. Your eyes look like they belong to a newborn fawn instead of to society's favorite insurance heiress. Turn to ice,

Julia! Make me feel like my proper place is under your boot!"

The obvious reply was irresistible. "I'm not wearing any boots." Julia couldn't help the smile that threatened to explode into laughter.

Derek put down his brush. "You just wrecked my concentration, lady. I'm going down to get a soda. Want one?"

Julia nodded. A minute after Derek left the room, the speakers went silent. Then Stravinsky's *The Firebird* filled the room.

Julia had to resist the impulse to pull the sheet up. Derek would have considered such modesty childish and gauche. He walked in and casually handed her an open bottle of cold soda, saying, "Drink all you want now, because I don't want to have to keep rearranging you."

It was a sentiment with which Julia heartily concurred. He sat down on the bed next to her feet; in spite of the veneer of sophistication which Julia had acquired over the past three years, nothing had prepared her to cope with the feelings his closeness was arousing. She peeked over at him; his face was a blank, as if his thoughts were a million miles away. She hastily swallowed some more of the icy liquid, then told him she was ready to begin again.

She suffered the quick adjustments that to Derek were no more than routine, then put the proper aloofness into her eyes. There were no more breaks.

As on the previous Thursday, when the artist sensed she was tiring, he abruptly stopped, told her to dress, and went downstairs to wait. He was withdrawn and unapproachable on the ride back to campus; Julia dared not introduce any idle conversation as they drove.

Derek walked into his lecture course Tuesday morning just as the bell signaling the beginning of the time period sounded. He did not begin speaking, but instead searched the auditorium until he found Julia's eyes. He grinned at her like a little boy expecting praise, held up his left arm with its expensive Swiss watch, and wiggled it back and forth. Julia mouthed a silent "Bravo" and soundlessly clapped her hands. Everyone in the hall twisted around to try to figure out what was going on. Of course they all knew who Julia Harcourt was. Veblen's probably her latest lover, many of them told themselves. A number of female eyes lit on Julia, jealous of her presumed position.

Julia, embarrassed, became even more eager for that afternoon's class. The anticipation of revenge had never been so sweet. When she walked into the studio at seven minutes past two, Derek was already there, leaning against the desk with his accustomed grace and languidly chatting with Ryan Kennedy. She held her picture close to her body, so that he couldn't see it.

Her instructor immediately turned to her. "2:08. Do I get a medal?"

"Am I going to have to hear your disgusting self-congratulations for the rest of the term?" she retorted, her left hand resting on a shapely, blue-jeaned hip. She glanced at Ryan and Lucy Ramirez, who were the only two students in the room, then thought, why the hell not! She went on, "From that little pantomime show this morning, half your lecture course probably thinks we were arranging an assignation!"

"Weren't you?" Ryan lost no time in asking.

"Our esteemed instructor was proudly showing me that he had managed to get to class on time," Julia explained as she took her seat.

"She chewed the hell out of me last week," Derek said to the confusion of several more students who were just coming in and had missed the beginning of the conversation. "Julia's posing for me. I committed the grievous sin of arriving ten minutes late to meet her. As penance, I've resolved to get to my classes at the appropriate hour. A major undertaking," he concluded solemnly.

Julia flashed him a mischievous look.

"Passed and intercepted," Derek said with a grin. "I told you I had the feeling that you'd been waiting to get back at me for the comments I made last time. Does anybody have any objection if we let Miss Harcourt go first again?"

The other members of the class, clearly fascinated by the ambiguous relationship between their professor and the school's most famous student, were only too willing to see what would come next.

Julia, a broad smile on her face, triumphantly put her painting on the easel. Most of the students were puzzled at the portrait. It was obviously a painting of the mother of the current governor—a grande dame of the Boston élite, she was known more for her hard-driving encouragement of her son than for her beauty. To put it kindly, the lady was plain. Her husband, now a successful businessman, must have married her either for her intelligence or for her position in Boston society. She had rather small eyes, a receding chin, and a humped nose. Even the skillful makeup she used could not hide all her faults. And in the last few years, she had put on rather too much weight!

Yet Julia had somehow managed to subtly correct her physical shortcomings—to turn her into an attractive older woman. She had glamorized her just enough for the whole picture to become just a little bit outrageous.

Derek studied the picture for longer than his accustomed twenty seconds, then burst out laughing. He mockingly bowed to the artist.

"I'll bet you enjoyed every moment of painting that, didn't you!" He shook his head ruefully. "Obviously," he told the class, "Miss Harcourt has seen examples of my early work." He cocked an eyebrow at Julia. "Yes?"

"Some of my parents' friends had their portraits done by you. I've seen them hanging in their living rooms." Julia was a little relieved by his reaction. As much as she had eagerly anticipated springing this picture on him, she had worried that he would be angered by it.

She smiled at him, warmly and openly. "I have to admit you're a good sport."

"I don't have any choice—it's damn near perfect!" Some of the students in the class still looked mildly bewildered. Their instructor elaborated, "Miss Harcourt has painted a rather heartless parody of my early efforts. You all know that I began as a portrait painter. Maybe you also know that when I was starting out, I found it—uh—expedient to flatter my subjects. In all modesty, I must tell you I was brilliant at it!" he laughed. "Rumor has it that my first commission came from a lady who was rather more than a friend. As a gentleman, I won't comment on that allegation; but let me assure you that if the lady in question hadn't been pleased with her portrait, I could have been the world's greatest lover and she wouldn't have recommended me to her friends." He grinned. "Not as a painter, anyway!" His students laughed as he went on, "I think it would be kindest to say that I accentuated the positive and politely looked the other way when it came to the negative. But my past has now caught up with me. I only wish it were possible for all of you to see some of those portraits, so you would know what a first-rate job Julia's done. Not as good as I did, of course," he teased, "but first-rate nonetheless."

Julia wanted to seem as cool as ever in the face of his praise but it was impossible not to glow with pleasure. "Are you pleased because I complimented what you did, or because you think you took me down a peg?"

"Oh, both, Mr. Veblen." Julia gave him her most innocent look. "Since you like it so much, do you want to keep it?"

"Hmm. That's not a bad idea. If my ego ever threatens to become dangerously over-inflated, I could look at your picture as an example of my humble beginnings." To Julia's surprise, because the offer had been made in jest, he picked up the portrait and placed it behind the desk.

The other students had chosen more conventional targets; their efforts received the unanimous appreciation of the class and their professor.

When time was nearly up, Derek told them, "I can see that you all liked this assignment. And I was worried that you were overly impressed by authority!

"Okay. For next time, why don't you all try something abstract. Portray an emotion for me. Then we'll all sit here and try to figure out which one you chose."

A chorus of groans and protests arose from his students. "What's the problem? You don't like the assignment?"

Justine Brandon spoke up. "It's not enough time. We all have other courses." Her six classmates chimed in with woeful tales of papers due, readings already put off for far too long.

"God, what a sense of power you give me!" Derek laughed. "You have no idea how tempted I am to give you just the one week so that I can feel like a dictator."

"And you always paint those lurid protests against torture and violence," Julia said reproachfully. "You should be ashamed."

"Oh, I am! Thoroughly!" But Derek hardly sounded

it. "Okay, you win. Two weeks." Julia waited to see if he would really take her picture along with him; and in fact, he picked it up along with his notebook as he walked out the door.

Julia spent most of the next few days at the library, catching up on reserved reading that she had put off in order to work on the portrait for Derek's class. Her mind was not particularly receptive to the idea of painting. She was leaving that Friday after her international relations class to go to New York. Her father and Maggie Rasmussen would be getting married Saturday night, and Mr. Harcourt had made the occasion a command performance. Even her brother Edward and his elegant wife Nancy would be flying in from California for the wedding.

When Julia had called Maine the previous week to see how her sister-in-law was feeling, Allie had offered to drive down to New York instead of flying, and pick up Julia on the way. Only this made the whole trip palatable. As Julia packed on Friday, she recalled the previous afternoon's session at Derek's house.

She supposed things were settling into a routine. He met her promptly at noon, and the two drove in silence to his house. Julia had been all set to return to the bantering relationship of the previous Tuesday, but Derek's expression was forbidding. By now Julia made no attempt to second-guess his moods; she simply adapted herself to them.

She undressed while he put some music on the stereo; Thursday it was Bartok. Then Derek came upstairs, again clad in jeans, and with swift, impersonal movements posed her as he wished. If his hand casually brushed against a bare breast or carelessly touched a thigh, it seemed to have absolutely no effect on him. Only Julia's years of practice at hiding her emotions enabled her to endure it. She told herself again and again that a ridiculous adolescent infatuation was the last thing in the world she needed, but that didn't slow her rapid heartbeat or erase the stabs of desire she felt when his hand stroked her skin.

And as before, when she began to fidget, he stopped immediately and went downstairs to wait for her. Then they drove home, again in silence. Perhaps Derek's aloofness was a polite way of stressing that although he found Julia an interesting subject to put on canvas, she held no great fascination for him as a person. Certainly, she thought a little disappointedly, I don't appeal to him physically.

Tom and Allie arrived at her apartment about noon. Julia offered to drive down to New York, but Tom was in the mood to stay at the wheel. Julia and Allie ended up sitting in the back, gossiping and laughing. About halfway to New York, everybody decided that it was definitely time for lunch. They pulled off the highway to one of the towns along the way. When Tom offered to get sandwiches to go from a deli in the middle of Main Street, the two women were glad to let him, grateful for the time it gave them to talk.

"Tell me how school is coming. How are you getting along with the famous artist?" Allie asked.

Julia debated whether or not to confess to Allie just how she had managed to wind up in Derek's tutorial. Inevitably, the whole story came pouring out. Her sister-in-law sensed that Julia was a bit annoyed with her father for showing the picture of Jill Harcourt to Derek Veblen.

"Now that's unfair," Allie commented. "Your father isn't among my heroes, as you perfectly well know, but he was quite right in this case. I suppose he brought the picture along as a back-up maneuver. The two of you should have skipped the attempts at bribery. You know, you're lucky Veblen didn't walk out on the spot."

"Hiram Felker stopped him," Julia admitted. "Maybe you're right. I guess the picture was the only reason he let me into his class. But let me tell you, I've paid for it. Veblen can be nasty when he wants." And Julia repeated some of his painfully harsh judgments.

"But he liked the last thing I did and it was a parody of his own early work. And, umm—there is one more thing, Allie. I'm posing for him."

This admission brought forth a flabbergasted yelp from Allie. "What! You're kidding! He doesn't do portraits anymore. Besides, you make it sound as though you two are barely on speaking terms."

"We don't have to talk for him to paint me," Julia replied drily. "To tell you the truth, we hardly exchange a word during our sessions. He sends me upstairs to—" She halted in mid-sentence. She hadn't intended to blurt out *that* part of it.

"Julia?" Allie's look was quizzical.

"Oh well, you might as well know. I'm posing, well—" She stopped and blushed, unable to get the rest of the sentence out.

"Is naked the word you're looking for?"

Julia nodded. "He's—he's a great artist, after all," she said defensively. "And—and it's not as if he has any interest in me."

"If he has no interest in you, why is he painting you?" Allie asked with flawless logic.

"He's always telling me to look cold, unapproachable. I think it's the contrast. Hot on the outside, cold on the inside. You know." Julia couldn't help but be rather disconcerted at the turn the conversation had taken.

Allie's look was knowing indeed, her mouth a bit twisted. "Do you sleep with him?"

Julia's whole body slumped. "Not you *too*, Allie!" She sounded terribly hurt.

Her sister-in-law's arm went around her. "I'm sorry, honey. It's just that—well—I grew up in Boston, don't forget. Gossip had it that more than one man refused to let Derek Veblen paint his wife's or daughter's portrait because the man had a reputation. I admit he's lived like a hermit for the past several years, if what you read is true. But teaching in a university, surrounded by nubile young creatures like you, is hardly reclusive. I just don't want to see you hurt—again. He's never made a pass?"

Julia had not told her sister-in-law about that searing kiss in his office. She wasn't very good at lying to Allie, so she simply shook her head and tried not to redden.

"When, Julia?" Allie had not been fooled.

"It wasn't—it didn't mean anything," Julia explained hesitantly. "He was already angry about—about being dragged down to Felker's office. And when I saw him again, he read me the Riot Act. I got annoyed and I provoked him. He—he just kissed me, that's all. It was like some sort of punishment."

Allie gave a disgusted snort. "And do you think he would have done that if you'd weighed two hundred pounds and looked like somebody had flattened your face with a steamroller?"

"No, I suppose not," Julia admitted. "But it was my reputation. I guess he figured I was fair game." She shrugged. "I can hardly blame him for that. And nothing's happened since. He might as well be painting a statue. He touches me, looks at me—but he has absolutely no reaction, Allie." Her voice was raw as she choked out the last sentence.

"But you *do*. Have a reaction, I mean."

"Yes."

And then suddenly Allie began to giggle, and Julia looked at her, perplexed and wounded.

"I'm sorry, honey. But I was just thinking about the last time we talked, when you said you were afraid you wouldn't be able to respond. Well, you respond. At least that's one worry taken care of!"

Julia's smile was sheepish. "You mean, one worry traded for another. But nothing will happen. In the first place, he's not attracted to me; in the second place, he's thirty-three years old, he thinks of me as a child; and in the third place—"

"Hmm?"

"In the third place, I was so reluctant to take off my clothes that he must realize that I'm not as sophisticated as he thought. It's gotten to be a joke. Every time I let the expression he wants fade from my eyes, he'll say something like, 'How's your latest lover, Julia?' or 'Did you ever consider publishing your personal ratings of the world's princes?' I think he knows that I'm not—that I don't—"

"One can only hope he acts appropriately in view of that knowledge," Allie said sharply and changed the subject to less sensitive matters as Tom came into sight, bags of sandwiches clutched in his hands. None of the three was in any great hurry to arrive in Scarsdale. Tom drove at a leisurely pace as they ate, and they pulled into the ancestral home, as Tom called it, at about dinner time.

The next day, the day of the wedding, they lounged around. Julia's father emerged from his room at two o'clock, looking distinctly hung over after his bachelor party the night before.

"Somebody should have told me," he said woefully, "that I'm too old for this sort of thing. If I don't get it together, I'm going to catch hell from Maggie for my failures tonight." He looked over to Julia. "You ignore that, right?" he teased.

She made a face at him. "Is Mrs. Rasmussen a hot ticket, Dad?" she gibed. "She always looks like she wouldn't want to mess up her makeup." Then Julia's conscience tugged at her. It hadn't been a very nice thing to say to a man on the day of his wedding.

"I know you don't like Maggie very much, Julia. No one could ever take the place of your mother, I realize that. But you have more in common with your future stepmother than you know. The Maggie you see on the surface is no more the real woman than the Julia people see on the surface is the real you. I happen to love her, and she loves me. If she's cool to you, maybe it's just because she's intimidated. You have that effect on people, you know."

Her brothers' and sisters-in-law's eyes were on her; Julia knew she had to make some reply. "Okay," she admitted, almost contritely, "what I said was catty. I'm sorry. We won't have that much to do with each other and I'm sure we'll manage to get along all right."

The remainder of the day passed agreeably enough. Julia took her time dressing. The plan was to leave for the city at 4:30 to allow plenty of time before the 6:00 ceremony.

When the Harcourt clan was gathered downstairs its patriarch announced proudly that they made a fine looking family. Suddenly some long-lost daughterly impulse welled up inside Julia. She knew that her father's remarriage tonight was an emotional milestone in her life. For the past eight years, she had been the most important woman in his life. Perhaps he had not been the most attentive of parents and had substituted expensive gifts for the time he might have spent with

her. But she felt that on some level he truly loved her
and acted on behalf of what he perceived as her best
interests.

She gave her father a hug, and said lightly, "You're
looking extremely distinguished tonight, Mr. Harcourt.
Oh! Did I get makeup on your dinner jacket?"

He was touched by this show of affection. Julia was
sure his eyes were misty as he told her, "No. You know
you hardly wear any. Julia—don't ever think that
because I'm remarrying—you're second in my life."

"Of course Maggie will come first, Daddy. Don't be
silly. But if you're trying to say that you'll be around if I
ever need you, I know that." Her voice became husky.
"I know you always try to do what you think best,
and—"

"My God!" Tom broke in. "No more! This is a
wedding celebration, not a wake. Let's get going or
your bride is going to wonder where the hell you are,
Dad."

Julia had to admit that everything had been tastefully
and beautifully planned by Maggie, and certainly
everything went smoothly. Her father and new stepmother were married by the mayor, who was an old
friend of the groom's. Julia personally preferred a
religious ceremony, and promised herself that if she
ever married, she would have one.

The ceremony was followed by a formal dinner and
dancing, with champagne flowing like the waters of
Niagara Falls and more food than even the ravenous
Allie could consume. Julia resolutely charmed all of her
father's colleagues and friends, and obligingly posed for
photographs when the members of the press finally
badgered their way in. The party continued long past
the hour when the bride and groom made their escape.

The family collectively staggered into the Harcourts'

Scarsdale home at three in the morning and it was late morning before any of them awoke. At about two o'clock, there was a complex round of good-bye kisses, and the blue Volvo, with Tom, Allie and Julia safely inside, headed back to New England.

Melinda was having dinner when Julia arrived back at the apartment. Julia had planned to study that evening, but Melinda wanted to know all about the wedding. The psychology reading would have to wait. For the second night in a row, she all but crash-landed on the bed.

Chapter Seven

Derek was not pleased with Julia's appearance on Monday afternoon. "You look like a hag," he said bluntly. "What the hell have you been doing with yourself?"

Julia was trying to summon up the inner resources to make some scathing retort when he continued, "Oh right. Your father's wedding. I saw the pictures in the Sunday paper. Did you pick up any new names for your little black book, Miss Harcourt?" He was grinning at her, waiting to see if she would rise to the bait.

"No," was the airy reply. "Although I was propositioned a few times." Julia, tired and rather cranky, was quite unable to prevent what came out next. "Not everybody finds me as unappealing as you do, Mr. Veblen."

He stared down at her for a moment, and Julia waited for the polite denial of her statement. But

Derek only lifted his shoulders before telling her that she was clearly too worn out to pose. He unceremoniously sent her home to rest.

Julia dejectedly concluded that he was right. She walked back home, and fell asleep while reading a singularly boring account of the history of Southeast Asia.

For the next few weeks, Julia's life fell into the sort of routine that once would have horrified her. During her first three years of school, there had been no pattern to her existence. She had cut classes when she thought she could get away with it, had studied as little as she could to earn respectable B's, and done papers at the last possible moment. All her energies were thrown into weekend trips to New York to hobnob with her father's social set, or frequent dates with young men from nearby Harvard or other Ivy League schools. In retrospect, Julia could see that the price she had paid was to forfeit close relationships with fellow students; she had also learned far less from her courses than she might have, and she regretted it.

All that was changed now. She was spending Monday and Thursday afternoons posing for Derek; these sessions continued as before. The two of them rarely exchanged more than a few words during an entire afternoon. Derek would be coolly impersonal; Julia strove desperately to match his indifference and probably, she felt, outwardly succeeded.

Derek always took the same route back and forth from his house, and Julia came to have a dozen favorite trees she would look for along the way. She delighted in watching the foliage change from week to week, until it hit its colorful peak in late October. And when she would arrive at Derek's each Monday or Thursday, she would insist on taking a walk all around the house, looking at the woods from every angle. As a fellow artist, Derek could hardly object to this exercise, but Julia clearly sensed his impatience with her perusals.

She watched the progress of the portrait with interest. Apparently he worked on the background while she was not there. Although she was posing on a twin bed in an almost bare room upstairs, the portrait showed her on a large brass bed which she soon realized was the one in Derek's room. Somehow that disconcerted her far more than the actual fact of posing undressed for him.

Prince Abrahm had called her twice after her return from New York, but Julia had stuck to her decision not to date him again. Several other young men, former escorts or friends of friends, asked her out as well, but she declined every invitation. She had neither the time nor the desire to accept any of them. She occasionally attended campus functions with Max, or went out to dinner with him. As time went on, she began to have more and more difficulty fending him off. He was too old, he said, to have to confine his lovemaking to sporadic necking in automobiles. He cared for her a good deal and desired her too much to be satisfied with adolescent encounters. Julia enjoyed his company, but not the pressure he put on her to sleep with him. She was reaching the point where she was ready to end the relationship.

Usually Julia went out with Melinda and her friends, or with people she knew from the Art Department. There was no dearth of activities on campus, from basketball games to plays, lectures and concerts. Two or three times she saw Derek at these functions, always accompanied by the attractive anthropologist she had seen him with earlier in the semester.

But the greatest part of Julia's time was taken up in

studying. Her international relations course required her to read at least 250 to 350 pages per week of heavy, factual material. In addition, the instructor had provided a lengthy list of optional readings. Julia, determined to make up for all the years when she had paid absolutely minimal attention to what went on in the world around her, tried to read it all. Her paper on the Chinese legal system was coming along well; her professor, impressed with her intelligence and interest, had even arranged for her to borrow materials from Harvard on the subject.

She diligently kept up the journal of her dreams, and found that her professor had been right; she could now remember at least one or two dreams every morning. To Julia's dismay, quite a few of them were about Derek Veblen. She recorded them faithfully and in detail, but the object of her nighttime fantasies was referred to simply as D. From the content of some of these dreams, Julia fancied that she had seen too many foreign films or read too many popular novels where the activities in the hero's bedroom were described graphically and with great relish. Certainly she had never actually done in real life most of the things that the Julia Harcourt of the middle of the night was doing! And even worse, she often dreamt of being married to Derek—of sharing his life, doing the mundane things together which husbands and wives took for granted. She hated to have to wake up in the morning.

Real life had its compensations. Best of all to Julia was the feeling that Derek was pleased with her work for his tutorial. She had had difficulty deciding what she would paint for his assignment about the abstract portrayal of emotion; she had not begun until after her father's wedding. But she found that Richard Harcourt's remarriage had indeed marked some sort of ending for her. It gave her a sense of release to know that a certain stage of her life was behind her.

She dredged up the feelings she had experienced as a child; at first this was a melancholy, painful exercise for her, but gradually she found herself remembering and reminiscing on all the happiest moments of her girlhood. Picnics with her parents; trips to the zoo; running around a field, chasing her brothers' stray baseballs; her earliest attempts to draw and paint. Julia wondered why all the joyful moments seemed to have been repressed until now.

So that was what she tried to put on canvas—a child's innocent, perfectly serious delight with her world. Julia was skeptical about how successful she had been, but Derek and her fellow students had no problem interpreting the picture.

Derek's subsequent assignments for the course asked the students to attempt subject matter or modes of expression which they never would have tackled of their own accord. Julia's horizons were widened; her talent stretched almost against her will. Once, Derek asked them to sketch themselves at different ages: five, ten, fifteen. The happy child of five or ten presented no difficulty to Julia, but it was painful to portray herself at fifteen. Once, she would have avoided the hurt and drawn an idyllic picture of a squeaky clean teen-ager. But she knew Derek would never let her get away with that. His sarcastic, lashing reaction was quite tangible to Julia's vivid imagination. So she drew the picture honestly, and her professor's words of praise more than compensated for the ache that had filled her as she sat down and forced herself to draw the lonely, lost Julia of fifteen.

She abandoned the portrait of herself at seventeen in a Paris salon. It no longer seemed productive to dwell on how ugly and awkward she had been, or to blame her father for trying to glamorize her. That was all in the past now.

Julia was absolutely bewildered by the contrast between Derek's behavior toward her in class and his behavior toward her during their sessions at his house. Now that he was pleased with her work, he was unfailingly charming, encouraging and teasing during the Tuesday afternoon tutorial. During the last month, she could remember only one occasion when he had subjected her to his stinging tongue.

Yet when they were alone, he was so distant and curt that if Julia hadn't known better, she would have been prepared to swear that Derek Veblen had an identical twin brother. Her attempts at casual conversation or at humor were met with detached non-responsiveness. Julia was forced to put it down to artistic temperament; probably his mind was completely preoccupied when he was working.

It had been an exceptionally pleasant autumn in New England; crisp, sunny days were interspersed with nights cold enough to turn the foliage into a brilliant panoply of color. But, thought Julia as she walked behind Derek to his van one Thursday in the middle of November, their good luck appeared to be changing. She had bundled up in her boots and new winter parka, snuggling the fur hood around her face. The sky was a whitish gray, the thick clouds so oppressively low that she felt caged in by them.

Snow flurries began to swirl around them as they left to make the trip north to Concord. Derek made no comment on the weather, and Julia was so cowed by now from his previous lack of reaction to her stabs at conversation that she said nothing either.

It was snowing in earnest by the time they reached

his house; several inches were on the ground in Concord. But after all, it was only mid-November. There was seldom heavy snow this early; Julia could remember winters when she had hoped for a beautiful white Christmas only to be disappointed by the lack of snow.

Julia undressed, then lay on her back for a few moments to watch the snow fall directly above her onto the curved skylight. The studio was dreary and shadowed. When she heard Derek's footsteps on the stairs, she self-consciously pulled the sheet over the lower half of her body.

It was the first time Derek needed to set up additional lighting. Of course, it had occasionally rained during the fall, but somehow never on Mondays and Thursdays. Up until today, sunlight and the overhead lighting in the room had sufficed. But now the artist began dragging over the bright television lights which had been shoved into one corner of the studio.

It seemed to Julia that it took him forever to be satisfied with the effect the lights created. He kept staring at her body, trying to duplicate the look of the bright sunshine with these artificial substitutes.

She could feel herself beginning to perspire, whether from the heat of the lamps or from a sense of tension caused by his constant scrutiny, she wasn't sure. Finally, with a low grunt of satisfaction, he walked over to lower the thermostat, and began to paint.

Julia never had a very good idea of how much time was elapsing during these sessions; her only gauges of the hour were the music she listened to and the position of the sun in the sky. Today there was no sunshine, and she was completely unfamiliar with the atonal, strident modern pieces he was playing.

The warmth of the klieg lights probably tired her

sooner than usual; she waited for Derek to call a halt. But unlike all the other afternoons of posing, he kept on painting, a frown of concentration on his face.

Julia knew how it felt to be totally wrapped up in a piece of work. When it was going especially well, it was almost impossible to stop. So she stared out at the falling snow, and tried not to think about how achy and hot she was.

"For God's sake, stop fidgeting, Julia!" Derek's impatient command cut into her thoughts.

"Sorry." Julia willed herself to be still.

Ten minutes later, he stood up and stretched, a look of disgust on his face. "You're as twitchy as a Mexican jumping bean today," he accused. "What the hell's the matter with you?"

"What time is it, Mr. Veblen?" Julia asked with a look of long-suffering acceptance on her face.

He lifted his wrist to check, and was immediately contrite. "I can't believe it! It's nearly five. Hey, I'm sorry. No wonder you're tired."

"It was all coming together, wasn't it? I've never seen you so absorbed." Julia could not help the note of pleasure in her voice. They had exchanged more words just now than they had during the last two weeks.

"Umm. I hate to quit. If we took a break, do you think . . . ?" He didn't bother to finish the sentence, but looked at Julia with irresistible eagerness.

She was concerned about the snow, which had fallen unabated for the last four hours. But when he favored her with such a winning expression, there was no way on earth she was about to refuse him anything.

"I feel really grimy. Can I take a shower before we start again? And have something to drink?"

"Fine. Take your shower and then come downstairs. My mother's always sending me fresh oranges from

Florida. I bought her a condominium down there," he explained, "and now I'm constantly deluged with the damn things. I'll squeeze a few dozen." He began to walk toward the stairs, then laughed over his shoulder, "She sent an electric juicer too!"

Julia adjusted the shower to lukewarm, then stood and reveled in the feel of the cool water on her body. She would have loved to wash her hair as well, but Derek would be impatient at the time it would take to dry it. So, after emerging from the shower and wrapping a towel around her body, she contented herself with a thorough brushing. She reapplied the light covering of makeup she wore while she posed, slipped on Derek's robe, and went down to the kitchen.

He had produced not only fresh-squeezed orange juice, but some delicious Danish as well. Julia all but attacked it in what she supposed was a most unlady-like manner.

"From an Italian bakery in Boston," Derek told her. "The manna of my childhood—when we could afford it."

Julia took in the mocking tone of voice and wondered if she was supposed to feel guilty because she had never known what it meant to want something and not to have it—except for Mark, of course. She said lightly, "But now you can have anything you want, can't you?"

She honestly had not realized what a loaded question it was until she noticed his eyes traveling over her body. "Can I?" he asked softly, his eyes glowing with amusement.

Julia, confused by yet another of his total changes of mood, hastily swallowed the rest of her orange juice and, avoiding his eyes, told him she would meet him upstairs.

When he followed her up five minutes later, he was once again the cool professional. He repositioned some of the lights and his model and went back to work.

Julia, her aloof stare intact, gazed out the window. It was quite dark now, and the moonlit snow was falling even more heavily than before. She listened for the sound of snowplows, but heard nothing.

It was eight o'clock before Derek finally announced that he was too tired to continue. "I hate to stop," he added regretfully, "but I'd better get you back home."

Julia waited a moment for him to leave, but he simply sat and studied what he had accomplished thus far. At last she pulled on the robe and went off to dress. When she came out of the bathroom, he motioned her over to look at the picture.

"Well?"

There was no point in being less than truthful. "I don't like it very much. Oh," she added quickly at his sudden scowl, "I'm not saying it isn't—brilliant—for what you wanted to show. But I don't like to think of myself like that—anymore."

"Don't you?" The tone was curious. "I would have said that you were as cool, as removed from the world, as ever."

"That's not fair and you know it!" she denied hotly. "My work in your class—"

"I'm not talking about your work, I'm talking about you," Derek cut in. "You still strike me as being just as icy cold as the day in my office—" A grin appeared on his face.

Julia strongly suspected that this was teasing and not criticism; nonetheless, she didn't much care for it. Every instinctive defense clicked into place. She turned on her heel and imperiously descended the steps.

Derek, laughing, followed. He tossed her the furry

parka, and pulled on his ski jacket. But when he went to open the door, the casual amusement quickly faded from his face. There was a loud curse as he shut the door again.

"There must be nearly a foot of snow out there. Where the hell did it come from?"

"The clouds, I imagine," Julia said with ill-disguised sarcasm.

Derek walked into the bedroom, punched the buttons on the phone as if he meant to punish them. Julia followed him, anxious to know whom he was calling. "Sandy! The driveway? What?" There was a long silence as Derek listened. "Right. Yeah, I understand. I will. Bye." He gently replaced the receiver.

"It looks like we're not going anywhere," Derek sighed. "That was Sandy McCoy, the guy who plows me out. This damn snowfall's screwed up most of New England. There are idiots who tried to drive without snow tires or chains stranded from one end of the state to the other. The roads are hopeless. All traffic except for emergency vehicles has been banned until further notice. Does that about sum it up for you?"

Julia paled. She tried to sound nonchalant as she joked, "Better to be stranded in your nice comfortable house than in a car somewhere in the middle of Route 128!"

But she felt far from comfortable about the situation. The intensity of the physical attraction she felt toward Derek had grown, not diminished, as the weeks passed. She had the awful feeling that she could easily make an utter fool of herself if she weren't careful. Her chin lifted with defensive coldness as she looked at Derek.

"For God's sake, Julia, don't go all icy on me." He grabbed her arm and began to pull her out of the room. "I think we'd better talk this over. Come on."

In the living room, she was pushed into a chair; Derek sat down across the brass coffee table from her.

"We could be here together for more than one night, you realize that?" Julia nodded her understanding of the situation. Derek went on wearily, "All right. I'm not going to avoid the issue, even if you seem to want to do that. Julia, you happen to be a very beautiful woman, and I'm as human as the next guy. If you think it's been easy to keep my mind on painting with you lying sprawled out in front of me— Oh hell! Look—will you go to bed with me?"

Julia had never been so absolutely dumbfounded in her life. In the first place, it was the most abruptly direct proposition she had ever received. And in the second place—she verbalized the thought that had immediately come to mind: "But—but you're always so impersonal."

"What does that prove? Answer the question. All you have to say is yes or no."

Julia looked down into her lap and shook her head. "But I don't—I've never—" she began, and then was unable to manage another word.

His eyes were burningly skeptical when she looked up. "Come off it! You don't expect me to believe that you've never slept with anyone! If I don't appeal to you, fine. Just say so. But don't give me a lot of crap."

"It isn't *crap,* and I don't expect *anything* from you, and I don't give a damn *what* you believe!" Julia shouted, hurt and goaded by his cynical words. "And the answer to your clumsy proposition is no. N. O. Okay?"

He grinned. "It wasn't clumsy, just straightforward. I just don't happen to believe in seduction."

Julia continued to glower at him, now even angrier because he seemed to regard the whole thing as a joke.

Then suddenly he was next to her, sitting on the arm of the chair, and saying softly, "I should trust my instincts more. It's been very difficult to reconcile the Julia Harcourt I've gotten to know with the promiscuous princess of the papers. So. You don't sleep around." He lifted her chin and their eyes met. Julia found his smile absolutely devastating, and when he drawled with wicked languor, "How very disappointing!" she began to smile back.

"I can see I'm doomed to a very frustrating evening," he said ruefully. "Let's do the next best thing and have something to eat."

Derek lazily got up and went into the kitchen. Julia stayed seated for a few minutes, trying to bring her thundering senses under some sort of control. She reacted to Derek even when he was twelve feet away, but intimate conversation elicited a craving that was humiliating in its intensity. *He* seemed to be able to turn such feelings on and off at will. Certainly his last words were spoken in a relaxed manner which hardly summoned up a picture of rampaging desire.

Julia could feel the heat in her body dissipate, and wondered idly if one's temperature actually rose in such circumstances. There was no point in trying to retreat into her usual shell; she knew that Derek would poke merciless fun at her if she tried.

And I considered myself sophisticated; I thought I could handle anyone! Julia mocked herself. It gave her a certain shameless pleasure to know that Derek found her attractive—no, more than attractive. Beautiful and very desirable. But she didn't want to be desperately hurt by what could turn out to be no more than a one or two-night stand.

She would not dwell on the pleasures she was saying no to. She was sure she had made the right decision.

With a calmness she hadn't possessed a few minutes before, she got up to help Derek fix dinner.

He had found two T-bone steaks in the freezer and was slowly sautéing them with butter and scallions. When Julia entered the kitchen, he was beginning to cut up raw vegetables for a salad.

"No end to your talents," she teased. "I see you can cook."

"One of us has to!" he retorted. "Too bad I didn't get snowed in with Julia Child instead of Julia Harcourt."

"I do beg your pardon, Mr. Veblen, but I've had Cordon Bleu cooking lessons," Julia informed him, and then stuck out her tongue for good measure.

"Lady," he warned, "I can find a much better use for your tongue than insulting your betters. Now beat it, and let me make dinner." He gave her a shove back into the living room.

Julia occupied the half hour until dinner was ready by studying the art collection in the living room. She wondered how he had managed to afford such treasures. An early cubist painting by Max Weber, all angular color depicting a New York City scene, hung next to a watercolor of the Maine coast by John Marin. An oil painting by Georgia O'Keeffe, the flower she had painted was so enlarged that it looked abstract, was on the same wall. Other paintings by American and European artists were arranged in groups. With the exception of one late nineteenth century work by Cézanne, they all were twentieth century creations.

Derek also owned several works of sculpture and the brass cocktail table in the center of the room was a work of art in itself.

In a glass case mounted on one wall were a large

square of white cloth and some heavy chains. Julia guessed that the cloth might be part of Christo's Running Fence, a project in honor of the Bicentennial, consisting of a fence made out of heavy cloth that snaked across part of the Northern California countryside. It had run into a tangle of bureaucratic red tape and Julia seemed to remember that ultimately the wind had destroyed it.

But the chains totally mystified her. She would have to ask Derek what they were. Her tour of what she was beginning to think of as Derek's museum was interrupted by his shout of, "Julia! Get your tail in here. Dinner's ready and I'm starved."

Hardly the most polite fashion in which to be summoned in to dinner, but she wasn't about to stand on ceremony. She was equally famished. The steak, salad and baked potatoes looked mouth-watering.

She pointed to the potatoes. "The second oven's a microwave?"

"Good for people who want to eat quick but forget to put the meat in. Well go ahead. I've already noticed you eat like a horse." He was putting the food on his plate.

She stabbed the smaller steak. "Like a healthy, all-American girl, you mean."

The two dined in silence, much too concerned with eating to bother with conversation. Derek had come up with a bottle of California Cabernet to go along with the meal. Julia gulped it thirstily.

Since he had cooked, she offered to clean up. "I think I'm getting the worst of the deal though," she told him. "Your kitchen is as bad as your office used to be. How did you manage to make so many things dirty?"

"Talent." Without a backward look, he made his escape from the kitchen.

Later Julia found him upstairs at the desk in his studio, making notes for a lecture. He apparently hadn't heard her come up the steps; not wanting to disturb him, she went back down into the living room. She called Melinda to explain the situation, then began to read one of the books she had with her. Thank goodness she had stopped at the bookstore to pick up several more paperbacks for her international relations course before meeting Derek. At least she would be able to get something accomplished tonight.

He came downstairs about eleven o'clock. "I made up the bed in the studio for you. Tired?"

In fact she was barely awake. She had found it difficult to concentrate on her book detailing the history of the Middle East. "Umm. Yes." She rose sleepily from the couch, where she had been curled up, and started toward the steps.

His hand on her shoulder as she passed him halted her progress. "Don't I get a good-night kiss?" he questioned huskily.

Julia stiffened, but his hand was already under her chin and his mouth on hers. His embrace was warm and gentle, not at all aggressive. And then he ruffled her hair as if she were a ten-year-old, and ordered, "Upstairs, sleepy head."

Julia had repeatedly pushed away the realization that she was falling in love with Derek. But at that moment, as he turned away to go into his room and she climbed the stairs to the studio, it was no longer possible to run away from it. Indeed, she had no desire to. He had treated her in a teasing, solicitous manner which left little doubt that he felt something for her too. He never hid his emotions the way she did. Julia knew that if he cared for her, he would say so. She could only hope. . . .

She didn't want to fall asleep that night. It was too pleasurable to imagine that Derek was part of her future, to fantasize about what sort of life they would lead together. But her body wouldn't let her mind have its way. Inside of five minutes, she was sound asleep.

Chapter Eight

Julia awoke to the smell of freshly brewed coffee. She stretched lazily, and looked above her out the skylight. Flakes of snow swirled in the stiff breeze; the wind had blown most of the snow off the skylight. It was impossible to tell if the snow were continuing to fall, or if she were seeing the effect of what must be gale force winds.

"Finally awake?" At the sound of Derek's voice, Julia turned to look toward the steps. No Derek. Her gaze traveled further, until she was looking over her shoulder at the corner where his makeshift office was located. He was sitting there, looking at her; a notebook and pen lay on the desk top. A coffeepot sat on the floor next to him.

The previous night, she had washed out her underthings, hung them in the bathroom to dry, and fallen into bed, naked. Now Derek walked over to say good morning, and Julia instinctively pulled the covers up.

She strugggled into a sitting position, wrapping the sheet behind her.

Derek sat on the bed beside her and began to nuzzle the back of her neck. "Hi. I've been working up here and watching you sleep. You snore."

Julia tried to stay calm in the face of the fire he had lit in her. "I don't. What time is it? Derek!" She squeaked as he gave her a sharp nip on a bare shoulder. "Don't do that."

"Hmm. So this morning it's finally Derek," he drawled, drawing a bit away from her. "Almost eight-thirty. But forget your psych class. We're not going anywhere."

"What's been happening?"

"It snowed all night, twenty to twenty-five inches, all over the state. The wind's blowing like a hurricane. The drifts have made matters twice as bad; the police are having a hell of a time digging idiots out of them. Some are as high as a house. In short," he told her, "I have you at my mercy for a little while longer."

To Julia, that was a delightful prospect, but she was much too shy to say so. Instead she asked, "The roads are still closed?"

"Uh-huh. And the forecast is for another storm to blow in from Canada." He smoothed her tangled hair. "Do you mind?"

Julia's reply was low and husky. "No."

"And am I allowed to make love to you this morning, Miss Harcourt?" he asked teasingly.

A part of Julia wanted desperately to say yes. She had dreamed often enough of this moment, and her body had begun to tremble with urgent arousal. But it seemed so cold, so calculating, to come right out and say, "Yes, I want you," when there had been no mutual declaration of love.

Finally, after a lengthy silence during which Derek simply sat there and waited for her reply, Julia said haltingly, "Why don't you just—start. You know I wouldn't—stop you."

"I told you," he said firmly, "I don't believe in seduction. I won't take responsibility for your actions. Especially when you tell me you're so damn innocent. *You* have to decide what *you* want."

"Then—no. Not yet." She peeked up at him, worried about his reaction to her refusal. "Are you angry with me?"

Derek's response was to kiss the tip of her nose and smile at her. "Of course not. Disappointed maybe. But I don't have rights to your body. Although if I sit here much longer," he muttered, "things are going to get out of control. Get some clothes on and come have something to eat."

As soon as Derek left the room, Julia ripped out a piece of paper from one of her notebooks and scrawled down the details of the only dream she could recall from the previous night. Much of it had slipped away already, but she remembered that she had been forced to marry some unidentified man, and had gone to a tropical island to honeymoon with him. On her wedding night, however, her lover had been Derek, not her husband. In the dream, this all made perfect sense. Indeed, she never even bothered to ask what had become of her husband!

Julia showered and dressed, her mood totally euphoric. The combination of passion and consideration with which Derek was treating her was more potent than any artificial stimulant she could imagine.

While she ate, Derek gave her more details of the snow emergency. Day-to-day life had ground to a virtual halt. Businesses and schools were closed; even doctors were permitted to practice only on an emergency basis. The highways were littered with smashed-up or stranded automobiles and trucks; frozen bodies had been pulled out of more than one of them.

"And finally," Derek concluded, "we have no phone. The wind must have kayo'd the lines."

"I called Mel last night to let her know I was all right." Julia looked out the window, admiring the beauty of the ice-covered trees and shrubs. "You sure are isolated out here."

"We won't starve. There's plenty of food in the freezer." Derek intercepted Julia's glance toward the small freezer beneath the refrigerator and shook his head. "No, not that one. Downstairs, in the basement. I hate to shop, so I go as seldom as possible. I've got a butcher who knows what I like better than I do myself; he wraps the stuff up, marks it, and I throw it into the freezer."

"And cook it in half an hour in the microwave."

"Right." A thought struck him. "I've never given you the guided tour of my art collection."

"I looked around last night, before dinner. Can I ask some questions, Professor Veblen?"

"Shoot."

"Well, first, is the white cloth from Christo's Fence?"

Derek nodded. "Very good. A friend sent it to me. And second?"

"Second—" Julia looked at him timidly, afraid he would be angry with her next question.

"Second?" he repeated.

"Where did you *get* all that stuff, Derek? I mean, how could you afford it?"

His expression turned brooding, and Julia instantly regretted her curiosity. She was about to tell him to forget the matter, when he said cynically, "From my wicked past, Julia. I'm going to tell you the truth. As much as I enjoy owning all of it, I don't much care for how I acquired it. Oh, a few things I bought; others were trades or gifts from the artists. But the majority—the majority were presents from very wealthy, very bored women whom I painted, and more often than not, slept with. I was ambitious and impatient for wealth and fame. I wanted my mother out of her old, walk-up apartment. I was tired of being poor. I don't suppose someone like you would understand."

"I'm not so sure about that, Derek," Julia murmured. "You're telling me you let them give you expensive gifts in return for amusing them, relieving their boredom. You used each other. It's not very pretty, but it's hardly a major sin either. And when you'd made enough money, you did what you really wanted to do."

"When I'd made enough money! Bull! I enjoyed it—at the time. I liked it when women threw themselves at me. I liked the expensive suits and fancy cars and yacht parties, the critics' acclaim and the fact that royalty wanted me to paint them. I got the Weber from some filthy rich widow who was delighted when I admired it. She said it didn't look anything like New York City to her and why would he paint something like that? Can you believe it?"

Julia shrugged. "Sure. So what made you give it all up?"

"My mother told me I was no better than the scum on 42nd Street. I was furious, but I took a good look at my life after I cooled down. I didn't much like what I saw. Here I'd traveled around the world, seen slums and killing and racism, and never given them a thought."

Julia smiled. "Did you want to add, 'Just like you, Julia'? They say a reformed sinner is the best proselytizer, Derek. Are you out to convert me? Because if you are, I think I should tell you you've already succeeded."

His dour mood evaporated. "One out of two isn't bad," he said cryptically.

Julia looked at him, puzzled.

"I've made you into a social critic, Miss Harcourt. Now do you want to tell me how I get you into my bed?"

Julia giggled. "Well, you could always use those chains. What on earth *are* they, Derek?"

He was once again the charming raconteur. "Oh! My insane friend Seamus O'Hannigan, the mad Irishman."

"The conceptual artist?"

"Yes. He lives in New York. Lying down on the floor and letting people step all over you is not the type of art I choose to do, but," Derek shrugged, "to each his own. Seamus seems to want to see just how outrageous he can be and still make money at it."

"The chains?" Julia prompted, laughing.

"A gift. He had himself tied up with them, then asked the people attending the exhibition it was part of to feed him. He sent me the chains with a note that read: 'To Derek, a souvenir for a scoundrel who probably would have let me starve.'"

Julia was by now in near-hysterics. "Well? Would you have?"

"He weighs 250 pounds. Would have done him good."

Still laughing, Julia got up to take the dishes into the kitchen. That Derek had been willing to share such personal feelings with her was heady indeed. He was sitting at the table smoking a cigarette when she came back in. She remarked off-handedly, "I've never seen you smoke before."

"Your fault, Miss Harcourt. I've pretty much given it

up, but in moments of great stress—" He took a long drag on the cigarette and blew the smoke in her direction.

Julia went to load the dishwasher.

They spent the morning working, Derek upstairs, Julia in the living room. She found some cold cuts for lunch, and half-pretending that she was Derek's wife fetching him for a meal, went upstairs to ask him if he were ready to eat.

A deceptive calm had settled outside, and Derek suggested a romp in the snow after lunch. When Julia protested that she would get soaked and had nothing to change into, he asked her if she had ever heard of an automatic clothes dryer.

They bundled up in boots, parkas, and gloves, Derek adding a ski hat while Julia pulled her hood over her head. The first order of business was, of course, to build a snowman. Derek had brought some small garden tools out with them; as might be expected of an artist, he was not content to merely roll around some snow, pile a second ball on top of it, and stick chunks of wood into the whole thing.

He arrogantly took command of the act of creation, briskly ordering Julia to sculpt the snow according to his notions of how a modern snowperson should look. She was often up to her thighs in the wettish white drifts, and moved clumsily at best. Why was *she* the one who had to wade about searching for pine cones and sticks, while he stood and barked orders like some lord of the manor? When Derek snapped out imperiously, "You call that an arm? What kind of an arm is that?" she meekly asked how he wanted it, and as soon as his back was turned, whacked him hard on the head with a smartly thrown snowball.

"You'll pay for that," he growled, and backed off to

pelt her with a barrage of white missiles. At first Julia
was able to score a few hits of her own, but the
snowball fight soon turned into a rout. She stood there,
helpless, hands in front of her face, begging him to
stop. In a fit of temper at his tactics, she was ready to
storm off into the house when he finally took pity on
her and ceased the punishment.

Derek was completely taken aback by this. "What'd
I do?" he asked, all charming innocence.

Julia was nearly in tears. "First of all, you're bossy.
You act like Michelangelo sculpting David. If I can't
have any input on the snowman, I won't help!"

He nodded. "Maybe. Don't cry. What other sins did
I commit?"

"What—what were we having? A friendly snowball
fight, or a massacre?" she said angrily.

"Mea culpa," Derek laughed, and pounded his chest
with his fist. "I'll give you five free shots, how's that?"

Julia doubted that he was serious, but she quickly
took him up on it. After he had casually swatted away
the first two harmless snowballs, he invited, "Come
closer. You have a lousy arm."

Infuriated by the taunt, she moved in to stand
perhaps six feet away from him, and hurled a snowball
as hard as she could. He easily brushed it aside.

"Maybe you should forget the snow and just hit me.
Would that make you feel better?" he teased.

Julia clambered over, and tried to push him into the
snow. It was clearly a tactical error. She found herself
flat on her back a second later, with Derek towering
over her. She looked up at him, out of breath and
furious with his tactics.

"You're very alluring like that, you know that?" he
said softly. He sank to his knees beside her. "Correction. Totally irresistible."

Julia was in no mood for what he clearly had in mind.

She tried to get up, only to be quickly pushed back into the snow. Derek's mouth covered hers, and began a gently possessive probing that quickly neutralized her pique. That she was soaked to the skin mattered not one whit. Her arms reached hungrily around his neck, and she responded to his kiss with wanton passion.

A single thirty second embrace was all she was permitted. He smoothly drew away, telling her, "I'm too old for this kind of stuff. Let's go inside, honey. This isn't the most opportune time for either of us to catch pneumonia."

He stood and pulled Julia to her feet. She absently noted that it had begun to snow again. Inside she was firmly ordered to strip off her sopping wet clothing, with Derek marching her into his room and shutting the door behind him as he left. She found a robe to put on, and handed him her clothes.

"Now get into the bathtub and soak for a while. I'll throw these into the dryer in the meantime. When it buzzes, you'll know it's time to come out."

Julia obeyed. She acknowledged that she half-wanted him to follow her into the bedroom, but it seemed that he had been completely earnest when he told her that the decision would be up to her.

She edged her body into the steaming water, and then melted with relaxation. Soon her eyes closed and she let herself drift into a near-doze. It was only when she realized that Derek had come into the bathroom to turn out the lights that she opened her eyes again.

"Derek?" He didn't seem to be anywhere around. The water had gotten cool, so Julia climbed out of the tub and wrapped herself in a large bath sheet. Then she switched the light back on.

Nothing happened.

There was a knock on the door. "Are you alive in there?"

Julia opened it and walked out, still clad in the huge terry cloth towel. "No electricity, huh?" she asked ruefully.

"Cheer up. At least the stove is gas. But the oil burner's thermostat is controlled by electricity. So no heat." He cocked his head over to the fireplace. "I knew I had this put in for *some* reason. Besides the purely sybaritic, that is."

He went off to the kitchen as Julia felt the implications of the situation sink in. No heat, fireplace in the bedroom, one bed. Terrific!

When he came back, he was holding her still-damp clothing. "Should have put in a gas dryer, too!" he joked. "I can dig up some stuff for you to put on." A quick search of his closet produced a woolen workshirt and a pair of his jeans. "Cheer up," he said to Julia, who had winced at his choice of attire for her. "At least you'll look so shapeless in that get-up that not even a sex starved teen-ager would want you."

"Thanks a heap."

He smiled. "Anytime, ma'am."

Alone, Julia reluctantly put on his clothing. The shirt came down to her knees; the pants were so loose that they slid to her hips. She rummaged around and found the sash of a bathrobe, slipped it through the belt loops, and tied it in a bow at her waist. She let the shirt hang over the jeans, then rolled up the cuffs of the pants so that she wouldn't trip on them. The sleeves of the shirt received similar alteration. Finally, she borrowed a pair of his socks and put them on her much smaller feet.

There were several kicks at the door and Julia went over to open it. Derek stood with his arms full of wood. He dropped the logs by the fireplace. "You look sensational," he teased, and went down to the basement for more wood.

By the time dinner was ready—Derek had baked

pork chops in a white wine sauce and made rice and a frozen vegetable to go along with it—the house was distinctly chilly. They carried their meal into the bedroom and sat on the rug to eat it. A Coleman lantern, generally used for camping, had been pressed into service to provide light.

As they ate, they listened to an all-news station on the portable radio. The police were still working to rescue stranded motorists and clear away wrecked vehicles. There was no chance that the roads would be clear for at least another twenty-four hours.

Derek and Julia spent the evening side by side on the king-sized bed, reading. Or, thought Julia wryly, in her case it was a matter of trying to read. Every now and then Derek got up to poke the fire or throw another log on it.

Finally Julia couldn't stand it a moment longer. "Derek," she managed to ask, "where am I going to sleep tonight?"

"If you want to sleep on the floor, I won't stop you. But the bed is a lot more comfortable, Julia," he said indifferently.

"But the floor's a lot safer, Derek," she mimicked viciously.

"If it's me you don't trust," he said wearily, "you have nothing to worry about. I won't touch you. If it's *you* you don't trust—well, that's another matter entirely, isn't it?"

"You think I'm being silly, don't you?" Julia accused.

"No. Not really." The tone was impatient. "I suppose I just don't understand what you're so afraid of. I wouldn't hurt you, Julia, you must know that."

Julia rolled over and turned her back to him. She didn't want to discuss it anymore. What she wanted to hear was "I love you" and it hadn't happened. There was an exasperated mutter from behind her, and Derek said, "Okay. Let's try to get some sleep." He went over to the bureau to fish out two pairs of ski pajamas, then entered the bathroom, leaving her to change in the bedroom.

She hastily did so, and silently took her turn at the sink when he had finished. Without another word exchanged between them, Derek put out the lantern, closed the window which had been left open for ventilation, and got back into bed.

A few minutes later his breathing was deep and regular. Julia wished that she could fall asleep so easily. She moved as far away from him as she could and tried to ignore his presence. It was a futile exercise. She had to resign herself to the dull ache, the painful longing. It was a form of self-torture to lie there and fantasize about making love with Derek, but she did it anyway.

By the next morning, the house beyond the bedroom was almost as cold as the outside. A check of the phone confirmed that it was still not repaired. The extra eight inches of snow added by the second storm, which had continued off and on into the night, had ensured that the emergency would continue beyond that evening. Derek switched on the radio. The governor had made a statement that if there were no further storms, the roads might be open by the next morning. In the meantime, he warned that anyone driving without permission would be arrested. "And shot at dawn," Derek added sourly.

The enforced closeness of that Saturday inevitably led to frayed nerves and short tempers. Julia was edgy and fidgety and it seemed to drive Derek beyond endurance. He smoked one cigarette after another, viciously poked the fire more often than was necessary, and snapped at Julia every chance he got.

He wouldn't let her come into the kitchen with him to fix meals; it was obvious to her that he wanted to be alone. In the afternoon he put on his outdoor gear and went outside to shovel snow. Julia had hung her own clothing in the bathroom, but with the heat off it hadn't dried yet. She watched him through the bathroom window; he was attacking the snow as if it had fallen purposefully onto his property in order to torment him.

She envied him the exercise. Why should she have to stay inside while he got to go out? She resolutely hunted through his things until she found a few extra sweaters to put on, and went outside as well. Derek had cleared off most of the front walk; his next target would be the half-buried van. For several minutes he didn't notice Julia's presence, but spotted her as soon as he stopped to rest.

"I told you to stay inside," he lashed out. "Get back into that bedroom."

"I'm sick of the bedroom," she raged back. "It's claustrophobic."

"Damn it, Julia, don't argue with me. I'm in no mood—"

"You're in a rotten mood. And so am I. You must have another snow shovel around here. I'll help."

For a minute he glared at her, and Julia thought he might try to pick her up and dump her back in the house. But he silently thrust the shovel at her, and went inside. Julia began to clear the rest of the walk, and a few minutes later Derek emerged with a second shovel.

They worked side by side, in silence, to finish the walk and dig out the car. By the time this was accomplished, both were too exhausted to bicker.

"Now let's just hope the wind doesn't cover it all up again." Derek put his arm around Julia's shoulder and they walked to the house.

Inside, he presented her with a faded, gray and white

Middlesex University sweatshirt, a pair of sweat socks, and athletic shorts which had definitely seen better days.

"Fetching!" was the tongue-in-cheek comment as Julia emerged from the bathroom. Her right hand was hidden under the sweatshirt, clutching the too-large shorts to hold them up.

"What can I use to put around my waist?" Julia said grumpily. "And my knees are cold."

"Why not take off the shorts," Derek laughed, "and I'll warm your knees for you."

"Funny!" Julia went to his closet and began rummaging through it. "This is a dreadful tie, Derek," she said, holding up a multicolored, floral creation. "I'm appropriating it."

"Help yourself. I think one of my friends gave it to me. I've certainly never *worn* it!" He was sprawled out on his bed, watching her. She turned her back to him, lifted up the sweatshirt, and tied the offensive cloth around her middle.

"I never thought I'd miss watching television. But the next best thing—" Derek clicked on the portable radio and tuned in a college football game from Atlanta. He became totally absorbed in it.

With a shrug, Julia lay down on the bed and picked up one of her school books. Derek glanced over at her, then opened up the drawer of his night table and took out an ear plug for the radio. He lay back on the bed, eyes closed, listening to the game.

Julia studied. After a while, she was sure he was asleep. After shoveling snow for three hours, it wouldn't have been surprising if he had collapsed on the doorstep instead of merely dozing off on the bed. She yawned. Maybe he had the right idea.

When she woke up, the room was lit only by firelight and Derek was gone. A peek out the door confirmed that he was in the kitchen. She padded out to discover that dinner was almost ready. Derek had cooked thin slices of veal in lemon sauce; Julia helped him carry the food into the bedroom and they enjoyed the dinner and a white French wine in companionable silence.

The evening radio news conveyed the information that the police hoped to lift the embargo on automobile travel the next morning. Back roads would be plowed as quickly as possible. The electric and phone companies were working around the clock to restore service to their customers.

They sat on the bed, reading, until midnight; then without a word Derek got up and went into the bathroom to change. Julia took her turn when he was done. When she came out, he was staring into space, smoking a cigarette. She mumbled a low good night as he put more logs on the fire and extinguished the lantern.

She was as restless as a kitten. As hard as she tried to stay still and fall asleep, it just wasn't happening. She twisted and turned, willing herself to forget that Derek was only inches away.

Finally he uttered the first complete sentence either of them had spoken all night. "Damn it, Julia, will you keep still?" His voice was a guttural growl.

"I'm sorry," she whispered. "I can't sleep."

"Now I wonder why not," he taunted acidly.

Julia snuggled up under the covers, curling her body into a tight ball. She forced herself to stay absolutely rigid. At last—it seemed like an hour later but was probably closer to fifteen minutes—she was assured by Derek's deep, even breathing that he was sound asleep.

Overcome by a craving just to be nearer to him, to touch him, she slid over to his side of the bed. No reaction from him. Timidly she slipped an arm over his shoulder and snuggled up against his back.

"Just what do you think you're doing?"

At this angry bark, Julia nearly jumped out of her skin, drew away, and said the only thing that came to mind. "I thought you were asleep."

He rolled over to face her, his features clearly visible in the light from the fire. "And were you planning to ravish me without my knowledge?"

His smoldering eyes and half-smiling mouth aroused her almost as much as physical contact would have. After two days of frustration, she simply could not endure any more. Her voice was an uncertain whisper. "Yes."

"Julia, this isn't fair to you. You can't make a rational decision."

"Stop it, Derek, this is the wrong time to be noble," Julia choked out. She moved closer to him, burying her face in his neck, her mouth caressing the smooth skin.

For a moment he lay perfectly still, and Julia was afraid he would push her away. But then one arm reluctantly reached out to stroke her body and, with a muffled curse, he rolled over onto his side to press her close against him. Her mouth was captured in a sizzling, rough kiss which told Julia that he was far beyond the point of stopping.

If Julia had any hesitation about what she was doing, all notions of holding back vanished when he moved his mouth from hers to nip her ear and whisper, "You know I'm falling in love with you, don't you?"

Julia had no opportunity to reply in kind. His mouth was exploring hers and she was so alive with happiness that she could feel her eyes tearing under the closed lids.

Any inhibitions that she might have felt fled. Derek was kissing and caressing her with a tender passion that was all giving, no taking. She wanted desperately to please him in return, and some sixth sense told her exactly how to move, where to touch, what to do.

He stopped to remove the top of her ski pajamas, accomplishing this with slow deliberation. Clearly he enjoyed making both of them wait a bit before continuing the lovemaking. He yanked off his own pajama top, then stretched out again, holding Julia against him, kissing her, taking his time.

When the phone by his bedside rang, he uttered an angry curse, followed by "Now the damn thing decides to work!" Julia tried to pull away but Derek muttered "Let it ring!" and held her tighter.

The unknown party on the other end of the line was tenacious. By the eighth ring Derek lay back, disgusted. He seemed to have no intention of picking up the phone, so Julia reached over his body to grab it.

She said huskily, "Derek Veblen's residence."

Her father's voice crackled over the line. "Julia? Is that you? What in the name of God is going on up there?"

Julia tried to sound casual. "Hi, Daddy. Nothing's going on. We were asleep. The snow—"

"What the hell do you mean, you were asleep. Asleep where?" He sounded ready to explode.

"Nothing happened, Daddy. The fireplace is in the bedroom, and there's no heat, so we're both sleeping—"

Again her father cut her off. "I've been trying to get you since yesterday. Melinda told me—what the hell are you doing there?"

"Will you let me finish one single sentence," Julia yelled. Silence from the other end. "I was posing for Derek. We got snowed in. He's a perfect gentleman. Okay?"

Julia glanced over at Derek, who was lazily laughing at her end of the conversation. Her father had been screaming at such a pitch that Julia decided Derek could probably hear his end, too.

Her father was far from satisfied. "Let me speak to him."

Julia covered the mouthpiece of the phone to whisper to Derek, but he had obviously heard the barked out order from Richard Harcourt, and took the phone from her.

"Richard," he drawled. "So nice to hear from you. Thanks for the material on the scholarships. Now what can I do for you?"

Julia could make out her father's answer. "What the hell are you doing with my daughter?"

"Well actually," laughed Derek, "you didn't call at the most opportune time, Richard. I was in the middle of making love to her. Now if you'll excuse us—" He hung up the phone to break the connection, then picked it up again and tossed the receiver with its offending dial tone under a pillow on the floor.

Julia was in shock. "How could you tell him that? He goes absolutely berserk on the subject of my virtue, Derek, he—"

"Every father's daughter is a virgin, eh?" He smiled a decidedly cynical smile. "Well, why not? You sure as hell fooled me. Now come back over here and let's finish what we started, Julia."

His curt, sarcastic tone was like a knife under her rib cage. "What—what are you saying, Derek?" Julia managed to whisper.

"Oh come off it!" he said impatiently. "If the idea of your whole virginal performance of the last two days was to make the third act that much better, fine! I have no objection to erotic games, Julia. But I'm tired of waiting."

Too stunned to cry, Julia said blankly, "Is—is that what you think it is? A game?"

"Darling," he drawled, "give me credit for some intelligence. I can tell the difference between an inexperienced virgin and a woman who knows all the right moves. You make love like a pro."

"But—but I wanted to please you. You told me—you said you were in love."

Derek exploded in disillusioned anger. "I bet you thought that was funny, didn't you? That I was gullible enough to believe—" He reached for his cigarettes and viciously struck a match. When he spoke again, his voice was deadly calm. "For a minute there, I really had myself convinced you were a vulnerable, innocent little fledgling. Poor victimized Julia. The newspapers print such scandalous garbage about her. Hell, you must have made it with every millionaire's son from Boston to Bangkok."

"And what about all those Boston matrons you had affairs with, Derek?" Julia retorted angrily. "Where do you get off—you haven't exactly led a life of untarnished virtue!"

"At least I was honest about it! And I got away from that type of life," he thundered. "Besides, it's different for a man."

In Julia's present mood, that chauvinistic statement was the last straw. Still topless, she furiously picked up her pillow and stalked toward the door.

The temperature in the studio must have been in the 20s, but for a few minutes Julia was so hot with rage and hurt that she scarcely noticed. But as she lay huddled under the covers, the cold began to penetrate. She began to shiver, yet nothing would make her go down to that bedroom again. To think that she had been penalized for responding with all her heart—her love. The tears started.

She was sobbing silently when Derek came up to get her. She stiffened, ready to argue with him about returning to his bed. But he simply picked her up, and she choked out, "Don't touch me." He snarled, "I wouldn't make love to you if I'd already paid the hundred bucks. But I won't let you freeze to death either!"

He dumped her on the bed after having almost fallen down the steps with her in the dark, then turned his back on her and went to sleep.

Chapter Nine

Melinda walked into Julia's room and watched her roommate in silence. An expression of deep concern was on her face.

"Julia," she said softly, "you can't sit there crying that way. Please. Try to eat something."

Julia shook her head. The tears rolled down her cheeks, but she was catatonically still and made no sound, except for an occasional shuddering sigh.

That morning, Julia had awakened to the sound of Sandy McCoy's snowplow clearing out Derek's driveway. Apparently he had also helped Derek put chains on the tires of the van.

Julia's pride demanded that she not break down again in front of him. He offered no breakfast and she took none, but waited in the bedroom. Her own clothing was finally dry; she put it back on. The only words between them were Derek's curt "Let's go."

That was at 10:30. For the past three hours, she had

been in this near-paralyzed state. Melinda was still
standing in the room, trying to decide what to do, when
the doorbell rang.

Mel recognized Derek at once, of course; the
middle-aged man with him was a complete stranger.
The latter held out his hand to her. "You must be
Melinda. I'm Julia's father. May we come in?"

Mel shook his hand, and quickly invited them into
the apartment. Her offer of coffee was accepted with
appreciation.

"Is Julia in her room?" Richard Harcourt looked
toward the half-closed door.

"Yes," Melinda began hesitantly. "But she's in no
shape to come out, Mr. Harcourt."

It was the wrong thing to say. Richard Harcourt's
face reddened he shot Derek a furious glance and
stormed into the bedroom.

Julia looked at him blankly. Her father. How nice.

All the anger drained out of him at the sight of her.
He sat on the bed next to his daughter, put his arm
around her shoulders, and asked quietly, "Julia, baby.
Are you okay?"

His kindness and gentleness were her undoing. She
turned into his arms, and indulged herself with a
tempestuous fit of unrestrained sobbing. Fifteen minutes later, when she had finally calmed herself and
stopped, his shoulder was sopping wet.

"Get yourself cleaned up, honey," he said tenderly,
"we're going down to Maryland."

This non sequitur produced a near-hysterical giggle
from Julia. "Maryland? What are you talking about?"

"You're getting married. Now don't argue. It's all
arranged. Your godfather is meeting us at the airport
and he'll perform the ceremony." This news was
delivered in a calm, matter-of-fact manner, as if he had
just observed that the ground was covered with snow.

It took a moment for Julia to piece together what this was all about. She looked at him as if he were a refugee from a mental institution. "You can't be serious! To Derek? He—"

"He happens to be waiting in the living room. He's perfectly agreeable. Now get yourself together, honey."

"No." The word was spoken in a clear, firm voice. "I don't know how you blackmailed *Mr.* Veblen into this, but—"

"Derek!" Richard Harcourt called imperiously into the next room. "Get in here!"

Derek strolled in, dressed in a gray corduroy suit, and smiled warmly at Julia. He told Richard Harcourt, "I'll take care of this." She looked at Derek suspiciously, her hurt and anger for the moment forgotten in the unreality of the situation.

He closed the door and seemed to consider just how he should go about convincing Julia to go along with her father's order. Finally, he suggested, "Humor him, Julia. He's very upset."

"Since when do you worry about my father's mental state?" Julia jeered.

"In his present frame of mind, he's quite capable of hiring a hit man to rub me out, Julia." He grinned at her. "I know you're angry, but surely you don't want to see me dead."

"I wouldn't bet on that!" she snapped. "This whole thing is ridiculous. After the things you said to me, do you really think—"

"Just cool off, for God's sake. I admit I have a bad temper. I apologize for last night. Let's just take it one step at a time, okay? Your father will calm down eventually."

Julia tried to read the expression in his eyes, but saw only detached determination. "Are you saying we should go through with this today, and then get an annulment some time in the future?"

Derek shrugged. "It's an option."

"Of course, the merchandise is a little shopworn. Isn't that right, Derek? What possible grounds could there be for an annulment?" Julia asked sarcastically.

Another shrug. "I'm not a lawyer. Coercion, perhaps? We can worry about that some other time."

"You don't seriously believe that he'd try to have you *killed?*" Julia asked scornfully. "My father's not a maniac!"

"Like you said last night, he's irrational on the subject of your virtue." This statement was accompanied by a mocking smile. "Come on, Julia. What's a trip to Maryland?"

"I'm not going to live with you!" Julia seemed unaware that with this proclamation she had just agreed to the marriage.

"I didn't invite you to! We'll give you half an hour to shower and dress and then one of us is coming in here!" Derek strode out, leaving Julia to ponder the whole mad scheme in solitude.

Well, why not? Derek obviously didn't take it seriously. In a few weeks her family lawyer could straighten the whole mess out. By then her father wouldn't be ranting and raving about murder for hire. She shook her head. She had never known him to be *that* fanatical about her! Maybe marriage to Maggie had warped his mind.

Julia decided to wash her hair, and it was close to an hour before she was ready to leave. When she emerged from the room, Melinda, Derek and her father were joined in friendly conversation around a plate of sandwiches.

She had put on an elegant wool suit, with a lacy feminine blouse; her hair was twisted back into a sophisticated bun. An unusually heavy coat of makeup hid the circles and redness around her eyes.

During the entire surrealistic trip, Derek and her father talked together like the oldest of friends. Julia sat silently, listening to them proceed from the subject of the scholarship fund Richard was setting up to a discussion of art collecting to her father's often repeated war stories.

Her godfather, who was actually a cousin of her mother's named Joshua Sibley, met them at the gate as they stepped off Richard's private plane. Her Uncle Josh, as Julia had always called him, was a judge in Maryland, which had no waiting requirement for marriage. He had arranged the use of a small room for the ceremony, which was over in fifteen minutes. Julia hazily remembered promising herself a religious ceremony, but then, this hardly counted. It wouldn't be a real marriage.

Julia's father had brought along Jill Harcourt's wedding ring for his daughter; Derek coolly slipped it on her finger. But his reaction to the words "I now pronounce you husband and wife" was far warmer. Julia's lips were taken in a thorough, probing kiss that totally flabbergasted her and to which she refused to respond. Then Derek winked at her, as if to say, "That was for the benefit of our audience."

Richard flew back to New York, where he dropped off his daughter and new son-in-law so they could catch a plane to Boston.

Derek's car was at Logan Airport in Boston; Julia could not quite figure out how her father and Derek had wound up in *his* car at *her* apartment. She was not about to ask. Derek had been broodingly uncommunicative while they were alone, and Julia acknowledged that her own mood was not much better.

She was sure that he would drop her off and let her

go upstairs to her apartment without so much as a good-bye. In fact he did not say "good-bye"; what he said was "See you tomorrow at noon." Julia looked at him as if he were deranged. Surely after all that had happened he didn't expect her to continue posing for him?

The expression on her face was as good as saying the thought aloud. Derek said calmly, "The heat's back on, Julia; you won't get cold."

"That isn't the point!" she fumed. "You surely can't expect me to—"

"I want to finish the portrait," he told her arrogantly. "I'm not going to touch you," he grinned, "except in the line of duty." He studied his new wife's implacable visage. "For the sake of artistic expression," he coaxed.

"No."

"Julia. It will be the last time. Please."

She softened. "You promise nothing will happen?" she said reluctantly.

Derek held up two fingers. "Scout's honor."

"Oh, all right then." Without a good night, she hopped out of the car and slammed the door behind her.

Julia lay on the bed, waiting for Derek to come upstairs. It was, she thought peevishly, as if absolutely nothing had happened between Thursday and today. The routine—the silent drive, the music, the waiting downstairs while she got ready—was unvaried. Apparently he had changed the sheets on the bed; they looked unslept in. If she had not known better, she could easily have convinced herself that she had imagined the whole awful/ecstatic weekend. But the knowledge that she loved him desperately in spite of the things he had said, and the ache to be held by him, could not be dismissed.

Derek climbed slowly up the stairs and over to Julia's

bed. He began adjusting the sheet from behind her as she stared in the other direction. When his hand stroked her hair, she stiffened.

Then he walked around the bed to stand in front of her, and Julia saw that he was wearing only a robe, apparently with nothing under it. Utter panic assailed her. "You promised—" she sputtered.

"Yeah," he laughed. "Scout's honor." He sat down and traced a finger along her jaw, her neck, her collar bones. "I never *was* a member of the Boy Scouts," he said huskily.

"No, Derek, I don't want—"

"Yes, Julia, I *do* want!" he mimicked.

And then he was lying beside her, his hands caressing her intimately, his mouth ravaging hers with a series of hungry, quick kisses, and the token resistance she had initially put up melted away. When he picked her up to carry her down to the bedroom, she buried her face against his shoulder, loving the smell of his skin and the feel of it against her mouth. "You said you didn't believe in seduction," she whispered.

"You're my wife now. I reserve the right to seduce you any time I feel like it!" he growled back.

Julia walked out of the bathroom, her mind confused. Derek lay on the bed, half covered, smoking a cigarette. She looked uncertainly at him as he motioned her to lie down next to him.

"Why didn't you tell me, Julia?" he asked quietly.

She did not pretend to misunderstand the question, but thought it was hardly fair. "You're the one who said I was so experienced," she reminded him.

"You said there were no grounds for annulment. How was I supposed to know you didn't mean it?"

Julia said nothing, just damned him with reproachful eyes.

"For God's sake, Julia, I'm not a rapist!" he said angrily. "You responded passionately enough in the beginning. I didn't realize you were actually frightened." Suddenly the tone was softer. "I thought you were holding out on me, and I lost my temper. I'm sorry I forced you."

Julia sat motionless. She supposed she could understand his side of it, but that didn't lessen her pain at what she had experienced. His furious anger at her last minute resistance had been even worse than his actual physical possession of her.

Julia's soundless accusations were meant to goad Derek, and succeeded completely.

"Do you have to sit there like a martyr?" he yelled. "What on earth do you want? Am I supposed to be eternally grateful for the precious gift you've bestowed on me?"

Julia continued to stare at him in silent condemnation, enjoying the fact that he had lost control of himself.

"All right," he went on in a low, enraged tone. "Don't speak to me. So you've done everything in the book with God knows how many men, but you saved a little bit of yourself for your husband. I'm honored. At least I got something the rest of them didn't!"

With that, Derek stormed out of the bedroom, slamming the door behind him. Julia didn't know whether to laugh or cry. It gave her a sense of satisfaction to know that *something* had gotten under his skin. She suspected that he felt guilty over what had happened; certainly he prided himself on being a good lover. Furthermore, for a man who made honesty a moral imperative, he had been undeniably deceptive. Yet his reaction to her reproaches seemed all out of proportion, even given his emotional makeup.

At the same time, Derek's insistence that she was

some kind of promiscuous tramp wounded her. How could he profess to be half in love with her one minute, and then be so cruelly cutting the next? She was the same person, wasn't she? Of course, he thought she had lied to him, teased him, played with his feelings. She could understand his resentment, and admitted to herself that her silent goading hadn't helped. But why did he always assume the worst of her? What had she done to make him so cynical about her?

Derek's class on Tuesday morning was a review of the course material in preparation for the midterm exam the following week. Julia was unable to concentrate on any of it.

Yesterday had been bad enough. When Derek had returned to the bedroom, his manner had been icy. He all but dragged her home, and dropped her off at her apartment without a word.

But her roommate's casual "Congratulations! You're on Page 1" had been the start of something worse. Julia had grabbed the newspaper; at the bottom of the front page was the headline, *Insurance Heiress Weds Artist.* The article had begun:

Richard Harcourt, Chairman of the Board of Harcourt Commercial Insurance Corporation, has announced in New York the marriage of his daughter, society beauty Julia Elizabeth Harcourt, to internationally acclaimed artist Derek Veblen. Mrs. Veblen is also the daughter of the late Jill Carver Harcourt. The couple met at Middlesex University, near Boston, where Mrs. Veblen is a student of her husband's.

When Julia had walked into class that morning, she

felt hundreds of eyes on her, and for once she was bothered by it. A few people yelled out best wishes or congratulations, but she knew what they were really thinking: Why the hurry? How come there wasn't a big jet-set ceremony in New York City?

Derek had sauntered in a bit late (back to his old habits, Julia thought sourly). A hushed silence had greeted his entrance. He looked around at the expectant faces, his eyes turning cold for a moment as he spotted Julia. Then he drawled, "Have I made enemies of all the young men in this class by taking Miss Harcourt off the marriage market?"

Laughter greeted the question, along with a few shouts of "Yes" and "Congratulations." Derek had quickly turned to business, and begun his rapid-fire review of the course work thus far.

Julia was positive that the absence of any statement to the effect that he was a lucky man had been noted by his audience. And that was humiliating. Did they think she was pregnant, or that Derek had married her for her money?

She dreaded the afternoon's tutorial, and even considered cutting it. But Derek would have been outraged and she had been at the painful end of his lashing tongue too many times recently to risk further chastisement.

The students had been assigned the task of executing something in the pop art mode. Julia's acrylic on canvas painting depicted a number of politicians packaged like soap flakes or dry cereal for the marketplace.

Julia was relieved by Derek's impersonal manner. He followed his usual habit of chatting with his students for several minutes, then critiquing and discussing their work. A freewheeling conversation about the pop art movement concluded the session.

He treated Julia no differently than his other students, except that he called her by her first name. When she came forward to display her work, he mentioned to the class that he hadn't seen it, and casually draped an arm over her shoulder while he studied it.

Thank God he had liked it! Julia could not have borne a harsh judgment from him; she felt much too vulnerable.

He had dismissed the class a half-hour late, then softly added, "Mrs. Veblen. Will you stay after for a few minutes?"

Julia waited until the others had left, then hesitantly looked at him. "Yes, Derek?"

He said mockingly, "Alone at last," and took her into his arms to kiss her. Julia, off-balance and more than a little resentful of his changeable moods, stood frostily still and clamped her mouth shut.

"I can see I'm going to have to make up for my sins of yesterday," Derek told her with a laugh. "My sister Ramona called last night to invite us for Thanksgiving dinner. My mother's flying in from Florida. I'd like you to meet my family, Julia."

"What for? We'll be divorced soon enough!" Julia began to gather up her things.

"Not so fast! You had better understand a few things, Julia." His voice was uncompromising. "I have no intention of trying to annul our marriage or of getting a divorce. And I'll contest any attempt by you to do so."

"But you said—" Julia gasped, shocked.

"*You* said. Not me. I merely admitted that it was an option." He took her books from her hands and threw them down. "And I don't much care for our living arrangements. We'll go to Albany Thursday morning, stay over that night, and when we come back, you're moving in with me."

When Julia began to protest, a hand was clapped firmly over her mouth. She refused to give him the satisfaction of struggling, but stood rigidly still, glaring at him. "And another thing, Mrs. Veblen. I intend to make love to you Thursday night, and I guarantee that there won't be any complaints about the performance." His hand was replaced by his mouth, and this time Julia was unable to resist. His words had aroused her, and within fifteen seconds she was clinging to him, kissing him back eagerly, pressing her body to his. When his mouth left hers to travel to her ear and whisper, "Thursday, not now," she blushed furiously.

Unable to meet his eyes, yet terribly aroused, she murmured, "Why not now? Don't you want to?"

"Of course I want to. I should think it would be obvious. But I wasn't very gentle with you yesterday, Julia," Derek answered seriously. "I think your body could use a few days to recuperate. Hmm?"

She nodded, warmed by his thoughtfulness, the bitter words of the day before pushed to a hidden corner of her mind. His tender expression gave her the courage to question him.

"Why did you marry me? My father didn't really threaten—"

"Another time," Derek interrupted. "I don't want to discuss it now. We'll only end up arguing." He took her hand. "Come on. I'll drive you to your apartment."

He began to pull her out the door, stopping only when Julia's breathless "But my books—" made him glance back to the spot on the floor where her things had been carelessly tossed.

During the short drive back to Julia's apartment, Derek told her to be ready at ten o'clock Thursday morning; she should pack a small overnight case since they would be staying in a motel near his sister's that night. "And look pretty for me, Julia," he concluded the list of instructions with a smile, "but not Julia

Harcourt knock-'em-dead. You're my wife now, not a jet-setting celebrity."

She might have taken offense at such a highhanded order, but his smile and teasing tone precluded it. She was no more anxious for another argument than he seemed to be.

Derek arrived promptly at ten o'clock on Thursday morning, accepted a cup of coffee before they started out, and surveyed his young wife with approval. Julia was wearing a soft blue ultrasuede jumper with a feminine beige blouse; elegant leather boots, slightly darker than her blouse, came to the below-the-knee hem of the jumper. Apparently Derek didn't want her to appear too sophisticated, so she eschewed exotic hairstyles to simply catch part of her hair in a clasp in the back, and let the rest fall to her shoulders, as usual.

"You look beautiful" was his simple comment, and to Julia it was compensation enough for the time she had spent deciding what to wear, how much makeup to use, and how to wear her hair.

"I have to match the elegance of my escort," Julia said lightly. She had never seen him so formally dressed. In a pinstriped suit, blue shirt, and coordinated striped tie, he looked more like an attorney than an artist. And as handsome as a god.

"I call this my gallery suit," Derek explained with a half-smile. "I wear it for exhibitions of my work. Seventy-five percent of the people probably expect some half-crazed madman in rags to show up; I like to watch their reaction. And I wore it last year"—the smile became cynical—"when I prostrated myself before a Congressional committee to plead for more money for the arts. Other than that, it tends to hang in the closet."

"What's the special occasion today then?" Julia asked.

"Ah! The arrival of the matriarch. I catch hell from my mother unless I'm suitably attired."

As they walked out to the van Julia asked Derek to tell her about his family. She never knew from one day to the next what his mood would be, so the casual, good-tempered behavior of today was a relief.

"My sister is a teacher, a musician. She teaches elementary school music, and gives private lessons. My brother-in-law—"

"Allen Moran, isn't it? Doesn't he work for the Governor, in Albany?"

"Right. But he isn't going to be on the Governor's staff for much longer. With two sons ready for college, he can't afford it. He's had offers to join a consulting firm where he can make much more money." He shot her a lecherous glance. "My nephews will *love* you. I'll probably have to tie them up to keep them from attacking."

They talked easily and impersonally for the rest of the trip to New York's capital city.

Derek's mother had arrived earlier that week and it was Mrs. Veblen who answered the door. She was a small, silver-haired woman, now slightly plump but still quite lovely. Her son received a fierce hug, or more accurately it was the other way around; Derek had lifted his petite mother clear off the floor.

Derek introduced Julia to Clementina Veblen; the latter greeted her new daughter-in-law with a distinctly cool nod and even cooler handshake. Julia had been prepared to kiss her mother-in-law hello, but quickly changed her mind.

Ramona Moran was a female version of Derek; tall, slim, dark. Her reception for her brother and his wife duplicated her mother's example. She clearly adored her younger brother but was suspicious of Julia.

Had it not been for the friendly welcome extended by Allen Moran and Derek's two nephews, Walter and Charles, Julia might have started to feel like she was a carrier of the Black Death. True to Derek's prediction, Walt and Charlie devoured Julia with their eyes, quite openly telling their uncle that he was an old man who didn't deserve such a knockout of a wife.

Nonetheless, it was quite obvious to Julia that Derek's two nephews idolized him. Their father might be a nationally respected expert on social welfare programs but their uncle Derek was a far more glamorous figure to them. His new young society wife only added to the image.

The male portion of the family soon retired to the living room to watch one of the many Thanksgiving Day football games, and Julia was left to cope as best she could with her female in-laws. There was still a lot of cooking to be done. Dinner would be served at five o'clock and Julia was thankful that they had stopped along the Mass Pike for something to eat.

Mrs. Veblen at first persisted in talking to her daughter in Italian; Julia had to smile at this ploy because she spoke the language fluently. But to admit it would be disastrous. She was certain that it would only embarrass her mother-in-law if she knew that Julia could understand her dark mutterings about Derek's fancy wife.

Ramona put a stop to her mother's rudeness; she might not care for Julia, but at least she had the good manners to be civil to her. Julia successfully maintained a facade of eager friendliness, pitching in to help with the slicing, peeling, chopping and beating.

As the food cooked, the Veblen clan kept up a lively

conversation that jumped from current events to family concerns to art and music. Mrs. Veblen had forcefully insisted (above the strong protests of her grandsons) that the television be turned off. Julia was, for the most part, silent; she appreciated the fact that Derek sat next to her on the couch, his arm protectively around her. Allen occasionally directed a question or comment to her, for which she was grateful.

Julia helped serve and clean up as well, and felt that she had made a small dent in her mother-in-law's determinedly negative opinion of her. As for Ramona, after dinner she had followed Julia into the bedroom where she had gone to freshen up, and apologized for her earlier coldness. "I guess I think no one's good enough for my baby brother," she admitted. "But you aren't anything like I expected, and Derek is obviously nuts about you. So welcome to the family." Julia responded with a kiss and her thanks. She was genuinely touched by Ramona's kindness, even if she had her doubts about the accuracy of her opinion about Derek's feelings.

After dinner, with everyone well-fed and relaxed by wine and conversation, even Mrs. Veblen seemed to loosen up. Julia had never seen Derek so genuinely at ease; a pang of jealousy shot through her that his family could have this effect on him when she could never hope to.

When they left at nine o'clock the hugs and kisses included even Julia. To her amazement, her mother-in-law told her that she should call her "mama, like the rest of the family." Julia could not resist replying in perfect Italian that she would be honored to do so. For a moment there was shocked silence from Ramona and Mrs. Veblen; then the latter laughed and told Derek that he had chosen a wife as strong-willed as his mother, and had best take care with her. His reply—

"Oh, I'm learning that the hard way, mama"—was calculated to spare Julia's blushes.

"What was all that about your speaking Italian?" he asked, puzzled, on the way to the motel.

"Your mother and sister were talking about me when all of us were in the kitchen. In Italian. And your mother wasn't very flattering, I can assure you," Julia laughed. "Of course she didn't realize I understood any of it, and *I* wasn't about to clue her in!"

"You charmed the hell out of all of them," Derek said, sounding very pleased.

Julia looked at Derek, all provocation and sensuality. The wine had gone to her head just a bit. "Aren't you going to thank me for making such a big hit with your family?"

"Oh, yes," was the smoldering reply.

Their room had two queen-sized beds in it; Derek flung his coat and suit jacket on one, stripped off his tie and shirt and left them to join the other garments, and went into the bathroom. Julia could hear the sound of his electric razor, and waited on the other bed, fully clothed. Excitement mingled with fear; she savored both emotions.

Derek emerged from the bathroom to pick Julia up off the bed, put her on her feet, and slowly undress her. Soon the rest of his clothing joined the heap on the second bed and, clicking off the lights, he threw back the covers of the first bed and gently lifted Julia onto it. Then he was beside her, ordering her to lie on her stomach and kneading her back and shoulders in a firm, lovely massage that made her want to purr.

What followed was an assault on her senses so total that Julia could hardly bear it. She felt as though every inch of her body had been caressed either by his hands or his mouth, but when she reached out to touch him, he grabbed her wrists and laughingly growled at her that if she tried it again, he would tie them up. Her meek "Yes, Derek" seemed to satisfy him.

He had brought her to the point that she was ready to beg him not to tease her anymore when he stopped cold, lit a cigarette, and lay back on the bed to smoke it. Julia waited patiently beside him, aware that his own arousal would not let him delay the inevitable for long.

Derek began slowly to make love to her again, lightly stroking her body, taking her mouth with lazy, drugging kisses. This time, when she reached out to caress him, he did not stop her. But almost immediately he lost control of the situation, and possessed her with a rough, fierce passion that had Julia closing her eyes tightly to experience more intensely the feelings he was arousing in her. She dug her nails into his back and moaned softly, only half-aware of what she was doing.

And afterward, as she snuggled next to him while he smoked another cigarette, he asked in a teasing voice, "And is the lady pleased?"

Her body was trembling and still highly sensitive, and she knew it was impossibly trite, but she truly had never imagined that she could respond as she had. She whispered, "You know I am." Warm blue eyes surveyed him adoringly.

"Me too." He stubbed out the cigarette and lazily stretched. "God, but you turn me on. Your body, the way you kiss me—"

And then Julia saw a frown cross his face and he subtly withdrew from her. When he looked at her again, his expression was harder, and it frightened her. "Well, how did I do? Or as you once put it, how do I *measure up?*"

"Derek, please don't," Julia begged. "I've never done anything like this—"

"Damn it, don't lie to me!" he interrupted.

"I swear it, Derek, please—" Julia began again, in a stricken voice.

"I can learn to live with your past, but I can't stand it that you're not honest with me," he said in a dangerous, controlled tone. "How about it? Do I score a ten?"

Julia, hurt beyond caring by his words, thought only of hitting back. "Let's see now," she spat out. "There was that Belgian prince—he was worth a seven. And the California senator whose marriage I allegedly broke up—you wouldn't *believe* some of the things we used to do in his Jacuzzi. But the Indian prince I met in Bombay was the best. Those eastern men *really* know how to make love—he was right off the scale!" She glared at him. "I'd give you about—an eight!"

He was tight-lipped, furious. "Right." He angrily rolled off the bed, threw all the clothes from the second bed onto the floor, and climbed in.

Chapter Ten

Silent automobile trips were getting to be a way of life, thought Julia. She could become resigned to *that*. But Derek's lack of trust was too painful to be borne. She did not know which was worse, his male chauvinism in condemning her allegedly sinful past or his lack of faith in her honesty. She sensed that he cared for her; that he was strongly attracted to her physically was not in doubt. And God knows, Julia told herself, in spite of everything, I love him to distraction. But what possible chance do we have for a happy marriage under the circumstances?

She took a deep breath and let out an audible sigh. Derek looked over at her, frowned, and lit another cigarette. At least, she thought, I won't have to move in with him now. With hostilities at a renewed peak, Derek would never want her to live with him.

That particular supposition proved erroneous. Derek

pulled into the parking lot of her apartment building, and calmly announced that he would help her pack up her things. But Julia refused to meekly obey him.

"Derek," she said in a low, beseeching tone. "I have midterms next week. I won't be able to study if—if we're at each other's throats this way. Please believe me when I tell you it upsets me terribly. Derek?"

From the way her husband was staring out the window, Julia wondered if he had even listened to her plea. Finally he turned to her, a bland expression on his face.

"Fair enough. There's no reason why we have to fight," he said indifferently. "But you're still my wife and I won't have every university gossip from here to Boston dissecting our living arrangements. Isn't that reasonable?"

Damn his mercurial nature! How could he be so cool all of a sudden? Oh, Julia could see his point of view, but she could not picture the two of them getting along smoothly in Derek's small house. "It's no good," she protested. "We'll just fight and I'll get upset and I'll louse up my exams. It's—"

Her reply was cut off by the feel of her husband's mouth against her neck. He knew perfectly well that he could always get around her by making love to her, and she resented it. She stiffened; a frosty look came into her eyes.

"Please," she moaned. "Don't you know that every time we make love, we end up yelling at each other. I've studied hard this term and I don't want to blow it because—"

"Right. You're absolutely right," Derek interrupted. "We'll call a moratorium on that." He moved back to his side of the front seat. "Don't make me drag you, Julia. Please."

"You won't lose your temper with me? And you'll let me study? And you won't try to seduce me?"

"No. Yes. No. Satisfied?" Now Derek was grinning at her, and Julia felt herself smile almost against her will. He did not give her time to reconsider her capitulation. He was out of the car and urging her to hurry up before she had even agreed to come back to Concord with him.

She joined him on the icy blacktop and allowed him to take hold of her elbow as they half walked, half skidded to the door. Derek helped her pack her things, then waited while she wrote a note to Melinda. He backed the van close to the front door; they loaded it up and were on their way in under an hour.

Everything was repeated in reverse at the other end. An antique chest had appeared in Derek's bedroom (Julia still could not think of it as *their* bedroom) and her husband had cleared out some closet space for her as well, but the amount of room made available was sadly insufficient for her wardrobe.

"It's what I deserve for marrying an heiress with expensive tastes," he said mournfully. "What the hell do you *do* with all these gowns? All I ever see you wear around school are jeans, or pants and sweaters."

"I used to have a very active social life, Mr. Veblen, before I got tangled up with you!" Julia said with mock disgust.

"But you don't miss it," Derek stated flatly.

"No," came back the quiet admission.

"Let's store this stuff upstairs then. I have more storage space up there. Now. Let's find a good spot for the portrait of your mother. Maybe on the wall next to the kitchen?"

Julia's face began to heat up. "It's not good enough to hang with—with—with—"

"You're stuttering, darling." He lifted her chin, pondered the uncertain, questioning look in her eyes. "I'm not going to be able to keep my hands off you if you look so vulnerable," he sighed.

Julia twisted her head away, embarrassed, as Derek took her arm. "It *is* good enough, Julia. It was good enough to get you into my class, even though I was absolutely furious with you at the time."

"You're sure?"

"Fishing for compliments?" he teased. "Do you want me to tell you you're very talented? Okay, you are—in more ways than one," he said softly, and went down to the basement to fetch a hammer and picture hook in order to hang the portrait.

When this had been accomplished, Julia marshaled her courage and brought up the subject of sleeping arrangements. "I'm not sharing a bed with you, Derek," she told her husband defensively. "We would wind up—you know—and then we'd fight, and—"

He held up his hand to silence her. "Okay, say no more. You sleep upstairs. I don't give up my bed for anyone!"

Julia nodded. For the first time she began to feel that she would get through her midterms without a domestic crisis.

Her instincts proved correct. Derek was the perfect roommate. He left her in peace to study, and would even have done all the cooking had not Julia made it clear that she was not a princess to be waited on hand and foot. A housekeeper came in once a week to clean, so they had only day-to-day tidying to do.

Her art exam was Tuesday, her psychology exam Wednesday, and her international relations test, easily the most terrifying of the three, on Friday. She had a mountain of material to review for the last exam, and the task of sorting it all out in her head was yet harder.

She gratefully accepted Derek's help. On Wednesday, over dinner, he began to ask questions about the areas her professor had covered up until then. He helped her to make sense of the course work, uncover trends, develop ideas. They talked all of Wednesday evening and again on Thursday evening. Julia felt closer to her husband than she ever had before. Had he not maintained a relaxed, slightly distant, definitely professorial manner toward her, the impulse to come to his bed would have triumphed. But she knew that *that* would only end in disaster. She did not want to have to walk into her exam on Friday a nervous wreck.

Derek left Friday morning for New York where he had promised to give several lectures in conjunction with a retrospective of his work at The Museum of Modern Art. He was staying on to visit some English friends who would be in town, and would return to Boston Sunday night.

Julia took the opportunity of an empty weekend to finish the term paper for her international relations course. By Friday afternoon she was feeling utterly delighted with herself. She was sure she had gotten A's on all her exams; it gave her a sense of accomplishment that she had never before experienced. She only regretted the semesters she had frittered away with parties and people who bored her.

All day Saturday she wrote; books and notes surrounded her on Derek's bed. The only interruption was a pleasant one—a phone call from her husband. She had been upstairs in the studio, retrieving some notes she had left there; when the phone rang, she dashed downstairs to the bedroom again, grumpily wondering why Derek didn't have an extension installed in the studio. She grabbed the receiver, "Derek Veblen's residence."

"Oh? And isn't it Julia Veblen's home also?" her husband asked.

"Derek! How did the lectures go?" Julia felt absurdly pleased by his call.

"Very well. And your exam?"

"I think I aced it. Talking with you helped so much. And I'm working on my paper today; isn't that virtuous of me?"

"Umm. I wish I hadn't promised to spend tonight and tomorrow with Roger and Stephanie. But they're flying back to London—"

"I understand," Julia said huskily. "But you'll be back tomorrow night?"

"Right. See you then, darling."

"Yes. Bye, Derek." She hung up, her energies recharged, and threw herself back into her writing.

By that evening the paper was completed. She had only to type it on Sunday.

Why did I have to come down with flu *now*, Julia asked the Fates on Sunday morning. She lay in bed, miserably nauseated and quite unable to get up. Unable to fall back to sleep either, she suffered silently until almost 10:30. The feeling of sickness had abated somewhat by then, and she was able to make it down to the kitchen to force some tea and toast into her protesting stomach.

Miraculously, she began to feel much better. She was an excellent typist, and by late afternoon the forty-five-page term paper—footnotes, bibliography and all—was finished. She surveyed the completed product with pride.

By now ravenously hungry, she went to the kitchen to fix herself a sandwich. Her eyes lit on the large appointments calendar which was tacked up on Derek's bulletin board. Sunday, December 3. Sunday?

Under the pressure of studying for exams, Julia had lost track of certain things. She moaned to herself that it was impossible. One couldn't become pregnant the very first time, yet from the age of fifteen her body had been so regular—until now.

Could a woman feel morning sickness so early? They say every woman is an individual; there are no rules. Julia supposed anything was possible.

Of course she would have to tell Derek. For some reason she found it difficult to imagine how or when she would do so. Perhaps it was because he lived in a house clearly built without children in mind. He probably didn't want any. He must have assumed she was on the pill—until he found out she was a virgin. Or, being a man, more likely he had never considered the matter at all.

Julia reproached herself for not having visited the University Infirmary to prevent this, then remembered that Derek had made such a point of *not* seducing her before they were married that it had honestly never occurred to her that he would do so afterward. In any event, it was too late now to bemoan her lack of foresight. She would have a pregnancy test, but she already knew what the result would be.

In her own mind there was no question; she would have the child, whether her husband wanted her to or not. It was the son or daughter of the man she loved, but beyond that, she placed too much value on life to snuff it out because it had made an appearance at an inconvenient time. But suppose Derek disagreed? He always seemed to get his way with her. Could she be sure she would stand up to him?

By eight o'clock she was feeling distinctly queasy once more. She thought food might help and began to fix herself a hamburger, but the smell as it cooked had her running to the sink, afraid she would be sick. She abandoned the idea of eating. How long would this keep up?

When Derek came home at ten o'clock, Julia was lying on his bed watching television, feeling absolutely dreadful, trying to get her mind off her physical condition. Her husband greeted her with a kiss on the head, and asked if she had finished her paper.

It was all she could do to get out the word "Yes".

"You could look at me when you talk to me," he replied, irritated by her lack of response. "Or did I commit some new sin I haven't heard about yet?"

Julia silently shook her head and tried not to retch. "Is something the matter?" Derek asked, but it was more an attack than a question. Julia shook her head once more.

"In that case, would you get out of *my* bedroom? I'd like to relax!" Julia fled up the stairs; she could hear his muttered curses as she left.

She lay in bed for what seemed like hours, finally making herself go back downstairs for a box of crackers. She munched a few, felt a little better. She decided to take the box up with her, since it seemed to help.

Derek appeared at her bedside at eight o'clock the next morning. "If you plan to make it to your nine o'clock class, your majesty, you'd better get your tail out of bed. I've got an appointment at 9:15 and I'm not waiting around for you." With that, he turned on his heel and stalked downstairs.

How she managed to shower and dress in fifteen minutes, Julia never knew. She nibbled some crackers, gathered up her books and term paper, and went to find Derek. He was waiting on the couch, a dour look on his face.

Another silent ride. Why couldn't she summon up the courage to say "I'm pregnant and I feel awful"?

But there was no sense in making announcements until she was certain. The University Infirmary provided the new blood tests for early detection of pregnancy. It was easy enough to make sure.

Meanwhile, Derek was driving too fast, and every time he jammed on the brakes, Julia felt that much more miserable. He dropped her off in front of the building where her psych course met and, without saying good-bye, hit the gas pedal and sped away at a velocity considerably above the fifteen miles per hour campus speed limit.

But instead of going straight to class, Julia went to the Infirmary to have her blood drawn. She was told that she could call for the results first thing in the morning. Then she went to her psychology class, to find that her instructor had returned their exams, and she had received the A she'd hoped for. It improved her mood.

Derek's tutorial was not meeting until the following Tuesday; he had given his students an extra week for the current assignment because of midterms. Julia went over to the Fine Arts Building to paint. She was working on an abstract watercolor, and enjoying this foray into a type of art she had not previously been drawn to. It was a few hours before she realized that her stomach was beginning to travel into her throat again. She put down her brush, overcome by a sudden spell of dizziness. Was it going to go on like this for months?

Derek would not be finished until six o'clock; Julia cleaned up and went into the ladies' room to lie down on the couch there. At 6:30, she woke up with a jolt. She had slept for nearly an hour and a half.

Derek's office was locked; there was no sign of him. With calm resignation, Julia walked back to her old apartment; this was as good a time as any to pick up her car. It was still sitting in the parking lot, undriven since the November blizzard. Melinda had arranged for some teen-agers to dig it out.

The station wagon started without any trouble, and Julia skidded out of the lot and began to drive back to Derek's house. Funny, she didn't think of it as *her* home. She drove carefully, not wanting to insult her sensitive stomach. Only when she reached the still icy back roads near Derek's did she realize that she had never had snow tires put on the car. She began to slide all over the pavement, and a sudden attack of dizziness made her lose control of the car completely. She wound up against a tree.

Sniffling with self-pity, she backed up the car, relieved that it still ran. She all but crawled the next three miles to her husband's, and barely made it up the slight incline of the drive. He was calmly eating dinner when she walked in the door. One step into the kitchen had her reeling from the smell of the food.

He was not about to let her run away. As she backed out of the room, he lazily got up to follow her, his long strides efficiently covering the distance between them. He pointedly looked at his watch, and Julia, resigned, sat down on the couch.

"Where the hell have you been? It's nearly eight."

"Driving home. You didn't wait for me," Julia said miserably. She wanted the conversation over with so she could go lie down and suffer in peace.

"You're the one who's always harping on the time. I waited around for half an hour. Then I figured you weren't going to show up. Where have you been?" The tone was overbearing, imperious, as if she were a harem slave who had offended her lord and master.

Ordinarily Julia would have attempted to put him in his place with an icy retort, but she simply did not have the wherewithal. "I fell asleep in the ladies' room. Then I drove home," she mumbled.

"You fell asleep? That's a novel excuse," he said drily. "A romp with your latest lover might be closer to the mark."

Julia had no intention of staying there and listening to his accusations, but when she tried to get up, he roughly pulled her back down. The room tilted slightly, and she was glad to sit once more. She doubted whether she could make it up the steps just now.

"I have something to show you," Derek said in a venomous voice. A trip to the bedroom produced a wrapped-up painting. Derek removed the brown paper and held up a stunning Picasso abstract oil for Julia's inspection. She stared at it, speechless. Only millionaires could afford to buy such works of art.

His explanation confirmed her impression. "A wedding present from your father. I stopped in to see him when I was in New York." The painting was casually tossed onto an upholstered, overstuffed chair. "That's worth a few laughs, isn't it, Mrs. Veblen? I was a damned saint last week. I expect to come home to an appreciative, loving wife, and what do I find? An ill-tempered, distant bitch! Maybe you were right in the first place. We *should* be talking about a divorce!"

Julia managed a cold "Sure. You take care of it," and fled to her room. This time Derek seemed delighted to let her go.

The next morning, while Derek showered, Julia sneaked into the kitchen to phone the Infirmary for the results of her pregnancy test. Positive. But with Derek taunting her with talk of a divorce, there was no way she was going to announce the news. She speculated on his possible reactions and wasn't prepared for any of them.

There was the "We'll stay together for the sake of the child" speech. Or "How can I be sure it's *my* child?" Then again, he might ask how she had let it happen, or tell her she'd have to "get rid of it." Even contrition would be no good. If he wasn't going to trust her—now he was accusing her of engaging in on-campus love affairs—there was no basis for a real marriage. Mental anguish plus physical misery turned her into a stoic robot. It was even too much effort to keep up her dream journal.

She was ready to leave by 7:45. Derek had made himself bacon and eggs for breakfast. Julia avoided the kitchen while he finished eating. When they walked outside, his eyes immediately fixed on her car.

"What on earth happened to you?" he said, sounding as annoyed as if she had done some personal damage to *him*.

Talking turned her stomach. She managed, "I skidded. No snow tires. Plowed into a tree."

He muttered something under his breath, then said aloud, "You aren't driving *that* anymore. Come on."

Julia waited in Hayes Theater until the beginning of class; Derek was in his office, going over his notes for that day's lecture.

When he appeared on the stage at 9:10, his usual charming smile was missing. He launched into his material without even a hello to his class, clicking the slides on and off at a pace almost too rapid to follow. When several students urged him to slow down, he snapped out, "Write faster!"

The class was over half an hour early. Julia heard a girl behind her moan, "What's with *him* today?" and to her left, a fellow art major jeered, "What happened, Julia? Lovers' quarrel?" She silently shook her head, still mildly nauseated from morning sickness. Everybody seemed to be staring at her; she had never been so glad to get out of a room as she was to leave the auditorium.

As on the previous day, by lunchtime she felt fine, at least physically. She had reading to do, but was unable to keep her mind on it, so she spent the afternoon painting. She was careful to arrive at Derek's office promptly at five o'clock. In the mood he was in, she did not want to give him further cause for complaint. Had Melinda not already found a new roommate, she would have returned to her old apartment.

A list of midterm grades was posted by his door, but her mark—A—failed to cheer her up. She was about to knock when Derek came out, looked at her coldly, and strode out to the van so briskly that she had to run to keep up with him.

At home, her husband shot her a withering stare. "Are you making dinner tonight, madam?" He pointed to the counter. "I took some veal out of the freezer."

"Yes. All right." Anything to avoid another argument.

"Fine. Call me when it's ready." With that order, he stalked out of the room and up the stairs.

It was no easy task for Julia to prepare the meal when the very smell of the food outraged her stomach. But she did so anyway. She could only hope that it would taste okay; sampling the fare as she cooked was beyond her resources.

She called Derek in to dinner, then sat and toyed with her veal, pilaf and salad as he ate. A glass of soda was all she could get down.

"Aren't you going to eat that?" Derek took her lack of interest in the food as a personal affront.

"No. I—I had a big lunch. Do you want it?"

He silently switched their plates and ate her portion. "Very good," he said curtly. "At least you didn't lie about one thing—you *can* cook!"

Julia received the sarcastic gibe in silence. She felt too awful to fight back.

Derek pushed his empty plate away with a dramatic gesture. "Coffee?" he demanded arrogantly.

And Julia had had enough. "Make the lousy coffee yourself! I don't want any!" She stormed away from the table, and he made no attempt to stop her.

Wednesday was no better than Tuesday, and Thursday no better than Wednesday. At least she was feeling slightly less sick each morning and afternoon; perhaps one could get used to anything. Her international relations professor returned her exam on Wednesday; Julia could not help but feel proud of the A- she had earned. But Derek's hostility dampened her enthusiasm for study. She began to write in her journal again, recording bizarre, frightening dreams that clearly related to her pregnancy.

Wednesday night Derek had dropped her off in Concord, then told her he was going back to Boston to have dinner with friends. Relief at being left alone for the evening mingled with hurt at being excluded from the invitation. But she hid all these feelings, and climbed out of the van with an indifferent, "Have a nice time." He gunned the accelerator and skidded down the drive. She had stayed up for hours, but still managed to be asleep before he returned.

Julia was painting in one of the studios in Sherman Hall late Thursday afternoon when footsteps behind her broke her concentration. She turned to see Max Nyquist; she hadn't talked to him since her marriage to Derek.

"How's the blushing bride?" he asked, and Julia picked up a bitter note in his voice. She ignored it.

"Fine. And yourself? Your class going all right?" she returned politely.

He placed himself between Julia and her painting, commenting, "Not bad. Obviously Derek's taught you a lot—in more ways than one. Hmm?"

Julia refused to rise to the bait. "It was nice of you to stop by to say hello, Max, but—"

"What was I, Julia? The second string?" Now he sounded really angry. "Why didn't you tell me I didn't stand a chance! You must have known I was in love with you!" His hands grabbed her shoulders. "At least let me kiss the bride!"

Julia tolerated this with stiff detachment, wishing that he would hurry up and finish before she got sick. They were interrupted by an angry voice from behind her.

"What the hell is going on here?" Max drew away to look over Julia's shoulder straight into Derek's eyes. His face turned beet red.

"If I ever catch you so much as *looking* at her again, Nyquist, I'll flatten you." The level of Derek's voice was deceptively low. "Now beat it!"

Max exited with alacrity. Gallant of him, thought Julia sourly, to explain that *he* was kissing *her,* and against her will into the bargain!

Julia had never seen her husband look so furious. "I'll just clean up the brushes—" she began in what she hoped was a placating voice.

"Forget them," he said through clenched teeth. "We're going home."

He grabbed her arm so tightly that she was sure there would be bruises on it. She had left her coat and books in his office. Derek all but threw them at her, and did not even bother to put on his own coat. "Now move!" he ordered.

Julia had no intention of resisting. Even once they were in the car and he was able to take out his anger on his fellow motorists, he continued to look absolutely livid. She only hoped that he would cool down by the time they arrived home.

She was well aware that the little scene he had witnessed had unfortunately reinforced every suspicion he had about her, every accusation he had made. She had the feeling that if she tried to explain now, he would become positively enraged.

The forty minute drive had no effect on the intensity of his reaction. Once they were inside the house, Derek turned to Julia and said in a voice that absolutely chilled her, "Get into the bedroom and get undressed."

For the first time, she was actually physically frightened of him. In this mood, he was like a stranger. Ashen-faced, she obeyed. God knows what he would do if she provoked him by resisting.

She was tremblingly unhooking her bra, her fingers clumsy with apprehension, when he walked in, half undressed. "Share the wealth, eh, Julia?"

He gave her no time to reply, even had she wanted to, but picked her up and threw her onto the bed. He lay down on top of her, making her body take the full force of his weight. His kiss was meant to be punishing; her lips were ground against her teeth with coldly deliberate fury. In a moment she was gasping for breath, terrified not only for herself but for her unborn child.

She managed to free herself of his mouth, and in tears choked out, "Derek, for God's sake, the baby—"

He lifted his weight off of her and stared into her eyes. "What?"

Some corner of her mind realized that she finally had his attention. "He was kissing *me*. I hated it! I'm pregnant. I'm sick all the time."

At this disjointed recitation, Derek rolled off her, and sat on the edge of the bed to mutter, "Of course."

He turned around to look at Julia, and she could see that he was actually shaking. "It *is* the truth?" he asked weakly.

"I've—I've never lied to you—about anything, Derek. I—I swear it!" The words were punctuated by sniffs.

"Oh, God," he groaned, "I must be crazy. I was ready to—" He did not complete the sentence, but went back into the living room, put on his clothes and coat, and walked out the door.

Julia told herself that it was just as well. He would drive around for a while and get hold of himself. She needed to do the same; she was still shivering from the scene that had just taken place.

But Derek did not return that night or the next morning. Julia heard nothing from him. She went to her Friday classes as usual, driving as if the back roads were eggshells, immensely relieved once she came to the main streets, which were clear. She plucked up enough courage to stop by Derek's office in the afternoon, but he was not there.

On the way home, she stopped at an auto store in Concord, purchased snow tires, and sweet-talked the manager of the service department into putting them on right away.

When there was still no sign of Derek by Saturday morning, Julia knew that she could not bear to wait alone. She had to be with people who cared about her. She waited until the morning nausea had passed, then packed a suitcase and headed north.

Chapter Eleven

By that afternoon she was in Maine, at Allison and Tom's house. The minute Allie opened the door, Julia burst into tears. Allison led her to the couch, and held her while she sobbed. Eventually Julia was too wrung out to continue; her sister-in-law persuaded her to drink some tea and talk.

The whole story of her marriage came pouring out. Allie was looking angrier and angrier, but by the time Julia had finally finished, a thoughtful expression had come into her eyes.

"You should have told him about the baby right away, Julia. But beyond that," she said quietly, "you say you're in love with Derek. Why?"

"A good question," Julia laughed nervously, "in view of what he's put me through. Why doesn't he trust me?"

"First you answer my question, then we'll see if we can answer yours," Allison answered patiently.

"Well, I suppose because he has this—this burning commitment—he really feels things. You can see it in his work. And he's sensitive." She felt herself blush. "He's an incredible lover when he wants to be—sweet, and giving, and passionate. And he's taught me so much." She glanced at Allie. "But it isn't just hero worship. I'm sure of that."

"So. You love him because he's emotional and passionate about life and about his work."

"He can be perfectly rational and logical, Allie," Julia objected.

"About things which don't concern him personally, I bet," Allison pointed out.

"Maybe. What are you trying to say?"

"I'm trying to say that your husband is obviously anything *but* rational and logical when it comes to you, Julia. If he told you he was falling in love with you the night you almost went to bed with him—if he told you that, he wouldn't change his feelings. It would be out of character."

"It's no good," Julia replied in a depressed voice. "That was before he assigned me the part of the promiscuous tramp in the farce we've been acting out." Bitterness had crept into her tone.

"Julia." Allison was reproving. "I repeat, if he loved you then, he isn't the type of man who would suddenly stop loving you, no matter *what* he thought. It would take a very cold, rational type of person to do that, and from all you've told me, Derek is primarily emotional. It's what makes him a great artist."

"So? Even if he *does* love me, what kind of a marriage can we have if he won't trust me?"

"Give it some time, honey! He has to come to his senses sooner or later." Allison poured herself some more tea, sipped it pensively, and went on, "You know, Julia, you aren't exactly an ordinary girl. Derek was raised in a poor family in Boston. I know he's traveled all over the world and met a million famous people, but your youth stays with you." She smiled. "Take it from me. I know. Your whole family intimidated me in the beginning. Still does. Your name has been splashed all over the papers for over three years now. You've had marriage proposals from half a dozen super-eligible bachelors. Julia Harcourt—media goddess. What man *wouldn't* be unsure of himself with a woman who has the image you do? Never mind that most of it's garbage." Allison continued, "Julia, Derek had quite a reputation as a Don Juan when he was still in his twenties. Then all of a sudden, he stops painting portraits, holes up in Concord, and paints these devastatingly intense pictures of his. And while he's becoming internationally famous for it, he's living as a virtual hermit. Wouldn't you say that was rather strange behavior?"

"It wasn't quite *that* bad, Allie. He has close friends he continued to see. Besides, he feels things deeply. He once told me that his mother chewed him out about his life and he came to hate himself for it. Sometimes," she concluded ruefully, "he overreacts."

"Sometimes he overreacts!" Allison shook her head. "What an understatement! Three years of painting out his guts as some sort of penance for his sins, and you can still sit there and not understand why he doesn't trust you? Julia, the man is obviously crazy about you. He's emotional and possessive and jealous of every man he imagines ever touched you. What I don't understand is why he couldn't tell you were inexperienced."

Julia had conveniently forgotten to mention that part of the story, implying that only newspaper and magazine publicity had convinced him of her lack of virtue. But now she blushingly confessed, "He said—he

said I knew all the right moves—that I made love
like a pro. He said he could tell the difference. Oh,
Allie."

"He was probably all psyched up to play teacher.
Poor Derek!" Allison was laughing.

"Poor Derek? Poor Julia! He all but labeled me a
'technical virgin,'" she said, outraged at the memory
of it.

"Yes. I suppose he would," Allison observed.
"Look, Jules. You can't love a man for being emotional
and sensitive, and then turn around and condemn him
when those same attributes result in behavior you don't
like."

"But he's so mercurial. I've never known anybody so
moody. He's passionate one moment, insulting the
next. Or furiously angry, then teasing. It—it throws me
off-balance. I never know where I stand."

"But neither does he," Allison said wisely. "You've
never told him you love him. Give him time, he'll figure
things out."

"You really think he loves me?" Julia asked hesitantly.

"Of *course* he loves you. And your dark past is
driving him right up the wall! You should have been
clumsier in bed," she kidded.

"I guess I should go back to Concord and wait."

"No. No, I wouldn't do that. Let him cool off first."
Suddenly Julia turned as pale as the proverbial ghost.
"Oh God, Allie, suppose something's happened to
him."

"Julia, your husband is a very famous man. It would
be all over the newspaper. I wouldn't worry on that
score. If he could seclude himself for three years to
paint, he can take three days—or three weeks—to work
out his feelings. Be patient. He'll show up."

"But he doesn't know where I am!" Visions of

Derek, searching through all of Massachusetts for her, floated into her mind.

"He'll find you. He'll call your father, probably. If you like, I'll phone Richard and let him know where you are."

Julia nodded. "Please. But I—I'd rather not speak to him. Tell him as little as possible?"

Allison gave her a hug and headed for the phone.

Had Julia not been apprehensive about her personal situation, the next week would have been as close to idyllic as she could have wished. Her nausea gradually abated, until a few plain crackers in the morning sufficed to get her going.

Allison jokingly admitted that her advanced state of pregnancy prevented her from potting. When Julia suggested that her enceinte state be preserved for posterity in oil, Allie enthusiastically agreed. Julia worked more from photos taken by Tom than from life because Allie was uncomfortable sitting for more than short periods of time. But she would lie on the bed in Julia's room, where the easel was, and talk as her sister-in-law painted.

As for Tom, he was delighted that his sister was keeping his wife company for a while. He was sympathetic and supportive, cheering Julia up when each day produced no word from Derek, making her laugh with tales from their childhood.

Julia was far enough ahead with her work that missing a week of school did not worry her; she had taken along two paperbacks for her international relations course but was none too diligent about reading them. She had forgotten her journal, but tried to record her dreams faithfully nonetheless. It was difficult; for the first time in months she had trouble remembering them each morning.

On the seventh day of her stay, a cold, clear Friday, Richard Harcourt called. Allison had gone out for a walk; she insisted that it was important to be in good physical condition for her baby's birth, so Julia answered the phone.

"Hi, runaway wife," her father teased. "Just thought you'd want to know that your husband is on his way to Maine."

Julia's heart began to patter erratically. "He called you?" she asked weakly.

"Umm. Seemed to think you'd be down here. He was surprised when I told him you weren't." The teasing tone vanished from his voice. "The truth is, he sounded really shaken when I told him you weren't here, Julia. It was all he could do to ask where you might be, so I put him out of his misery and told him. He'll show up in a few hours, I suppose."

"Well, thank you for calling, Daddy," Julia said quietly.

"Right. And, honey, everything will work out. I don't know why you quarreled, and I don't suppose Derek particularly wants you to know this but I think maybe you have the right. I flew up to Boston the night after your damn husband cut the line on me. Had to get the governor's permission to even land there. Frankly, I was ready to hold a shotgun to Derek's head. I called him from the airport and went so far as to mutter some dramatic nonsense about getting the local thugs to break every bone in his body. He laughed at me. Told me he would be more than happy to marry you. He even drove down to pick me up. The only condition he made was that he would handle things in his own way. Somebody should tell him," Richard Harcourt chuckled, "that he blew it."

It was reassuring to have her father's word that

Derek had not been pushed into the marriage against his will.

She murmured, "Thank you, Daddy. And good-bye."

"Bye, honey. Take care of yourself—and the baby."

Allison returned fifteen minutes later. "We're going to have company," Julia told her.

"Derek?"

"Um. Allie, I'm so nervous."

Allison looked at her watch. "He won't be here before two. You can go to your room then, and let me test which way the wind blows."

"I shouldn't involve you—" Julia's voice reeked of indecision.

"But you already have," Allison finished. "Why don't you paint?"

Julia was soon immersed in the portrait, stopping only to have a sandwich at lunchtime. The painting of Allie was turning out beautifully. Her sister-in-law was a loving, intense girl, and Julia had captured this on canvas. But when an angry knock sounded against the front door, her heart lurched and she almost dropped her brush.

Quickly she got up to close her door, then changed her mind and left it slightly ajar. She wanted to hear what was going on. Allison took her time about answering the door and the knocking continued unabated.

"Where's my wife?" she heard Derek demand arrogantly.

Allison's quieter voice was hard to pick up, but she could just make out her sister-in-law's response, "You must be Derek. It's so nice to meet you."

"It's mutual," he snapped. "Now that the damn formalities are over, where's Julia?" Julia heard his footsteps approaching the staircase.

Then Allison's voice again, but this time louder and firmer. "Not so fast. We have a bit of talking to do—"

"Like hell! Lady, I don't care if your baby was due last week, if you don't stop blocking the staircase, I'll pick you up and—"

"*Mister* Veblen. You will do nothing of the sort! You will kindly keep in mind that this is *my* house and that *you* are a guest here! Now get into the den because *I'm* going to talk, and *you're* going to listen!" In spite of her tension, Julia had to smile.

Footsteps trailed away from the bottom of the steps. Julia resisted the impulse to creep down and listen at the door of the den. Better to wait up here, and let Allison soften him up for her.

She heard the two of them downstairs about forty-five minutes later, and all the edginess she had felt when Derek first arrived returned. But then the front door opened—was he leaving? Julia sat on her bed, paralyzed by indecision. She was about to call down to Allie when she heard the door again, and then Derek's footfall on the steps.

He didn't bother to knock, but walked in carrying a painting, avoiding her eyes. Then he held it up for her to see, and said in a low voice, "I would like you to look at me like this, Julia."

It was the nude portrait of her, but instead of the cold, self-contained woman he had begun to paint, this Julia Harcourt looked out from the canvas with a glowing, loving look in her eyes. More than that—Julia realized that her likeness was inviting the observer into bed.

Julia felt like a fool for blushing, but the picture was so unrelentingly erotic and sensual that she could scarcely help it. She continued to stare at it, and when Derek put it down to walk over to the bed, she stared at her lap instead.

"That sister-in-law of yours is unbelievable! I'm

lucky I escaped intact," Derek said lightly. Then, huskily, "Julia, please say something."

"What does it matter what I say?" Julia answered quietly. "You never believe me."

"I suppose I deserve that, Julia." He sat down beside her, and she moved away from him. "Darling—" he reached out a hand to touch her, and Julia could feel him stiffen when she flinched.

"Julia," he said firmly, "I know you love me. You'll probably be mad at me, but you already are, so what's the difference! I read your journal for your psych course. I assume that I'm the 'D' you dream about all the time?"

Julia was utterly mortified. "You had no business doing that!"

"I know," Derek admitted. "But I found it with your books upstairs, and opened it to see what it was and I'm not sorry." He adopted a confidential tone. "Your dreams should be rated X, Mrs. Veblen. I was shocked!"

Julia made the mistake of looking at him then, and the wide grin on his face broke down all her resistance. She flung herself into his arms, murmuring, "I love you so much." She raised her head for his kiss, which was slow and hungrily passionate. Then he took his mouth away to nuzzle her throat while his hand gently rubbed her neck. "I don't know why you should. I've put you through a lot of grief. But I thank God you do."

Julia said nothing, just snuggled closer.

"I love you very much, Julia. You know that?" her husband went on softly.

Julia nodded, mumbled "Um" into his neck.

He held her for several minutes, until Julia pulled away a little and broached the subject that had destroyed their attempts to live together. "But you don't trust me."

"I didn't. I admit it. I was like an animal, fighting off anyone who got near my territory. I'm very irrational at times, Julia. When your father called me, and threatened to leave me splattered all over a snow bank unless I married you, I never even argued. I knew I was in love with you. I told myself that once you were my wife, all the men you'd had before wouldn't matter. I manipulated you into agreeing to the marriage, and I'm ashamed of it. I never had any intention of it being anything but permanent. And once you were my wife, all my overblown ideals about not taking you to bed unless you wanted it went straight out the window. Nothing could have kept me away from you. You have to understand that I'm very emotional, Julia. I was haunted by every lover I thought you'd ever taken. It drove me crazy when you denied it. If I'd stopped to think—"

"Yes?" Julia whispered.

"After I almost raped you—no, don't 'Oh, Derek' me because I probably would have, I went totally berserk when I found Nyquist kissing you—I went out and got roaring drunk. I stayed in a flea-bag Boston hotel, and came back Saturday night to find you gone. At first I was ready to go chasing all over creation to haul you back, but I noticed some of your books on the floor of the studio, and that's when I found the journal."

"I still say it's unfair," Julia muttered, embarrassed over the intensely personal things she had recorded.

"Unfair, hell! Why shouldn't you have been dreaming about me for months? Ever since you walked into my office in September, I've been fantasizing about taking you to bed. Oh, I admit at first it was purely physical. Not only did I find you beautiful, but your aloofness was an unconscious provocation. And yet I was appalled at myself for making a pass at you, my twenty-two-year-old student, for God's sake!"

He leaned over to kiss her, as if to reassure her that the age difference no longer troubled him. Then he continued, "I wanted to paint you almost from the beginning. It never occurred to me to do anything *but* a nude portrait. Your refusal threw me—I suppose I began to see you as a woman, not a newspaper story. And that made it twice as hard for me to keep my hands off you."

"You didn't," Julia reminded him. "You touched me all the time, and it aroused me like crazy."

"*I* had no way of knowing that; you were as cold as an iceberg. It dented my confidence to think I had no effect on you, because I was already falling in love with you. Then we got snowed in. I realized you were attracted to me, but you seemed so innocent, I wanted to be patient. And then when it's finally about to happen, and you turn out to be imaginative, and sensitive, and absolutely fantastic in bed, I blow the whole thing!" He shook his head ruefully. "I'm deeply, deeply sorry, Julia. I thought I was being so damn noble when I finally decided I would have to learn to live with your lurid past. Until I read that journal, I had no idea you loved me. And then I knew I had some more thinking to do."

"And?" Julia prompted.

"Once I told you I should trust my instincts where you're concerned. Only I'm so in love with you, and so jealous, that I find that hard to do. Now I understand that you responded as you did because of your feelings for me. Even before your sister-in-law got hold of me—"

"What did she tell you?" Julia demanded tensely.

"Oh, about Mark Glenndale, and your year in

Europe. About how you really are, as opposed to what you allow people to see. I understand you better because of what Allison told me, but please believe that my respect for you and trust in you were absolute before I even walked in the door. It only took me a week," he said self-deprecatingly, "to get to that point. And in case you're wondering, she told me what she thought of me. She was right on target. She's very perceptive."

"Derek—" Julia peeked shyly up at him.

"Umm."

"Are you always—so hot and cold—moody?"

"No."

"No?" Julia sputtered. "That's all you're going to say? Just no?"

"What *should* I say? That it's your fault? That I've been at war with myself? Julia, I love you. I freely admit that I'm too possessive and I'm not always easy to live with, but I'm not usually a raging manic-depressive either. And now am *I* allowed to ask *you* anything?"

"Turnabout's fair play. Go on."

"Why didn't you tell me you were pregnant? I thought about you all the time I was in New York, and you were so warm on the phone. Then I come home—" He shook his head, remembering how he had misinterpreted her response to him.

"I'm sorry. I should have. But deep down, I suppose I thought you wouldn't want the baby," Julia admitted. "I was afraid to tell you, and then you started talking about divorcing me."

He smiled tenderly. "Julia, it's the only act of creation I can't perform alone. I'm an artist. Of course I want children, especially with you, because I love you. How could you imagine otherwise?"

"Well, your house," she pouted. "You had it custom-built, and it only has one bedroom."

He roared with laughter. "Only Julia Harcourt could come up with a reason like that! Darling, it was all I could afford. The land was very expensive. I had plans drawn for a much larger house, figuring I'd add the rest when the time came, if I had the money. How intelligent of me," he drawled, "to marry an heiress."

"I'd pay in a minute, Derek, but I don't have any money," Julia said innocently.

"But you do. I told you I saw your father when I was in New York. According to your mother's will, upon your graduation from college or your marriage, if your father approves, you inherit close to three-quarters of a million dollars."

Julia was staggered by this news. "That's just like him! He never told me! *Does* he approve? Or do we wait until January?"

"Your father is a dyed-in-the-wool conservative who finds my politics execrable. Other than that, we get along fine. He seems to have this peculiar notion that I can handle you. Thus his approval. I didn't tell him he's very much mistaken!"

"Derek Veblen," Julia said incredulously, "you know perfectly well that you've turned my life upside down since we met! You've stormed my defenses, made me feel things I've never felt before, and all you have to do is touch me to turn me into a little lap dog! If that isn't handling me—"

Derek's eyes roamed over his wife, who was clad in a scoop-necked tee shirt and tight jeans. Julia, glowing with love, waited for him to come to bed and make love to her. He simply stood there and watched her. It seemed that it was up to her to make the first move.

She let her eyes rove over his body, enjoying the fact that he was becoming aroused by her thorough examination of him. The things he had told her were sinking in now, and with them a sense of utter contentment and joy. He loved her, wanted her and the baby, trusted her, and God knows, she adored *him*.

A wide smile lit up her face, and she mischievously unfolded herself to kneel on the bed, slowly removing the tee shirt.

"Professor Veblen," she said in her huskiest, most siren-like tone, "what would I have to do to get an A in your tutorial?"

"You're taking it pass/fail, remember?" he grinned.

"Derek!" she complained. "You've ruined it all!"

"Oh! Sorry, darling. Start again," he invited cheerfully, as he came over to sit on the edge of the bed, casually removing his boots. Then he looked at Julia expectantly.

She stretched out languorously, and did as instructed. "I would do anything to get an A in your class, Mr. Veblen," she said vampishly, trying not to laugh.

He stretched out next to her and began playing with her hair. "Are you propositioning me, Miss Harcourt? Offering me the use of your luscious body? Inviting me to commit unspeakable acts upon your person?" he whispered, nibbling her ear.

"Absolutely," Julia whispered back, giggling. "Are you going to take me up on it?"

"You bet I am," said her husband, gathering her in his arms.

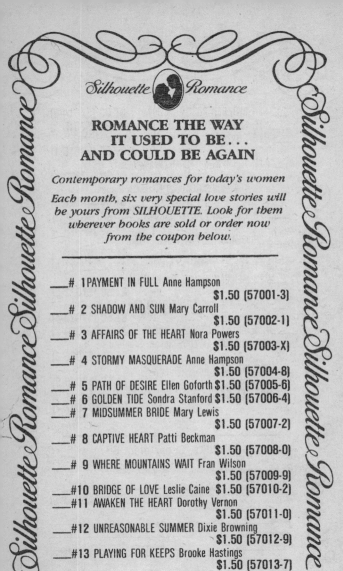

Silhouette Romance

ROMANCE THE WAY
IT USED TO BE...
AND COULD BE AGAIN

Contemporary romances for today's women

*Each month, six very special love stories will
be yours from SILHOUETTE. Look for them
wherever books are sold or order now
from the coupon below.*

"Look at me . . . Judas."

Val opened her eyes. To her horror, she saw an air gun, like the one used to give booster shots to children, in Shiloah's hand. The light glinted off the ominous metallic tip of its dart.

"You will publicly deny that there was any truth to what you wrote about the Children of Last Days Light," he insisted. "You'll say you made it up and those anti-cult nuts gave you doctored photos."

Val's chest heaved as she gasped for air. He was demanding nothing less than professional and spiritual suicide! She vigorously shook her head.

"Cooperate with the Lord, or you'll force me to use this again." He waved the gun in her face, his own angular face dark with anger. "God hates rebellion as the sin of witchcraft, and you, Tamar, are guilty of the gravest rebellion. Don't push me."

Val swallowed hard. *Dear Lord, help me. Show me what to do.*

UNA MCMANUS was born in Dublin, Ireland, and came to the United States nearly twenty years ago. Una makes her home in Columbia, Maryland, with her Pennsylvania Dutch husband and their three strapping sons. She enjoys telling earthly stories about divine love because the greatest Teacher of all was a storyteller. She formerly wrote for **Heartsong Presents** as Elizabeth Murphy.

Books by Una McManus (Elizabeth Murphy)

HEARTSONG PRESENTS
HP125—Love's Tender Gift
HP138—Abiding Love

Tender Mercy

Una McManus

Heartsong Presents

To my three beloved sons
John, Mike, and Matthew

A note from the Author:
I love to hear from my readers! You may write to me at
the following address: **Una McManus**
Author Relations
P.O. Box 719
Uhrichsville, OH 44683

ISBN 1-55748-829-0

TENDER MERCY

Cover illustration by Jean Brandt.

PRINTED IN THE U.S.A.

prologue

Kent, Ohio, January 28

*I crossed the sea and brought you home, my
beloved. Why, then, am I more afraid for you
than ever? You insist you're over the Children
of Latter Days Light cult and their false prophet
of doom, Father Elijah. Just like that. As
quickly and easily as snapping your pretty little
fingers. You left their influence behind in
Ireland and they can never touch our lives
again. Or, at least, that's what you try to tell me.*

*Oh, Val, I don't think so. In the past two
months, I've tried to explain. But you, my love,
won't listen. Having ears, you hear not. You
may really believe you're over this thing—this
cult manipulation that put you in such danger—
but I think you're mistaken. It's not that easy.
Recovery and healing take time.*

*But you say you don't have time. You say you
need to keep up this frantic pace in your
graduate studies to make up for time you "lost"
while in the cult. You give yourself no time for
mending, or for letting the Lord mend you.
When I try to talk to you about this, you only
listen half-heartedly, tolerantly, fidgeting or
drumming your fingers on the breakfast table,
eager to get on with your schoolwork. I try to
tell you that months of cult conditioning don't*

5

just disappear overnight. You may still be vulnerable to their devious psychological manipulations, should you be unfortunate enough to run into them again.

Since you won't listen, my diary listens for you. I thank God for this outlet, this faithful friend who served me so well during my days in Alcoholics Anonymous. From the time I first met you, Val, I've admired your determination to survive against all odds—not the least of which was growing up the daughter of an alcoholic mother who did not (and probably could not) love you. I'm eternally grateful for the way you took a chance on love with me. It wasn't easy to let me slip that ring on your finger. I saw the terror in your eyes when Reverend Tillman pronounced us husband and wife. Who can blame you when all you've known of love is abandonment?

Yes, Val, I admire you greatly. I love you, more than I ever thought possible to love any human being. But running away from the pain of your cult experience is not the better part of valor. It's denial. And you've lived with denial for so long, so very long, you don't recognize it.

But I do. I'll stand guard like a sentinel. I vowed to be worthy of your trust in both good times and in bad. I'll protect you. I'll defend you. And if bad times do come, I'll keep my promise. I will not abandon you.

Please hear me now, my love—I will not abandon you.

one

Joel Bennigan's sandy brows furrowed, and he tightened his grip on his book as he studied his wife of thirty days. She wasn't listening. Nor had she listened the last time he'd brought up this subject. Val sat across the table, shoulder-length chestnut curls framing her face, eyes downcast, slim finger drawing musical circles around her empty coffee cup.

"Val, this is important."

She sighed impatiently and continued tracing the rim, more vigorously this time.

"Sweetheart, escaping a cult is one thing, but recovering is something else," he said slowly, choosing his words carefully. "Experts say recovery can be difficult. Listen to this," he urged, reading from a page he had marked. "'Most returning cult members suffer a predictable pattern of problems—nightmares, lack of self-esteem, loss of faith in God, phobias, inordinate fears, difficulty in thinking and making decisions, compulsive over-achieving to compensate for joining the cult. . .'"

Val looked up. The second her gaze met his, Joel felt a familiar electrical current course through his body. His heart always lurched when his wife looked at him with that intensity which turned her eyes deep forest green. Despite their Christmas wedding—Val, glorious in white satin trimmed with fur and glistening with raindrop pearls—Joel could still hardly believe that this beautiful woman with the jade green eyes was now his, to have and to hold, forever. How could God have blessed him so? He, a lowly assistant pastor, willing to forgo the joys of marriage should the Lord's service have required that sacrifice? Surely his marriage was proof that divine

7

generosity knew no bounds.

Val inclined her head and regarded him steadily for a moment before she spoke. "I'm not having any cult-related problems, Joel, and I wish you'd stop assuming I do. I don't like being treated like a returning prisoner of war."

The morning sunlight crept through the window and gathered in buttery pools on the glossy oak tabletop—the kitchen table they'd picked out together. Joel reached across and cupped Val's hand. It felt small and warm, almost fragile. But he knew the spunky strength behind his wife's petite appearance.

"Forgive me, Val. I don't mean to offend. But it's wise to know the psychological landscape, so to speak, in case we come across any problems." He deliberately stressed the word *we*. Above all, he wanted Val to know she wasn't alone. That he was with her until death parted them, as he'd solemnly vowed.

Val deliberately made her voice cool and languid. "I don't think *we* are going to undergo any problems—post-cult or otherwise, Reverend Bennigan—unless you stop splitting the Oreo cookies, eating the cream side, and leaving the rest!"

Momentarily, Joel was stunned into silence. He gaped as Val's eyes widened innocently, her eyebrows arched, and the smile disappeared from her rosebud mouth, leaving her face as expressionless as a poker player's. He frowned, puzzled, and searched her face for some trace of humor. Nothing. Could she be serious? Then he discerned the ghost of a smile playing at the corners of her mouth.

"Enough teasing, you pitiless woman!" he cried, leaping from his chair. In one long stride he reached her side of the table and scooped his astonished wife into his arms. "Come with me, and you'll never be hungry again . . . for Oreos . . . or anything else!"

Val threw back her head and laughed as he hoisted her small frame to his chest as if she weighed no more than a sack of flour. Her eyes glowed with enjoyment, and she tossed back her hair and let out a hoot. "Gotcha!" she crowed. "I found six abandoned, sorry-looking cookie halves in the tin this morning." She turned to him and waved an accusing finger. Her eyes sparkled.

"Guilty as charged. And I'm not ashamed to admit they were scrumptious." He injected joviality into his voice even though his intentions were turning serious. He could feel his heart thumping against his rib cage as he carried her into the living room.

"Put me down, Joel. I'll be late for class," she said as she snuggled into the crook of his neck. "Right now."

Joel Bennigan was not convinced. "Make me." His shirt collar was unbuttoned and he could feel her breath warm against his neck.

"You asked for it, you chauvinist cookie-gobbler," she retorted as she began to tickle his sides, mercilessly.

"Hey, no fair! You know how ticklish I am."

"My gain, your loss." She continued to torment him.

"Stop! Stop!" he wailed, taking great delight in feigning discomfort as he fell backwards onto the fake bearskin rug in front of the fireplace, carefully cradling Val in his arms all the while. "Now, Mrs. Bennigan, exactly who is at whose mercy?" he taunted as he tightened his embrace, pinning her arms at her sides.

Val gasped for air. She struggled briefly, then grew still as Joel's piercing blue eyes looked intently into her eyes, his face only inches from hers. She caught her breath. At times like this, it seemed Joel's gaze could penetrate to and cherish the very mystery of her being. He didn't so much look *at* her as *into* her. For one sweet, terrifying moment, the boundaries between them dissolved, and their souls touched. A certainty of love beyond words washed over Val. This was the closeness she yearned for. Suddenly, feeling a little too vulnerable, she tried to draw away.

"Perhaps I am at your tender mercy . . . for now, that is," she said. With a great lurch, she tried to disengage herself, without success.

In one fluid move, Joel flipped over, covered her body with his, and gazed down into her flushed face, beginning to lose himself in those pools of liquid green that reminded him of new grasses, wide oceans, and the deep green of a daffodil leaf full of the promise of new life. "You're already late for class," he murmured as he moved his lips closer to hers.

"I know." She closed her eyes, resisting no longer.

"And we don't care . . . do we?"

"Um-m-m . . ." Whatever she had been about to say was lost as he took possession of her mouth in a passionate kiss.

❧

Val ran across the grassy Kent State commons toward the journalism building, clutching her books to her chest. She'd completely missed Professor Weston's class. Fortunately, he rarely questioned absences, especially Val's. She'd been a favorite of the cantankerous professor since her story about the Children of Last Days Light, the undercover investigation that had resulted in her being trapped within the cult for a nightmarish three months until Joel had rescued her from their house in Dublin, Ireland.

Weston's two-semester class had the reputation among graduate journalism students as the most challenging course in the program. Val understood why. Weston was demanding, painstakingly thorough, and possessed no tolerance for excuses. Although he didn't share Val's Christian faith, and made no bones about saying so, he respected her and treated her work fairly. For that, she was thankful.

The bitterly cold Ohio wind nipped Val's nose and cheeks. She pulled her down jacket tighter and quickened her pace. She was also thankful that Joel hadn't awakened last night when her nightmare had recurred. Neither had he awakened the night before. Val shivered as she tried to forget the dream that haunted her sleep.

It was always the same. She ran down an endless maze of cobbled streets, each street leading into another just like the last. Maybe she was back in Ireland. Ancient European buildings towering overhead leered down at her through their empty windows. She felt piteously small and defenseless. The sun beat down on the cobblestones while she ran as fast as she could, pushing her weary body on by force of will alone.

Behind her, she could hear the faceless, dark cult figures pursuing her relentlessly. They were angry. They wanted to hurt her, and hurt her badly. She had betrayed them; now, she must pay.

Frantically, she pounded on doors, calling and pleading for help. No one answered. The houses and streets were deserted. The sun hammered down, sapping her strength. Not far away, the violent sounds of enraged voices rang through the still, hot air.

Just when she couldn't run another step, she found an unlocked door and darted inside. Panting, she took the old, winding staircase two steps at a time. In a tiny room on the third floor, she crouched behind a large, wooden chest in front of a wide window. She felt safe at last. Surely they'd never find her here. She held her breath for fear her breathing would betray her hiding place.

Then she heard the cult members downstairs. They'd found the unlocked door! She curled into a ball, desperately trying to make herself smaller. She trembled as heavy boots echoed on the stairs. Her heart froze as the footsteps came nearer . . . nearer . . . nearer—finally bursting into the room. She jumped up and opened her mouth to scream, but terror had closed her throat and no sound came. The cultists advanced, their faces featureless and dark, hidden behind their black executioner masks, their dark gloved hands grasping for her. In one final bid for survival, Val flung herself out the window, surrounded by the shattering of glass and the timeless sensation of falling. Taunts and cruel laughter drifted from the window. . . .

Each time the nightmare returned, Val woke up with a start, her palms cold and sweaty, clutching the edge of the blanket to save herself from falling. She would lie awake in the darkness, her heart racing wildly, her thoughts chaotic, as Joel slept peacefully beside her. She was thankful he slept so soundly. Even though the nightmares had become a regular occurrence, she didn't want him to know. It was the *last* thing she wanted.

Why? Joel has to be the most devoted husband in the world. He loves me. Why can't I bring myself to tell him? Val quizzed herself as her hurried footsteps echoed along the halls of the Merrill Building, which housed Kent State's journalism department. Breathless, she slipped into the back of the large lecture hall. Dr. Dorsey's taped lecture on ethics in journalism had already begun. The professor's round, expressionless face peered from ten identical monitors suspended from the ceiling over the heads of a hundred students. Dorsey's course, although boring, was required.

Quietly, she took a seat, rubbing her gloved hands together and flexing her cold toes inside her fur-lined boots. She hadn't told her husband about the other "post-cult" problems that had been silently plaguing her life. Several, such as inordinate fears and recurrent nightmares, were listed in that counselor's book he'd read aloud this morning. She'd been listening intently while feigning disinterest.

"Inordinate fears" . . . like being afraid of the dark. Ever since leaving the cult, she'd been as frightened as a nervous child. Some nights Joel would stay up late working on his sermons. If she went upstairs before he did, she'd find herself standing at the bottom of the stairs in their tiny, rented house, paralyzed by fear. It seemed as if the darkness overhead was not empty at all, but filled with apparitions and unseen horrors. Even after she'd flip on the light switch for the second floor, the fears would persist.

She'd force herself to climb the first three steps, her heart hammering so wildly she could barely hear anything else. Nevertheless, she'd stand still, straining to hear any telltale noises from upstairs. *This is ridiculous. Get a grip,* she'd reprimand herself. But no amount of reasoning or self-talk helped. The eerie sound of the wind moaning through the weeping willow trees at the lower end of the yard only heightened her anxiety.

Each time, she'd turn and hurry back to the well-lighted kitchen where Joel sat at the table, poring over his books and Bibles. She'd settle into the easy chair nestled in the corner and read an inspirational romance until her husband declared himself finished for the night. Then she'd climb the stairs, her arm safely linked through his. He always said he appreciated her company, but she really didn't have to stay up with him. She always replied that she wanted to be near him. He never questioned her motives.

Just like the guy, she thought fondly. *Pure, honest, and uncomplicated. That's why I can't tell him.* How could he love a woman so laden with lingering problems, problems that made her feel like a freak? Maybe he'd even regret having married her. Worse, he might even feel sorry for her, and she couldn't bear that thought.

And there was her inordinate fear of the cult leaders—the mysterious, all-powerful Father Elijah and his snake-eyed son Shiloah. And that angry bear of a man Jeremiah. Val shivered at the memory of the bulky, black-haired leader who spewed hate and had been about to claim her as his cult "wife" when Joel had shown up. Although Jeremiah had made her skin crawl, she'd never guessed that in addition to his role as a cult leader, he ran guns for the Irish Republican Army and supplied the terrorists with money. Not until Joel had proved it to her, literally shoving the evidence under her nose. She owed her husband so much.

She shook her head and fought down the feeling of nausea that accompanied the memory of Jeremiah. *What if Joel hadn't come? What then?* She couldn't bear to think what might have happened. Would she still be trapped inside the cult . . . "married" to Jeremiah? She blinked back tears that prickled her eyes.

Joel's book was also right about the difficulty in thinking and making decisions for some ex-cult members. Ever since she'd come back from Ireland, Val felt as if she were moving, living, and walking in slow motion. Her brain seemed set on two-second delay; she was always a beat behind. Even the simplest decision seemed hard. What to pack for lunch, for instance. Tuna or cheese? Ketchup or mustard? This morning, at least, since he'd "delayed" her, Joel had packed her lunch.

Val stared at the TV monitor as Dr. Dorsey droned on about copyright law. His face swam before her eyes. She could follow his train of thought only with the greatest difficulty. But that wasn't the boring Dr. Dorsey's fault; Val had the same problem in all her classes. Difficulty concentrating also coincided with her return from the cult. It was frightening. How much other damage had the cult's mind manipulation done? Even if the effects were only temporary, temporary was too long.

What about her low self-esteem, for example? A self-deprecating chuckle caught in her throat. *What* self-esteem? She even lacked the self-confidence to reveal the depth of her readjustment difficulties to her husband—the person who loved her most. *If he really knew me, he wouldn't love me. How could he? Joel may say his love is forever, but do I dare put that love to the test?*

What about loss of faith? She still clung to trust in a loving and kind God, but sometimes she couldn't help wondering how He could have let something so terrible happen to her. Where had God been when she had walked the streets of Dublin, cold and terrified? How could He have let her be so deceived in His name? Surely He could have saved her. . . . Of course, He had sent Joel. *I suppose that counts.* . . .

Dr. Dorsey was still rambling on electronically. Val closed her eyes. She breathed deeply and tried to visualize herself safe in her heavenly Father's lap. *Dear Lord,* she prayed silently, *thank You for this wonderful Christian man You've given me to cherish and love. I'll do my best to be a good wife, but Lord, I can't risk revealing all my secrets. I can't confess these fears. I just can't lose the man of my life again.* . . .

Briefly, the image of her father's face hovered in her mind's eye. Marc Packard—the young, devoted father who had filled the emptiness in her girlish heart created by a neglectful, alcoholic mother. Marc Packard—the U.S. Army officer who had stepped on a land mine during the early part of the Vietnam War. Marc Packard—the daddy who had never come home. Who had left her. Or at least, that was how Val's young heart had perceived her loss.

I can't take a chance on losing Joel, too, Lord. Please understand that. I need You to heal the after-effects of the Children of Last Days Light. I need Your grace, Lord. Please. Take charge of the whole sorry mess. . . .

She must have dozed off, because when she suddenly awoke, the majority of the students had already left the room. The TV monitors were blank. Dr. Dorsey had disappeared. The class lasted two hours—she must have slept for over an hour! Well, she wasn't going to improve her grade point average like this.

Val sighed, straightened up, and fished in her backpack for her brown paper lunch bag. She opened it and discovered a ham, cheese, and pickle sandwich on whole wheat, wrapped expertly in plastic wrap just like a deli sandwich. *Thank you,*

Joel, she murmured silently as she began to unwrap the plastic.

Then she noticed the piece of red paper stuck to the underside of the sandwich. She peeled it off its Scotch tape mooring and unfolded the heart-shaped piece of construction paper.

As her eyes scanned the text, she felt her heart start to race: "To Val," read Joel's unmistakable angular print, "my beloved wife, I will cherish you forever. Please write my promise on your heart: I will never abandon you, my love."

A lump the size of a boulder formed in Val's throat. She sat a long time, alone in the lecture hall, staring at the words, until her tears made the ink run. This man was in love with her, was devoted to her; yet, she couldn't come clean with him. What was wrong with her?

two

Kent, Ohio, February 2

*I think Val listened to me this morning—maybe
just a little. She accused me of patronizing her.
What were her words? Oh, yeah—"wounded
returning prisoner of war." Not a pretty picture.
Yet . . . what if she has been wounded by the
cult? She denies any post-cult problems, but she
seems burdened with a heaviness, a depression
that wasn't there before.*

*Would she tell me if she were having difficul-
ties? I hope so. I think so. But I don't know for
certain. Part of me doesn't want to find out.
Maybe that's why I'm writing in my journal
about this; I need to reveal truths to myself that
I'd rather ignore.*

*I've got to warn Val about "floating." I came
across that term in one of the books the anti-cult
people sent me—the books Val won't read.
"Floating," I learned, is a confused state of mind
that temporarily afflicts some people who leave
cults. From what I gather, it's a kind of mental
and emotional limbo. The ex-member feels
trapped between two lives. Painful, but, unfortunately, common.   What's frightening is, floating
is so easily triggered. Meeting up with an active
cult member can plunge the ex-member into this
state. Or maybe reading Bible verses the cult
distorted, or even hearing melodies of the hymns*

17

*they sang (usually with words changed to suit
their own purposes).   One ex-member described
floating this way: "Leaving a cult is like awak-
ening from a deep sleep and gradually regaining
consciousness.   During the semi-conscious stage,
when ex-members are struggling to find themselves again, they can lose their footing, float,
and even return to the cult.   Ex-members and
those who love them should be aware of the
danger of floating and be ready to meet it with
reason, information, support, and prayer."   Amen
to that.   I'm ready, willing, and by the grace of
God, able to fight in this spiritual warfare for my
wife's well-being.*

*Periods of floating eventually fade, the
experts say.   Then the person is usually in no
further danger of being lured back into the cult.
The literature says that short but intense periods
of uncertainty can persist for up to a month, or
sometimes longer, after leaving a cult.   Dear
Lord, what are we going to do?   How can I
protect my wife?*

Lord, help us!   Both of us!

≥∝

The dark, rainy night had blanketed Kent by the time Val had
finished her last class and begun her short walk home. As she
turned the corner of Main and Water, yellowish halos of street
lights shimmered against the raven-black ribbon of road.
Things appeared distorted and fuzzy-edged, as if she were seeing through dark glasses. That's why she couldn't be sure it
was him. But even the possibility that it could be knocked the
wind out of her. She clutched her book bag tightly and stepped
into the shadows of a darkened doorway, struggling for breath.

Finn O'Dwyer! She had caught a glimpse of his lined, stony
face in the lamplight before he'd whipped around, his raincoat

billowing about his wiry body like Dracula's cape, and ducked into Filthy McNasty's Bar. *Finn O'Dywer? In Kent?* Val rubbed her throbbing temples. She'd only seen the thug once when, at Joel's insistence, she'd witnessed Shiloah and Jeremiah's meeting with an IRA representative. That representative had been none other than O'Dywer.

She'd seen the cult leaders give money—money she and other disciples had slaved to raise by peddling Father Elijah's writings—to this weasel of a man. That money, she'd learned, was used to fund terrorist activities. Joel had patiently explained Father Elijah's doomsday plan to promote terrorism and mayhem, not just in Ireland, but in other countries as well, in order to hasten the end of the world. Then Father Elijah and his chosen few, so he claimed, would rule the world for a thousand years.

Of course, as a new disciple, she hadn't been privy to those details. Cult doctrine was doled out in small, bite-sized pieces so new members wouldn't choke, start doubting, and leave. She saw the cleverness in the cult's method of indoctrination, but she still felt like a fool, an utter fool, for having allowed herself to be duped in the first place. . . .

She flattened her hand over her hammering heart and breathed deeply. *Dear Lord, help me calm down,* she prayed. *"The Lord is my light and my salvation, whom shall I fear?"*

Yet God had seemed very far away since her return, almost as if she'd left Him behind on the cult doorstep. She hadn't gone near the house on Oak Street. She hadn't gone on TV or spoken out publicly against the Children of Last Days Light. She hadn't even discussed her experiences with Joel's Bible study group. Her fear of the cult was still too real, too raw. During her darkest moments, she feared they could reach out and snatch her away again.

But no one from CLDL had tried to contact her. Certainly, no cult member had tried to snatch her. Her brief experience with them was over. Finished. A closed chapter of her life.

Wasn't it?

❧

"Joel, what's wrong?"

Her husband sat at the kitchen table, his face buried in his hands, his powerful fingers threaded through his tawny hair, making it stand up on end. His head snapped up. "Oh, Val, I didn't hear you come in."

She threw down her heavy book bag and rushed to sit beside him. After her jittery experience on the way home, she drank in the comfort of his nearness like a thirsty sponge. She studied his angular face, his classically straight nose, his crisply etched lips that usually broke into a full-bodied smile so easily. But no smile played on his lips tonight. Her heart softened at the tolerance she always saw in his face, a deep sympathy for other people's pain and uncertainty. His kindness was just one of the things she loved about Joel Bennigan.

"What's wrong?" she asked again, her voice soft as she placed one hand lightly on his well-muscled shoulder. "Has Mrs. Sommers died? Didn't James Phillips make it through surgery?" In her new position as a minister's wife, she was beginning to appreciate how deeply parishioners' problems weighed on their pastors.

"No, no. They're both fine. James' tumor was benign. This is worse, Val. It's a sickness of the soul. . . ."

"Tell me." She cocked her head as he shot her a troubled look. *What could have happened?* Even though his piercing blue eyes looked tortured, his gaze moved, even thrilled, her.

Joel snatched her hand and pressed a kiss into her palm. A shiver of delight followed his touch. Her heart felt like it was bursting with love, even as she witnessed his anguish. Joel truly was a good shepherd who walked with his sheep through the dark valleys of their lives. She saw him hesitate, as if he were carefully choosing his words before he answered. She waited, willing the tight muscles in her shoulders to relax. Whatever the problem, she'd help him bear it.

He closed his eyes and took a deep, shuddering breath. "Kevin Milford went back to the cult."

Val gasped. Her hand flew to her mouth. A dark, yawning chasm opened in her stomach, as if she were trapped in an elevator dropping twenty floors at once. "No! No! It can't be true! He—he was doing so well. . . . He'd been out three or four months. . . . They couldn't possibly have . . ."

The young freshman's anxious face flashed across her mind. After Joel had talked him out of the CLDL, Kevin had suffered agonizing bouts of doubt and fear that he'd lost his eternal salvation by walking out on God's "true prophet," Father Elijah.

Joel nodded wearily. "Yes, I thought he was doing well, too. At least well enough to stay out of their clutches."

"How did they do it, Joel? How did they get him again?" She had to know. *If they could lure Kevin Milford back, then maybe* . . .

Joel's large hands framed her face. His touch was almost unbearable in its tenderness. The naked vulnerability she saw in his eyes embarrassed her, but she did not pull away nor lower her gaze.

Suddenly, with a guttural moan, he pulled her roughly to him and crushed her to his broad chest. "They won't get you, Val. They'll have to climb over my dead body."

She said nothing, but buried her face against the heaving of his chest as he struggled with his own emotions. Trembling, she clung to him like a mountain climber clings to the rope. She could feel raw fear tense Joel's muscles and shorten his breath. She hoped he couldn't sense the panic surging through her—the deep, sickening feeling that something terrible was about to happen.

❧

"I could have done more to help him, Val," Joel said miserably as he stirred the hot chocolate Val placed before him. His hand dwarfed the silver teaspoon that had been a wedding gift from his mother.

Val stood with her back against the sink. "You were counseling him regularly. And you're a wonderful counselor, Joel. You did all you could."

Hunched over his blue ceramic mug at their small oak table, he looked like a man who could forgive the failings of others, but not his own. When he raised his head, she couldn't bear to see the anguish that ripped across his features.

"You don't understand, Val. I knew the symptoms. And I didn't act quickly enough. Kevin Milford was floating. . . ."

"Floating?"

"Yes," he said with a deep sigh. "It often happens to people who've recently left cults. It's a period of intense confusion. The person wonders if he did right in leaving and can hover between two lives—and possibly float back into the cult."

"You figure that happened to Kevin?"

"I don't figure; I know. The last time we met, he said, 'What if Father Elijah really is God's end-time prophet? Then I've lost my soul by turning away from God's anointed.'"

"Did he really say that?" Val gripped the edge of the sink behind her back. She didn't like what she was hearing.

Joel nodded. "Oh, I reasoned with him from Scripture and refuted those verses Father Elijah takes out of context," he went on wearily, "but I think Kevin was floating because he'd bumped into Gilead last week. She was recruiting outside the student center. . . ."

"Like she was the day I let myself become bait."

"Right." Joel grimaced.

Val felt guilty as she remembered he'd never approved of her hare-brained idea to allow herself to be recruited into the cult so she could write an insider's exposé for her Investigative Journalism class. Just one more way she'd failed him.

"Gilead can be very persuasive," she noted, deliberately keeping her voice even and calm. "Did she lure him back in?"

"I suppose she did. She triggered his floating, anyway. Some cult researchers say the recruiter's influence is a type of hypnotic suggestion—very compelling, even if the person knows better. An ex-member needs lots of time away from all cult contact. Recruiters can still find ways to press the right buttons to trigger massive amounts of guilt and fear."

Val nodded slowly. "I remember that hypnotic look." Inside, she shivered at the memory of her own helplessness under the evil gazes of the men—Shiloah and Jeremiah—who ran the cult house in Kent. A chill ran through her body and goose bumps rose on her arms. There was something strange about all cult members' eyes, she realized. The ones who had been in a long time had unwavering, intense gazes; *hypnotic* was a good word for it. The newer disciples looked spaced-out.

"Kevin was having other problems too," Joel continued. "I can't break his confidence, but they were typical post-cult issues."

Val's heart warmed at her husband's practice of ethical standards. "I met Kevin a few times myself in the Student Union," she said. "He told me he was flunking out. I tried to assure him that with tutoring, he could bring up his grades."

"The cult capitalizes on weak areas, such as failing at school. The whole experience probably wrecked the poor guy's concentration. I should have spoken to the dean about it. . . ." Joel's words trailed off into the silent night until the only sound that broke the silence was the humming of the electric clock on the wall.

Val stiffened as she remembered how he'd tried to warn her about her own "weak areas" before she'd gone to the cult's brainwashing weekend in their isolated camp in Michigan. *I know you don't want to hear this,* he'd said, *"but they'll go for your jugular. Your alcoholic mother, for example. She did a number on you, even if you can't see it . . . or won't admit it. You still carry around a truckload of guilt about her."*

Disturbed by that memory, Val shifted her weight from foot to foot, crossed her arms, and rested her forehead in her open hand. Her eyes felt tired, and she wanted to hide her face from Joel. Even now, she remembered the shame that had washed over her at those words. She'd felt as if Joel had told her she was damaged goods. *Once the daughter of a drunk, always the daughter of a drunk,* she'd thought at the time. With prickly defensiveness, she realized that at some deep level, she still thought that. Somewhere deep inside, she felt defective. Perhaps part of her would always feel unloved and ashamed.

"Val, what's the matter?"

She hadn't noticed Joel getting to his feet or crossing the room. Now he stood before her, his hands on her shoulders. She stared glumly at the unbuttoned collar of his red flannel shirt. "Oh, I don't know," she said, feeling as weak as a rag doll.

Her face flushed. She couldn't meet his gaze, not when she was remembering her angry words when he had suggested she join an Adult Children of Alcoholics' group. He'd even offered to go with her to the meetings. "No matter how much you deny it, your mother's alcoholism wounded you and, until you start dealing with that, it's an area the cult can use," he'd said. She'd as good as told him to mind his own business. Her wounded pride had turned into raw fury. He'd lost his temper, too, and stormed out. But she had gone on to the cult's weekend retreat, and the next thing she'd known, they'd had her trapped, impaled firmly on the hook of never being good enough to win her mother's love.

"Val?"

She felt Joel's grip tighten as he shook her gently. But she couldn't respond. She felt as if she were a million miles away, sinking into some lunar sea of inadequacy. His broad hands cupped her face and raised her gaze to meet his. A startled cry broke from her throat when she saw the depth of love in his eyes.

"Val? I know the news about Kevin Milford has upset you, but I think it's more than that."

It seemed to take all her concentration just to shake her head negatively. She closed her eyes and sighed. When she opened them, Joel was still studying her. His hands felt warm and comforting, an anchor to reality.

"Val, this isn't good," he began, speaking softly as if he were afraid she might break, like a piece of fine china. Gently, he stroked her hair. "I think you're having some kind of floating or post-traumatic stress syndrome. We need to get you some help."

Val felt her backbone stiffen automatically at his words. She pulled out of Joel's grasp and found her voice. "I'm all right."

"No, you're not. Your eyes are glassy. You look frightened."

"I was just . . . shocked to hear about Kevin, that's all. I'll be fine in a minute."

Joel's mouth hardened into a straight line. He wasn't letting her off the hook that easily. "There's a group of Christian counselors in southern Ohio who run a recovery center for ex-cult members. You can stay for a day, or a week, or a month, however long it takes. Let's fly down, Val. We'll go together. It's not a sign of weakness to seek help when you need it."

"I don't need it!" Val hated the brittle anger she heard in her voice. Counseling? Laying all her cards on the table? Where Joel could see them? She couldn't risk that. *He thinks he loves me, and he does, to a certain extent. But if he really knew me, how could he love me? I'm only fooling myself to think he loves me that much.* Again the needle on Val's internal emotional compass swung around to the same old point north, that belief that had guided her all her life: *If my own mother couldn't love me, I must be unlovable.*

She jerked away from him, her back arched uncomfortably over the sink in an attempt to distance herself from him. "I don't need therapy, Joel. I'd be fine if you'd quit making me feel like a crackpot."

He grabbed her upper arms, hard enough to make her flinch.

"Val, don't you see? I'm suggesting getting help because I love you, because I don't want . . . I don't want you to float back into the cult like Kevin did."

"Now you're insulting me!" Val placed both hands on Joel's chest and shoved hard.

Graciously he released her and stepped back, spreading his palms in a conciliatory gesture. "Almost all ex-cult members float when they first leave," he said gently. "I want to protect you. . . ."

Anger flushed Val's cheeks. She needed to nip this therapy idea in the bud. She needed to continue to hide her difficulties, her "weak areas" as he so tactfully put it. *Don't talk, don't feel, don't trust.* How easily the old rules that had governed her alcoholic home came back!

Nevertheless, part of her wished she could bring herself to trust her husband fully. Part of her ached to throw herself into his arms and let everything tumble out—the nightmares, the mental drifting, the confusion, the feelings of worthlessness . . . but she couldn't. That level of trust was too different, too new, and much too dangerous. Rejection would surely follow.

She'd never felt safe enough to trust anyone completely, she realized. As a child, whenever she'd reached out to her mother, rejection had been swift and sure. Val had learned her lesson well, and it was too hard to change that pattern now. The very thought frightened her as if she were standing on the edge of a cliff and Joel was on the other side, promising to catch her if she jumped. Vertigo blinded her. Fear paralyzed her.

Instead, Val did the only thing she knew. She hardened her heart against Joel's pleading eyes, voice, hands. She jerked away from him, snatched her purse, and bolted for the front door.

"I need time alone!" she snapped. "Don't follow me."

three

Val checked her watch. She'd been wandering around downtown Kent for three hours. At 12:30 on a weekday night, the small college town was practically deserted. Since Kent's criminal activity didn't extend much beyond underage drinking and joyriding in Daddy's car, Val wasn't worried about her safety.

Thankfully, the stinging, sleety rain had stopped. The full winter moon, as round and luminescent as a big pearl, scattered its eerie white light over the sleepy town. The old flour mill gleamed like the burnished tower of a fairy-tale castle against the velvet cocoon of navy sky. In the middle of town, Val stood on the bridge spanning the Cuyahoga River, transfixed by the soothing music of the black waters.

How long can I keep my secrets? she wondered. *Is it possible to dodge and weave such central issues forever and still have a marriage? Wasn't marriage the sharing of everything? That's what Pastor Tillman had said when she and Joel had stood before him on their wedding day. Well, it may be. But I can't share everything. If I do, I won't have a husband for long.*

She gathered her burgundy down-filled jacket closer against the cold night air and began walking, more to keep warm than to reach a destination. She wandered by the Pufferbelly Restaurant, a converted train depot where she and Joel often ate Sunday brunch, then past the student housing on Elm Street. She ambled by Brady's Coffee House and peered in the windows at the few sleepless patrons who still sipped coffee. She thrust her cold, gloved hands deep into her pockets and wound along the narrow, tree-lined side streets, picking her steps carefully on the sections of sidewalk not cleared of snow and ice.

At the corner of Oak, she paused, staring down the street where the Children of Last Days Light lived. She drew in a frosty breath. This street, lined with old frame houses and towering, ancient trees, looked no different from any other in the Tree City. Yet, how her one trip to the CLDL house had forever changed—and perhaps ruined—her life. She turned away, then thought then reconsidered. *Why should I be afraid to walk down this road? Am I going to allow Father Elijah and his gang of spiritual thugs control my life forever?*

She swiveled, squared her shoulders, and strode as confidently as she could along the bumpy sidewalk. The swells, dips, and cracks in the pavement were caused as much by decades of freezing and thawing as by expanding tree roots. As she passed the cult commune, the most run-down house on the block, she stumbled over a huge gnarled root hidden by the snow and tumbled into a pile of snow. Jagged icy particles snuck into her gloves as she tried to break her fall. She jumped up and clapped her hands together, hoping to dislodge the unwelcome intruders.

"Well, well. If it isn't little sister Tamar!"

Val's blood turned as cold as the ice when she heard her former cult name. She hadn't seen a living soul on the street a moment ago. Now a tall, lean man stepped out from behind a massive oak tree in the cult's snow-covered yard.

A small cry escaped her throat. She blinked, unwilling to believe her eyes.

Shiloah!

In the pale moonlight, Father Elijah's son looked even more gaunt than she remembered. His dark, thinning hair was caught back in a shoulder-length ponytail, as he had worn it when she had met him in Dublin. His narrow lips gave him a mean, hungry look. The moonlight turned his pale green eyes into silver shards, glinting like knife blades over his sharp, high cheekbones. Val felt transfixed by those unblinking eyes.

Hypnotic. Joel had said their eyes were hypnotic. I must look away! She tried to break his gaze, but found she could not. Her heart began to beat wildly. Her hands, chilled a moment ago, were sweating, even inside her woolen gloves. Her knees felt weak.

"Poor little Tamar," he crooned, his voice as smooth as snake oil. "You've come back to us so you can save your soul from eternal damnation."

The thought flashed through Val's mind that this was the voice of the serpent in the Garden of Eden. She could understand how defenseless Eve must have felt. "No . . . I haven't . . . I was just out for a walk." But it was no good. No matter what she said, her words sounded absurd and pathetic.

"How could you leave the Lord's work? Do you want to burn in hell with the rest of the lukewarm, weak Christians?"

"No! What I mean is . . . the Children of Last Days Light aren't the only ones doing God's work." *Val, Val, it's a mistake to even talk to this guy.* With every word she uttered, she felt herself sinking deeper into a defenseless quagmire. But she couldn't seem to pull away. What was it about the way he looked at her that made her feel she was a vile sinner? "Father Elijah is a false prophet!" she blurted.

"Well, well. Is that so?" A snide chuckle underlay his words, as if he were talking to a mentally incompetent child. "And who do you think *you* are to pass judgment, Tamar? Who are you to place yourself above God's end-time prophet? *You*— the faithless woman who deserted her post in the army of God and left countless souls to perish? *You*—who aren't worthy to be called a child of God? How dare you judge us!"

Val's head began to spin. Shiloah's angry words had opened a flood of painful feelings. He'd ripped the scabs off old emotional wounds, and started them bleeding again. With all her willpower, Val tried to resist him, but like notes in a horror movie's music score, each utterance plucked an automatic response of fear from her heart. His words and phrases, like half-forgotten melodies, took her back to her cult days. The all-pervasive fear that had filled her life then—fear of God's wrath, fear of eternal punishment for failing Him, fear of Father Elijah's anger—seized her again.

She licked her dry lips and tried to take a deep breath. All she could manage were shallow gasps. *Just concentrate on breathing, Val. He can't hurt you. The Lord is my light and my salvation. Stay calm.*

Shiloah stepped closer. "If I'm not part of God's end-time movement, then why are you so nervous?" he taunted. "Little sister, why have you betrayed the truth? Jesus is coming soon, His wrath in His hand. Why have you deliberately chosen to fail God and incur His judgment?"

With great effort, Val closed her eyes. Shiloah stood so close, she could feel his stale breath on her face. She felt as if her body were swaying like a leaf in the breeze. In her imagination, Shiloah's leering face metamorphosed into the face of her mother, Joan Packard.

Instead of Shiloah, she could hear her mother bark the same sentiments: *Defective. Unlovable. A disappointment as a daughter.* Mrs. Packard's taunts rang in her head. All her life, Val had tried to block out her mother's words, but they always came back. *I never loved you. How could I? You're an unlovable failure.*

Like a shark smelling blood, Shiloah escalated his attack. "What about the Lord's word, 'By their fruits you shall know them'? Think about all the souls who've been saved through our ministry." He cocked an eyebrow and narrowed his ice-cold eyes. "How many souls have you won since you returned to the world like a dog returning to its vomit, Tamar?"

"But—but . . ." Val fought back her tears. *Lord, please,*

please make him stop.

"Just as I thought."

Her mind raced. *What about the guns? What about the money given to terrorists?* She'd seen it with her own eyes. But with Shiloah looming next to her, the words stuck in her throat like lumps of ice. Even now, he intimidated her. In his presence, she felt as tongue-tied as a child caught lying. Her confusion surprised and stunned her. Cold panic crept along her spine. She couldn't think straight. Why *had* she left the group? She couldn't remember. Her mind seemed empty.

Empty. Blank. Except for one word that sounded like Joel's voice earlier that night. One lone voice shouting one word across the wilderness of her addled brain: *Floating.*

Was she floating? Like Kevin Milford? Surely that couldn't happen to her! She was too strong, too sensible for that kind of psycho-babble. But floods of self-doubt assaulted her. She dropped her purse and clasped her temples. Her head ached.

"Sister, you don't look well," said Shiloah, as he placed his open palm at the base of her spine.

Val flinched. Evil surrounded this man. "Leave me alone!" she cried.

"Come back to us, Tamar. For your soul's sake."

"No!" Her voice rose shrilly. "*No!*"

Suddenly, as deftly as if he were changing costumes in a play, Shiloah became the perfect gentleman. "Forgive me, my dear. I forgot my manners. No man of God should leave a sister in distress out on the street. Come inside and let me fix you a cup of tea. Then you can go home. I'll even drive you."

Run, Val, run! Every fiber of her being screamed at her to flee. She closed her eyes. She felt so tired. So confused. She remembered hearing that people stuck in snowstorms should keep moving. To stop, to lie down, to rest meant death by freezing. But she felt so sleepy. . . . Briefly, in her mind's eye, she could see herself back in the cult, singing their songs, reveling in that blissed-out, mindless comfort of being part of God's only chosen ones. The security. The acceptance. How she had wanted to believe those things were true and real.

But it was all a lie.

Or was it?

What if she'd made the biggest mistake in this life and the next by leaving God's work? What then? Fear sliced through her like an icicle.

"Tamar, you really don't look well," Shiloah said, guiding her toward the front door with its peeling yellow paint.

Her mind went as numb as frostbitten fingers. Thinking had become too much effort, like trying to walk through knee-high slush.

"Come inside, Tamar. We'll take care of you."

The words echoed in Val's head: *We'll take care of you.* Nice, comforting words. Why did they sound like the voices of demons?

❧

Kent, Ohio, February 3, 12:30 A.M.

Where are you, Val? Are you in danger? Dear Lord, cover her with Your protection. Place Your angels around her to guard her and lead her home safely.

How could I have been so stupid? When am I going to learn? You were trembling like a frightened, trapped bird, Val, and I drove you away. Your eyes were wide with fear. Forgive me! I'm a big, clueless dolt.

You needed time alone. You didn't take your car or my pickup. I watched from the window as you walked toward downtown. Do you know that although you aren't tall, you carry yourself in a way that makes you seem tall and stately? In a

*fairy tale, you'd be the princess. I'm not too
worried about your walking alone, my princess.
Kent is safe at night, even for women who need
time away from their clumsy husbands.*

*I can't imagine that you'd put yourself in
danger by going anywhere near the CLDL house.
At least, not if you were in your right mind. But
that's exactly why this "floating" worries me. It
may not make much sense to someone who hasn't
been trapped inside a cult, but the experts agree
it's real. And it's dangerous. I certainly saw
that with Kevin Milford.*

*Oh, Val, I'm afraid for you, and I'm mad at
myself. What if telling you about Kevin
triggered the floating response in you? Or if my
insistence on therapy made you feel rejected?
Perhaps you still believe your mother's lies that
you're flawed and unlovable. I'm sorry if my
words reminded you of hers. You are no more
flawed—or no less forgiven—than anyone else,
Val. You're lovable and loved, not only by me
with my puny kind of love, but by the all-
embracing love of God Who loved you perfectly
from before time began.*

*I'm not sure what to make of the panic that
crossed your face when I mentioned going to the
rehabilitation center. I forced the issue. Until
you deal with your core issues, you'll be vulnerable to the cult. Vulnerable to floating, or
regression, or lingering guilt about breaking
away. Like poor Kevin.*

*I need to surrender that fear to the Lord.
Why? It's simple. Because the Bible tells us
fear is not of God. Fear gives rise to anger, and*

tonight, I felt twitches of anger when you wouldn't see things my way. Paul tells us love is patient. It bears all things. It believes all things. It hopes all things. This is what I must learn to do, by God's grace. To hope, to believe, and to patiently bear with you, Val, until you see your need for help. Like any recovering alcoholic will attest—myself included—before you can find a solution, you've got to admit you have a problem.

You try so hard to hide your inner turmoil, my love. But I catch glimpses of it. You've looked so tired lately. Haven't you been sleeping well? And your distress over Kevin Milford. Is the CLDL's hold so strong, their deceptions and manipulations so devilishly clever, that you were afraid they could lure you back too? Have I been completely blind? Oh, God, I'm afraid for Val. . . .

I'll wait, no matter how long your healing takes. I want to listen to you and help you feel heard. Please, Val, reach out for help. I'll be there, I promise. I'll support you in every way. But you need another Christian brother or sister to minister to you. We can't do this alone. I love you too much. You're flesh of my flesh now. Bone of my bone. But I'll wait . . . whatever it takes, I'll be there.

It's after one o'clock now, and there's still no sign of you. I should have gone after you. I know you said you needed to be alone. But I shouldn't have listened. . . .

Maybe you stopped by your old roommate's apartment. Maybe you're at Brady's. Even if they're closed, I doubt they would have thrown you out. It doesn't seem likely that you would have gone by Dan and Mary Milford's house this late. I'll make a few calls. I'll drive by all our favorite walking spots. . . .

God, show me. Where is she? Where is my wife?

four

Val moved like a sleepwalker as Shiloah guided her toward the house. She watched herself climb the icy wooden porch steps as if she were hovering above her body. Everything seemed to be happening in slow motion.

Her mind blurred and she could focus only on small, insignificant details: the aged yellow paint still peeling off the front door, the window screens still hanging in tatters, the steps still creaking beneath her feet. But the overall significance of what she was doing—the absurdity and danger of letting Shiloah lead her into the house—kept evading her, slipping from her mental grasp like a silver fish glimmering at the top of the water one second, then disappearing into the murky depths the next.

Strange how this place hasn't changed. The click of her low-heeled boots echoed down the hollow, wooden hallway and a frigid, empty feeling spread throughout her stomach. Shiloah ushered her into the living room.

"Home, sweet home," he said, his tone cordial. He leaned over to snap on the lamp perched atop a small wooden table holding pamphlets, the only furniture in the room. Pale yellow light spread across the threadbare lime green carpet. *The light orange walls still look sickly,* Val decided. *No, nothing's changed with the Children of Last Days Light. So why on earth am I here?*

"Make yourself comfortable. You look beat." Shiloah shucked off his old Army jacket and disappeared into the kitchen.

Val cocked her head, marveling a little over his sudden

change of attitude. She knew Shiloah was playing the "good guy, bad guy" routine, alternating between attacking and comforting her in an attempt to confuse and throw her off guard. She'd read about that technique in accounts of Communist brainwashing. He wasn't pulling any wool over her eyes, she thought with a glimmer of self-satisfaction.

Then why was she here? To prove to herself that she could withstand his tricks? Possibly. To put her head into the lion's mouth just to test her own strength? Probably. Val sighed. She didn't know anymore. All she was sure of was her physical and emotional exhaustion. She sank down on a faded yellow paisley floor cushion next to the table, curling her legs beneath her body and resting her head against the wall. Weariness overtook her. *I'm not under their influence. I'll go in a minute. Just after I rest my eyes. . . .*

"Your tea."

At Shiloah's voice, Val jumped. Her eyes flew open. How long had she been dozing? She accepted the steaming mug. "Chamomile?" she asked, inhaling its flowery aroma.

"Yes. I thought it was a bit late for caffeinated." Shiloah sat down, cross-legged, opposite her. The dim light emphasized the skull-like appearance of his face. He appeared older than his forty years; his thin lips grimaced in a death-mask smile. *Ghastly.*

Val shuddered and turned her attention to the warm mug between her hands. "Thank you," she said as she took a sip. "But I really must be going. My husband will be worried."

"Of course."

Maybe it was the warm tea reviving her. Maybe it was the partial return of common sense, but suddenly, alarm shot through Val, as if she'd just awakened from deep, dreamless sleep to find her house on fire. She shouldn't be here. She must be *crazy* to let this happen. Stupid! This man was not to be trusted. Her defenses bristled. No, she hadn't made a mistake leaving Father Elijah and his band of lunatics, and she had to make that clear to Shiloah.

"I think it only fair to remind you that I've left your group, Shiloah. Please don't ask me to come back. Father Elijah is a false prophet," she stated firmly, looking him straight in the eye. She felt better immediately. *There! I've made it clear where I stand. What did Joel call that? Oh, yes, drawing your boundaries.*

"I understand perfectly." Shiloah bared his yellowed teeth again.

Val frowned. *That's odd. Why is he smiling?* Shiloah—the great son of the great prophet, all fire and brimstone—never smiled. Well, maybe once . . . when he had handed money over to Finn O'Dwyer back in Dublin.

Terrorists! How could you forget? Shiloah aids terrorists!

That word and the image it evoked jolted Val back to full awareness. She started, as if a hypnotist had snapped his fingers and shattered her trance. The scales fell from her eyes. *I almost allowed myself to float right back into the cult state of mind!* she realized with horror. *I've got to get out of here and fast!* More than anything, she wanted the safety of Joel's arms.

Thoroughly frightened, she jumped to her feet and spun toward the door. In her haste, she never saw Shiloah retrieve the air gun from under his baggy sweater, aim at her leg, and shoot a man-sized dose of tranquilizer into her bloodstream. She heard the whoosh of air and felt a sting. Suddenly, her legs turned rubbery and she lurched forward, landing on the carpet with a dull thud.

She landed with her face away from Shiloah. The room was spinning. Behind her came a reedy, hyena-like laugh. Shiloah's cackle floated farther and farther away, as if Val were falling down a deep, dark hole, tumbling toward the center of the earth. Her mind scrambled to make sense of what was happening. But even when the realization finally came, she couldn't believe it. *I've been drugged! Joel, help me! This can't be happening!*

It seemed to take an eternity to turn her head toward Shiloah, each movement an effort. At last, she met his gaze. His green snake eyes glistened with evil. *God, save me!*

Then a terrifying blackness engulfed Val's body and mind, blotting out her consciousness as quickly as a snuffer extinguishes a candle.

≈

Val felt as if she was swimming sluggishly through thick, murky water. She struggled, only to sink back into the dark depths again and again. Finally, with a burst of almost superhuman effort, she broke through to the surface. She found herself gagged and bound, lying on the stone floor of what she thought was a basement. The inky blackness pressed in on her oppressively, like a smothering hand. *How long have I been lying here?*

The cold, damp floor had chilled her to the bone. Coarse, thick rope gnawed at her wrists, bound and jammed behind her back. The rope tying her ankles had been looped to the cords around her arms so that her body formed a tight, uncomfortable curve, making it impossible to get to her feet, even if she had known how to go about freeing herself. She ached all over. Her head throbbed mercilessly.

With a jolt, the memories of how she'd gotten here scurried from the corners of her dazed brain and solidified into one tall, menacing figure. "Shiloah!" she called. But the cloth binding her mouth muffled the cry to a whimper. No answer came. She could feel no other human presence in the darkness.

Fear thickened around her and crawled up her back, raising goose bumps all over her body. Her neck became rigid with tension. In a useless effort to calm the pounding of her panicked heart, she took deep breaths.

She strained to see something, anything. As her eyes grew

accustomed to the darkness, she could make out two small, bar-covered windows high on the wall she faced. Outside as well as inside, all she could see was looming darkness. *This can't be real. It's just a nightmare.*

But it was real, and she knew it. Primitive fear surged through every cell in her body. Blind panic fought against drugged grogginess. Her heart hammered. Cold sweat covered her face. She struggled to separate her hands and arms and break her bonds. But the more she squirmed, the deeper the rope cut into her skin. She realized that the sleeves of her sweater had been shoved up and the rope binding extended from her wrists to her elbows.

Time and time again her fingers stretched to their limit and painfully scratched and picked at the rope, searching for some loose thread to unravel. Even when her fingertips were worn raw and her nails ragged, they still couldn't get a grip. Her shoulder muscles screamed painfully, protesting the unnatural position of her arms.

After an interminable amount of time, she found herself gasping for breath and stopped her thrashing. Exhausted, she lay there, tensed like an animal caught in a trap. Her heart continued to pound. Tears of fear and rage spilled down her face, gathering in the folds of the gag that bit painfully into her mouth.

Dear Lord, help me! Sensing the futility of struggle, Val closed her eyes and began to pray in earnest. *I'm in big trouble! Don't desert me now. I need You. . . .*

Outside, a winter storm had blown up. Icy rain hurled against the aluminum siding, clattering like bones. The wind moaned through the trees. It tore at the shutters, slapping them back and forth, and howled up and down the street like a mourner who refused to be comforted. The basement itself seemed like a beast crouching over her, breathing its stale, mildewed air into her face.

Val began to shiver uncontrollably. Try as she might, she couldn't stop the shaking. With a sickening lurch of her stomach, she assessed her situation. *I'm a prisoner of the cult. I have no idea what they want from me or plan to do with me. And Joel doesn't know where I am!* At that thought, panic rose in her throat like bile.

Is he looking for me? Is he praying for me? He must be. She knew her husband's spiritual habits well enough to know he'd turn to prayer first. That comforted her. Words from Psalm 91, which she'd read that morning, formed in her mind: "Because you have made the Lord your refuge, the Most High your habitation, no evil shall befall you. . . . For He will give his angels charge of you to guard you in all your ways."

The ancient words of the Hebrew psalm seemed to be addressing her, as if God Himself were comforting her, promising her His protection. *Yes, Lord, I believe. Help my unbelief,* she answered silently. A great "Amen" resounded in her soul. She took the promise of God into her soul and believed it with all her heart.

Suddenly, she didn't feel alone in the darkness anymore. She sensed a divine Presence beside her, around her, within her. The One who had generously given her the gift of life, and even more generously had redeemed her through the death of His Son, would not abandon her now, she knew.

He will keep me in all my ways. He promised. A feeling of liquid warmth spread throughout Val's being. *Although to the natural eye, I'm lying huddled and chilled on the floor of an old stone basement, already the angels are bearing me up in their hands.*

❧

I must have fallen asleep again. Val's shivering had stopped. Still groggy, she peered up at the cereal box-sized windows. Faint gray shades of dawn crept through the filthy glass. The brittle brightness of the light told her that last night's rain had turned to snow.

On the outskirts of town, a freight train wailed. She knew that early-morning sound well and drew some small solace from its familiarity. *Ouch!* She flexed her arm muscles painfully. The skin around her wrists and up along her forearms felt raw, perhaps even bleeding, though she couldn't see her arms to ascertain the damage. *What's to become of me, Lord? Help me to trust You.*

She surveyed her dismal surroundings. She was lying in a small room in a basement, the type used for canning or storing preserves in the last century. The heavy black door leading to the rest of the cellar was closed. The walls were made of gray boulder-like stones; the floor, flagstone. Spiders had strung their webs in every conceivable location. *There must be hundreds of cobwebs,* she noted with a shudder. *That means there must be thousands of insects and crawling things to get caught in them.*

She bit her lower lip. A new wave of anxiety flooded her. She hated, detested, loathed creepy, crawly things. Nervously, she visually checked as much of her body as she could see— her burgundy down jacket, her blue jeans, her black leather boots. All seemed clear of trespassers. *Well, at least that's something to be thankful for.*

As the hours crept by and the light through the window grew stronger, she fought down the frequent panicky feelings by reminding herself of God's promise of protection. She'd just started reciting Psalm 91 for the umpteenth time, when she heard footsteps outside on the porch. *This room must be on the front of the house.* She heard loud banging. *Someone's at the front door. Could it be . . .* She strained to hear above the frantic beating of her heart.

Then she heard it. The most welcome, wonderful sound in the world—Joel Bennigan's voice!

"Open up! I know she's in there!" he called loudly as he

banged on the front door.

Oh, thank God! He's sent me an angel. Instinctively, Val began struggling to free herself to run to Joel. A flood of adrenaline blinded her to the pain of the rope tearing her flesh. "Mmph . . . in here, Joel!" she mumbled through her gag.

Suddenly, the front door creaked open and Shiloah's voice boomed, "I tell you, Bennigan, she's not here!"

"I'm not moving until you get her."

"Listen, man. You're crazy. Get off our porch or I'll call the cops."

Val stopped struggling and willed herself to lie still. She could hear the anger rise in Joel's voice. "I'm the one who'll be calling in the law!" he thundered. "You've got her in there. What trick did you use?"

"Hey, I've no idea what you're jabbering about."

"Get her!"

Val heard a thud, as if Joel had driven his fist into the door jamb.

"Bennigan, destruction of property is a crime. Now, why don't you take yourself off home? Unlike you lazy church folks, we're busy—warning the world of coming judgment. Anyway, why would we want your wife after she wrote those lies in *The Irish Times?*"

Val gasped. In the swirl of events, she'd completely forgotten her article—and the bad press it had given the cult. Originally published in Ireland, her exposé had been reprinted in several American publications. Even *Time* magazine had printed a small blurb. Although the flurry of public interest had died down as quickly as it had flared, she knew Shiloah wouldn't forget. Her blood ran cold. *Revenge!* A terrified voice at the back of her mind shrilled. *They want revenge!*

She heard Joel again, more agitated this time. "The only judgment you're gonna see anytime soon is the law smashing down on your head when I've figured out what you've done to my wife!"

"Just get out, Bennigan." Contempt and triumph dripped from Shiloah's every word. "I don't see your search warrant."

"You haven't won the war. I'll be back for my wife."

He's leaving! Val's mind screamed in panic. *No! Joel, don't go! I'm in here! I'm in here!* Furiously, she tried to propel her body forward. "Mmph . . . Joel, wait! No! No!" she yelled into the gag. But she couldn't be heard and she couldn't budge herself more than a few inches. *The door's probably locked anyway. I'm trapped.*

Her heart sank as she heard Joel's booted feet lunging down the porch steps. "You and your cult of devils haven't heard the last of me!" he shouted. As if in reply, Shiloah slammed the front door so hard the shock waves ran right down to the basement.

Val closed her eyes against the torrent of tears as she imagined her husband, her angel of salvation, walking away, pounding down the path, each step taking him farther away from her. She could make out the crunch of his boots on the new-fallen snow. A few moments later, she heard the engine of his Jeep turn over.

Oh, Lord. Don't fail me. Not now.

Joel's engine idled for a while, maybe five or ten minutes, Val gauged. *What's he doing out there? Waiting for me to come out? Does he really know I'm here? Or is he just trying to fake Shiloah out?*

Suddenly, with a roar of dreadful finality, Joel gunned the engine and tore away.

five

Minutes later, Shiloah flung open the door to Val's dungeon. In the dim early morning light, he looked longer, leaner, and even more sinister. His skin had a pallid cast and his long, ponytailed hair looked as if it could use a good washing. His stooped shoulders reminded Val of a dark Dickensian character. He thrust his hands into the pockets of his green Army jacket.

"She trusted in God. Let's see if God will come and rescue her," he sneered, echoing the words of those who mocked Christ on the cross. "Maybe you've been trusting in the wrong God since you left the family, *Tamar*."

His sharp emphasis on her former cult name rankled Val. She wanted to cry out, "I'm not Tamar. I never *was* Tamar, except under psychological duress. I'm *Val—Val Bennigan*. And nothing you can do can change that."

But, of course, she couldn't speak. The gag still bound her mouth. By now her lips felt chapped, her throat parched, and her tongue swollen from thirst.

Shiloah reached behind him and produced two folding metal chairs. He opened them and flung them into Val's prison. She flinched as the metal screeched across the stone floor.

"Yes, Tamar, it's time me and you had a little talk. You've been leading souls to damnation long enough." He jerked Val to her feet and shoved her down onto a chair. She landed with a thud that knocked the breath out of her.

Positioning his chair opposite hers, Shiloah plopped down. Elbows on knees, he leaned forward until their faces were only inches apart. "You can't turn traitor and get away with it."

His eyes narrowed. "Even Judas paid with his neck."

Val felt her eyes grow wide and round with fear. She tried hard to breathe normally.

"The newspapers might have given their thirty pieces of silver for your little collection of lies, which, by the way, didn't hurt us as much as you might have hoped. We have friends in high places, you know. Very high places." He raised an eyebrow imperiously. "Now I'm here to give you the rope to hang yourself."

Val shook her head from side to side and squirmed as far away from him as her chair would allow.

"What rope, you might be asking yourself," he continued, resting his razor-sharp chin on his long, laced fingers and regarding her intently. "Don't you know?"

Val shook her head again.

"Oh, come on now. You're a smart cookie, Tamar."

Again, she indicated the negative.

"All right then, just think about it. Besides your labor and all that money you've come into recently as Mrs. Joel Bennigan, what do you have that God wants for His end-time work? How could you make amends for the damage you've done His prophet, Father Elijah?"

What's he talking about? The story has already been printed. I can't go back and undo what's been done.

Shiloah paused. His evil gaze seemed to bore into Val's soul. She winced and looked away. Immediately, his hand shot out, grabbed her face, and wrenched it back so that his pale eyes locked on hers. "You will recant your story," he hissed.

Recant?

"You will publicly deny that there was any truth to what you wrote about the Children of Last Days Light," he insisted. "You'll say you made it up and those anti-cult nuts gave you doctored photos."

Val's chest heaved as she gasped for air. He was demanding nothing less than professional and spiritual suicide! She closed her eyes and vigorously shook her head. Again, his hand snared her chin.

"Look at me, Judas."

Val opened her eyes. To her horror, she saw an air gun, like the one used to give booster shots to children, in Shiloah's other hand. The light glinted off the ominous metallic tip of its dart. She shuddered. *So that's how he drugged me!* Her stomach lurched as she remembered the sickening whooshing sound and the suffocating blackness that had followed.

"Cooperate with the Lord, or you'll force me to use this again." He waved the gun in her face, his own angular face dark with anger. "God hates rebellion as the sin of witchcraft, and you, Tamar, are guilty of the gravest rebellion. Don't push me."

Val swallowed hard. *Dear Lord, help me. Show me what to do.*

"To bring your obstinate heart into submission, we've chosen to give you a taste of the coming judgments of God, the mighty plague He will pour out on the waters of Egypt." Shiloah's pupils dilated, his eyes appearing almost black, like two lumps of coal. He dug deep into his right-hand jacket pocket and produced a glass vial of purple liquid. "The plagues of Egypt," he announced solemnly.

Val's mouth felt dry. Her mind raced. *The plagues of Egypt— swarms of locusts, hordes of frogs, outbreaks of boils, rivers turned to blood, the death of every Egyptian firstborn—all of which convinced the Pharaoh to let Moses lead the Children of Israel out of Egyptian bondage. What had they to do with twentieth-century America and the CLDL? He's insane!*

As if he'd read her thoughts, Shiloah cocked his eyebrow. "No, I'm not mad. I'm just a servant of the Lord sent to mete out His wrath on this wicked and perverse generation. I don't like inflicting God's punishments." He sighed, looking almost pained. "It's a heavy burden I must bear—like my father—for our God is an avenging angel, a consuming fire, and the sender of plagues."

Val blinked in amazement. How cunningly he could twist the Scriptures. *Does he really believe what he's saying? And what's in the vial?* Her eyes flew to the small purple container in his hand.

Again, as if he could read her thoughts, he lifted the glass vial. "Tamar, *this* is the Ebola virus from the rain forests of Africa." Once more his features contorted into a death-mask grimace.

Val's stomach turned. *How did he get his hands on a deadly virus? Did the cult steal it from a lab?* Then she remembered what he'd said about her article: *We have friends in high places. Very high places.*

"Oh, we also possess an ample supply of its cousins—Lassa from Africa, Sabia and Machupo from South America. Our government classifies them as the most dangerous biohazardous materials in existence." He smiled, an effort that only twisted his mouth in a hideous leer. "But we have allies in places you'd never suspect—true believers who know the world deserves the coming judgments."

Val swallowed hard. *This can't be true. He's just trying to scare me.*

"The Lord sent an interesting array of plagues to Egypt. Do you remember when Moses turned the waters to blood? Well, this time, God, working through Father Elijah, will turn the waters into biohazardous waste."

Stunned, Val could only shake her head.

"But I'm getting ahead of myself. A Judas like yourself has no need to know the divine plans. All you need to know is how to make reparation for your sin. First, you'll publicly recant your *Irish Times* story. Something like a reverse Benedict

Arnold. Second, you'll divorce Bennigan, take his money, and give it to God's work."

Leave Joel? Never! She'd rather die! Val clenched her teeth and shook her head violently. *No! No! No!*

"Perhaps I haven't made myself clear enough, Tamar. You don't have any choice but to obey. And here's why." He dangled a key on a chain. A silver door key attached to a round pink disk containing a wedding photo.

The key to her own front door! *He stole it from my purse!*

"If you don't submit to God's plan, my dear Tamar, we'll pay a little visit when your precious Joel isn't home. It would be so easy to slip a few drops of our friend Ebola into his orange juice in the refrigerator. He does like juice, doesn't he?"

Joel! They mean to get at me through my husband! Val could feel the blood drain from her face. Shiloah was a raving lunatic, and both she and Joel were in trouble—*big* trouble.

"What's particularly interesting is the grisly, yet quick and efficient, way Ebola kills those who refuse to honor Father Elijah," Shiloah continued, his tone frighteningly calm and clinical. "Moses turned the rivers into blood; Father Elijah will turn the blood into rivers. Imagine this scenario: Your Joel ingests the virus, which he will, if we decide to infect him. In two days, he gets a headache and those pretty blue eyes of his become bloodshot." He rose to pace the cramped confines of the small basement room.

"Red blisters cover his skin. Then, boom! Moses strikes the water. Your husband's flesh rips. Blood leaks uncontrollably from each body orifice, including those pretty eyes. He coughs up black vomit, sloughing off parts of his windpipe, throat, and tongue in the process. His organs fail. His body is gripped with seizures. His liver decomposes. Within a few days, he'll die in his own river of blood. As the infidel perishes, the virus will liquefy much of his tissue."

He's enjoying this, Val thought, her mind barely able to comprehend the horror.

"So, my dear, comply with us. Or else, just like Dorothy and the wicked witch, we will . . . melt . . . your precious Joel Bennigan!"

Melt your precious Joel. . . . The words reverberated in Val's head. Until this moment, she'd been so wrapped up in her own plight, she hadn't given a thought to Joel's safety. Joel—the man who loved her, who had risked his life to rescue her from the cult, who gave her life meaning. Now, because of her, his life was at the mercy of Shiloah! Against her will, the hideous, bloody scenario Shiloah had just described forced its way into her imagination.

It was too, too horrible. Beyond comprehension, beyond belief. *Joel! My beloved, I never meant to put you in danger.* . . . Nausea gripped and twisted her empty stomach. Feeling as if she were falling headlong down an empty elevator shaft, she fainted.

❧

Cold white light blurred against gray stone was the first thing Val saw when she came to. *Perhaps I've died, or maybe I'm just dreaming.* But the sharp pain in her head and the chill from the stone floor told her she was alive and very much awake. When she glanced up from where she'd fallen and saw Shiloah still sitting on the edge of his chair, watching her like a bird of prey, she knew she was trapped in a living nightmare.

"Yes, the details are quite unpleasant," he said, continuing his monologue as if she'd experienced no lapse of consciousness. He made no effort to help her back onto the chair. "Unpleasant, but necessary, I'm afraid. Judgment is always necessary."

He held up the vial of purple liquid. The suffused, hazy basement light seemed to give it an ethereal glow. "Only the work of God's true prophet holds back the plagues . . . for the moment, that is." Then his eyes narrowed and his gaze focused on Val. So much evil lurked in those eyes that raw fear formed in Val's throat like a lump of ice. She couldn't even swallow.

"You must be asking yourself, 'How do I know that's not purple Kool-Aid in that vial? How do I know that really is the deadliest virus known to man?' Good questions, Tamar. Questions that God has given me the wisdom to anticipate.

"The Bible clearly praises those who have not seen and yet believed, but you've already proven yourself to be a sister of little faith, so the Lord has told me to give you a demonstration."

That could mean only one thing. He was going to infect her! Val shrieked through the gag, squirming and twisting her body in a futile effort to get away.

"Hey, hey, little sister. Don't worry. You won't be my guinea pig. Not yet, at least." Shiloah rose to his feet and strode out the door. Val could hear him rattling around in another part of the basement.

He returned, carrying a small, glass aquarium with an orange plastic lid. Inside was a metal wheel, the type she'd seen in the cages of small pets. *A hamster cage?* Shiloah set it down on the floor about six inches from Val's face, slid the lid to one side, reached in, and yanked out the straw covering the floor.

A small brown gerbil, stunned by the sudden removal of his bedding and protection, huddled against the glass wall. His eyes, like tiny black beads, seemed to be staring straight at Val. *You poor creature. We're both at his mercy.*

Shiloah withdrew a pair of disposable rubber gloves from his pocket and pulled them on with a snap. Then he produced an eye dropper. Working slowly and deliberately, he uncapped the vial, inserted the dropper, squeezed the rubber bulb, and removed several purple drops. Deftly, he balanced the dropper, recapped the vial in one swift motion, and returned it to his pocket.

That done, he grabbed the startled gerbil and lifted him out of the cage. Expertly, he cradled the rodent in one hand, using his thumb and forefinger to pry the animal's mouth open. Val's body stiffened in shock. *Don't!* she pleaded silently. But before she could blink, Shiloah had squirted the deadly virus down the gerbil's throat, thrown him into his cage, and clicked the orange lid closed. Immediately, he pulled a small plastic freezer-bag from his pocket, slid in the dropper, and sealed the top of the sack.

"Now I'll leave you two alone so you can consider the ramifications of refusing to cooperate with God," Shiloah said, holding the plastic bag away from his body. "Your husband will die like a rat if you don't do as I say. Not even modern medicine will be able to save him."

Val stared at Shiloah in abject horror. His jaw had clenched, and he'd set his mouth in a tight, straight line. He radiated hatred. She closed her eyes and listened to him leave, locking the door. She swallowed against her nausea. *Is he trying to trick me? Did he really douse that gerbil with a killer virus?*

Against her will, Val forced herself to watch the small animal. He seemed to be acting normally, sipping at his water container, running on his play wheel. Val found herself mesmerized by his antics. *It was only colored water,* she decided. *Just another scare tactic.*

But just then, without warning, the gerbil tumbled headfirst off his wheel, landing on the floor of the cage with a sickening thud. Val watched as he writhed in agony, his terrified squeaks filling the room. Suddenly, his skin seemed to burst, as if he'd sprung a dozen leaks all over his body. Blood poured out, pooling under him. Val couldn't watch anymore. Panic like she'd never known welled in her throat. Fighting back the dry heaves, she clamped her eyes shut and prayed that the animal would die quickly.

It's true! It's true! she repeated to herself over and over. She could barely comprehend the ramifications of that fact. Icy fear twisted around her heart. *They have the means to carry out their threat and kill my husband. What choice do I have but to go along with their demands? Even if I managed to escape, they could infect Joel. . . .*

Val kept her eyes tightly closed. She could hear the gerbil thrash uselessly. After many excruciating minutes, his movements became slower and weaker. Finally, they ceased. She couldn't bear to look.

Lord, help me! I trust You. You promised never to leave me. But what am I to do? Surely you don't expect me to cooperate with the godless demands of these people! But if I don't, I'll be signing Joel's death warrant!

Suddenly, she saw her situation from a higher perspective. These smarmy fanatics might be ahead . . . for the moment. But God was still in control. A Scripture verse came to mind— one she had committed to memory after a particularly moving sermon on grace that Joel had preached shortly after she'd met him: "Blessed be the Lord God of Israel, for He has visited and redeemed His people. . . . Through the tender mercy of our God . . . the day shall dawn upon us from on high to give light to those who sit in darkness and in the shadow of death."

Well, she certainly was sitting in darkness, with death a very real possibility. But God had promised rescue and salvation, hadn't He? Could she believe that? *I want to believe, Lord. This situation looks totally impossible, but I want to trust Your Word.*

She remembered reading about the leap of faith. She hadn't quite understood the concept at the time. Now it was beginning to make sense. She felt as if she was standing on the precipice of a cliff, with nothing but the thick, smothering darkness closing in on her. God was asking her to jump . . . into His strong, loving arms.

Suddenly, like a light coming on, she got it! The Lord wanted her to trust Him, implicitly, without reservation, without having any other reason to trust except His promise. Could she trust God's promise to see her through this safely? That He had this crazy situation in hand? Hadn't He rescued her from the clutches of this evil cult before, through Joel's intervention? Was anything too hard for God?

Val drew a deep breath, hoping it would inflate her courage. She looked up at the bright light streaming through the small windows and remembered the blinding blackness she'd seen there last night. *Yes, Lord, I trust You and Your tender mercy. I'll play along with their deadly game, knowing—somehow—You'll rescue me.*

When Shiloah returned and, looming over her with his fists on his hips, asked the inevitable question, Val blinked back her tears and nodded her head twice. Only then did he untie and remove the stinking gag from her mouth.

"I want to hear you say it," he snarled.

"I'll do whatever you want," she said, trying to avert her eyes from the bloody gerbil cage at Shiloah's feet. "I'll recant my story publicly. I'll come back and work for you. I'll give you money. Anything, only, please—don't hurt my husband."

Lord, I'm taking the leap of faith. I've stepped off the cliff. Please, catch me!

six

It's been twelve hours—half a day, half a lifetime—since I went to the cult house. Val's there! I know she is, and I know she'd never go willingly. But how do I convince the police? Officer Owens listened without sympathy. He wouldn't budge on official policy. Says Val must be missing for twenty-four hours before I can file a missing person report. What kind of useless rule is that? If the CLDL has kidnapped her, she could be in Mexico by then! When I mentioned that, Owens cautioned me not to let my imagination run away with me!

In the old days, I'd have had a few choice words for him. As it is, it took all my Christian resolve to turn the other cheek. The police won't—or can't—help. It's maddening. Like most law-abiding citizens, I suppose I've taken for granted that the law would help me when I needed help. Now I find it won't. At least, not for another twelve hours. Well, I can't wait twelve hours to find my wife!

I told Owens I'd be back. He just smirked and said that most wives walk off their anger and return home long before twenty-four hours have passed. But he's wrong. This is no marital spat or temper fit. Val is in trouble!

55

*I waited up all night, listening for her
footsteps on the porch. I drove like a madman to
the house on Oak Street at the crack of dawn and
squared off with Shiloah. Then I swung by the
campus; she didn't show for any of her classes.
No one—not even her former roommate Tess—
had seen her.*

*That's when I called the national cult hot-line.
At least, those folks were sympathetic. Of all the
people I've talked to, they seemed to understand
my anxiety best. They know I'm not "imagin-
ing" things.*

*In fact, I was told that they've had reports
that the CLDL is stockpiling guns and munitions
for the apocalypse Father Elijah claims is
coming soon. No surprise there, but it does
scare me. Is the old coot stockpiling to arm his
terrorist friends? Or to blow himself and his
followers sky-high? Or will he open fire on the
good people of Kent someday? How far will
these nuts go? As far as mass suicide—like the
one at Jonestown? Or the inferno at Waco?*

*Was she kidnapped? Did she float back to
them? God in heaven, don't You care? How
could You have let this happen to . . .*

❧

Joel flung down his pen. He despised his anger at God, but
there it was, bubbling up inside him, spilling out onto the page
of his journal. The pen clattered across the green- and gold-
flecked kitchen linoleum and came to rest in front of the sink,
the very spot where Val had stood the night before.

He jumped up from the kitchen table and bent over to snatch
the pen, wrenching his left knee, the one that had been most
severely injured in his college football accident. "Ow!" he

bellowed in pain.

He doubled over, clutching the throbbing knee, and sank to the floor with a groan. *Not now, Lord! I've no time for this!*

Impatiently, Joel scooted over to the refrigerator and grabbed an ice pack. Glumly, he sat on the linoleum, not wanting to risk putting weight on the weak joint, and nursed the ice to his knee. He checked his watch. *5:30 p.m. Time for the local evening news.* He reached up and snapped on the small black-and-white set Val insisted on keeping near the sink. She liked to watch the news while washing dishes. *Always the journalist,* he thought as the appliance sprang to life.

His hand froze in midair.

Val's voice was speaking to him from the TV. Her face filled the screen.

"Everything I wrote about the Children of Last Days Light was a bunch of lies," she said, looking directly at the camera. She didn't blink. She didn't look nervous. Neither did she look drugged.

What on earth .... Joel dropped the ice pack.

"The anti-cult fanatics put me up to it. They supplied me with doctored-up photos of an alleged terrorist transaction between two of our beloved leaders and an actor who posed as a member of the Irish Republican Army. It was all lies. I was deceived. My good intentions were exploited by these fanatics. I hope everyone who read my article will forgive me and listen to the truth spoken by Father Elijah."

They're forcing her to do this!

The reporter didn't miss a beat. "Are you telling us, Mrs. Bennigan, that you're recanting your story about the Children of Last Days Light's aiding of terrorists in Ireland and possibly in the Middle East?"

"Exactly. Every word was fabricated."

"I see. And have you rejoined the group?"

"Oh, yes. They're my true family. They've forgiven my

wrongdoing and have accepted me back with open arms."

"Tell me, Mrs. Bennigan, is there any truth to the rumors that the group is stockpiling weapons out on the property it owns in Brimfield called Mountain Manor?"

"None at all. These kinds of accusations are just vicious rumors spread by the enemies of God's work. I can vouch for that, since I was once a monger of lies myself. If you want my advice as a former reporter, don't even dignify those rumors by asking about them."

"A *former* reporter, Mrs. Bennigan?"

"Oh, yes. With the end of the world so near, how can I waste my time working at a secular job? I must devote every moment to God's work."

"Your husband is the associate pastor of Faith Bible Church, isn't he?"

"Yes."

Joel could detect no flicker of emotion on her face. She might as well be talking about the butcher on Main Street.

"Will he be joining you in this work?" probed the reporter.

"No," Val answered, her tone neutral. "Father Elijah teaches the truth of the Bible when he orders us not to yoke ourselves with unbelievers. I'm afraid my husband does not believe Father Elijah is God's end-time prophet, so I'm . . . divorcing him."

Joel's mouth went dry.

"I see. Very interesting. Thank you, Mrs. Bennigan." The freckled-faced young man spun around to face the camera. "This has been News on Five. Back to you, Mike."

Joel heard no more after that. He sat on the floor, immobilized and stunned. *I don't believe it. She's been set up. They threatened her, had a gun to her back . . . something!*

That wasn't his wife talking. He'd been with Val when she'd written her exposé. She'd come along on the stake-out of the IRA-cult connection at his insistence and had been convinced of the cult's evil doings. She'd seen the photographs of Shiloah and Jeremiah passing money to Finn O'Dwyer. No way she could deny it. And divorce? Impossible!

The telephone rang. Hoping against hope it might be Val, he jumped up and snatched the receiver off its cradle on the kitchen wall.

"Son, are you all right?"

His shoulders slumped when he heard his dad's voice instead of the voice of the woman he loved. He'd probably seen the telecast. His grip tightened around the telephone to distract himself from the shooting pain in his knees. "I've been better, Dad."

"Don't worry, son. There's got to be some rational explanation for this. Something's not right here."

Joel sighed. "I know. They're threatening her or blackmailing her, or—or something," he finished weakly.

"This reeks of Satan."

"Yes, Dad. It does."

"Then what are we waiting for? There's only one thing to do—fight! But not with guns. We'll need all the spiritual weapons the Lord gave us. Let's call an emergency prayer meeting at church."

"That's the best idea I've heard all day."

"OK, son. You take half the telephone numbers on the prayer chain list. I'll take the other half."

"Dad?"

"Yes, son?"

"This is war."

&

Val didn't know how she'd managed to do it. No, that wasn't quite right. She did know, only too well. She'd put on the greatest act of her life to save Joel.

But she'd wanted to shout the truth into the camera—that Father Elijah and his Children of Last Days' *Darkness* were more diabolical than she'd ever dreamed possible. She'd wanted to tell every viewer in the broadcast area that she loved her husband as her own flesh and blood and, more than anything, she wanted to go home to him.

But across from her, behind the TV camera, Shiloah had stood, holding a vial of purple liquid, running his bony finger up and down the glass. He had never token his lightless eyes from her face.

Dear Lord, forgive me for what I've just done and the lies I've told. But what other choice did I have?

After the young TV reporter had left the cult house with his camera crew, the *Kent-Ravenna Record Courier* called. Then the *Cleveland Plain Dealer* and the newspaper from Cincinnati. Shiloah invited them all for personal interviews. His self-satisfied smirk sickened her. But it also frightened her. She couldn't look at that man without remembering the bloody gerbil cage.

He couldn't seem to put that purple vial away. *What if he drops it? I guess he'd look at that like he views terrorism— something that will hasten the end of the world and usher in the cult's rule. There's no reasoning with a deranged mind.*

The evening dragged on with media interviews. Even the national press got in on the act. *Time* magazine called to confirm the story—that she had perpetrated a hoax about a perfectly innocent religious group. *Yes, yes, I did it.* She'd told the lie so often, she was almost beginning to believe it. In fact, at times she did let herself partly believe it. She'd read that a person can lie more convincingly if he believes the lie himself. *It's like a game of bluff,* she thought. *A game I've got to win.*

At some point in the evening, Shiloah brought the other cult members in to meet with the press people. *He isn't one to pass up an opportunity for good public relations,* thought Val. Petite, red-headed Gilead gushed over Val, weeping with joy over her return. Several nervous new disciples said they'd never believed those terrorism stories anyway, that Father Elijah, the true end-time prophet, would never lead them astray. But it was Kevin Milford who broke Val's heart.

"You've seen the light, just like me," he said as he hugged her.

Val put her hands on his shoulders and held him away from her to get a good look at him. The former freshman looked more anxiety-ridden, if that was possible, than she'd ever seen him. His long, dark hair hadn't been combed in quite some time. Stale body odor wafted from his person. Painfully thin, he seemed to be wasting away.

She struggled to keep up the true believer act, when what she really wanted to do was to grab Kevin and make a dash for it. "Yes, I've seen the light, Kevin."

"Don't call me Kevin anymore. That's my devil name. My real name is Job." A trembling smile fluttered across his haggard face.

"Job," Val echoed, keeping her voice devoid of emotion so as not to betray her grief over this tragedy. But her conversion was an act; Kevin Milford's was not. "Why did the Lord give you that name?" She was surprised to find how simple it was to slip back into the cult language, their way of looking at the world. She found she could put on her cult persona as easily as slipping into her winter boots.

"Shiloah told me that in the Old Testament, Job was arrogant toward the Lord. Like when I figured I knew the Bible better than Father Elijah, and I deserted God's work. God punished Job, but He brought Him back into His sheepfold just like He brought me back to the Family. Sister Gilead was His instrument." Kevin flashed a nervous smile at Gilead.

"Amen to that, brother!" shrieked the redhead, bounding over to hug Kevin furiously. "Amen and amen! Thank God He rescued you from the claws of the devil."

Dear God, please save Kevin from this darkness, this shadow of death, Val prayed silently. "Job," she said sweetly, "can you share with me how the Lord brought you back to the Family?"

Kevin warmed up to her request. A momentary sparkle shone in his dead-looking eyes. "Well, Val—oh, sorry, I mean Tamar, it's like this. I got to thinking, what if Father Elijah really is the prophet of God? What then?"

Val flinched at the flash of panic that crossed the young man's face.

"I'd lose my soul and burn in hell for all eternity for deserting God's work," he continued, the pained, anguished look returning to his pinched features. "I was afraid to stay out in the world, so I came back, with Gilead's help."

"I see," said Val. "Praise the Lord, brother Job!" She hugged him, using the opportunity to close her eyes and squeeze back the tears that threatened. *Lord, teach this son of Yours that You're not an angry God, out to get him for every mistake, hunting him down as if he were a scared rabbit. Show him that You are love, truth, and justice. Lord, help me to believe it more fully myself.*

Darkness had fallen outside when the reporters finally left and Shiloah gathered the dozen or so cult members to sing and chant the invocation of Father Elijah's name.

"Father E, Father E, who do we love? We love Father E!" Each disciple tried to outdo the other in fervor and volume. Val was sure neighbors down the street could hear the racket.

She particularly hated the chant because, with its hypnotic effect, it had the tendency to lead the disciples into a group trance. She'd seen the pattern before. Once the followers had reached a suggestive trance-like state of mind, the leader— Shiloah, in this case—would start preaching or reading Father Elijah's angry, rambling epistles. The sequence made perfect sense psychologically. Brainwash them while they're suggestible.

Immediately, Val started fighting the mind-numbing repetition by focusing her attention on the coat hook at the back of the living room door. She'd chosen the coat hook at random. The object of her attention didn't matter, she knew that much from her psychology courses at college.

That's why she was the first one in the room to see the door open. A half-uttered chant stuck in her throat, like a fish bone that no amount of hard swallowing could dislodge. Her knees began to shake, threatening to buckle beneath her.

She nearly choked as Jeremiah came crashing through the door, bear-like, his shoulder-length black hair and chest-long beard matted and dull. He covered the distance between himself and Val in three hefty strides and clamped his beefy arm around her.

"Praise the Lord!" he thundered. "He's brought back my prodigal wife!"

seven

Val caught her breath sharply. "Jeremiah!" She tried to break away, but he held her firm. "Where did you come from?" *It doesn't matter where the hairy ape came from, you idiot. He's here now and your goose is cooked.*

"Nice of ye to worry about me, sweet Tamar." The refrigerator-sized man had lost none of his throaty Irish accent. He curled a thick finger under Val's chin and forced a kiss on her clenched lips.

All around them, CLDL disciples broke into applause and shouts of "Hallelujah!" Val struggled free of Jeremiah's clammy embrace.

His flinty gaze lingered possessively on her mouth. The scars on the squared cheekbones above his full black beard looked like they'd been put there by a switchblade and gave him a mean look. "It's God's will that you marry me—or He'll smite ye for foolish disobedience," he said sternly, angry thunder rumbling in his voice.

Jeremiah's God was an angry bear, like himself. Val knew this from her time with him in Dublin. Like the other disciples, she'd cowered under his angry tirades. She'd witnessed his consorting with an IRA terrorist. She'd read his police rap-sheet and knew his real name, Garret Foley. But what was he doing here? The last Val had heard, Jeremiah was still in Ireland.

She shrank back. Like many cult members, he exuded a foul body odor. In cult talk this condition was dubbed "divine fragrance." Father Elijah's followers didn't have time for regular showers. She looked from Jeremiah to Shiloah and back again. *How much does Jeremiah know? The virus? The black-mail? The charade? He's one of Father Elijah's right-hand men. He must know everything.*

Shiloah strummed his guitar slowly, a knowing grin twisting his thin lips. "A wedding!" he cried. "Let them be married tonight!"

"Yes! Yes!" shrieked the disciples. Gilead's voice dominated the others. "Amen! Let it be done tonight as the Lord says. Father E! Father E!"

"Is it the Lord's will?" Jeremiah asked Shiloah, with his question, acknowledging the lean man's superior rank within the strict hierarchy of the family.

"Yes," said Shiloah. "God just told me so."

Val swallowed hard, trying to conceal her revulsion. The room seemed stiflingly hot, and the clammy smell of unwashed bodies threatened to gag her. *Lord, give me wisdom, the wisdom of Solomon.*

She backed up, standing halfway between the two leaders. "Much as I want to do the Lord's will," she said as firmly as she dared, even though her heart was pounding, "I cannot marry dear brother Jeremiah until I am free from the infidel, Joel Bennigan." Val scanned the faces of the two dozen disciples crowding around her, hanging on her every word. Their faces were mostly young and impressionable. They believed her, she realized in amazement. Since she'd recanted to the media, the newer disciples had begun looking up to her as a kind of returning hero.

She realized she was putting Shiloah and Jeremiah on the spot in front of the freshly caught disciples who might not condone adultery, at least not yet. Later, when their consciences had been sufficiently seared, they would believe that anything the group wanted or needed was morally permissible, and even morally good.

Shiloah's serpent eyes narrowed. Val knew she'd trapped

him. But while she might have succeeded in forcing him to keep up the charade in front of the new disciples, she feared what he'd do later—when he had her alone.

He cleared his throat. "Yes, sister Tamar, you're quite right. I'm impressed with your spiritual maturity. Although we're not bound by the laws of this evil world, we should not flaunt our spiritual freedom and bring scandal to God's work."

He nodded to Jeremiah, who only scowled back. "So, I'm afraid you must wait to be wed, brother Jeremiah and sister Tamar. I understand the hardship this delay entails, but we must all sacrifice for the cause, even to the point of death!"

"Amen!" bellowed the group in unison.

Shiloah's eyes darkened and rested on Val. "But in Father Elijah's eyes, you are betrothed. Is that clear?"

"Amen!" roared Jeremiah, snatching Val's hand.

Shiloah reached out and clamped his claw-like fingers on Val's shoulder. She flinched. Even his touch sickened her. "We're so glad you've come back to your true family, sister Tamar," he said loudly, loud enough for every disciple in the room to hear. "You're one of us now . . . until death do us part."

His hidden message to her was unmistakable.

"Do we love sister Tamar?" Shiloah pumped up the group, spinning around with his arms outstretched. "Don't we love having her back?"

"Amen! Amen! We love you, Tamar! Hallelujah!" the group roared.

Oh, you misguided sheep. This isn't love. It's a cheap sales technique, Val thought. But she smiled brightly and widely as was expected of a loyal disciple of Father Elijah. She remembered how these forced group declarations of "love" had touched her deeply during her first visits. For a while, she really had believed they loved her. Every new disciple did. The countercult people called it "love bombing," overwhelming the new recruit with affection to win him over.

Seizing the moment, Shiloah began to strum quietly to the rhythm of the cultic chant. The dull, monotonous beat quickened as the atmosphere in the room became charged. The tension and excitement quickly escalated to a feverish pitch. Disciples flung their arms in the air and swayed back and forth hypnotically.

"Father E! Father E! Who do we love? Father E!"

The chorus grew louder. Val yelled louder than anyone. But she clamped her eyes shut. That way she didn't have to witness the garish freak show all around her—the glazed eyes, the frozen smiles, the shrill hysteria. And Shiloah exploiting it for all he was worth. Neither did she have to look at the hardened face of her "betrothed." As it was, his fleshy, hot hand on her shoulder sent chills down her spine.

How much longer could she keep up this pretense?

॰

It was three in the morning when Shiloah finally called a halt to the relentless chanting and allowed the group to retire. Many faces were tear-stained. Emotions had run high and raw for hours. Val could see that exhaustion and spiritual stupor had set in among the flock. Obediently, the disciples filed out of the living room and up the stairs: males heading toward one side of the house, females to the other.

"Hold it, Tamar. You, too, Jeremiah."

Val stood with eyes downcast, lacing and unlacing her hands behind her back. She prayed silently and waited while Shiloah drummed his fingers on the neck of his guitar. When the last disciple had left, he jerked his head toward Jeremiah. "Shut the door," he barked.

He turned his steely gaze on Val. "Good show, Tamar," he hissed, cocking an eyebrow. "Very good act. If I didn't know your disbelieving heart so well, I'd be convinced myself."

"I intend to keep my end of the bargain," Val said, her voice resigned. "I recanted my story, just as you ordered."

"And you will continue to recant, incessantly, to whomever will listen," snapped Shiloah. "As soon as the business day starts, our lawyers will file divorce papers on Bennigan. We'll trump up some photographic evidence so we can nail him for adultery and get more money."

Val bit down on her lip to suppress a cry of anguish, clenching her hands so tightly that her fingernails burrowed painfully into the soft flesh.

"You will sleep, eat, and work next to Gilead," Shiloah continued, never missing a beat. "She'll keep a close eye on you. Don't let the thought of escape even cross your mind. Remember, we have your key. One false move, and Bennigan's history. Got it?"

Val nodded numbly. Jeremiah stood behind Shiloah, his beefy arms crossed over his massive chest. He looked like a bouncer or a hit man who'd nail her if she took one step out of line. He witnessed the exchange without so much as a raised eyebrow. *He knows everything. And he certainly doesn't believe that nonsense about it being God's will to marry him. He's just lusting after me. . . .* She shuddered.

"You will recruit and raise funds with the other disciples, as usual. But you will be under strict surveillance. You need to prove your new conversion to the world before . . ."

Jeremiah grabbed Val by the waist, crushing her to his body. "I want her before that."

"All in good time, brother Jeremiah. All in good time. We must observe a little propriety and not cast our pearls before swine."

Jeremiah grunted, his big paws squeezing Val's flesh painfully. "OK, you're the boss. But just don't make me wait too long."

"Just as long as serves our purposes, brother."

Jeremiah raked Val's body with his eyes. One side of his

cruel mouth turned up in a mocking leer. His lewd smile chilled her heart. Suddenly, he roughly thrust her away from him and stormed out of the house.

❧

Somehow, Val knew Joel would show up. After three hours of fitful sleep, fully clothed in a sleeping bag on the floor beside Gilead's bed, Val bolted downstairs as soon as she heard his voice.

"I demand to see my wife!" rumbled the familiar deep baritone.

She watched him from the top of the stairs. He looked as dreadful as she felt. His handsome face was drawn and pale. Stubble shadowed his jaw. Her heart went out to him. Apparently she wasn't the only one who'd slept in her clothes. Joel's blue cotton shirt was a mass of wrinkles. He hadn't even bothered to button his jacket against the cold. His hair looked so disheveled, she wanted to run her hands through it to smooth it. She used all her willpower to keep herself rooted to the spot and resist running down the stairs and flinging herself into his arms.

Shiloah stood in the open doorway with his back to Val. Jeremiah lounged up against the wall, his arms crossed, looking like a black bear waiting for the kill. He noticed Val first. "Well, if it isn't the little lady herself," he said. "C'mon down, darling. See if you can get the message across to this bumpkin."

Joel jerked his gaze upward. "Val!"

The misery she saw lining his face splintered Val's heart into a thousand shards. She couldn't bear to witness such pain, knowing full well that she'd caused it, and dropped her gaze to the bare wooden steps.

"Val! What have they done to you?"

She willed herself to remain utterly motionless. She couldn't trust herself to say a word, not even a greeting. If she opened her mouth, the whole, unbelievable story would tumble out. She'd fling herself against Joel's chest and beg him to save them both . . . and Shiloah would be ready to make good on his threat. From where she stood, she could see him slip the purple vial halfway out of his pocket.

Instead of replying, she tightened her grasp on the wooden banister. Her hand was cold and trembling. *How can I go through with this? How can I pretend I don't love Joel anymore? How can I make him believe that? What if I can't do it?*

Memories of the blood-spattered gerbil cage flooded her mind. She could do nothing but fulfill the cult's orders. She had no future. The only thing that mattered now was to save the life of the man she loved most in the world.

The panic she'd briefly forgotten in sleep rose again and threatened to engulf her. She felt like a frightened child who, more than anything, wanted an adult to come and make the nightmare stop. But she wasn't a child. She was a wife who bore a grave responsibility to her husband—to preserve his life, even if it cost her own life or deprived her of his love. And if she played her part well, Joel's love for her would surely die, strangled by her own hand.

Greater love has no man than this, that a man lay down his life for his friends, Val recalled. *Or a wife lay down her love for her husband? Did it work that way? Please God, help me to pull this off. I'm doing the only thing I know to save my husband's life.*

She swallowed hard, squared her shoulders, and descended the stairs with as much dignity and aloofness as she could muster. She ran her hand through her tangled mass of chestnut hair and straightened her navy sweatshirt. She didn't meet Joel's gaze again until she stood in front of him in the open doorway.

He reached out and touched her cheek. Oh, the comfort of

his touch, even for one second! The temptation flashed across her mind to blurt out the truth, or at least to send Joel a secret, pleading look to let him know this was all an act. *No! That would put him in unspeakable danger. For his own safety, he's got to believe you—one hundred percent!*

The hardest thing she'd ever had to do was wrench herself away from Joel's hand in mock revulsion. "Don't touch me! I'm not your wife anymore!" She watched his face crumple like a paper bag. She longed to wipe that pain away with a touch of her hand and whisper that these words were lies. But she couldn't. All she could do was stand like a pillar of stone and gape in silent horror at the damage she had done to her beloved.

His sky blue eyes pleaded. He reached for her again. "What have they done to you, my love?" he rasped.

Side-stepping his hand, she said, "I've come back to the Family of my own accord. They're my true family. Father Elijah is God's true prophet. I must follow my conscience." Val's words sounded mechanical and rehearsed, even to her own ears. She hoped they were convincing enough to satisfy Shiloah.

"I don't believe you, Val."

Despite his protests, Val noticed dejection, almost resignation, in Joel's voice. His shoulders slumped. Was he beginning to buy her charade? His jaw muscles tightened, and he ran his hand through his sandy hair. He seemed to be favoring his left leg. Val's eyes narrowed. Had his old injury kicked in again? Her heart lurched. He looked like he was in pain, but fighting not to show it.

"Put a lid on it, Bennigan," Shiloah snarled. "It's true. You didn't think you could really fight God, did you?"

Joel's intent gaze never wavered from Val's flushed face. She felt her eyes grow large and liquid. Part of her hoped that he would somehow read the truth there—that he still was, and always would be, the only man she would ever love. *But giv-*

ing him hope is signing his death warrant. Instantly, she jerked her gaze away. And not a second too soon. Jeremiah was studying her closely, too closely.

"I do believe our little sister Tamar has something else to tell you, Bennigan," he said, vile amusement traveling downward from his black eyes to his leering mouth. "Something about your extra-marital dalliances. Tut, tut, and you a man of the cloth. Did you think you could pull the wool over God's eyes as well as your wife's?"

Her stomach clenched as Val prepared to utter so great a falsehood. "Yes, Joel, I found out about—" her voice cracked slightly, but she recovered quickly and took a quick breath before continuing "—your affairs, and I cannot longer live with an unfaithful man. I'm drawing up divorce papers today. . . ." Her voice trailed off miserably.

"You'll pay dearly for those dalliances, Bennigan," Shiloah jumped in, his voice laced with contempt. "Adultery ain't cheap, especially when there's documentation to prove it."

"What. . . " Joel began through gritted teeth.

Val watched his fists clench and unclench. *What torments must he be going through? Forgive me, my love.*

Suddenly, Jeremiah lunged forward, grabbed her by the shoulders, jerked her body against his chest. She fought and quelled her instinct to resist and allowed him to wrap his beefy arms around her. Unable to face Joel, she buried her face in Jeremiah's ample chest.

"See? She's mine now, Bennigan," Jeremiah taunted. "All mine."

Val heard Joel gasp and take a step forward.

"Hold it right there!" Shiloah's voice rang out. "The little lady obviously doesn't want you here, Reverend. Neither do we. Get off our property."

Joel's breath sounded labored. Val heard him back out the door onto the porch.

"All right, I'll go," he said, his voice hoarse and pained. "But I don't believe this act for a minute. I love you, Val. Remember my promise—I won't abandon you. I'll come for you, no matter what. You're my wife, forever."

"Get out!" Shiloah bellowed, slamming the heavy oak door in Joel's face.

Only then did Val wriggle out of Jeremiah's grasp and dart up the stairs.

"Ain't revenge sweet?" Shiloah goaded her.

Their cruel laughter lanced Val's heart like a sword. At the top of the stairs, she doubled over, clutching her abdomen, and sobbed silently.

eight

As soon as the sound of Joel's pickup faded, Val stifled her sobs and slipped quietly back into the women's bedroom. To her relief, the others were still sleeping soundly. *And no wonder they sleep like logs,* she thought. Every one of them lived in a state of perpetual exhaustion. But at least they couldn't witness her present distress.

Val checked her watch and glanced out the window. At 5:05 A.M., Kent was still shrouded in a mantel of darkness. Shivering with misery as much as with cold, she climbed back into her sleeping bag, hoping to use the quiet moments to sort out her thoughts before Gilead awakened and started monitoring.

It began as a small ghost of an idea that crept out of the corners of her mind as she lay in the borrowed sleeping bag near the window, her eyes moist with unshed tears, watching the last stars of the night shine hard as diamonds in the cold blackness. Their beauty reminded Val of the emotion she'd seen in Joel's eyes when he'd stood at the door. He loved her. It showed not only in his eyes, but in his face, his voice, his actions.

Witnessing that love again gave her new hope. His words kept ringing in her head: "I'll come for you." What did he mean? Was he going to kidnap her? Would he hire deprogrammers to nab her on the street and spirit her away in a windowless van? While every fiber of her being cried out to be rescued, she knew any such action would ensure Joel's death.

Or would it? What if they kept going in that windowless van—or whatever vehicle the deprogrammers used? What if they didn't return home to their house in Kent? Shiloah's

74

trump card, his lynch-pin upon which his blackmailing hinged, was the fact that he owned a key to her house. But what if she and Joel never returned there? Maybe they could disappear without a trace, and, when they were safe, contact the police, the FBI, the Center for Disease Control, and whatever other authorities had jurisdiction over deadly viruses. What if . . .

As Gilead snored, Val plotted. She must get a note to Joel explaining the need for their immediate escape and disappearance. Perhaps the countercult people would hide them. Val knew about the nationwide network of people working against cults—mostly parents who had lost children to one group or another. Surely, they'd help. Then maybe she could persuade a prosecutor to file charges against Shiloah. It must be a criminal act to possess deadly viruses.

But her immediate task was to protect her husband's life while saving her own. How could she get the message to him? Either Gilead, Shiloah, or Jeremiah watched her like a hawk, every waking moment. She didn't even know how she'd manage to write a note without being found out. Shiloah had taken her purse, her money, her checkbook and pen—everything. She had the clothes she'd arrived in and a borrowed toothbrush and comb. Nothing more.

But she could ask for a Bible, couldn't she? Surely they wouldn't deprive her of that. She could point out that her not having a Bible, notebook, and pen wouldn't look good to the younger disciples. Every disciple was expected to take notes when Shiloah or Jeremiah lectured. If she could just get her hands on pen and paper, then she could write a note and somehow get it to Joel. Maybe she could even ask for a few Father Elijah letters, just for good measure. . . .

Wait! That's it! Shiloah had ordered her to do some fundraising with the other disciples. That meant selling the Father Elijah letters on the street in Kent, or up on campus. Some of the disciples were being bussed to Cleveland because the begging went better in bigger cities. But, if and when she was assigned to Kent . . .

Of course, Brady's! Why hadn't she thought of that before? Joel always stopped in for one or two cups of coffee before going to his office at the church. In fact, they often ate breakfast there. Neither liked to cook, and Brady's was an enjoyable way to start the day together—sipping freshly brewed coffee and reading the Scriptures.

Jagged pain tore at Val's heart at the memory of the happy, intimate times they'd spent in that old landmark coffeehouse. With its rough plank floors and its wooden swinging doors, it always put her in mind of an old Western saloon. It wasn't fancy, but it was *their* place. In fact, the first time they'd ever spent together, outside of church, had been at Brady's. Joel had bought her lunch—a Reuben sandwich and a cup of the best espresso she'd ever tasted. They'd talked about cults, in fact. *How ironic.* At the time, she'd been researching the subject for Professor Weston's journalism class, and Joel had offered to help since he knew quite a bit about the subject. . . .

All the love she felt for Joel welled up inside and filled Val with renewed, aching longing. Every moment they'd spent together came flooding back in a great wave of desire for him. Her heart beat faster. Tears blinded her eyes. The stars didn't glimmer anymore; they swam. Deep, tortured sobs wracked her body, but she didn't dare cry aloud for fear of waking Gilead. Her chest ached as she tried to swallow her roiling emotions. She bit down hard on her lower lip. *When I'm safe in Joel's arms again . . . then I'll cry. . . .*

She waited silently as the darkness began lifting and the promise of escape etched itself upon the dawn.

❧

"Hurry! Hurry! Souls are going to hell while you dawdle!" Shiloah roared from downstairs. "This isn't a trip to the mall! The world needs to be warned that the end is coming soon.

Get a move on, brothers and sisters!"

By 7 A.M., each disciple had dragged on yesterday's clothes and had grabbed a peanut-butter sandwich off the kitchen table, eating on the run. The engine of the cult's restored school bus was already turning over as groggy disciples began boarding, burdened with satchels full of pamphlets, bound for another grueling day of pounding the snowy streets of Cleveland. Val and Gilead, however, would be selling pamphlets in Kent. Shiloah wanted Val in town so she could visit the lawyer as soon as an appointment was arranged.

Buoyed by her encounter with Joel and her subsequent strategizing, Val's mind was sharper than most. She mentally ticked off the names of the cult followers as they climbed aboard the bus—Mercy, Micah, Simeon, Jehu, and a few others whose names she still hadn't learned.

Boaz, an enthusiastic, flabby young man with a bulbous nose, was delegated to drive. As the most senior "new" disciple, Shiloah had entrusted him with this responsibility. Val knew that as Boaz proved himself faithful and unquestioning, he would be rewarded with more prestigious jobs and more status within the family. He would be declared a faithful "older brother," then a "trainee leader," and he'd get to lord it over the "babes," or newest disciples. Power was the coveted lubricant that kept the cult machine working smoothly. Leaders also got better food and more rest.

"Praise the Lord, sister Tamar!" cried Kevin Milford, the last to board the tan bus. "Work hard for Father Elijah. The end is coming soon! Very soon!" He gesticulated wildly with one thin hand while clutching a stack of Father Elijah pamphlets with the other.

Kevin's jerky movements and plastic smile reminded Val of a wind-up toy. He seemed to be in a permanent state of near-hysteria, either crying or laughing uncontrollably, or else staring off into space. *I've got to get him out of here,* thought Val, genuinely afraid for him. *He needs psychiatric help.* But she knew that, like a parent with a child making an emergency airplane landing, she needed to get her own air mask on first.

She noticed that everyone moved in a state of great agitation and urgency. Cries of "The end is near!" flew back and forth. *They talk like the end of the world is coming next week,* she thought. The cult had always emphasized the coming apocalypse, and Father Elijah ranted on about it interminably in his writings, but Val felt a new sense of immediacy she hadn't noticed when she had been with them in Ireland. *Something's new. What's happened? What new prophecy of doom has Father Elijah trumped up now?*

Val decided not to ask outright, but to watch and listen carefully.

Following Shiloah's instructions, Val and Gilead were to position themselves on campus in order to hit the students on their way to early classes. On the way from the bus, Val thought of his last words to them before thrusting a stack of pamphlets into their hands. "Father Elijah has been given a new rule from God," Shiloah had said, smirking. "You must raise three hundred dollars and distribute one thousand pamphlets before you can eat dinner. He who does not work, does not eat. We need to be on fire to save the world. The end is coming soon, sisters, and don't you forget that for a moment."

At fifty cents or a dollar a shot, it would take a lot of effort to collect three hundred dollars.

"Amen, brother!" Gilead had chirped, clapping her small hands and smiling her thousand-watt grin. She cocked her head at Val. "Ready to save souls, Tamar?"

With her red hair and darting brown eyes, the small woman reminded Val of a nervous sparrow. "Amen," Val had replied with as much enthusiasm as she could muster.

As they trudged up Main Street, bundled in winter coats and boots, Val wondered how much Gilead knew about the viruses and Shiloah's blackmail. By all indications, she believed Val's return to the cult was genuine. Although Gilead had been in the Family for several years, Val knew women weren't admitted to the inner circle of leadership. Indeed, Father Elijah had written that women were weak and inferior, mentally, physically, and spiritually. He even denied that women had souls. But that doctrine, like the one about promoting terrorism, was reserved for "mature" disciples.

I wonder if Gilead really believes that crock about women having no souls? Val sneaked a sidelong glance at her companion. She looked much younger than her twenty-odd years, even with the deprived life she led. Like all the lower-level disciples, especially the women, Gilead had an air of innocence and immaturity about her. *Like lambs led to the slaughter,* Val thought ruefully. It saddened her to see how devilishly the cult distorted and belittled God's role for women. There was no true equality in Christ for women within the confines of the Children of Last Days Light. From her study of how destructive cults worked, Val knew this was the case in almost all these groups.

Val's heart began to race as they approached Brady's. She'd devised a plan. Now it was up to God to make it work. She patted her stack of Father Elijah pamphlets—paper she could use to send a note to Joel—and secretly rejoiced. For once, the rambling, irate epistles of doom and judgment would serve a useful purpose. "Oh, Gilead," she said sweetly, "I'm sorry to be a bother, but I must duck into Brady's to use the little girl's room."

Gilead stopped, her small face creased in a frown. "Really, Val. You should have taken care of that at the house. You're wasting God's time, and these people don't have much time left before the end comes."

"I know, I know. Forgive me. I'll just be a minute. You can catch a few people outside while you wait." With only one entrance to the coffeehouse, maybe Gilead wouldn't feel compelled to accompany her to the rest room.

"Oh, all right. But hurry!" Gilead snapped and spun around, shoving a pamphlet into the hand of an unsuspecting passerby and then demanding a donation.

Val silently uttered a prayer of thanks as she hurried through the wooden swinging doors into the dimly lit interior of Brady's. Her boots clicked on the rough floor as she made her way toward the back. On the way, she scanned the early-morning customers. Several regulars nodded to her. Val smiled, but her heart took a nosedive. *No sign of Joel! Maybe he'll get here before I leave.*

On her way past the cash register, Val picked up a free pen. Margie, the proprietor, had thought it an enterprising advertising idea to imprint pens with the name and address of her business establishment. These were stashed handily in a nearby cup. Earlier, Val had considered the idea a great publicity stunt. Now, it might literally save her life!

After locking the rest room door, she sat down on the floor, opened a pamphlet, and began to write hurriedly: "Joel, my dearest, I'm being held prisoner. Shiloah is blackmailing me with your life. You're in grave danger. We must escape and go into hiding. Follow me and 'kidnap' me on the street. We must leave Kent immediately. Under no circumstances can we go home. I'll explain all when we're together. I love you forever, Val."

She chewed the top of the pen. No way could she adequately explain everything in the margin of one pamphlet. Anyway, there was no more time. *This will have to do. You'll have to guide him, Lord.*

Val gathered her pamphlets and slipped back out into the shop. Her eyes skimmed from face to face. Her heart beat furiously. *Where is he? He always stops for coffee at this time. Why not today?*

Her hands tightened around her stack of paper. She saw Gilead peering in the window, frowning. To appease her, Val handed out pamphlets to a table of bemused construction workers. "Father Elijah says the end is coming," she stated, feeling foolish. Her gaze darted around the room. Her stomach churned with anxiety and frustration. *No Joel.* She walked past the booths. Still no sign of him. Her breath seemed to have solidified in her throat.

He must not be coming. Val choked back a cry as she watched her carefully laid escape plan crumble before her eyes. She felt the nauseating sinking of despair. With one last, futile scan around the room, she weighed the advisability of entrusting her message to one of the regulars or even to Margie, but at that moment Gilead burst through the swinging doors. "Let's go! Now!"

Val hunched her shoulders, shoved Joel's pamphlet in her pocket, and followed Gilead out on the snowy sidewalk. The message was too important to leave to chance.

"Well, you took long enough in there!" Gilead complained. "Don't you care about lost souls and the end of the world?"

"Yes, I do. More than I ever imagined possible."

As they hurried toward the campus, the bitter wind chapping their faces, Val silently moaned to her heavenly Father. *Our plan didn't work. Why? Why did You let me down? How could You do that to me?*

She listened for a while to the soft crunch of the snow beneath her boots as she and Gilead climbed the hill to the campus. On the way, Val looked for a trash can where she could stuff the evidence. *Oh, I see. Maybe the problem was that it was my plan—not Yours. You know best, Lord. May Your will be done.*

&

Joel didn't go to Brady's for his usual cup of coffee that morning. He couldn't bear the place now. Not without Val. Not with all the happy memories of their times together languishing in every corner. In fact, he resolved not to frequent Brady's again until his wife came home.

Instead, he slipped into the chapel at Faith Bible and prayed on his knees in front of the cross hanging above the altar. His left knee screamed in protest, but he persisted. When his knees gave out, he fell on his face on the marble floor, waiting for the still, small voice to whisper something comforting. Where was God in this whole awful mess?

Except for the unremitting rumbling of passing traffic, he would not have known if time was passing or standing still. His injured knee throbbed. The death-like cold of the marble seeped into his large frame. The early silver light sifted lazily through the colored windows, suffusing the sanctuary with its hazy, ethereal glow.

Help me, Lord. I'm completely baffled. Do I call in the deprogrammers? Has Val been brainwashed back into the cult? Does she need rescuing? And why do You feel so far away from me, Lord, when I need You the most?

No answers came.

Outside, the birds sang their morning lauds in the trees near the chapel windows. *Lord, don't desert me now. . . .*

"I will never leave you nor forsake you." Suddenly the words of Christ etched themselves on Joel's heart with a new and deeper reality than they ever had for him before. He sat up, feeling ashamed for doubting that promise, no matter how badly he felt or how disastrous his situation. Joel sat back on his haunches, ignoring the pain in his knee, his fists balled on his jean-clad thighs. He stared, almost mesmerized, at the wooden cross. He remembered the Lord's own heart-wrenching cry of abandonment on the cross, "My God, my God, why have You forsaken me?"

You felt this way, too, Lord, Joel mused in wonderment. *I'm not alone.*

Heartened, Joel stood up gingerly. *God cannot be manipulated. He will answer in His way, in His time. Perhaps He's teaching me to trust Him more—to walk by faith, not feelings. To grow up a little spiritually,* Joel thought as he made his way out of the church.

Father, it's easy to preach faith, but hard to live it. Please give me the wisdom and humility to know what to do. Then give me the courage to carry it out. Even if it means kidnapping and deprogramming my wife.

nine

How do you file a missing person report on someone who's missing in spirit, but not in body? Does Officer Owens have a regulation to cover that? Thank God I stopped in the chapel to pray before tangling with that bureaucratic purist this morning. He insists there's nothing he can do if Val's living in the cult house of her own free will.

But she's not. I know my wife. At least, I think I do. But why did she lie on TV? Why is she filing for divorce, or threatening to? Charging me with adultery, of all absurdities! What's going on? What kind of control do these spiritual con men have over her? When I saw her on television, I figured they must be holding a gun to her head. But I saw no sign of physical force at the house this morning. If they'd been holding her by force, she could've made a break for it then. Or she could have told me, and I'd have carried her out of there.

I searched Val's face for some flicker of recognition of the bond of our love. Nothing. I looked for some secret sign that she was in distress and needed rescuing. Nothing. And, worst of all, when that black-haired gorilla grabbed her, she went into his arms—willingly! Or so it appeared.

84

Lord, what am I to make of this? Has my wife gone mad? Have I lost her? Who can I turn to for help? I can't press kidnapping charges against the cult. She'd deny them. I can't just go in there and grab her. There are too many cult members around, and I believe they're armed. Maybe I could petition the court to have her declared legally incompetent. Some people do that when loved ones disappear into a cult. But then the label hounds them for the rest of their lives. I couldn't do that to Val!

Is she incompetent? Is she brainwashed? Is she being held under the influence of mind-manipulation, like Patty Hearst or those American prisoners of war who were brainwashed by the Chinese? Do I call in deprogrammers and have her kidnapped? Is that the only solution?

I've read all the books on cult brainwashing. I've talked to experts. I know the theories and the techniques of mind-control. Even so, it's hard to believe it could happen to my own wife. For one thing, I guess I don't want to believe Val's mind has been tampered with, but I don't see any other reasonable explanation for the changes I've observed in her. She must have floated that night she left the house. She must have bumped into them and been lured into the house. . . .

But how could they have gained so much control so quickly? It's not meant to happen immediately. Even the anti-cult experts are puzzled by the speed.

Now I'm even beginning to wonder if there's any way she could actually believe what she's

saying. Could her cult conversion be for real?
Could she have been planning to return to them
all along? No! I won't accept that. I will not
abandon her to the cult. I'm bound to Val by
sacred vows—"for better or worse, in sickness
and in health, till death do us part."

This I vow also: If it costs my life, I'll save
hers. . . .

It was late morning by the time Joel arrived at the Bennigan
homestead ten miles outside of Kent. He was glad to see the
big old house. The few pleasure horses the family kept stood
at the white fence, watching lazily as his red Jeep cruised up
the winding driveway. *At least this place hasn't changed,* Joel
thought as he parked behind his father's black Taurus.

Despite the bright winter sunlight, his mother's carefully
sculptured bushes were still blanketed with powdery snow.
Joel's Texas Steer boots crunched the salt his father had thrown
on the walkway to prevent accidents. *Ohio winters go on forever,* he grumbled. *When will it end?*

His black mood lifted, however, as he stepped through the
back door into his mother's kitchen. The smell of Millie's
homemade chocolate chip cookies filled the air with the comforting, chocolaty smell he remembered so well from his youth.
He couldn't help smiling as he shook off his heavy jacket and
stepped toward the small, matronly figure hovering over the
stove.

"Mother, I think you've always believed you could fix any
problem by baking up a batch of chocolate chip cookies," he
said lovingly as he reached down to give Millie Bennigan an
affectionate hug.

"Can't hurt anything, son," she answered, pulling back to
place one plump hand on his stubbly cheek.

The compassion he read in her faded, blue eyes and lined

face made his throat catch. "No, it can't hurt," he echoed softly, brushing back a lock of her gray hair that had strayed from her knotted bun and fallen across her forehead. "How could I manage without my family?"

"That's why God gave us families. He knows our needs. Come on, everyone's waiting in the living room."

A worried-looking Robert Bennigan rose as soon as Joel walked through the sliding oak doors. Joel embraced his father and looked around. All his siblings were present, circling the wagons as it were. Matthew, the oldest, and his wife, Sarah. His three sisters—Faith, Hope, and Charity. Joel knew they'd all taken time off work or school to meet with him, and he felt humbled and grateful. Even Ruthie, his disabled foster sister, sat in her wheelchair, her frail eleven-year-old body folded in on itself like an accordion. His heart melted at her wide smile.

Swallowing against the hard lump in his throat, Joel stood in front of the white marble fireplace and extended his forearms, palms up, in a gesture of supplication. "Thank you for being here," he said, his voice growing husky. He dropped his arms. "You don't know how much this means to me."

"We're in this together, son," said Mr. Bennigan. "Let's get down to business. What's happened in the past few hours?"

Joel turned to face his father, but he turned too sharply and too quickly. Arrows of pain shot up his leg, and his weaker knee began to buckle. He grabbed for the mantel, but Mr. Bennigan's strong arms reached out to steady him. "Whoa! The old knees bothering you again?"

"Yeah, Dad. I hurt the left one the other night. Too much weight at the wrong angle."

"Have you seen a doctor?" Mrs. Bennigan asked, frowning thoughtfully.

"Naw, no time. I'll go later . . . when Val's home."

His mother's eyes widened in concern. She pursed her lips, as if in a conscious effort not to lecture. "I'll fetch some ice.

You sit down. Boss' orders."

Leaning on his father's forearm, Joel hobbled over to the green leather couch in front of the fireplace and plunked down beside Charity. "Thanks, Dad. You know how these aches come and go," he said, looking into his father's handsome face.

The older man frowned, his heavy salt-and-pepper mustache giving him a stern look.

"You've got to take care of yourself, son, or you'll be no good to Val or anyone else. You may be a warrior for the Lord, but at the moment, you're a wounded warrior."

Joel gave a wry grin and rubbed his knees. The left one throbbed fiercely. He never thought of that initial injury without a feeling of thankfulness and awe at the mysterious workings of God. A vicious college football sacking when he had been quarterback had ended his dream of playing professional football. Along with the dream had died all the perks of that life—the fame, glory, money, prestige . . . and fast living. How he'd suffered—or thought he'd suffered—at the loss of his life of easy decadence. What vanity! Such empty, meaningless vanity. But he'd been blind to that truth back then.

Still, God had used the injury to draw Joel into His eternal, loving embrace. Little by little, as he had undergone a year of physical therapy to learn to walk again, he'd found himself drawn to the Lord's team. Having experienced the fleeting nature of worldly success, he'd begun looking for something more lasting, or Someone. He had finally found that Someone through the pages of the Bible he'd so carelessly tossed aside when his life had been going well. *Thank you, Lord. Help me to trust that Your perfect will is being worked out through this seeming disaster with Val also.*

Joel looked into his father's warm, brown eyes. "I went to the house early this morning," he began. "Shiloah answered. Then Jeremiah joined him." Joel's fists clenched at the thought of the gorilla even touching Val.

Millie returned with several packages of ice. She drew up an ottoman and helped Joel swing his feet onto it. She gently placed the ice over his knees. "There, son. You'll feel better in a few minutes."

Joel closed his eyes and drew a deep breath as the cold penetrated his throbbing joints. "Thanks, Mother. That feels good."

"Go on with your story," she said, perching on the arm of the couch beside him. "Did you see Val?"

Joel frowned at the memory. "Yes, I saw her. I'd only been there a few minutes when she appeared at the top of the stairs."

"How did she look?" asked Charity. Of Joel's three sisters, Charity had been closest to Val.

"Miserable. Worn out. Black circles under her eyes."

"Did she talk to you?" Charity probed.

"Yes, I suppose so. What I mean is, it was Val's voice and Val's body, but it didn't seem like Val. It sounded like she was reading a movie script. A very bad script."

"What did she say?" asked Hope.

He shrugged. "You won't believe it. I didn't. In fact, I still can't."

"What?" Millie's voice cracked with fear. "What could she say that was so terrible?"

There was a long pause while Joel collected his composure. "She's . . . divorcing me."

The blood drained from Millie Bennigan's round face. "Oh, son. That girl loves you more than life. That's not what she wants. Something's very, very wrong here."

"That's what I want to think, too, Mother. She says she's leaving me because I don't believe in Father Elijah—can you buy that? It's preposterous! Then . . . then Jeremiah grabbed her and claimed she was 'his woman' now. . . ."

Charity gasped. "Not that hairy ape I saw on campus?"

"Yes. Can you believe it? But, the worst thing was, she

didn't resist him. He wrapped those tree-trunk arms around my wife, and she let him! She buried her face in his sweater and ignored me!" The humiliation of the scene flooded over Joel again. Somehow, he could have taken anything but that—seeing his wife go willingly into the arms of another man.

"And if divorce isn't bad enough, she's accusing *me* of adultery! Shiloah said they had photographs." Even now, as he said the words out loud, Joel couldn't believe them. He shook his head.

"This is not what it appears, Joel," said his father slowly, his voice gravelly. "The girl's been brainwashed. They've already used her to win public sympathy through making her recant the exposé. I think they're using these adultery charges to get at our family's money."

"Brainwashed," Joel echoed miserably.

"How else can her drastic personality change be explained? I think deprogramming is the only option, at this point."

There was an air of definitiveness about Mr. Bennigan's voice that caught Joel by surprise. He jerked his gaze to his father, who stood beside the mantel. "You really think that's the answer?"

"I'm afraid so. Your mother and I have been talking to a deprogrammer out in California, a fellow who goes by the name Deliverer. The more we talk to him, the more we're convinced it's the right thing—the only thing."

Joel leaned back against the creaking leather. He studied the green Oriental carpet for several minutes. "I'm not convinced she's been brainwashed," he admitted finally. "We can't just kidnap Val off the street and hold her prisoner in some motel until she recants her beliefs."

"But that's just the point," his father interjected. "They're not *her* beliefs. They've been forced on her. Deprogramming isn't a crime against her free will because the cult has stolen that. Without freedom of thought, there can be no freedom of religion. And freedom of thought requires freedom of choice, decisions made without psychological coercion."

"Think about it, Joel," his mom put in. "Even God respects our free will and does not force us to believe . . . not even in Him."

Joel stared numbly at the toes of his boots. "But this is my *wife* we're talking about," he blurted out. "Val's not a zombie. She hasn't lost her mind, literally speaking."

"I'm not saying she has," his father went on. "The word *brainwashing* is a clumsy term for the ideological conversions forced by Chinese communists. Belief in Maoism was the goal. Thought reform was the means. It's well documented that the cults use similar techniques. So whether or not we use the word *brainwashing,* we know Val's been subjected to conditioning and indoctrination. She's in grave danger."

Joel knew his father was at least partially right. Val *was* in danger. And she needed rescuing. But brainwashed? There had to be some other explanation. There had to be. "How could they have brainwashed her so quickly?" he pressed. "They only had her one night. Manipulating the mind takes longer than that."

Mr. Bennigan frowned. "I don't have an answer to that one. Perhaps she never broke the hold they had over her in Ireland."

Joel sucked in his breath. That was one possibility he didn't want to consider.

Mr. Bennigan studied his son's face. "What if you don't rescue her? The last time, they shipped her out of the country. What'll they do this time? The cult is stockpiling weapons on their estate in the woods outside Brimfield. That's only fifteen miles away. What if they take her there?"

"I don't know," said Joel weakly.

"They're either arming terrorists or preparing for an apocalyptic showdown," his father continued.

"Oh, Joel, she's in danger!" cried Millie. "They're merciless as well as mad. Who knows what they'll do to her? We can't just stand by and leave her in their clutches!"

"I'm afraid for her, too," said Joel, his shoulders slumping helplessly. "But kidnapping is illegal."

"Let's look at our options." Mr. Bennigan began counting off on his fingers. "First, there's voluntary deprogramming. Can you persuade Val to willingly talk to Deliverer?"

"No." Images of Shiloah and Jeremiah loomed before Joel's eyes like devils from the pits of hell.

Mr. Bennigan was not to be deterred. "Second, if we petition the court to have Val declared legally incompetent, the cult may have her out of the country by the time the order comes through. Even if we rescued her physically, we'd still need a deprogrammer to free her mind."

Joel nodded miserably. *If she were brainwashed, that is.*

"That leaves deprogramming. You know the facts, son. It's not completely illegal. Only the abduction part. Deprogramming is just talk—confronting Val with the truth so she can start thinking for herself again."

Joel grunted and raked his large hand through his tawny hair. "This Deliverer character, is he a Christian?"

"Oh, yes," his mother assured him. "He believes he's doing God's work when he frees a cult member's mind. And, Joel, we have to agree with him. We wrestle not against flesh and blood."

Mr. Bennigan cleared his throat. "I've interviewed this young man at length," he began. "Years ago, he was a top leader in the cult. Father Elijah trained him personally. Deliverer's inside knowledge of the cult is phenomenal. He comes well recommended."

Joel looked around at the ring of strained, anxious faces surrounding him. Their love for Val was a palpable, living force in the room. "Matthew, do you agree?"

His older brother nodded. So did his twin sisters, Hope and Faith, and his sister-in-law, Sarah. Joel glanced over at Ruthie. She was dozing in her wheelchair, basking in a beam of sunlight filtering through the high bay window. He thought of the sacrifices his mother made daily to care for this severely disabled girl whom no one else had wanted. Perhaps, like Ruthie, Val was trapped and helpless in a situation not of her making. Like his mother, Joel would make whatever sacrifices were necessary.

Charity snugged up beside Joel. She ran her hand through his tousled hair. "Remember when we were kids, playing out in the woods, and I wandered off by myself that time?"

"Yeah. You locked yourself inside an old, abandoned refrigerator."

"But you came looking for me," Charity said softly. "What if you hadn't? I was trapped. I couldn't get out of that refrigerator by myself."

Joel winced, a muscle jerking in his unshaven jaw. Her words shot straight through his soul. He looked deeply into his sister's open, vulnerable face. Her eyes glistened with tears.

"Maybe that's how it is with Val," she continued. "She's trapped. She needs you to come after her. Calling in the deprogrammer may be the only way." Charity's words chilled Joel, despite the warmth of the cozy room. He held her hand, stroking it gently. She'd hit a nerve. He wasn't convinced Val was brainwashed, at least not in the way cult members or prisoners of war usually were. Somehow, that didn't fit. Kevin Milford might be brainwashed, but not Val. There was something else going on with her. For the life of him, Joel couldn't figure out what.

He lurched forward, burying his face in his hands. The sudden movement registered painfully in his legs. He flinched, steeling himself to ignore the pain. He had too much else on his mind. Brainwashing or not, Val was trapped, as helpless as Ruthie and in as much danger as Charity had been, locked in that abandoned refrigerator. However the cult had lured her back, however they'd trapped her, she was at their mercy now. What would become of her? What could he do? *Oh, God, forgive me if I'm making a mistake! Deprogramming is a drastic action, but it's our only option.* Even as Joel prayed, he knew God was there. . . .

He raised his head and looked at his family. His mouth was set in a grim line, for he knew what love bade him do.

"Let's call in the Deliverer."

ten

Val stared glumly at the lunch Gilead laid out for her on the wooden bench—one cold fried chicken wing, one badly bruised apple, and one plastic bottle filled with tap water. She was famished and exhausted after a hard, cold morning of peddling pamphlets. With only one piece of stale bread for breakfast, this lunch was more than a little disappointing. But then, Val knew from experience that hunger was a way of life for the Children of Last Days Light.

"Save the bottle," Gilead chirped, apparently undaunted by the meager rations. Rebecca, the cult cook, fed the disciples on cast-offs from supermarkets and restaurants, even from dumpsters.

Gilead dug into her backpack and produced an identical brown-bag lunch for herself. Val could see from the crease marks that the bag had been recycled many times.

"Praise the Lord! Eat light—we're living in the end times!" Gilead said in a sing-song voice, flinging her arms up in the air in a gesture of praise. "Hurry, so we can get back to the Lord's work."

Val squirmed with embarrassment as students passing by stared at the strange picnic on the bench outside the library. She supposed that two shivering women, huddled over a couple of forlorn-looking apples and chicken wings, made a strange sight. Val's stomach growled. She bit into the chicken, as eager to hide her true feelings from Gilead as to satisfy her hunger pangs.

The menu hasn't changed. Val remembered the meals of squishy, brown bananas and Kool Aid. Peanut butter for dinner. A donut for breakfast. She knew it was an important part of the control regime: Keep the followers tired, under-nourished, and overwhelmed; the mind is easier to conquer when the body is hungry and tired.

As she chewed the mealy apple, Val wondered where Shiloah and Jeremiah were lunching. The Steak House or the Pizza Barn? Leaders enjoyed special privileges, paid for with the money collected by lowly disciples like herself.

"Praise the Lord for good food, Tamar." Gilead licked her fingers, then rubbed them on her brown wool coat. The coat was shabby. Val guessed that it predated the cult since Shiloah didn't allow money for clothes. "Let's get back to work. Time's a wastin' and souls are going to hell and the end is coming soon." Gilead jumped up and began to gather her pamphlets.

"How're you doing on your quota?" Val asked.

"I've sold about one hundred. And you?"

"Well, I'm not doing so well . . . would you believe about fifty?" Val's heart sank when she saw a frown darken Gilead's face. "But I have faith I'll collect my three hundred dollars before dark," she added quickly.

"Sister Tamar, are you taking Father Elijah's word seriously?" Gilead stopped stacking her pamphlets and shot a withering look at Val. Impatiently, she tossed her long red hair over her shoulder. "You need to work harder. The end is coming. The plagues of Egypt will soon be poured out," she said grimly.

Val was about to take a drink, but her hand stopped halfway to her mouth. *Plagues of Egypt?* A chill ran through her body. *That's what Shiloah had called the purple virus. The mighty plagues of Egypt . . . the Lord's punishment on this wicked generation . . . our God the avenging angel.* Some-how, Val had thought that the virus was solely a pernicious tool of blackmail, used on herself and maybe a few others to enforce the will of Father Elijah. She'd never thought . . . oh, no! It was too horrible to contemplate.

Still, she had to know the truth. Val threw out a little test. She took a sip of water and, without meeting Gilead's gaze, said as nonchalantly as possible, "Oh, yes. The river of blood."

"How can you be so calm when the Lord may bring down his plagues on this wicked world tomorrow? Really, Tamar, you've got to repent and get right with the Lord. You don't have a burden for souls. When the Lord smites the Egyptians and turns their blood into rivers, it will be too late to save them. And God will hold you accountable." Gilead's words seemed to tumble out in a great rush.

Tomorrow? The Lord might bring down his plagues tomorrow? That could mean only one thing . . . *the virus. Surely the cult wasn't going to . . .* Val's grip tightened around the plastic bottle.

"Gilead, you don't really think the plagues could happen *tomorrow,* do you?" She willed her voice to remain calm. She couldn't believe she was asking this question about a lethal, flesh-eating virus. But then, who would have thought such a virus could have ended up in the hands of madmen?

Gilead drew back, her brown eyes wide and frightened. "We know not the day nor the hour, sister. But when it happens, we must flee like birds to our mountain hideout. Shiloah says it's nearly time. Father Elijah will be coming soon to strike the waters of the wicked with his staff. C'mon, we've wasted enough time in vain babbling. God will punish us."

Val struggled to comprehend what she'd just discovered as she watched Gilead walk up to a small cluster of students coming out of the library. She thrust a pamphlet into each student's hand, announcing shrilly, "Repent before the plagues of Egypt destroy the wicked."

One Hispanic boy apparently didn't understand and asked his girlfriend for a translation. When he understood, he doubled over with laughter.

"It's not funny!" Gilead cried. "God will punish you for

rejecting His prophet!"

Snickering, the group moved away and Gilead marched on to her next victim. She cast a scornful glance over her shoulder as if to urge Val to hurry. Immediately, Val sprang to her feet and began distributing leaflets like a cartoon character in fast-forward, running from student to student, imploring them to buy pamphlets. The mechanical activity away from Gilead's scrutiny gave her a chance to think.

Gilead's right. This is no laughing matter. Val reviewed her terrifying experience with Shiloah in the basement less than thirty-six hours ago. She'd thought he was demented, bent on frightening her by threatening Joel. It hadn't crossed her mind that the virus could be part of a bigger plan—a sinister terrorist plot to be unleashed on the general public as part of Father Elijah's doomsday paranoia. Somehow, she'd blocked that idea. No wonder. It was too alarming, too bizarre, too full of terror. Even now, she didn't want to entertain the possibility that Father Elijah could be hatching a plan so hideously evil. . . .

But it fit, didn't it? She already knew the CLDL was promoting terrorist activities to hasten the end of the world. Maiming innocent men, women, and children didn't faze them. "Holy terrorism," they called it. Val had always thought this consisted of supplying guns and money to the likes of the IRA or Libyan extremists. But why wouldn't Father Elijah want to dabble in biotechnical terrorizing? What would stop him? Certainly not his conscience. Why wouldn't he release deadly virus into the water, if he thought God was telling him to?

Val stopped in her tracks. Her stomach knotted. *It can't be true! It can't!* She wanted to scream. Her pamphlets fluttered to the ground. She fell to her knees in the snow and scrambled to pick them up before Gilead saw. *Dear God, why are You letting me see this? Why me, Lord?*

Suddenly, the bloody gerbil cage flashed before her mind.

Rivers of blood. We know not the day, but it's soon. . . . Her stomach heaved. She threw herself behind a frozen rhododendron bush and vomited.

⋇

Val's head was pounding by the time Shiloah dragged her into the lawyer's office that afternoon. The smell of stale cigars in the small, dark, airless room only heightened the pain.

"Tamar, this is our attorney, Bill Lovel," Shiloah introduced them with a careless wave of his hand.

The bald, oily little man behind the desk didn't bother to stand or shake Val's hand. He merely grunted and motioned for her to take a seat on the grimy tartan couch.

"How much we doin' him for?" He directed his obscene question to Shiloah. Val felt invisible, a mere pawn to get what they wanted.

"His family owns Bennigan's Grocery chain all across Ohio. He should be good for a million, at least. If you've done your job and gotten the goods on him, that is."

A million dollars? They are going to take Joel for a million dollars? Val closed her eyes and rubbed her temples. *Lord, this can't be happening. Please tell me this isn't happening.*

"'Course I got the goods!" Lovel snapped. "What kinda operation you think I'm runnin' here?"

Val heard him rustling in a drawer. She didn't want to open her eyes. She never wanted to open her eyes again. Maybe if she kept them shut, she'd wake up and all this would have been a dream. A hideous, crazy dream.

"Piece o' cake," said Lovel, his voice syrupy. "That guy should learn to stay away from those female parishioners of his. Now ain't this a masterpiece?"

Shiloah let out a whistle. "I gotta hand it to you, Lovel. She's a beaut. His own wife will believe in his cheatin' heart when she sees this baby."

The next thing she knew, Val was being jerked to her feet

and shoved roughly over to Lovel's desk. When she saw the large black and white photos strewn across the surface, she gasped. She counted eight—all showing Joel in compromising situations with women. "How did you do this?" she cried.

"Hey, little lady, ain't much we can't do with computer technology," said Lovel, spreading his fat hands in a helpless gesture. He shrugged his shoulders as if to say it wasn't his fault—the computer did it.

"This is character assassination, and you know it!" Val blurted, tears welling up in her eyes. She pounded her fist on the desk, causing the photographs to jump. *How could they do this to the man I love?*

Shiloah caught her arm in a vise-like grip. "Tamar, you seem to be forgetting the purpose of our little visit to Mr. Lovel. Look at it this way, he's on your side. You just sign his papers and Joel will get no visitors . . . and nothing unusual in his orange juice."

Fear and anger knotted inside Val. These evil men held all the cards. *For now. Lord, I trust you. You're my light and my salvation, whom shall I fear?* She glanced from Shiloah's thin face to Lovel's paunchy one. Shiloah was grinning diabolically; Lovel bit off a chunk of chewing tobacco and spit into a filthy Styrofoam cup on his desk. Val noticed the trail of brown stains on his dingy white shirt.

It's come to this, Lord? These men are going to destroy my marriage? You can't let them get away with it! You can't! Her hands clenched into hard fists, her fingernails digging painfully into her palms. Anguish ripped through her, making her feel light-headed.

Trust the Lord with all your heart, and do not rely on your own insight, came a soft voice from within. Val felt herself flinch. She was forgetting Who was really in charge. *Oh, Father, forgive me for doubting You. Help me not to try to figure things out for myself.* As if in response, another thought whispered assurance: *Is anything too hard for the Lord?*

No, Lord, her heart answered. *I trust You to bring victory out of this evil situation.*

Val blinked, amazed at the calmness that had come over her. It was as though a mighty wind had rushed into her being, filling her, strengthening her to face the powers of darkness that surrounded her and the evil present in these men. She felt a strength beyond her own. "Very well, gentlemen, let's get on with this. Show me where to sign."

❧

On the floor next to the window, Val tossed and turned on her hard pallet. Gilead's heavy snoring filled the air. Six other women, mostly new recruits, lay passed out in sleeping bags on the floor. Since Gilead was the most senior sister, she got the only bed. Even after midnight, Val found herself too exhausted and overwhelmed to relax. She lay with her hands behind her head, gazing up at the frosty winter stars through the curtainless window, taking solace from their silent praise of their Creator and offering her own.

She kept turning the events—the momentous events—of the day over and over in her mind, like pieces of a giant jigsaw puzzle. How did they fit? Where was God's design in all this craziness? At first, she'd gone along with Shiloah in order to protect Joel. So far, that appeared to be a good strategy. They hadn't hurt her husband . . . yet.

All during the long, tedious hours of distributing tracts, she'd tried to come up with a way to warn Joel that his life was in danger—another note or possibly a covert phone call—although that would be difficult since she was never alone. And if she did happen to be successful in getting through to Joel, would Shiloah take his revenge on *her* when Joel arrived with the police? It would take only a second to splatter her body, or even Joel's, with the contents of that vial. Shiloah would be arrested, no doubt, but the damage would already be done.

And why wouldn't Shiloah resort to such violence when the chips were down? He himself had chortled that revenge was sweet. Moreover, he probably knew where Joel's parents lived; they were listed in the telephone book. The Bennigan family would make a nice, easy target with their well water. Many innocent people could be in jeopardy if she made a mistake. No, she decided, both she and Joel—even the whole Bennigan clan—had to be safely out of the cult's grasp before the police were contacted.

But since Gilead's revelation at lunchtime, things had grown even more complicated. Now Val knew Joel wasn't the only target. As far as she could tell, Father Elijah planned to re-lease this virus into the public water supply: *Turn the rivers to blood, the blood to rivers.* It all made such poetic sense in the minds of a madman. Now untold numbers of people were in imminent danger of being "melted," as Shiloah had put it so chillingly.

But when? And where? In Kent, or all around the country, or just in the fifteen states where the cult had houses, including the ranch in Oregon for children of cult members? Or maybe just major cities? She needed this information before she could stop the plagues.

She had to find out the details of the "plague of Egypt." She needed dates, times, and places. And, until she found them, she had to play along with their little game. . . .

But filing divorce papers, charging Joel with infidelity? That thought clawed at her heart. Lovel had thrown in mental and physical cruelty charges against Joel as well, probably for Shiloah's perverted amusement. Lovel himself was slime, pure slime. Apparently he did a lot of work for the cult, including suing parents who tried unsuccessfully to deprogram their children.

Deprogramming! She hadn't thought about that! Could Joel be thinking of bringing in a deprogrammer? Perhaps she'd put on such a convincing act that by now he believed she'd been brainwashed. How else could he, and his family, explain her drastic, overnight change? *Oh, no. That can't happen!* His kidnapping her—however much she wanted to be rescued right now—would ruin her plans.

Val flipped herself over onto her stomach and pounded her pillow softly. Gilead's snoring grew louder. *He can't have me kidnapped and deprogrammed, Lord. Not now! There's too much at stake! If I blow my cover, who's to say Shiloah won't get panicky and release the virus immediately? And how do I act with Joel? Do I resist the deprogramming and escape back to the cult at the first opportunity? Now, that's lunacy. Escape back to the cult!* Val chuckled grimly.

But then, everything's crazy. I'm deceiving the man I love in order to protect his life. I'm pretending to be a cult member so I can stop a lunatic from poisoning the public water. And now I'm suing my beloved for divorce and a humongous amount of money!

Suddenly, Gilead coughed and turned noisily. Startled, Val clamped her eyes shut, pretending to be asleep, and willed herself to stop thinking about escape—almost as if Gilead could not only read her mind, but could read it while she was asleep! Val realized that the hairs on the back of her neck were standing on end. *This is ridiculous. These people may be fruit and nut cases, but they're not omnipotent,* she chided herself.

But Val knew full well her nerves were just about shot. She didn't know how much longer she could hold up. *I can do all things through Christ,* came another thought from a Scripture passage Joel had taught recently. *Yes, Lord. I believe that. But please give me the strength I need. I can't endure on my own.*

eleven

Joel Bennigan fell asleep on his knees, his head resting on the edge of the bed, his clasped hands on top of the Bible in front of him. For most of the night, he'd been pleading for God to protect Val and to defeat the powers of darkness that surrounded her. He could almost feel the spiritual battle raging. Somewhere around midnight, fatigue overtook him.

The grandfather clock in the living room striking two roused him. Shaking off his drowsiness, he resumed his prayer. "Father," he began, feeling the warmth of the Holy Spirit begin to flow through him, "I pray that You will put a hedge of protection around my wife as You did around Job of old. In the name of Jesus, I rebuke and bind the powers of darkness that are attacking her. I claim the power of the blood of Jesus to cover Val and keep her from harm. . . ."

Joel leaned his forehead against the bed again. His face was wet with tears as he drifted into an uneasy slumber and began to dream. He was running, out of breath. His side ached. The thick, green forest around him seemed bent on hindering his progress. Gnarled old roots sprang up from the mossy earth and tripped him up. Ravens mocked him. Crooked, claw-like branches raked at his hair and face. He could taste the blood from the scrapes, but he pressed on. He was looking, seeking desperately, but for what? Or whom?

Suddenly, he came to a clearing in the depth of the forest. He stopped running and tried to catch his ragged breath. At first the reflection of brightness almost blinded him. He blinked and rubbed his eyes. *What is that massive white rectangle?* The full noontime sun reflected off its surface, dazzling him with the brightness. He rubbed his eyes with the backs of his hands, then noticed that his hands were trembling, slick with the sweat of fear. *Why?* An unknown terror closed around his heart like a hangman's noose.

Then he heard it. A voice. A pitiful whimpering from inside the bright white rectangle. "Help me, Joel! You're my only hope!" He lunged forward, grabbed a silver handle, and yanked with all his might. The door of the old refrigerator swung open and Val fell out, gasping for air. Her face was tear-stained, and her fingers, were bleeding from clawing the inside of the locked door.

He knelt and gathered her into his arms. *Don't let her die, Lord. Please. Not now. Not like this.* He cradled her face in his hand as his tears fell on her mass of chestnut hair. "Val, don't leave me. When I couldn't find you, I felt that part of me had died, as if someone had torn my heart out of my chest. I've been looking everywhere for you. . . ." *Please, God, don't let it have been too late.*

He drew a ragged breath and checked the pulse in the graceful curve of her neck. Love for her washed over him until he felt he was drowning. He raised Val's cool, limp hand to his lips and kissed her palm. His stomach tightened painfully. "Forgive me, my love," he cried. "Forgive me for not protecting you."

Her eyes remained closed, feathery lashes sweeping the pale cheeks. She looked beautiful, peaceful, like a child asleep. *Dear God, I want to grow old with this woman. I want to have children with her, Lord. You destined us to be together. Don't take her from me now. . . .*

Suddenly, he seemed to be outside his body, looking at himself cradling his unconscious Val in a forest clearing. A beam of golden sunlight pierced the tall, dark pines, suffusing them both in its glow. Part of him backed away until he could see both Val and himself resting in the outstretched hand of God.

He felt safe. Everything was in God's hands.

What does this mean, Lord? Joel asked, still deep in his dream.

Words from the Scripture imprinted themselves on his heart, words in which Joel found no relevance: *No city or house divided against itself will stand.*

What "house," Lord? What "divide"? Please tell me what You mean. Joel's anguish and sudden fear tasted metallic.

No answer came. But before his eyes, the forest scene took on a purplish cast. The color began at the sky and, like a child coloring a page in a coloring book, an invisible paintbrush swept back and forth until everything was that vivid hue.

Joel jolted awake. Sweat beaded on his forehead, and his heart hammered so hard, he could barely breathe. He looked down at his arms, where Val had lain in his dream. They were empty. Just like his life without her. One great lonely, aching void.

He continued kneeling, staring at his hands as if they no longer belonged to him. He noticed his fists clenching. His jaw tightened. His breathing shortened. He felt a great fury building within him, like black rain clouds gathering for a storm. Who did these people think they were, making off with his wife? Trapping her in their cult? Using her? Distorting the gospel and enslaving Val and other children of God with their false teachings?

His anger began to bubble and seethe. But it wasn't the self-absorbed anger of his rabble-rousing college years. Joel had been no stranger to the misdirected, frustrated, unholy anger of barroom brawling before he'd come to know the Lord. The anger that inflamed his blood now—tensing his muscles and making his breath ragged—was different. This was solid, purposeful, filled with zeal—not mindless hatred. This was the righteous anger of Christ overturning the money-changers' tables. The anger that propelled Christian soldiers onward in battle. This anger was the roar of the lion of God.

This was the anger that would help him win the war for his wife . . . or die trying.

∾

Val turned the corner of Main and Market and blinked. Perhaps the sun glaring off the snow had blurred her vision momentarily. Perhaps it was the result of getting only four hours of sleep in three days. Or the constant hunger that gnawed at her insides. But Val didn't think so. No, her eyes weren't deceiving her. Not today. Nor had they deceived her, she now realized, on that fateful evening before she'd walked out on Joel.

Finn O'Dwyer of the outlawed Irish Republican Army was in Kent, Ohio. She'd just seen him with her own eyes. He and Jeremiah had just walked into Filthy McNasty's pub, both men puffing furiously on cigarettes. Jeremiah's face was partially obscured by a black fedora, but Val recognized the bulky body. It had been the wiry O'Dwyer with his black curly hair whom she'd seen ducking into the same lewd establishment on her way home from class the night Joel had told her about Kevin Milford and she'd met up with Shiloah. There was no doubting it now.

What's going on here, Lord? Why have You allowed me to see this?

She peered back around the corner at Gilead, who was peddling pamphlets to the customers pouring out of the Downtown Deli. Originally, Val and Gilead had been scheduled to sell Father Elijah's writings in Cleveland that day. But, for some reason he didn't explain, Shiloah changed his mind at the last minute and ordered them to stay in Kent.

So Jeremiah, or rather, Garret Foley, probably thinks the coast is clear because there are no disciples in town today. Usually the leaders didn't openly flaunt their higher standard of living before the cold, hungry disciples. Father Elijah claimed enough "spiritual maturity" to live in open luxury, but his underlings put up more of a façade of leading "simple, revolutionary" lives to promote the cause.

Which cause? Terrorism? The end of the world? Pouring deadly viruses into the public water supply? She still couldn't believe that Father Elijah would go to such extremes to hasten the apocalypse and usher in his own thousand-year reign sooner.

Val rounded the corner to join Gilead. *She knows about the terrorism, if not the virus,* Val decided as she witnessed the determined, grim look on the womans' otherwise pretty face. *She's been in the Family for years, long enough to be trusted with this "higher knowledge," even if she is a woman. But like lying to collect funds, she probably passes it off as necessary for God's purposes. The end always justifies the means.*

Val couldn't help but wonder if Father Elijah himself believed his doctrines. Was he that delusional? Insane? Perhaps he suffered from some kind of paranoia. She'd read that some cult leaders actually did wholeheartedly believe their own claims. Others consciously ran a con game, raking in the money and the women.

Val knew that of the two, those who really believed their own lies were the more dangerous. That's when a tyrant could cross the line and became a fanatic like Jim Jones or David Koresh, bringing death on himself and his followers in the name of God. Or on the innocent people around them.

As far as she could make out, Father Elijah fell into the category of the self-deluded. Or satanically deluded, more likely. *After all, who is the father of lies?* she mused.

She wondered about Shiloah. He was ruthless and cunning, all right. His devotion to his father's goals ran like a fever in his blood, burning away all conscience. Yes, he was a true believer, firmly under Father Elijah's thumb his whole life. Val shuddered at the thought. What must his childhood have been like, growing up as the only child of the great prophet?

No wonder Shiloah was sick and twisted.

Jeremiah's scarred face flashed across her mind. Was he a true believer? If not, why was he with the cult? What was in it for him? It wasn't the easiest of lifestyles for an ex-con, but it did give him the satisfaction of wielding power, at least within the group. Jeremiah and Shiloah seemed cut from the same cloth, but there was something different about Jeremiah, something Val couldn't quite put her finger on. . . .

"Sister Tamar, you're not daydreaming, are you?" Gilead asked sharply.

"No, Gilead. I'm praying for help." *And that's no lie.*

"Enough praying. God wants our work, not our words."

Val picked up momentum with her distribution. She had found that a smile could open many pockets, and she silently prayed for each person who took a pamphlet, beseeching the Lord to protect them from the evil influence of Father Elijah. She wondered where the self-proclaimed prophet was right now. This morning, Shiloah had announced that he had come out of seclusion where, "like Moses in the desert," he had been listening to the Lord's end-time plans. Now he was en route east, planning a stop at each of the fifteen cult houses dotted across the country from San Diego to Boston.

Shiloah had warned the disciples to stay alert, ready to greet the mighty Father Elijah when he arrived sometime soon. "You know not the day nor the hour," he'd taunted. Gilead had burst into tears of ecstasy. Rebecca the cook had swooned and actually fainted. A visit from Father Elijah was an unprecedented favor.

Val had felt her stomach turn in revulsion, but her curiosity had been piqued. She'd only seen photographs of Father Elijah; she'd never met nor talked to him. Yet, because of this man, she'd lost her husband and thousands—maybe even millions— of people were in grave danger. Yes, she wanted to meet him. She wanted to see for herself what kind of human being could bring about such catastrophic wickedness. Above all, she needed to find out the details of his plan to put that wickedness into action.

Pamphlet trade was brisk outside the Deli, and Val wanted to meet her quota today. Yesterday, she'd gone without dinner because she'd failed to bring in the required sum of money. She joined Gilead and began passing out pamphlets, careful to ask for donations when a tract was accepted. The cult, she knew, never actually "sold" Father Elijah's writings.

I've got to hang in here until I learn the details of the dooms-day plan, Val reminded herself as she handed a pamphlet to a young woman with a toddler balanced on her hip.

"Please read it and donate to our work with young people," Val parroted the usual line.

The blond woman smiled. "And what work do you do?"

"We help drug addicts." *Well,* some *cult members used to be drug addicts.*

"Oh? Do you run recovery centers?" The woman tilted her head to one side, smiling at her daughter.

"Yes, we have fifteen centers spread across the country. We even have work in Ireland." *At least that's not an outright lie.* Val swallowed hard as the woman handed her a ten-dollar bill. She quickly went on to the next person. It would take many such donations to make her quota.

Forgive me, Lord, for spreading this false gospel and for collecting money for drug rehabilitation centers that don't even exist. Please don't let these people read this trash. I pray they all lose their pamphlets! Please help me uncover the plan quickly, today, so I can put a stop to all this.

　　　　　　　　　　　　　　☙

The winter gloaming had set in, and still Val had not collected her three hundred dollars. It was after dinnertime and her stomach growled in protest. Her teeth chattered with the cold although she'd begun running from person to person just to keep her blood circulating. Gilead, she noticed, had never let up. She was single-minded, totally focused on selling. It didn't seem to bother her one bit that she and Val had been out on the streets for twelve hours straight. They'd taken time to eat one cold hotdog each, but that had been their only break today.

By now they had worked their way up to the campus. "We can get the students going to evening classes," Gilead had said with her usual unstinting cheerfulness.

They started distributing tracts outside the student center, catching the students leaving the dining hall for class. That's where they were when Val felt a heavy hand come down hard on her shoulder. Frightened, she spun around.

"Jeremiah!"

His dark face creased into something resembling a smile. "Little sister Tamar, I'm glad to see you working so hard for the Lord." His breath reeked of alcohol and tobacco.

Val started to back away from him, but he grabbed her forearm and squeezed. "Hey, hey, I'm your leader, you know. You can't just walk away from your leader, or God will punish you."

"You know that's a crock," Val hissed. "Let me go!"

"Not until we've had a little talk so you'll be knowin' what your future position will be as wife of a leader." He laughed coarsely.

Val looked from Jeremiah, who seemed more huge and menacing than usual in his thick leather jacket and black fedora, and shot an imploring look to Gilead who was watching the exchange from twenty feet away.

"Hey, Gilead, the Lord has given me a message for Tamar!" thundered Jeremiah across the brick student plaza. "Can you manage for ten minutes by yourself?"

"Sure thing, Brother Jeremiah," she called back gaily, obvious deference in her voice.

"That's the nice thing about leadership, Tamar," he whispered as he slipped his arm around Val's tense shoulders. "The leader always gets his way. Always. Do I make myself clear?"

"Yes." Val's stomach tightened and her pulse raced with fear as Jeremiah steered her toward a wooden bench on the other side of the grassy commons around the plaza. The area was thick with trees, deserted, and dark. *Dear Father, protect me. Use this situation for good . . . please.*

As they walked, Val noticed Jeremiah's unsteady gait. Once he actually stumbled and only saved himself from falling by grabbing onto a large oak tree. Her eyes narrowed. *He must have been drinking all afternoon, ever since he and O'Dywer went into that bar. That could give me the advantage if I need to make a run for it.* The other time she'd seen him with the terrorist, the two men had been drinking in a bar in Dublin.

"Make yourself comfortable," he said, making a mock flourish toward the bench.

She sat down. *Thou wilt keep him in perfect peace, whose mind is stayed on Thee. I claim this promise as my own, Lord. Keep me in perfect peace so I can keep my wits about me and get the information I need.*

"So ye filed for divorce?" Jeremiah asked, plunking his huge body down beside her. His eyes raked her body crudely. The drink seemed to thicken his brogue.

"Did I have a choice?"

"Nope. I guess Shiloah's got ye over a barrel—or over a purple vial."

Val caught her breath. *So he does know about the virus.*

"And ye'll marry me soon," he grunted. It was a statement of fact, not a question. "After all, who are you to go against God's will?" He chuckled slyly. *He doesn't believe this stuff,* Val thought wildly, her heart racing with the thrill of her discovery. *He's not a true believer.* But if he wasn't indoctrinated—brainwashed—what was he? The possibilities sent chills down her spine.

"Hey, babe, whadaya say we get cozy and get to know each

other better? I've had a thing for you since the first moment I set eyes on ye. I ain't so bad," he crooned as he wrapped his arms around her.

Val flinched. The smell of whiskey was overpowering. It was time to play her trump card. "Jeremiah," she said as sweetly as she could manage, "can you explain something to me?"

"Anything for a kiss, darlin'."

Val stiffened. "Before any kissing, tell me why Finn O'Dwyer is in Kent. I saw you with him today, going into Filthy McNasty's." She dropped her gaze from his scowling face and pretended to study her stack of pamphlets.

Whack! She had never even seen his hand coming. Her cheek stung from his open-palmed slap. "You just keep your trap shut, d'ye hear me?" he snarled, his black eyes flashing dangerously.

Val's hand flew to her hot cheek. Tears stung her eyes. But despite her fear, a small voice in the back of her mind whispered with an excitement that bordered on euphoria: *He's hiding something. He has a secret, and its name is Finn O'Dwyer.*

Jeremiah stood up and jerked Val to her feet, giving her a hefty shove toward the student plaza and Gilead. "Get back to work, woman. And ye better keep yer silence, or I'll be taking my marital rights, with or without Shiloah's permission."

All his threats couldn't dampen Val's hopefulness. Knowledge was power, and now she had power over Jeremiah.

But that knowledge also put her in a dangerous position. A cornered bear could turn vicious. Or deadly.

twelve

Val hung onto two moist, soft hands—Gilead's on one side of her, Rebecca's on the other. The disciples had formed a large circle around Shiloah and Jeremiah, swaying in time to the cult songs the two leaders were strumming on their guitars. It was past midnight. After three hours of being confined with twenty people in the small orange living room, Val felt hot and oppressed.

"Any day now, any way now, we shall be released. . . ." Shiloah closed his eyes, carried away by the fervor of his misplaced faith. Val sang along with her whole heart. *Amen, Lord. That's my prayer. Release me. Release all of us from Father Elijah's madness.*

The circle moved together like a ripple on a lake. Overwrought emotionally, Rebecca wept softly as she sang. Gilead, Kevin Milford, Boaz, and the others kept their eyes clamped shut, their faces scrunched in earnestness. *They really believe,* thought Val.

There was one other person whose eyes remained open. Jeremiah. His hot, angry gaze was fixed on her. All night long he'd shot leering looks her way. Each time, her skin crawled. She lowered her head, pretending to be enraptured by the singing. *Resist the devil and he will flee from you,* she quoted to herself.

Now she felt Jeremiah's flinty gaze boring into her again. She looked up. His eyes appeared coal black in the dim overhead light. Val glared at him and then snapped her own eyes shut. She continued to move in time to the music and mouth the words to the cult songs, but within the privacy of her own mind, she struggled to put together the pieces of the "plague puzzle," as she'd begun to call it.

Jeremiah didn't want it known Finn O'Dywer was in town. That much was obvious. Neither did he want anyone leaking the information that he was consorting with O'Dywer. What was she to make of that? In Ireland, *both* Jeremiah and Shiloah had met with the terrorist. Why would Jeremiah meet with him secretly now? Didn't Shiloah know O'Dywer was in the States?

She had to find out. And quickly—before Jeremiah arranged a "secret" meeting with *her*. She shuddered at the memory of his arm around her shoulder and his beefy, bearded face so close to hers on the bench. . . .

Val sighed and kept singing. *Lord, how am I to find out this information? It's not something they'll just announce, especially when I'm around. I need a break, Lord. I need someone to slip up and tell me the plan . . . something, Lord, before . . . before it's too late for Joel and me.*

With a heavy heart, she turned her thoughts to her husband. Could his love for her survive this ordeal? After publicly rejecting him on TV as well as to his face, how could she possibly hope their relationship would remain intact? For his own protection, she was trying to convince him she didn't love him anymore. Yet it frightened her to think he might actually believe her charade. Still, that was a possibility. Especially after the divorce papers were served.

Dear Lord, what if he falls for my deception? Or what if I've hurt him so badly that when I finally get out of here and tell him the truth, he won't be able to forgive me? What if I've damaged our relationship beyond repair? How can I expect Joel to just forget and pick up where we left off when I've caused him such pain?

Val's heart started to pound. Her mouth felt dry as packing ice. Blinking back tears, she opened her eyes.

Jeremiah was watching her.

Suddenly Shiloah stopped the music in mid-song. His cold, green eyes scanned the surprised young faces surrounding him. If Jeremiah reminded Val of an angry bear, Shiloah was more like a calculating snake. And like a snake, he was always coiled—watching, tense, poised to strike and wound with his poisonous tongue and his counterfeit gospel.

"Praise God, brethren, I have great news for you tonight." Shiloah began to speak in a normal tone that quickly escalated in volume and tempo. "Great and mighty news, as glorious and cosmically important as the message of the angels to the shepherds in Bethlehem! News that will save the world from eternal damnation!" Shiloah's voice rose dramatically, then he paused, giving the faithful sheep time to absorb the full impact of his words.

"Tell us the good news, brother," said Jeremiah, as if on cue.

"Amen! Tell us!" echoed Gilead, followed by a chorus from the other earnest disciples.

Shiloah smiled, a slow, sneaky smile. *What a fake!* Val thought in disgust. *He thrives on this hysteria and adulation.* Jeremiah began strumming his guitar and built to an incessant, pounding rhythm that carried the chant to a feverish pitch.

Shiloah spread his arms wide. His gaunt, hawk-like face contorted into a sneer. In his black sweater and pants, he looked like a vulture about to swoop. "Blessed brethren, God is about to visit you. In three days, Father Elijah will appear, bringing with him God's plans for the end of this perverted and wicked generation. Behold, he brings God's wrath in his hand! And he will reveal God's plan to smite the ungodly with the plagues of Egypt!"

The group exploded into hysterical shouting and weeping. Gilead fainted. Kevin Milford began screaming uncontrollably, his voice shrill. Boaz beat his brawny chest and fell to his knees, begging forgiveness for his offenses against the prophet.

Rebecca wept loudly. Jeremiah gloated.

"We must prepare!" cried Shiloah, gesturing wildly, his long ponytail flying. He flung his arms into the air and shouted at the top of his lungs. "Repent! The end is near! Let us go forth prepared with our lamps burning. Let us fast from all food for the next three days. And on the third day, the light shall shine forth and all will be revealed to God's Children of Light in these last days."

"Amen!" shrieked the disciples.

Val could almost reach out and touch the self-importance that swept like a tidal wave through the group. They believed they were the chosen ones, the elite. They, and no one else. God had favored them above everyone. God's revelation was coming to them . . . in just three days. Father Elijah was the end-time prophet, and they were the recipients of direct revelation through him.

Swollen with pride, they followed as Shiloah and Jeremiah began the chant, "Father E! Father E! Who do we love?"

"Father E! Father E! We love Father E!" the disciples cried in unison.

Jeremiah threw down his guitar and began pounding the air with his clenched fist. He often assumed this posture during the chanting, but tonight his pounding seemed even more aggressive. "Father E! Father E!" he bellowed. "Who gives us the power and the glory, forever?"

"Father E! Father E!" the group responded with equal gusto.

"Who will smite the wicked?"

"Father E! Father E!"

"Who will bring the plagues of Egypt?"

"Father E! Father E!"

Val trembled inwardly as the atmosphere of intoxicating frenzy grew into a mad intensity of anger and hatred for the world outside the group. The faces around her, especially Shiloah's and Jeremiah's, contorted in rage. Before her eyes, the collection of bedraggled, dispirited misfits became a mob, hungry for blood and revenge. They were glorying in their delusion of being the chosen ones, the saved ones, the ones to call down the plagues of God upon the world.

Her stomach churned. She stood transfixed by what she was witnessing. *So this is how mob mentality takes over!* It was grotesque, obscene. Evil pulsed through the room, and Val could imagine the demons of hell throwing fuel on the fire and laughing hysterically. Death and destruction were the work of hell, not heaven.

This is also part of the drama and manipulation, she thought, closing her eyes to the horror around her. *We're being led like lambs to the slaughter.*

&

Joel sat down hard on the stone bench facing Kent State University's May Fourth Memorial. The four pink marble markers, commemorating the four students slain by National Guardsmen during an anti-Vietnam War demonstration on May 4, 1970, loomed before him like giant tombstones reaching for the sky. Joel liked the peaceful atmosphere of this quaint memorial tucked into the heavily forested hillside. He walked up here often. It was a good place to think.

It was also one of the places he and Val had frequented . . . together.

Since her disappearance, he hadn't been able to work. Or eat. Or sleep. Instead, like a lost soul, he found himself returning to the places where they'd spent time together. He took off his woolen cap and drove his fingers through his hair. He was lonelier than he'd ever been in his life. It had been three days since Val had disappeared into the cult, yet his loss swept over him in a fresh wave of grief.

Sitting here on this bench without her, Joel could almost hear her soft, sweet voice. He shut his eyes, wishing he could change the past. If only he'd been a better husband. If only he'd done a better job of protecting her. . . .

"Val," he whispered hoarsely. Then, more urgently, "Val."

But his only answer was the lonely chirps of a few birds and the guilt that dogged him. His pain solidified into a heavy mass inside, weighing him down like a millstone around his neck. It was becoming harder and harder to move, to keep going, to keep hoping as this bizarre scenario unfolded. He'd walked aimlessly around the campus all morning, hoping to get a glimpse of her since cult members often came here on campus to sell pamphlets to the students. If he could just see her, talk to her alone. . . .

He was listless, bone-weary, drained even of anger. He couldn't summon the energy to walk another step. Activities that had once brought him joy—walking the campus, visiting this memorial, sipping coffee at Brady's—were now so much dust in his mouth. Without Val to share the small pleasures, life was empty. Small pleasures like the crunch of snow, the crackle of a fire, the softness of their fireside rug. . . .

Almost against his will, his thoughts flashed back to their morning of love on that rug. That was the day this nightmare had begun. He'd tried over breakfast to read to her about the after-effect of cults, but had ended up chasing her around the house, a chase that had ended with her willing surrender. . . . *Dear Lord, how can I bear life without her?*

Joel raked his hand through his hair again and took a long slow breath. The morning air was frosty. *We're pledged to each other until death. Our love can't have ended so soon. . . can it?*

When Val hadn't come home and then had publicly denounced him on TV, something within him had died. Maybe he hadn't known his wife as well as he'd thought he did. Did he even know himself? He shook his head. All he could be sure of was that Val was gone.

He remembered sitting with her here, in front of this memorial, watching the soft tendrils of her long chestnut hair blow about her face. He'd marveled at God's artistry in creating a woman with skin so creamy, lips so soft, eyes like emerald or the finest jade. Looking into those green eyes always gave him a kick in the stomach each time she looked at him with the intensity of a woman in love. Almond-shaped eyes, flecked with the gold of a sun-tipped summer leaf. . . .

Now, whenever he walked downtown or went to his office at the church, people stared, embarrassed. Everyone knew his wife had run out on him. And why not? Val's face and voice kept turning up on TV, in the newspaper, on the radio. Now folks didn't know what to say. After all, Joel was usually the one doing the comforting. He felt ashamed and humiliated. Yet he chided himself severely for entertaining those feelings.

"Why, Val?" he demanded through bared teeth. "Didn't I prove myself trustworthy enough? Didn't I vow to love you forever? What more could I have done?" A wave of frustration, then anger as hot and honest as fire, swept over him. The muscles in his jaw clenched. He narrowed his eyes and took a ragged breath, feeling his chest tighten. *Why did you deny me, Val? Why did you take my love and fling it back in my face? Don't you know you're mine and I love you more than life itself?*

He grimaced and kicked a stone across the walkway separating him from the memorial. He felt like a wild animal caught in a trap. His fists clenched and unclenched as he stared into the cold, silver sky. His love for his wife rendered him vulnerable to the steely teeth of the cult trap closing around them both.

❧

Val wasn't sure why she felt such a strong compulsion to climb Memorial Hill. She glanced across the narrow path at her partner, Gilead, who was still deep in conversation with a potential convert. Every day Gilead met the same student at this spot—a young, homesick freshman from West Virginia. And every day, Gilead made a little more headway. If she played her cards right, soon the girl would capitulate, turn all her worldly possessions over to the group, drop out of school, and move into the house on Oak Street. *That's probably why Shiloah keeps assigning us to Kent,* Val realized.

Wearily, she counted her pamphlets as she climbed the hill, walking the winding granite path that meandered between the bald trees. The memorial markers came into view just as Gilead and her victim slipped out of view behind her. *Thirty pamphlets. Forty. Forty-two! I've only sold forty-two tracts today!* But what did it matter? Shiloah had decreed a strict fast until Father Elijah arrived, so she wouldn't get any dinner, no matter how many letters she sold. Already she was starving. Perhaps she could sneak away from Gilead long enough to buy something from a vending machine.

Val sighed and looked up from her counting. Then she saw him. She stopped in her tracks and, stepping off the path, hid behind a thick tree. Apparently, he hadn't seen her. He was sitting, hunched over, face buried in his hands, on their bench opposite the memorial. His rugged masculinity sent her heart skipping. He wore his heavy brown leather jacket with the red tartan scarf she'd given him for Christmas. His fingers were clenched in his thick, tawny hair, which looked like it hadn't seen a comb since the night she'd left.

I've hurt him so badly, Lord, she grieved.

She knew she should backtrack as quickly and quietly as possible. If she walked on the patches of snow between the trees, he'd never hear her footsteps. Yet she found herself unable to move away. Her heart raced faster. Longing for her husband swept over her like great waves crashing against the rocks. Tears filled her eyes. She should leave, now. She should not jeopardize him in any way. Father Elijah would be here the day after tomorrow. . . .

Instead, against her better judgment, she stepped out from behind the tree in full view of Joel, and ran toward him. It all happened so fast that everything was a blur. She flung her stack of pamphlets on the ground. They scattered and fluttered across the granite like so many brittle, lifeless leaves.

Joel leaped to his feet, then doubled over in pain, clutching his left knee, and sat back down with a thud. Amazement flooded his handsome, rough-hewn features. "Val?"

She dropped to her knees beside him, cupping her hands around his dear face. His eyes filled with tears, like a summer sky brimming with rain. "I'm sorry. So sorry," she whispered hoarsely.

"Why?" His voice broke.

Fierce love for him washed over Val as she heard the heartbreak in his voice—but that same love made staying impossible. For his sake. For the sake of countless others. She backed away, biting her bottom lip, but he caught her by the shoulders.

He drew a ragged breath. His clear blue gaze searched her face. "Have you forgotten my promise that I'd come for you? I will. You're my wife and I love you, no matter how many times you may denounce me."

I love you too, Joel. I love you so much it's killing me to leave you again.

"Don't, Joel. For your own sake, don't. For my sake, leave me alone!" Val could see the pain of confusion reflected in his eyes. She couldn't bear to look, but neither could she bear to look away. She was so starved for the sight of him.

"I want you back, Val. When you left, you tore out my heart and took it with you." His voice was low and husky, like long-napped velvet brushing against her skin.

The old, familiar yearning for him rose within her as he caught her chin and lowered his mouth to cover hers. For a moment she allowed herself to melt into his kiss, to mold herself to his body, to feel the utter rightness of their love. He was the other part of her.

Then she remembered the purple vial. The blood-red gerbil cage. She jerked back. "Stay away from me!" she cried, jumping to her feet and grabbing as many pamphlets as she could gather in one swipe. "Trust me, it's for the best," she added gently when she saw his face spasm in pain. She didn't dare explain further.

Then she bolted down the hill as if legions of demons were in hot pursuit.

thirteen

Joel had touched her soft skin. He'd breathed in the scent of her and felt her velvety lips yield to his. Then she'd disappeared as suddenly as she'd come.

Had he imagined her? Was his need for her so desperate that he'd hallucinated his wife back into his arms?

Of course not. The abandoned Father Elijah pamphlets were proof that it had really been Val. She had said she was sorry. For what? For leaving him? For loving him? She had warned him not to come after her—for his own sake. What did that mean?

Well, whatever it meant, he was going after her, and all the cults in the world couldn't stop him. And the two men sitting there across from him in his parents' living room were going to help him accomplish that task.

"They call me Deliverer," said the brawny, fiftyish Hispanic in a strong Latino accent. "But my real name is Mario Santos. This is my assistant, Karl Lupe. He was also once a member of the CLDL." He gestured to the kid, who looked like a quarterback and weight-lifter rolled into one, complete with thick gold hoop earring. Apparently Karl didn't speak much. He communicated with grunts.

"Where'd you get the name *Deliverer*?" Joel asked.

"A nickname given me by some cult members I rescued. I guess they kinda looked on me like an angel of deliverance."

"We see you that way, too, Mr. Santos," said Millie.

The family spent the next hour over coffee and homemade chocolate chip cookies, sharing with Deliverer the details of the last few days. He nodded occasionally. Once or twice he asked a question, but for the most part, he just listened thoughtfully, his huge hand curled under his chin.

"Uh huh. I've seen a lot of people float. They can get trapped back in the cult so quick it'd make your head spin," he said when Joel finished. "Cults thrive on ex-members publicly recanting. It makes the group look real good. Like they're victims of the media."

Joel felt the tension drain from his shoulders. He liked Deliverer. There was something honest and direct about him. The man had been sued by different cults, but he kept right on doing what he believed was right. "Do you think she could have been brainwashed?"

"Possibly. She could have floated and gotten herself nabbed. But in any case, this girl needs rescuin'. You know them maniacs have enough guns to mow down the entire population of Kent."

Millie Bennigan hid her face behind her hands and began to sob. Her husband sat down beside her and put his arms around her. Karl nodded sympathetically.

"OK, Deliverer, let's do it," said Joel, his jaw flexing in determination. "What do we do first?"

"We stake the lady out, figure out her routine, then we grab her. Karl, here, usually does that part." He nodded toward his massive assistant. "I'm not in the vehicle during the actual kidnapping. It's easier on me legally that way. Then we go somewhere secure, where the cult can't find us and we talk, and talk, and talk some more."

"What exactly do you talk about?" asked Joel.

"Stuff that'll open the ex-cult member's mind so something else can go in. I show 'em the other side, the stuff they never hear when they're inside. Deprogramming is simply tellin' the truth and gettin' the person's mind working again. Give 'em something to compare the cult with. When they start comparing, they start evaluating. Then they start thinking."

Joel's throat felt dry with sudden fear. In his mind, he was back on Memorial Hill, watching his beloved bolt away from him like a frightened doe. "What if we fail? I could lose her forever."

The older man regarded him kindly. Deliverer appeared to be street-smart, yet his brown eyes were soft with compassion. "We'll do what we can—from the human side of things, of course. Then we trust, brother. We trust like crazy that the Lord will do what we *can't*."

❧

Val didn't see the white, windowless van until it was practically on top of her. An Hispanic giant jumped out, shoved Gilead into a snow-covered lilac bush, grabbed Val, stuffed her into the cavernous blackness of the van, and sped away. Even above the roar of the engine, Val could hear Gilead's screams.

She knew who was doing the "rescuing." She sat up on the bare metal floor, still clutching her pile of pamphlets, and waited for her eyes to make out Joel's familiar figure in the darkness. Her only problem was, what would she do now? Much as she wanted rescuing, she couldn't risk leaving the cult until she knew Father Elijah's plans. Until that madman was put behind bars and the virus in the custody of the proper officials, neither Joel nor anyone else would be safe. But she couldn't tell her husband all this; he'd never let her go back.

Her thoughts raced. She *had* to return to the cult before Shiloah learned she was missing. She doubted if the deprogrammer would believe her story, even if she confessed everything on the spot. Her research for her journalism class had turned up a lot of facts, including the one about kidnapped cult members concocting all kinds of weird tales to lure their captors into letting down their guard.

Val knew that the deprogrammer would most likely insist on taking her to some secluded spot for a marathon talk session. By the time she could convince him she wasn't faking, her cover would be blown. Shiloah would know. She shuddered to think what would happen then, especially with all the pre-Father Elijah's visit hysteria.

No, she couldn't chance bringing Joel in on this. She had to escape.

Now!

Joel never knew what had hit him, Val decided later. One minute, he was scooting closer to her on the van floor—probably to wrap his arms around her and kiss her senseless, the next, he was being crowned over the head with nine hundred Father Elijah pamphlets. Val flung herself against the van door and violently yanked the handle.

Lucky for her the traffic light was red as she leaped to the ground and sprinted down the street toward a weeping Gilead. *Joel needs to hone his kidnapping skills if he's planning on doing this often,* she chuckled to herself as she ran into her partner's outstretched arms.

&

Deliverer's dark brown eyes opened wider, then narrowed as he spread his hands in utter amazement. "What do you mean, you couldn't tie her wrists? I showed you how! Didn't you learn to tie knots in the Boy Scouts? And why, may I ask, did you not lock the van door?"

Joel hung his head. "I didn't want to hurt her. She's not a criminal."

"I said, 'Bind her wrists.' I didn't say, 'Hang 'er.'"

Joel sighed, crossed his arms, and looked down at his mother's living room carpet. How could he explain his misgivings, his gut revulsion against snatching his wife off the street and spiriting her away as if the Bill of Rights hadn't been written? "Rescuing" a brainwashed cult member was one thing in theory, another in practice. When he'd kissed Val that morning, she'd certainly seemed to be in her right mind. .

"And the door?"

"I didn't think she'd try to escape," he said with a shrug. But she had. Joel ran his hand through his hair and wondered how many more times he could stand to watch in silent torment as his wife ran away from him. But her kiss on the hill . . . the love he had seen in her eyes . . . it had lit a flicker of hope inside him that would not die. He would not let it die. The flame might be small, but it made more sense to light a candle than to curse the darkness.

Deliverer smoothed his heavy black mustache. "This is not a church picnic, Mr. Tenderfoot. I can't help you and your wife unless you cooperate. You won't do 'er no permanent damage if you tie 'er up for a little while. Do I make myself clear?"

"Loud and clear." At least, it was clear to Joel that he needed to rethink his plan of attack.

Deliverer shook his head and sighed heavily, patting his shirt pocket for the cigarettes he'd given up the year before. Couldn't this guy do anything right? Under his breath, he muttered to himself in Spanish.

≥∙

Shiloah glared at Val as Gilead reported what had happened. ". . . but she escaped from Satan's hold," Val's partner concluded breathlessly.

Val could tell that the whole dramatic incident had served to bolster the girl's blind allegiance to the cult. Father Elijah constantly ranted about the persecutions they'd suffer as God's chosen. Deprogrammings were persecutions, and as such were proof of God's favor.

To her surprise, Val now found herself a hero. Everyone, with the exception of Shiloah and Jeremiah, believed she'd risked life and limb to escape and return to the arms of Father Elijah and his Children of Last Days Light. Val seized the opportunity and ran with it. "I thought I was a goner," she said. "Can you believe they were dumb enough not to lock the van door?"

"Praise the Lord, sister Tamar!" Boaz broke in. "You socked the devil in the eye that time!"

"Amen," echoed Shiloah, his narrowed, steely gaze never leaving Val's face. "And we'll sock it to the devil again." His thin lips bared in a wicked grin.

Val felt her stomach tighten.

"Bennigan receives his divorce papers within the hour," said Shiloah with a sneer.

❧

Joel didn't like himself when he brooded. But neither did he like it when his whole life collapsed around his shoulders like a shattered mirror. He'd left Deliverer and Karl at his parents' home in the late afternoon, apologizing for bungling the attempted kidnapping, and excused himself, pleading the need for solitude. Now he sat alone in the home he'd shared with Val, brooding—hating himself for it—but brooding just the same.

The house itself seemed to contain traces of Val. He could almost hear her laughter. Part of him expected her to burst in the front door any minute, full of chatter about her latest journalism assignment. He imagined her bounding down the stairs, or clattering pots and pans at the stove, or transcribing her recordings of Professor Weston's classes at the table.

Joel stood up carefully so as not to strain his aching knee and walked slowly into the kitchen. Val's tape recorder lay where she'd left it, on top of her pile of transcribed class notes. He picked up the small black machine and cradled it in his hand. It represented some connection—a visible reminder that she'd once loved him and been his wife.

The doorbell startled Joel out of his reverie. Leaving the recorder where he'd found it, he crossed the living room and threw open the heavy wooden door.

"Sheriff Wilcox! What are you doing here?" With a sinking heart, Joel saw the legal papers in the burly man's hands and knew the answer. *So she was serious about divorce. Lord, help us!*

"I'm sorry to have to do this, Reverend Joel, but it's my job," Ed Wilcox said, handing over the documents. "Is there anything I can do?"

Joel took the papers hesitantly, as if he were being handed a poisonous snake. "No, Ed. Frankly, I don't think there's anything anyone can do." Joel knew he shouldn't voice such lack of faith in front of one of the most faithful members of his church, but he was almost beyond caring. This moment had to be the darkest of all dark hours.

"Not quite," said Wilcox softly. "The Lord can still do something."

Joel's mouth twisted wryly. "Of course, you're right." But he didn't believe his own words. Doubts assailed him. Where was God? Why had He abandoned them?

"Faith ain't based on good feelings, Reverend. You told me that yourself when my missus was in hospital and the prognosis was bad. Don't you remember what you said?"

"Remind me," said Joel testily. He knew the man was only trying to help, but irritation at his efforts was beginning to rub at his gut like sandpaper.

"You told me to trust the Lord, not what was goin' on around us. You said faith don't rely on feelings and circumstance. Faith trusts the promises of God. Don't you remember how the Lord came through for me and my missus?"

"Yeah."

"Maybe it's time you took a dose of your own medicine . . . or mebbe I should say, 'Listen to your own sermons,' Reverend."

Joel noticed Wilcox was twisting his cap in his hands nervously. Usually the large, placid man didn't have two words to say. Well, that wasn't quite true. Wilcox usually said exactly two words as he and the now healthy Mrs. Wilcox left church on Sunday mornings: "Good sermon." Ed Wilcox was a man who had probably barely made it through high school. He certainly hadn't gone to seminary. Yet his childlike trust in God's care shamed Joel. *Isn't this the type of faith Jesus encouraged us to have? Unless you be as little children . . . .*

For a moment, just one fleeting instant, Joel put aside his irritation and allowed himself to be open to the conviction and correction of the Holy Spirit. But then his pride kicked in. He felt his face flush. He didn't like being "shown up" by a member of his own flock. Joel set his jaw. "Thanks, Ed. Good evening."

Joel could have kicked himself. From the crestfallen look on the older man's face, he knew he was being dismissed.

"You're a stubborn one, all right," Wilcox said slowly. "But God ain't finished working on you, Joel Bennigan. Mark my words, He'll refine you in the potter's fire and make a golden vessel out of you yet. I'll be praying for you and your missus."

"You do that," said Joel as he shut the door. *I need someone to pray for us. I can't seem to do that anymore, either.*

Leaning against the doorframe, Joel felt his chest tighten as he fought the dark emotions raging within him. His conscience condemned him. *It's easy to preach to others to have faith, especially when you're a pastor. So easy. Yet so hard to have faith when it's your life that's unraveling.*

He kneaded his throbbing temples with one hand, then looked down at the legal papers still clenched in his other hand. Clenching his teeth, he tore the envelope and read quickly. His jaw tightened. Not only was Val petitioning for divorce, but she was accusing him of adultery and emotional cruelty, and demanding a settlement of two million dollars! *What?* The words jumped off the page and hit him like a brick between the eyes. The preliminary hearing was scheduled for the following week.

Adultery? Two million dollars? He could feel anger gathering inside him. Shock quickly yielded to fury. The court date was scheduled too soon, way too soon. The cult lawyer must have an inside connection in the old boys' network, he realized. Val wasn't the only one being manipulated, if indeed she *was* being manipulated. Joel's breath came in ragged spurts that burned his throat. *Dad was right. They're after the Bennigan money. But why is Val lying for them? Why is she doing this to us? Lord, can't You stop this travesty? Where are You in all Your glorious omnipotence when I need You?*

He thinned his lips in anger. His mouth felt dry. His fist closed around the divorce papers, crumpling them into a hard ball which he flung across the room, aiming for the fireplace. Instead, the ball bounded off the mantel and landed on the fake bearskin rug, where he had held Val in his arms.

Uttering a word of despair, Joel grabbed his jacket from the clothes tree, and strode angrily out into the night, slamming the front door with enough force to rattle the windows.

fourteen

Joel ran the twelve blocks to the cult house on Oak Street at a punishing pace. His head pounded. His chest burned. His muscles strained. Most of all, his knees complained. But he didn't care. He gritted his teeth against the pain and pressed on harder into the frozen night air.

He wasn't sure yet what he'd do once he got there. Bang on the door and demand to see Val, he supposed. What did he hope to accomplish? Lure her out of the house? Maybe she'd run to him, throw herself into his arms, and confess that the divorce papers were a ghastly mistake, that she'd been forced to file them. Joel flinched as bitterness filled his mouth. Why had she kissed him on the hill that morning if she knew she was serving papers on him that afternoon? Had she chosen the cult over her marriage? Or did she have a choice in the matter?

He crunched the snow underfoot viciously. It would be nearly eight o'clock by the time he reached the house. The cult members generally spent their evenings singing those inane songs and hypnotizing themselves with that stupid chant. At least, that's what Val and Kevin Milford had told him in their more lucid moments.

He turned into the short gravel driveway of the cult house and took the porch steps two at a time, ignoring the pain in his knees. He pounded on the front door, once, twice, three times. Flecks of old yellow paint bounced off. Even over his pounding, he could hear energetic singing and guitar playing wafting from the house.

"Val! Val! Come out!" he bellowed.

No reply. The singing seemed to grow louder. *Shiloah's got them riled up tonight. How do the neighbors put up with this racket?*

"Val, I know you're in there!"

He pounded harder, this time with both fists.

Still no reply. If anything, the din from the living room increased.

"Val! We need to talk!"

Yes, the ruckus was growing. It swelled to a crescendo. *Shiloah's trying to drown me out! I'll show him!* Joel slammed his fists into the old oak door. *Wham!* He pounded the wood again and again, beating and hammering until his fists were raw. Then, furiously, he kicked at the door. The blows reverberated across the porch, but with the hysterical chanting and screaming inside, he knew it was unlikely they had been heard.

"I'm not leaving without you, Val! You're still my wife!"

Finally, spent and soul-weary, Joel leaned his back against the door jamb and let his body slide down to the porch floor, expelling his breath as he went. He buried his face in his stinging hands and tried to calm his emotions. A primitive grief washed over him. She wasn't coming.

Joel lost track of time. He drew his knees up to his chest and hugged them tightly to ward off the chill that was creeping through his body. *A person could freeze out here,* he thought. Only last week a homeless man had been found frozen stiff, huddling in the doorway of City Bank. But even the bitterness of an Ohio winter was warmer than the chill that wrapped its icy fingers around Joel's heart. Had he really expected her to respond to him? Bereft, his throat closed around emotions he could no longer deny, and he uttered the low, guttural sound of a man who'd just taken a body blow.

Suddenly, the door opened and Joel heard a metallic click. He spun around and found himself looking up the barrel of a rifle.

Jeremiah, cursing savagely, nostrils flaring, was aiming straight at his head. "She don't want you no more, Bennigan. Can't you get that through your thick skull? She's my woman now. Now get off our property before I blow your brains out!" he spat, his Irish accent broad and heavy.

Joel stiffened and swallowed against the taste of fear. The steel barrel inched nearer to his head. The hair on the back of his neck bristled. He considered fighting, but as quickly as the idea came, he dismissed it. Fists couldn't win against an M-16.

"You've lost," said Jeremiah with a sneer. "Get out of here."

Something told him Jeremiah was right. He had lost. Maybe Val really did want to be with this giant oaf. Carefully, with no sudden movement, Joel eased himself to his feet. He raised his hands, palms toward his aggressor. "I'm going, man. Cool it."

Jeremiah jerked both his head and the rifle in the direction of the road.

Joel shrugged and gave a bleak laugh. "What does it matter?" He turned away from the black bear of a man, not sure whether he'd take a bullet in the back, and not really caring.

&

Joel woke with a start. *How long have I been sleeping?* His leather jacket creaked. His neck ached miserably, and cramped spasms shot through his back muscles. He'd fallen asleep in the fireside chair last night. Chilled to the bone, he'd walked home, thrown himself into this chair, and stared into the cold, empty grate. As the hours had passed, his anger had dissolved into grief. He hadn't moved. He'd had no reason to stir himself. The balled-up summons lay where it had landed, mocking him silently.

Now the white morning light crept across the textured ceiling. *It must be past mid-morning,* he thought as he ran his hand across his stubbly jaw. He'd had sick calls to make this morning, plus a meeting with the local Pastors Against Hunger committee, but it was too late now. A muscle jerked in his jaw and his expression grew stony. They'd just have to go on without him. Maybe the world would just have to go on without him.

Mouth grim, he stared straight ahead, seeing nothing.

He was thirsty.

Not for coffee, tea, or water. No, for the first time in a few years, he thirsted for the oblivion of alcohol.

Don't be ridiculous, man! Joel admonished himself. *You're a recovering alcoholic!* He could hear old demons nipping at his heels.

Even so, he yearned to forget. He'd been so sure Val loved him as much as he loved her. She'd promised to be his forever. She'd accepted his ring, taken his name, and one month later, run away! His mind circled around one possible reason why, yet he couldn't bring himself to admit it.

Maybe she didn't love him after all. Maybe he wasn't enough for her. Whatever her reasons, however the cult had lured her back, Val hadn't loved him enough to stay with him. Wasn't the proof over there on the rug, staring him in the face, summoning him to the courthouse next week?

Once a drunk, always a drunk. What's the point of fighting it? Had his alcoholism caused Val's flight? Maybe not consciously, but the more he thought about it, the more it made sense that it might have helped drive her away. Her mother had been an alcoholic who'd drunk herself to death. Did Val fear history might repeat itself if he ever fell off the wagon?

He shrugged helplessly. *It doesn't matter now.* He knew he was wallowing in self-pity, but he was beyond caring.

The longer he sat there, staring at the paper ball, the louder and more insistent the demons became. If he couldn't have Val, what was the point of staying sober? Life without her was a vast desert of loneliness. Why not indulge himself and blot out the pain? *Why not?*

He tried to envision his future without the woman he loved. The emptiness of the house closed in on him. That's what the days, months, years would be like—hollow. He would grow old alone—a loveless man in an empty house, brooding about what might have been and what obviously wasn't going to be . . . now.

What does it matter? he'd said to Jeremiah last night. He repeated it to himself now. Without his beloved, what was the point?

I need a drink.

As Joel climbed into his red pickup, he told himself he was only going to Filthy McNasty's Bar for a sandwich, nothing more. They served the best cheddar cheese and French bread in Kent. With fries and pickles. He knew Nasty's lunch fare from his college drinking days when "pub grub" had been all he'd eaten for weeks while on a binge. But those were the days before he knew the Lord. Days when he had been tossed about by every wind of sensual pleasure that had blown through a party-hardy college town. Joel Bennigan, jock extraordinaire, had been king of Kent State football team and could have had any girl he wanted . . . .

The days before he knew the Lord.

The phrase rang hollow to him now. *Seems like I don't know You anymore. I certainly didn't know my wife. Maybe I don't even know myself,* he thought as he walked into the pub.

The dark, dank interior of Nasty's hadn't changed much. The grimy dark paneling still needed a good scrub-down. The faded girlie calendar from 1988 still hung on the wall behind the counter. The stale smell of booze and tobacco permeated everything. The place was crowded with daytime drinkers and ne'er-do-wells. Mitch, the aging hippy, still served behind the bar.

"Bennigan! Never thought we'd see you 'round here again!"

"Beer with a chaser," Joel growled. *So much for a sandwich and nothing more . . . .* He didn't want to encourage conversation with Mitch. He was in no mood to defend himself. All his old drinking buddies had mocked his conversion to Christ and hooted and howled when he'd quit drinking cold-turkey. He'd spent a week in de-tox and attended Alcoholics Anonymous every week for over two years.

Mitch tugged at the red bandana tied around his forehead. Streaks of gray now peppered his shoulder-length blond hair. "Whatever you say, Bennigan. You're the boss."

Am I the boss? Really? Seems like Father Elijah is in charge of my life.

Mitch hummed the words to "Mellow Yellow" under his breath while he pulled the handle of the Killian's Red keg. He placed the frosty mug on the counter in front of Joel, unscrewed a bottle of Jamison's Irish Whiskey, and poured a shot into a small glass. "Only the best for you, old buddy."

"Put a cork in it!" Joel snapped. He looked away from the man in shame. "Sorry, Mitch, I'm just not good company these days. Wife left me, you know."

"Yeah, saw it on TV. Weird, man."

"Yeah, weird."

"Sorry 'bout that, man. I'll leave you alone. Too busy breaking up fights today to talk anyway." Mitch swung his grimy dishcloth over his shoulder and moved down the bar to where a group of disheveled-looking patrons was arguing.

Mitch cared in his own way, Joel realized, but he didn't know the Lord. *And what kind of witness to Christ am I being? Not much.* He stared at the beer and whiskey in front of him. Beads of water ran down the mug. The glass felt cold to his touch. He could just imagine the malty taste of the brew, smooth, soothing, quenching the fire inside. . . .

He picked up the whiskey chaser. In the old days, he and his drinking cronies used to follow each beer with a shot of whiskey. "Snake bite" they'd called the combination. The object was to put enough alcohol in the bloodstream that even the bite of a snake wouldn't affect you. *Or was it so that you wouldn't care if a snake bit you?*

He couldn't remember. Nor did he care. He just craved the release the liquid would bring. After five or six snake bite combinations, he'd be free of all his troubles.

He'd down the whiskey first. More potent that way. He held up the small glass and swirled the golden liquid around. The track lighting over the bar refracted a prism of amber, wheat, and yellow through the whiskey. *Pretty poison.*

He stared at it, his mouth watering in anticipation. Mentally, he savored its biting taste. He could feel the burning sensation trickle down his throat. He could imagine the numbness spreading across his stomach, then out to the rest of his body.

He raised the glass to his lips.

The glass felt smooth. The liquor smelled potent and familiar.

Then he looked up and caught his reflection in the mirror behind the bar. For a split second, he didn't recognize the haggard, unkempt hulk of a man staring back at him. The dark circles under his eyes seemed painted on, like a Halloween mask. *Dear God, how far have I sunk?*

He flinched at the desperation written all over his face. His gaze dropped to the glass in his hand. He remembered when that hand had shaken so badly, he couldn't hold a whiskey glass, so he'd swilled straight out of the bottle. He remembered the same hand trembling as the nauseating waves of detoxification had racked his body.

His mind drifted and suddenly he saw another hand. A hand nailed to a cross. A hand that had suffered to redeem him. Was he going to return that gift with a slap in the face?

Dear God, what am I doing?

From somewhere in his addled brain, words of Scripture came back to him: "Do not get drunk with wine, for that is debauchery; but be filled with the Spirit." His grip tightened around the glass. He stared at it. No one was pouring booze down his throat. He could still say no. Like Mitch had said, *he* was the boss. God was letting him make the call. What an honor. A crazy honor. Was God nuts?

No, He only respected His creation's free will.

Forgive me, Lord. Give me the strength. I want to resist. Even if I've lost everything I hold dear, I don't want to fail You.

Joel put the glass down.

He'd studied enough pastoral counseling to know that his current rage sprang from hurt, the astonished pain that had been ripping him apart since Val's public denunciation on TV. Hurt that washed over him in great, crushing waves. But the oblivion of alcohol was not the answer.

He ran his finger around the lip of the small glass. It hummed like the pain of loss vibrating within his soul. But even so, to trust and love God only in the absence of exquisite pain was a fickle commitment indeed. And so far from the Savior's own example of sacrificial love stronger than death. Oh, how easy it was to trust when his faith wasn't being tested. But to trust only in good times was to make himself an enemy of the cross of Christ.

Joel thought of Peter, the impetuous, blustery apostle who obeyed Christ's command to walk out on the water. As long as he kept his gaze fixed firmly on the Lord, he was fine. But once he began to look at the waves—the circumstances around him—he began to sink.

Joel had been looking at the waves, and they'd nearly swallowed him alive. Now, like Peter, he lunged forward to clasp Christ's hand before he went under altogether.

At that moment something shifted deep in Joel's soul. His

way of looking at the world changed. He felt that his eyes had just been opened wider to see more of God's truth. He resolved, by the grace of God, not to insult his Lord any longer by looking at the waves. This was spiritual warfare, not a day at the beach. Wave-gazing was a luxury he couldn't afford. From now on, his faith would be more manly, less rooted in feelings.

He laughed and lifted his gaze heavenward. *Thank you, Lord.* A warmth enfolded him, as comforting as a roaring log fire on Christmas Eve. He felt cleansed and whole. His blood pounded with new vigor.

In one swift movement, he picked up both glasses and dumped their contents into the pot containing a large rubber plant beside the bar. He closed his eyes briefly. *Good riddance.*

"Saints alive, man, are ye daft?" boomed a heavily accented voice behind him. "That's a sin, that is, wastin' good drink."

Joel spun around on his bar stool to face his accuser. The small, dark-haired man with the wiry body of a street fighter stood scratching his stubbly chin. "For the love of mutt, what did ye do that for?"

The accent was Irish. Unmistakably Dublin.

"Be not drunk with wine. . . , but be filled with the Holy Spirit," answered Joel in the words of Scripture, setting the empty glasses on the counter and spreading his hands innocently.

"Another bleedin' religious nut! This country's crawlin' with them!" With a disgusted snort the man turned and swaggered back to his seat at the top of the bar, motioning to Mitch as he walked. "Gimme another Jamison's, for the love of Mick. *I'll* not be pourin' it on the bleedin' plants."

Joel stood up. His mind was racing. Until now, he hadn't been able to understand why Val had left, why she was lying, or what he should do. Now, thanks to a chance encounter, he began to see a pattern in events that were previously chaotic and random. Suddenly, he saw meaning where there had been no meaning before. He watched in startled awe as the pieces of the puzzle started to click into sequence, like tumblers falling into place in a combination lock.

He stepped out of the bar into the bright winter sunlight, reflecting off the snow-covered streets. The raw February wind still whistled through the alleyways and around the corners, but there was a promise of spring in the clear blue sky.

Joel lifted his gaze. "Thank You, Lord, for using even my weakness for Your glory."

fifteen

Joel decided to leave his Jeep parked and walk the three blocks to Brady's. It seemed only natural to go there now. Everything had changed, although outwardly nothing had changed except the everyday miracle of a recovering alcoholic resisting temptation and putting his trust back in his Lord.

As he walked, Joel's step felt lighter. His knees ached less. The air seemed fresher; the noonday light, clearer. Hope wrapped her wings around his heart and whispered the age-old promise that all would be well in God's time. Happily, Joel thrust his hands deep into the pockets of his leather jacket and hunched his shoulders against the brisk wind. He hummed a song of praise. His mind cleared. His emotions quietened.

At Brady's, he ordered a Reuben sandwich along with an espresso coffee, a duplicate of the first meal he'd ever shared with Val. Eating the same food now would serve as a memorial, a symbol of his confidence that she would be home soon. *In Your way, Lord. In Your time.*

"Son, I've been looking everywhere for you!" Robert Bennigan's rich voice broke into Joel's musing. The large, gray-haired man took a seat across from his son. All around them, the lunchtime chatter and clatter of silverware continued as usual. The stricken look on Mr. Bennigan's face seemed out of place in the amicable atmosphere.

"Dad, am I ever glad to see you. Have a seat. Want a sandwich?"

"No, thanks. I've been calling your house for hours. Your mother and I have been worried sick about you."

"I'm fine. I wasn't so hot this morning, but I'm beginning

to see my way clear now." Joel blew the steam off his coffee.

"Deliverer's waiting back home. He wants to grab Val again."

Joel took a sip of the dark brew. The bitterness made him grimace. "Dad, could you pass the cream?"

Mr. Bennigan frowned. "We don't have much time, Joel. Deliverer says . . ."

Joel poured the half-and-half into his coffee and stirred until it was the color of rich mahogany. "Funny how people always ask if you want your coffee black or white," he said, idly tapping the spoon on the side of the mug. "I don't think it's ever exactly black, and it's certainly never completely white. Coffee can be brown, tan, beige, mahogany, walnut. . . ."

"Joel, what on earth are you talking about?" Mr. Bennigan clasped his large hands in front of him on the table and stared intently at his son.

"I won't kidnap her again, Dad."

"But why? I thought we'd agreed it was the only way!"

Joel put down his spoon and looked into his father's pale blue eyes. "I did agree, Dad. But now I'm not so sure. It's not all so black and white to me anymore."

"What changed your mind, son?"

Joel saw the kindness etched on his father's lined face. "I thought I could do it, but yesterday in the van, I couldn't go through with it."

"How so?"

"I couldn't tie her up like one of our horses, or lock her in the van as if she were an animal in a cage." Joel closed his eyes and relived the revulsion he had felt when the realization of what he was about to do hit him in the dark confines of the van. He shook his head and opened his eyes. "I know you and Mom think coercion is justified in a case like this—and I agree in theory—but it's not so simple when it comes to tying up my own wife."

Mr. Bennigan nodded slowly.

"Could you tie up Mom and lock her in a windowless van?"

After a moment's hesitation, the older man answered slowly, "I don't know, son."

"I appreciate your honesty, Dad." Joel picked up his fork and toyed with the sauerkraut topping his corned beef. "I felt so ashamed. . . ."

"Ashamed?"

"When Karl threw Val into the back of the van. Although it was dark, I sensed she knew I was there."

"You didn't touch her, then?"

Joel shook his head. "No. All I could think of was the time you taught me how to tie a horse's front legs together to hobble him. . . ."

"Oh, I see. You felt you were . . ."

Joel's glance pleaded for understanding. "She's a human being, Dad. I can't hobble her."

Mr. Bennigan placed his hand over Joel's, his somber gaze never wavering. "I understand," he said simply.

It was one of those moments of inexplicable, almost sacred intimacy that occurs sometimes between a father and son, Joel knew instinctively. One of the moments he would treasure in his heart as a pearl of great price. "Thanks, Dad."

"You're a fine Christian man, Joel. God gave Val a good husband, just as He gave me and Millie a good son. He'll guide you."

"'No follower of mine walks in darkness,' right?"

"Amen. In His tender mercy He sends the dawn to light our way," Mr. Bennigan rejoined. "So, how ya gonna get her back, son?"

"I don't know, Dad. All I know is God will open a way. Somehow, I'll persuade her to talk to Deliverer voluntarily. Maybe love can do what force couldn't. I'll fight for my wife . . . but I'll do it God's way."

Robert Bennigan nodded. "Well, finish your lunch and we'll

go back to the house and plan. By the way, do you have any idea how bedraggled you look?"

Joel ran his hand through his tangled hair and over his bristly chin. "Better do something about that, hadn't I?"

His father grinned, the blue eyes twinkling. "Hurry up, and I'll introduce you to a couple of marvelous new inventions."

❧

"Father E! Father E! We love you, Father E!"

Val froze as the revered cult leader shuffled into the living room. She could not believe her eyes. Leaning heavily on a cane, the wizened, old man was a far cry from the fiery prophet his followers had proclaimed him to be. *He's wasted and ugly!* Sparse white hair hung limply to his shoulders and a long, matted beard fell to his sunken chest. Beady black eyes scanned the room. A thin but attractive woman hung on his arm, smiling at him seductively.

Val's heart skipped a beat. She recognized the woman. *Martha! She's Shiloah's wife. Or at least, she used to be when we were in Dublin.*

Then it occurred to Val that Shiloah's wife had been absent. Val remembered the woman as silent and submissive, even more so than other cult women. She had seemed to exist only as an appendage of her husband, the cold son of the great fiery leader. Had she switched allegiance from son to father? Or had Father Elijah exerted his omnipotence within the group and claimed her as his own?

In either case, Martha belonged to Father Elijah now. That much was obvious. She slipped her arm through his and glared defiantly at Shiloah. Val remembered one of the Father Elijah letters, declaring that God's prophet could have any female in the group as his wife—any woman and as many women as he liked. "This is God's privilege to His anointed," he'd written.

Val tried not to gape, but it was difficult. She could feel the tenseness build as Shiloah stood, squaring off with his father, his fists clenching and unclenching behind his back.

"Father, what an honor," the son said.

"I have come to bless this house with my presence," Father Elijah droned, his voice gravelly but filled with hateful spite. "And with the presence of my new wife."

Val stood near enough to Shiloah to see the man's Adam's apple rise and slide back into place as he swallowed. *What's he trying to swallow?* she wondered. *Pride? Humiliation? Rage?* She scanned the rapt faces of the disciples to see if anyone else discerned the father-son drama playing out before their eyes. But after three hours of chanting, the group mood was charged to a drug-like high. Expectancy and excitement ran through them like a fever. Their prophet had come; they were oblivious to anything else.

Jeremiah started strumming the chords of the chant on his guitar as Shiloah took his father's other frail arm and led him and Martha to the center of the room. Boaz grabbed two chairs from the kitchen, and within seconds, Father Elijah and Martha were ensconced like king and queen.

"Father E! We love you, Father E!"

The chant grew louder and more feverish. Val tried to lip-sync while keeping her thoughts tightly focused on reality, not allowing herself to be lured into the hysteria surrounding her.

"Father E! Father E! Who will you die for?" shrieked Shiloah, his gaunt, pale face flushed an unhealthy red.

"Father E! Father E! We'll die for you, Father E!" screamed the disciples, punching the air with clenched fists.

Val trembled inside. *Lord, deliver me from the snares of my enemies, for I have put all my trust in Your promise.*

She drew a long, steadying breath. God would not fail her. She closed her eyes and swayed in time to the chant. But her mind was on Joel, his rugged, handsome face smiling at her the way he used to. She would be back in his arms again soon. *Dear Lord, please let it be.*

"Children, children, quiet now," crooned Father Elijah, raising his walking stick to silence the din. "I have come to tell you the word of the Lord."

Following Shiloah's example, the disciples sat down cross-legged, in a circle at the feet of their master. All attention was riveted on the ugly old man. Val could see his sunken chest swell with pride. He reminded her of a strutting peacock.

"Listen to God's prophet," he began, his voice suddenly gaining strength, almost as if he were feeding from the spirit of each person in the room, drawing their spirits into himself. "This wicked generation has refused to honor God's end-time prophet, so the wrath of the Lord is about to be poured out. He has ordered me to release the Plagues of Egypt."

"Amen!" shouted Shiloah.

"And the rivers shall turn to blood," boomed Father Elijah. "And the wicked shall be no more!"

"Amen!" yelled Gilead.

"Amen! Hallelujah!" roared the group.

Father Elijah raised a parchment-thin hand. "The Lord has told me the time is *now*. The end has come. We must flee like a bird to our mountain! Let us not waste a moment longer, children. Gather but a few belongings, for it is time."

Val's fear solidified in her throat like an ice cube. Where was he taking them? When was he going to release the plagues? She didn't dare ask as Shiloah herded them out to their restored bus like so many sheep.

❧

"Seems mighty quiet, Joel," Sheriff Wilcox said as Joel killed the engine. From their parking space on the street in front of the cult house, the place did indeed look deserted.

"Maybe they're chanting in the dark," said Joel as he jumped down to the street. He stood still and listened. "Can't hear a thing. That's strange. Usually by seven-thirty, they're hard at it."

Sheriff Wilcox started up the driveway. "I don't like the looks of this."

Neither did Joel.

The cult bus was gone. The house was dark. He pounded on the door. No answer. A chill began creeping up his spine. "What do you make of it?"

Wilcox grunted. "Looks like they've fled the coop, like it was doomsday or somethin'. That's what they preach, isn't it? The end of the world?"

Joel grabbed the burly man's arm in sudden awareness. "Their place in Brimfield! Do you know it?"

"Yeah. They bought the old Francesca mansion, way out in the country, didn't they? Big old house back in the woods. Hadn't been used for years. I've a hunch that's where they've been stashing all those weapons Shiloah's been buyin', but I can't prove nothing."

Joel massaged his brow. His head was pounding. "The fire-arms are owned legally?"

"So far, they check out. The FBI and ATF are both watching, but Father Elijah has his people trained well. Nothing irregular, at least not enough to nail 'em."

"At least not yet," said Joel grimly, his jaw tightening. "That may change after our visit to Brimfield tonight."

sixteen

The old bus lurched as Shiloah gunned it up the rutted dirt driveway of the hideaway. The drive snaked up and around clumps of pines that stood tall, like black sentinels in the clear moonlight. Val tried to forget the hunger clawing at her innards and focused on memorizing every detail of the terrain. If she discovered the secrets of the plagues tonight, she'd be escaping over this remote, isolated territory on foot.

She gasped as the vehicle careened over a small hill and Mountain Manor came into view. Nothing she'd heard about the creepy old mansion had prepared her for the sinister black hulk of a house that crouched like a vulture waiting for its prey. Turrets and spires clawed at the eerie moon-washed sky. The moon cast a long shadow over the old tiled roof. Like a living thing, the black shadow stretched and oozed past the sagging, once magnificent wooden porch, and unto the neglected lawn and snow-splattered bushes. Val shuddered.

The bus came to a screeching halt in the middle of the curved, gravel drive. Val looked up at the imposing marble steps that led to the ornately carved front door. *This must have been quite the place in its day, but completely secluded. Who'd ever think that dirt driveway led to a mansion?*

"It was once the home of a retired mobster," whispered Gilead. "The locals say it's haunted, but we don't believe in ghosts."

Right, thought Val, *with lunatics like Father Elijah, who needs restless spirits?* She felt chilled in her sweatshirt and jeans and hugged her arms to her chest, wishing Shiloah had given her time to grab her down jacket. She heard the crunch of tires on frozen gravel and craned her neck to see out the window. Father Elijah's black Lincoln pulled up in front of the entrance. Jeremiah, acting as chauffeur, jumped out and opened the back door for the prophet and his wife. Leaning heavily on his cane and flanked by his two loyal followers, Father Elijah ascended the dozen steps.

Shiloah turned in the driver's seat, his cold eyes scanning the busload of disciples. Even from her place near the back, Val could feel the tension he emanated. "Are we living in the end times?" he bellowed.

"Amen!" the group chorused.

"Then act like it!" Shiloah roared. "Get inside and listen to God's prophet!"

Two dozen bodies scampered off the bus, up the steps, and into the cavernous house. Val strained to see in the light cast by one overhead bulb struggling to illuminate what had previously been a huge entrance foyer. Dozens of booted feet echoed on the cold marble, which reflected dull white in the dim light. In the near-darkness, the mansion opened its throat like a hungry beast and swallowed them.

Val was swept along with the others into a huge, high-ceilinged room that had probably been a ballroom at one time. But there was nothing festive about the room now. Dank, moldy dust assaulted Val's nose. The huge expanse of pock-marked wooden floor was bare, except for a foot-high platform at the far end. An antique-looking needlepoint chair with massive lion-claw arms sat on the platform. *The prophet's throne, no doubt.* Outside, Val could hear the wind picking at loose roof tiles.

Something about the walls struck Val as strange. They seemed to be of a textured quality, as if covered with some kind of dull red cloth. Out of the corner of her eye, Val could see Gilead studying her.

"It's red sackcloth," Gilead explained.

"Oh?" Something about the yards and yards of red sent shivers down Val's spine.

"The prophets of the Old Testament wore sackcloth when they proclaimed God's coming judgments. We cover our walls in red sackcloth to remind us of the coming plagues of blood."

Val's stomach turned over. But she kept her face expressionless, willing even the tiniest muscle to remain motionless.

"We spent weeks dying all that burlap," continued Gilead. "I keep forgetting you weren't here at that time. You've been home only a few days, yet it seems like you never left." The girl squeezed Val's arm. Val steeled herself not to recoil.

"Yep, it sure does seem like an eternity," said Val in a hushed tone, following Shiloah's instructions to the disciples to sit in front of the throne in several straggly rows.

The wind began rattling the many windows, and frigid fingers of air seeped through the cracks and crevices of the old mansion. Val hugged her knees to her chest.

"Father E! Father E!" Shiloah started up the chant with fervent clapping of hands. The sound echoed around the cavernous room like an incantation to an ancient pagan idol.

After several long minutes, Father Elijah, now dressed in a long red robe, appeared in the massive doorway, leaning on a new, thicker wooden cane. Assisted by Shiloah and Jeremiah, he made his way unsteadily across the room and mounted the podium.

"Father E! We love you, Father E!"

The old man eased himself down into the chair. His gnarled hands wrapped around the neck of his cane. Val noticed its top had been carved into a gargoyle's hideous head. *The image of a demon,* she thought. *How fitting.* Father Elijah's sinister black eyes seemed to bore holes into whomever his evil gaze rested upon. He raised a bony hand to silence the chant.

"Children," he began, his voice as dry and cracked as the

bleached boards beneath his chair. "We are God's chosen people, for unto us and only unto us has He delivered the secrets of the end times."

"Hallelujah!" Jeremiah shouted, followed by a chorus of hysterical voices.

"The Lord has repeatedly told me in dreams and visions that we are to be as Joseph helping the Pharaoh of Egypt," Father Elijah continued, his eyes narrowing. "Just as Joseph worked with Pharaoh, we are to work with the powers of evil so that God's kingdom might be ushered in sooner! Then we shall rule and reign over all the earth when the Lord comes!"

"Amen! Amen!"

"So God has delivered into my hands the instrument for the Angel of Death." He gestured toward Shiloah who leaped to his feet, reached under the platform, and retrieved a black leather bag resembling a medical case.

Reverently, Father Elijah held the bag above his head. "Children, the plagues of Egypt which God has given us!"

Slowly, almost reverently, he lowered the bag, set it on his lap, and opened it. Then he withdrew a black metal cube that looked something like a safety-deposit box.

From her position on the floor at his feet, Val was unable to make out what was inside. But her heart lurched sickeningly when he held up a purple vial. The back of her neck prickled.

"God's curse on the wicked!" he announced with an evil grin.

Val held her breath until he put it back into the box. Suddenly, Father Elijah's wizened face darkened into an ugly scowl. "Shiloah," he bellowed. "Where is the seventh vial?"

Shiloah stood at his father's right hand, his gaze darting nervously around the room. Val could see his left eye twitch.

"Answer the prophet!" Father Elijah thundered, banging his cane like a scepter on the hollow wooden platform. "Where is the seventh holy vial?"

Shiloah cleared his throat, appearing to wither under the old man's venomous glare. He rooted in the leather pouch attached to his belt and produced the vial.

"Give it to me," snarled Elijah. "It is not for the son to know the hour and day. That secret is only for the father."

He snatched the vial and placed it in the black box. Then he fixed his narrowed gaze on Shiloah, who stood before him red-faced, looking like a chastened schoolboy. "The son must be subject to the father," Elijah said sternly. The prophet's gravelly voice echoed around the room. "Until the father is all and in all. Scripture says this of me, your prophet, and it must come to pass as it has been written. To teach you to subjugate yourself, God has taken away your wife and given her to me."

Val noticed Shiloah shifting uneasily from one foot to the other. She almost felt sorry for him, being humiliated like this in front of the whole group. She scanned the crowd for Martha. The young woman, her face hidden by lank, brown hair, sat up front. Her eyes were downcast.

"I came not to bring peace, but a sword. To turn father against son, wife against husband. Do you understand, O son of the great prophet?"

"Yes, father." Shiloah's left eye began to twitch again, more violently this time.

"Repeat after me, 'The son is subject to the father.'"

"'The son . . . is subject to the father,'" Shiloah echoed, his voice thin and reedy.

"Again! Louder!"

"'The son is subject to the *father!*'"

"Amen. You may sit." Elijah motioned Shiloah away. The younger man slunk to the outskirt of the group, his bony shoulders hunched, his gait dispirited. He avoided all eye contact.

"So, likewise, must each of you be subject to the father in your hearts," Elijah began, then launched into a tirade demanding obedience, loyalty, and honor to himself alone.

Val's stomach growled and she changed her position slightly to ease her aching muscles. The past three days had been brutal, and her body was screaming its protest. As Elijah's lecture droned on interminably, it seemed, she fought as sleep tried to overpower her.

". . . then the plagues shall come. . . ."

Val's head snapped up.

"I have dispensed seven angels of death around the country," Elijah said, his tone laced with pride and pleasure. "They are poised, ready to strike. When I give the word, like Moses raising his staff—" he thrust his carved walking cane into the air—"the waters of America's major cities will be stricken.

"Once the blood of the wicked turns into rivers, we shall immediately flood the national media networks with communications from terrorist groups all around the globe, each claiming responsibility," he continued, fiendish glee evident in his voice. "The country will be thrown into a state of emergency unlike any it has witnessed before. Any illusions about national safety will be shattered. Mayhem, rioting, paranoia, and persecution will prevail. But all these things must come to pass before the end."

He paused dramatically, the disciples hanging on every word. "We will not be suspected because the virus will not touch the waters of Kent. But if the agents of Satan attack us in our mountain sanctuary, God has given us guns. Let us defend this holy place lest the enemy thwart the plans of God! Let each one be prepared to die for the cause of judgment!

"And you, Shiloah," he said, his gaze resting on his son, "God has given you the great commission to spread the gospel of divine judgment. At dawn, you will board an airplane and travel the country, delivering one vial to each angel of death. We will fast and chant until your holy mission is complete. Do not fail your father, my son, lest the Angel of Death visit *you*."

Val's blood froze in her veins. Bile crept up the back of her throat. The room seemed to spin out of control. *He's either demon-possessed or stark, raving mad. . . or both.*

She had her information.

It was time to escape.

≈

From his crouched position outside the huge French doors at the north end of the ballroom, Joel could see the horror on Val's face. He glanced at the old, white-haired, red-robed coot lording it over the frightened disciples. What on earth was he holding up with such a triumphant sneer? Joel narrowed his eyes and strained to see. *Something purple. A glass vial?* Joel glanced back at Val. Whatever that purple stuff was, it terrified her. Why?

What was that false prophet up to?

Joel gritted his teeth, clenching and unclenching his jaw, his anger simmering. His knees were complaining again. He shifted his weight, careful not to make any noise. Whatever was going on, he didn't like it one bit. Val looked exhausted and pale. Dark circles ringed her eyes. One thing was certain. Contrary to her allegations on TV, she was anything but *glad* to be with the Children of Last Days Light.

Joel shivered, half wishing he'd brought Sheriff Wilcox, Deliverer, Karl—anyone who'd help him storm this rampart. But he'd decided to go it alone. He was determined to meet Val without force, without coercion, without threat of deprogrammer or lawman, and gently persuade her to return home. His plan was to catch her when she was alone. His Jeep, containing Wilcox and a walkie-talkie, was parked a mile down the road. Joel patted his pocket. His walkie-talkie and Val's mini recorder were still safely inside. He didn't know what he was going to record, but he'd seen the machine on the kitchen table and had grabbed it at the last minute. The tape inside was blank.

Wilcox had warned him about the possibility that munitions

were stockpiled at this hideout. That was a risk Joel was willing to take. He scanned the outside of the mansion and wondered where a bunch of lunatics would hide guns in a place like this. *There must be dozens of empty rooms where munitions could be stashed.* The building stood three stories high, and Joel could count ten windows spanning each level. *A haunted house of horrors.* In the bright moonlight, he could make out several new-looking barns out back, plus an assortment of vehicles, vans and older model cars, mostly.

He pulled his scarf tighter. A horrid squall had sprung up. Tree branches raked the upper-level windows. The sudden crack and scrape of a branch against the gutter made him jump. *Courage, man, or you'll be no good to Val or yourself.*

The moon slid behind a cloud, plunging the house into darkness. It looked like an evil monster, crouching over his wife and the other occupants of the ballroom. *Time to find an entrance to this mausoleum.* He stood and headed for the back of the building. . . .

Perhaps it was a moving shadow that caught Jeremiah's attention. Or maybe the twig that snapped beneath Joel's boot. But before Joel knew what had hit him, the bear had thrown open the French windows and yanked him inside.

"You never learn, do you, Bennigan?" he snarled and thrust Joel up against the wall so violently that flecks of moldy plaster rained down on their heads.

"I've come for my wife."

"Do ye hear that?" said Jeremiah loudly, gesturing toward Father Elijah. "He's come to steal the wife of God's servant."

Father Elijah stood and raised his cane. "And Moses smote the waters with his staff and the punishment of God fell upon the wicked! Let the same happen to this servant of Satan!"

Joel struggled against Jeremiah's great weight as the man pinned him to the wall. A couple of brawny male cult members jumped in to assist. Joel watched in horror as Father

Elijah advanced toward him, swinging his wooden cane in wide circles around his head. The old geezer seemed energized by evil that emanated from his black eyes. *What is that carved on the top? A gargoyle? The head of a goat?*

A shout died in Joel's throat as the prophet of doom swung the thick cane as if it were a baseball bat and smashed it down against his knees—again and again. Above the pain exploding in his brain, Joel could hear Val pleading for mercy. *At least she's still on my side,* he thought as the darkness seized and dragged him down.

seventeen

Joel struggled to emerge from the fog that shrouded his mind. Shafts of burning pain licked up his legs, knocking him back into the darkness. Rousing again, he clenched his teeth, waiting for the dizziness and nausea to pass. Staring down the pain, he clung to consciousness with the tenacity of a drowning man holding onto a lifesaver.

Groaning, he opened his eyes and tensed his legs. Pain exploded. *Will I ever walk again?*

His vision blurred. His head throbbed. He tried to rise, but discovered that his hands and feet were tightly bound. Turning his head, he tried to assess his situation. He could make out walls. An ornate marble fireplace. A bare wooden floor. The dank smell was overpowering. From the moonlight streaming through the window, he could see that he was lying on the floor of a small room, perhaps a former parlor or sitting room. From the height of the tree outside the window, Joel guessed he was still on the first floor.

The dust and mildew made him want to sneeze. He stifled the impulse, knowing the jolt would send more bolts of pain shooting up his legs. Drawing deep, shuddering breaths, he strained to listen. Somewhere in another part of the house, the Father Elijah chant was being sung with gusto reserved for the Marines. He wondered if Val were among the chanters. He'd heard her plead for him. His heart warmed. She still loved him. But how was he going to rescue her with a pair of busted knees?

The door opened and Jeremiah's dark frame filled the doorway.

"Like I say, Bennigan, some people just never learn," he sneered, his arms crossed over his grungy Army jacket. "But I'll learn ye."

He lunged at Joel's legs with the butt of an M-16 rifle, stopping just inches away from his throbbing kneecaps. Joel stiffened. Abruptly, Jeremiah straightened up and laughed. "Yankee chicken! If we were at home, my IRA boy-os would make short work of those knees."

Suddenly Jeremiah stopped short. His huge body stiffened. He seemed startled by the call of an owl outside, or what Joel thought was an owl. Three short hoots, then a long one.

Jeremiah's hand snapped to his forehead in salute. He muttered something in a foreign language.

"What?" Joel rasped, jerking his gaze upward to meet Jeremiah's flinty eyes.

"God save Ireland," snarled Jeremiah, scowling, as he turned to go, "in Gaelic. Say your prayers before Father Elijah gets his hands on you, stupid Yank. He's got some interesting experiments in mind."

A moment later, he stuck his head back in the door. "Don't try to escape, Bennigan. I'll be back . . . when you least expect me, like a thief in the night." Chortling, he pulled the door closed.

What now, Lord? Joel closed his eyes and reminded himself of the lesson of Peter walking on the waves. *Don't let the circumstances distract you. Keep your eyes on the Lord. Eyes on the Lord at all times.*

Joel found himself relaxing. Things *were* in God's hands. This Joel believed without reservation. The God mighty enough to sculpt the ocean, yet tender enough to care about each of His children personally would bring victory out of this mess. Joel closed his eyes and breathed deeply, drawing strength from the image of Jesus stretching out His hand to save the floundering Peter.

Be still and know that I am God. Now where had that verse come from? Oh, well, there wasn't much else he could do in this situation anyway. He continued to fiddle with the rope that bound his hands behind his back. Again, more insistently this time, the thought returned. *Be still.*

Joel concentrated on the sounds surrounding him, the night noises outside, and the chanting down the hall. He listened while his fingers worked stealthily and silently, picking and worrying, worrying and picking. The thick rope was knotted securely, but several strands at the end had begun fraying under his constant assault.

Be still and know. . . .

"Ok, Lord. I get the message," Joel whispered.

He heard footsteps dash past his window. *Val? No, they were too heavy. Men? Maybe. Two of them, even.* Joel held his breath and strained his ears. Several long minutes later, he heard what sounded like a barn door quietly open and close again.

Then, nothing. He expelled his breath with a whoosh and resumed picking the rope. He'd managed to work a few strands through the knot, weakening the hold. Now he concentrated on pushing more frayed ends through.

What was THAT noise? The grating sound of wood against wood. Nearby, a window had been opened. More footsteps, muffled. Then a soft thud as someone climbed in the window and landed on the floor. *A burglar? An intruder? Hardly likely when the ballroom is filled with cult members.*

Joel strained to hear above the blood rushing in his ears. He could make out two sets of footsteps, heavy footsteps. Whoever they were, they were working almost silently. Things were being passed through the window. Joel could hear whispers, but not words. The creaking of wooden crates being stacked one atop the other. The passing and stacking continued for some time. He counted ten boxes. Then the sound of scurrying down to the barn. Then more passing through the window. Ten more boxes, or crates, or whatever they were. Suddenly, something heavy and metallic clattered to the floor and a loud curse rang out in a heavy Irish accent.

"For the love of Mick, ye nearly broke me toe!"

For the love of Mick, why are ye pourin' that drink on the plant?

Finn O'Dwyer! Joel recognized the wiry, black-haired terrorist he'd seen in Filthy McNasty's Pub right away. . . .

He flinched as the door to his room burst open, and Jeremiah flung himself into the room. In two strides, he stood close enough to take aim at Joel with his rifle. Seconds later, more footsteps echoed down the hallway and Shiloah entered. "Is the prisoner under control?"

Jeremiah straightened, as if standing at attention, his rifle crossed against his chest. "Yes, brother. He's been subdued. He'll be ready when Father Elijah calls."

This answer seemed to satisfy Shiloah. He cast a cold eye at Joel, then a stony glance at Jeremiah. "Keep close guard," he snarled. He turned and disappeared in the direction of the chanting.

"One word outta you and I'll blow yer brains out," growled Jeremiah, aiming his rifle at Joel's head. Then he gave a derisive snort. "Father Elijah or no Father Elijah."

Then, as quickly as he'd appeared, Jeremiah was gone.

Joel knew now the source of the heavy, metallic sounds. *Guns.* Possibly more rifles like Jeremiah was using. The moving of munitions continued through the window, and Joel went back to working the rope. A strange sense of peace pervaded him, body and soul. His mind was clear. The pieces of the puzzle were coming together, revealing the picture more and more clearly.

Be still.

Joel stopped. Jeremiah and Finn O'Dwyer were talking in

hushed tones near his window. Joel could make out a bit of their conversation. "Guns . . . Ireland . . . smuggling. . . ."

Steeling himself against the pain in his legs, Joel fidgeted one last time with the cords around his wrists. He tugged. Once, twice. The knot gave way. *Praise God!* He threw off the rope and rubbed his raw, bleeding wrists. Quickly, he sat up and untied the rope around his ankles. Tremendous pain throbbed in his knees. He tried to stand, but couldn't.

What now, Lord? I can't even walk.

Joel knew Jeremiah's pattern. Joel waited until the footsteps retreated into the barn. Then, using his elbows, he dragged himself to the window. Sitting with his back against the wall, he reached for the frame. He took his time, so he could noiselessly open it about six inches. Retrieving Val's tape recorder, he pressed the record button and held the machine up to the open space, praying it would pick up the whispered conversation over the chanting in the background.

Outside, the wind riffled through the tall pines. A branch clacked against the side of the house. Before long, heavy boots quietly crunched snow and gravel. The men returned and resumed passing boxes of guns through a window several rooms down. Through the open window, Joel could pick up their conversation.

"Him an' his holy terrorists," O'Dwyer whispered forcefully.

"He's got Martha now," came Jeremiah's voice. "The ol' geezer's stolen everything from his son."

"Aye, 'tis a strange state of affairs. And him praying for the end of the world, yet."

The pair fell silent. The faint sounds of creaking boxes and rattling munitions continued, so faint that Joel felt assured no one in the ballroom would have heard a thing.

"Are we nearly done?" asked Finn plaintively. "I want out of here before that loony kills us all in the name o' God. 'Tis one thing to die for Ireland, but I'll not be spillin' me blood for a madman."

"Ten more boxes of AK-47s, fifteen Mac 10s, and 30 Uzis."

"All bound for the Aye-rabs?"

"Naw. We'll leave arming the Arabs to Father Elijah. We'll use these guns on the Brits back home." Jeremiah chuckled under his breath. "The old geezer's finally flipped his lid. But before we leave Father Idiot Elijah, I wanna git that little filly Shiloah promised me. She might not want me now, but she will, later...." He laughed lewdly.

Joel's hand tightened around the tape recorder. *Watch it, buster! That's my wife you're talking about!* The blood started to pound in his temples. Time was running out. He had to move—now. He slipped the recorder into his pocket and quietly rewound it a little. Then, propelling himself by his elbows and upper arm strength, he dragged himself across the floor, out the door, and up the dark hallway toward the ballroom and the incessant chanting.

He must be working them up for something big. How long can they keep it up?

Bursts of pain went off like fireworks behind Joel's eyes as he inched his way along the long, narrow hall. He kept close to the wall and occasionally used his feet to move himself along, but putting that much strain on his legs nearly blinded him with pain. *Dear God, help me.*

Sweat, beads of liquid pain, poured down his face by the time he reached the ballroom door. He hoisted himself up on one elbow and grasped the handle. At first, the heavy brass handle refused to yield. Gasping for breath, Joel leaned back on his haunches, ignoring his screaming legs, and in one movement, yanked the door open and threw himself several feet into the room.

Through pain-filled eyes, he saw Val jump to her feet, her hand to her mouth. Several female disciples huddled together, crying out. Others, including Kevin Milford, moved toward him.

Father Elijah's voice rang out commandingly. "Leave him to me!"

Suddenly, Joel flashed back to his dream, the nightmare in which Val had been blotted out by a purple haze . . . and the Scripture that had made no sense to him at that time.

The final piece of the puzzle snapped into place.

Thank you, Lord, for the ammunition. Now help me to shoot straight.

"Father Elijah," Joel said, easing himself up into a sitting position against the wall. "I've come to warn you."

The old man stood over Joel, slapping his cupped, gnarled hand against the demonic-looking head of his cane. "Oh?" He raised a white eyebrow.

"A house divided against itself cannot stand," said Joel forcefully. Again, that sense of perfect peace fell over him. The words came easily, as if he were reading from a cue card. "Your house is divided, Father Elijah. At this very moment, your top man is pilfering your property and plotting against you."

"Prove it." Elijah slapped his hand more menacingly against the cane. The sound reverberated around the room. Joel could feel the tension crackle.

"Here. Irrefutable evidence." He produced the recorder, adjusted the volume to its loudest setting and pressed the button.

"The old geezer's finally flipped his lid. But before we leave Father Idiot Elijah . . ." The sound of Jeremiah's voice seemed to expand and fill the silent room.

The prophet stiffened visibly. His face darkened.

Joel stopped the tape and rewound it further. "We'll use these guns on the Brits back home. . . ."

"Blasphemy! Curses on Jeremiah's head!" roared Father Elijah.

"Ah, curses on your own head, you bedeviled old madman."

Joel's head snapped around. Jeremiah loomed in the doorway, his rifle trained on Father Elijah. He aimed, but hesitated. His face went blank.

Shiloah lunged for his father, perhaps to knock him out of harm's way, but before he could reach the prophet, Finn O'Dwyer stepped out from behind Jeremiah and fired with incredible speed and accuracy. The old man's lifeless body slumped in the ancient chair.

Shiloah stopped in his tracks, his face contorted with shock, terror, abandonment. His left eye twitched furiously. Lamenting like a howling dog, he threw himself across his father's crumpled body while the two Irishmen fled toward the barn.

eighteen

Val entered the hospital room with trepidation. Her heart thumped wildly. She hadn't had a chance to say a word to Joel before he had passed out. With all the commotion when the police and ambulances had arrived—including that high-speed pursuit of Jeremiah and O'Dwyer in their truck full of guns—then the helicopter landing of the emergency squad dispatched from the Center for Disease Control to handle the virus—she'd been jostled out of the way.

Now here she was, alone with her beloved. At last.

She stood in the doorway. Joel lay sedated, his eyes closed, the green cotton blanket tucked neatly around his chin so that only his head was visible. His tawny hair against the pillow gave him a leonine look. A courageous, faithful lion who'd gone to the gates of hell for her.

She closed her eyes and breathed deeply. "Greater love has no man than to lay down his life. . ."

What more proof did she need? But while she finally allowed herself to fully trust her husband's love, a single niggling doubt remained. *Lord, please don't let our marriage be beyond redemption.*

As if he'd heard her prayer, Joel opened his eyes. A smile spread across his features, and he held out his hand to her. Shakily, she stepped into the little gray room, closed the door, and knelt beside his bed.

"Oh, Val," he whispered hoarsely. He reached for her and pulled her up to him.

"I'm so sorry, Joel." Tears crept down her cheeks as she brushed the hair back from his face. "They said they'd kill

167

you. They could have done it, too. So I went along with them."

"Of course you did, my love." He drew her to him.

She didn't resist. It felt so good and natural to flow into his arms and rest her head against his chest. Where she belonged. "They had a hideous virus, Joel."

"The purple vial?"

"Yes." A sob caught in her throat. "They had our house keys. They threatened to break in and put the virus in your orange juice if I didn't do what they said. Oh, Joel! The virus eats flesh. Shiloah used it to kill a gerbil in front of my eyes. It was horrible . . . there was blood everywhere . . . and they were going to kill you the same way!"

She felt his arms tighten protectively around her. She pressed her face against the crisp cotton of his hospital gown and listened to the soothing rhythm of his heartbeat. "I wanted to escape . . . but then I found out Father Elijah was planning to release the virus around the country as part of his doomsday plan. I had to find out the details so he could be stopped."

"My brave, brave Val." Joel wiped the tears from her face with the pad of his thumb. "You did the right thing."

"But I'm so sorry I had to hurt you in the process. . . ." Val felt herself choking on her own words. "Do . . . do you . . . can you ever forgive me?"

"Will the sun rise tomorrow? Will the stars set tonight? Is not God's love everlasting?" Joel shifted his weight onto his elbow and cupped Val's face in his hand, gazing tenderly into her eyes. "But . . . there's nothing *to* forgive, Val. And even if there was, of course I'd forgive you. I love you. Anyway, what kind of fool would hold a grudge against the woman who saved his life?"

"Oh, Joel, I was so afraid you wouldn't! The public humiliation, the trumped-up divorce charges. . ." A tortured cry escaped her lips. "And your poor knees! It's all my fault!" She buried her face in her hands and began to sob.

"Don't be afraid, my love. You mean more to me than a couple of intact kneecaps. Anyway, my legs will heal. They have before." With that, he gathered her to his chest.

She clung to him with trembling arms. Her heart cried out with gladness, *Oh, Lord, thank You for Your amazing, ceaseless wonders. Thank You, thank You, thank You!*

"It's all over now," he said, gently stroking her hair. "What terror you've been through."

Val sniffled. "Joel, I'm sorry I didn't tell you about my postcult problems. If I'd dared to trust you more, maybe . . ."

"That's in the past," he said, his voice husky. "But, in the future, no more secrets? OK?"

"No more secrets."

"We belong to each other, for better or worse," Joel whispered, his breath warm against her ear. She reached up and touched his face. It felt wet with tears. He pressed his lips to hers, caressing her mouth, whispering, "Until death do us part, my beloved."

&

Kent, Ohio, February 9

I've got to hand it to Deliverer. The man knows his business. He visited my hospital room while Val was here today. All three of us talked. Really talked. He told us things about Father Elijah and the Children of Last Days Light we never knew. Elijah abused Shiloah from the time he was an infant. Shiloah's mother committed suicide when the boy was quite young.

Father Elijah went on to create an idol in his own image, a false god of anger and hatred that destroyed him and many around him. I pray it's not too late for Kevin Milford. Tonight, he's under psychiatric care.

Val admitted she'd been floating the night she bumped into Shiloah (who, from what I hear, has entered some kind of catatonic stupor—but even he is not beyond redemption and prayer). Even before that night, she'd been having nightmares, flashbacks, difficulties concentrating—the usual gamut of post-cult problems. But she never told me. She was afraid I'd reject her as "damaged goods," she said.

Well, once that fear was out in the open, it seemed to evaporate like rain puddles under the noonday sun. I looked her straight in those gorgeous green eyes and assured her that her problems are mine, as mine are hers (including months of physical therapy before I can walk again.) "Fair trade," I said, "post-cult problems for gimpy knees." She threw back her head and laughed, the full-bodied, uninhibited laugh of a woman who knows she's loved and cherished. A laugh that made my heart soar.

My wife has come home to me, for good.

A Letter To Our Readers

Dear Reader:

In order that we might better contribute to your reading enjoyment, we would appreciate your taking a few minutes to respond to the following questions. When completed, please return to the following:

Rebecca Germany, Editor
Heartsong Presents
P.O. Box 719
Uhrichsville, Ohio 44683

1. Did you enjoy reading *Tender Mercy*?
   ❏ Very much. I would like to see more books by this author!
   ❏ Moderately
   I would have enjoyed it more if _____

   _____

2. Are you a member of **Heartsong Presents**? ❏Yes ❏No
   If no, where did you purchase this book?_____

   _____

3. What influenced your decision to purchase this book? (Check those that apply.)

   ❏ Cover   ❏ Back cover copy

   ❏ Title   ❏ Friends

   ❏ Publicity   ❏ Other_____

4. How would you rate, on a scale from 1 (poor) to 5 (superior), **Heartsong Presents'** new cover design?_____

5. On a scale from 1 (poor) to 10 (superior), please rate the following elements.

___ Heroine   ___ Plot

___ Hero   ___ Inspirational theme

___ Setting   ___ Secondary characters

6. What settings would you like to see covered in **Heartsong Presents** books? _____

_____

_____

7. What are some inspirational themes you would like to see treated in future books? _____

_____

_____

8. Would you be interested in reading other **Heartsong Presents** titles? ❑ Yes   ❑ No

9. Please check your age range:
   ❑ Under 18   ❑ 18-24   ❑ 25-34
   ❑ 35-45   ❑ 46-55   ❑ Over 55

10. How many hours per week do you read? _____

Name _____

Occupation _____

Address _____

City _____ State _____ Zip _____

Heartsong Presents

Settings Around the Globe!

Volume 2

___*River of Peace* by Janelle Burnham—The year is 1930. Ida Thomas has taken the job of schoolteacher in the remote village of Dawson Creek, British Columbia. Will she find a man she can truly love and know peace like a river? HP100

___*Search for Yesterday* by Mary Hawkins—While Hilda Garrett manages her family's sprawling farm in Austrailia, she is determined to discover the identity of her birth parents. Rance, the young minister who is helping with the search, must leave, though, to resolve his own mysterious past. HP129

___*A Change of Heart* by Nancy Lavo—When Laura Wells's father is unable to accompany her on a much anticipated Caribbean cruise, Graham Kirkland agrees to chaperon Laura and her bubbly friend, Kathi. Turbulent waters are ahead as Laura must learn to release her anger toward God. HP133

___*Distant Love* by Ann Bell—Although retired school librarian Rebecca Sutherland is preparing for a two-year position on Guam, she and fire chief Andy Hatfield team up to unravel the mystery surrounding a local tragic fire. They discover romance and real love after fifty, even separated by half the world, can happen to them too. HP137

·····Heartsong·····

Any 12
*Heartsong
Presents* titles
for only
$26.95 **

CONTEMPORARY ROMANCE IS CHEAPER BY THE DOZEN!

Buy any assortment of twelve *Heartsong Presents* titles and save 25% off of the already discounted price of $2.95 each!

**plus $1.00 shipping and handling per order and sales tax where applicable.

HEARTSONG PRESENTS TITLES AVAILABLE NOW:

······ Presents ······

*Temporarily out of stock.

Great Inspirational Romance at a Great Price!

Heartsong Presents books are inspirational romances in contemporary and historical settings, designed to give you an enjoyable, spirit-lifting reading experience. You can choose from 152 wonderfully written titles from some of today's best authors like Colleen L. Reece, Brenda Bancroft, Janelle Jamison, and many others.

When ordering quantities less than twelve, above titles are $2.95 each.

Hearts❤ng Presents
Love Stories Are Rated G!

That's for godly, gratifying, and of course, great! If you love a thrilling love story, but don't appreciate the sordidness of some popular paperback romances, **Heartsong Presents** is for you. In fact, **Heartsong Presents** is the *only inspirational romance book club*, the only one featuring love stories where Christian faith is the primary ingredient in a marriage relationship.

Sign up today to receive your first set of four, never before published Christian romances. Send no money now; you will receive a bill with the first shipment. You may cancel at any time without obligation, and if you aren't completely satisfied with any selection, you may return the books for an immediate refund!

Imagine. . .four new romances every four weeks—two historical, two contemporary—with men and women like you who long to meet the one God has chosen as the love of their lives. . .all for the low price of $9.97 postpaid.

To join, simply complete the coupon below and mail·to the address provided. **Heartsong Presents** romances are rated G for another reason: They'll arrive *Godspeed!*